GIRL
IN THE
SHADOWS

D1146599

The Dollanganger Family Series
Flowers in the Attic
Petals on the Wind
If There Be Thorns
Seeds of Yesterday
Garden of Shadows

The Casteel Family Series
Heaven
Dark Angel
Fallen Hearts
Gates of Paradise
Web of Dreams

The Cutler Family Series
Dawn
Secrets of the Morning
Twilight's Child
Midnight Whispers
Darkest Hour

The Landry Family Series
Ruby
Pearl in the Mist
All That Glitters
Hidden Jewel
Tarnished Gold

The Logan Family Series
Melody
Heart Song
Unfinished Symphony
Music in the Night
Olivia

The Orphans Mini-series
Butterfly
Crystal
Brooke
Raven
Runaways (full-length novel)

The Wildflowers Mini-series
Wildflowers
Into the Garden (full-length novel)

The Hudson Family Series
Rain
Lightning Strikes
Eye of the Storm
The End of the Rainbow

The Shooting Stars Mini-series
Shooting Stars
Falling Stars

The De Beers Family Series
Willow
Wicked Forest
Twisted Roots
Into the Woods
Hidden Leaves

The Broken Wings Mini-series
Broken Wings
Midnight Flight

The Gemini Series
Celeste
Black Cat
Child of Darkness

The Shadows Series
April Shadows
Girl in the Shadows

The Early Spring Series
Broken Flower

My Sweet Audrina
(does not belong to a series)

VIRGINIA ANDREWS®

GIRL IN THE SHADOWS

POCKET
BOOKS

LONDON • SYDNEY • NEW YORK • TORONTO

First published in the US by Pocket Books, 2006
A division of Simon & Schuster Inc.
First published in Great Britain by Simon & Schuster UK Ltd, 2008
This edition published by Pocket Books UK, 2008
An imprint of Simon & Schuster UK Ltd
A CBS COMPANY

1 3 5 7 9 10 8 6 4 2

Simon & Schuster UK Ltd
1st Floor
222 Gray's Inn Road
London WC1X 8HB

www.simonandschuster.co.uk

Simon & Schuster Australia
Sydney

A CIP catalogue record for this book is available
from the British Library

ISBN 978-1-84983-308-0

Printed and bound in Great Britain by
Cox & Wyman Ltd, Reading, Berks

GIRL
IN THE
SHADOWS

Prologue

Most people don't think about the way night falls around them. They go along their merry way and suddenly think, Oh, it's dark outside. They are truly unaware of how the shadows thicken and begin to ooze toward each other, merging, melding, clasping their invisible hands together to unite and flow forward to surround us. They rarely notice that the birds have retreated to their quiet places within the inky corners of the forest, nesting calmly with patience and optimism. Birds don't suffer through nightmares as I often do. They believe the sun will always return and the clouds will eventually be gone. All that they know, they have inherited. They do not separate their knowledge from themselves. It is who or what they are and they are comfortable with all of it. You can see their contentment and their confidence in the way they fly.

I envy them for that, for their comfort but mostly for their self-assurance, their wonderful trust in themselves and in the promises Nature makes, whether it is the promise of the seasons, the promise of the rain, or the promise of the sun itself. They glide and slice through their day, carving a world of beauty for themselves.

Mrs. Westington said that even though we are the more complex and the higher form of life for which all of this supposedly has been created, we still covet the simplicity that animals, that even insects enjoy. Their lives are so uncomplicated.

"They don't need the guidance of the Ten Commandments in order to avoid sin," she said.

"But," I asked, "are they capable of real happiness or do they just plod along in a mechanical manner? Do they have ambitions? Do they dream and hope? Do birds, rabbits, foxes, and snakes smile? Do they really ever experience rapture, ecstasy, contentment?"

"Oh, I don't know if they do or if it even matters. More important," Mrs. Westington replied, "you should ask, do we? We have our moments, even our days," she said, "but it doesn't last. Before long, we're envious of others or we're upset with someone we love or we're bored, disgusted, and disappointed. Notice the coming of night?" she asked when I'd mentioned my thought, punctuating her reply with her tiny, coughlike laugh. "Most of us don't even notice the day, much less stop to smell the roses or look up at the stars in awe of their dazzling beauty. My husband was oblivious like that. He never stopped to enjoy what he had. He was always in pursuit of something more and it was never enough. I wonder if he found enough in the grave."

Sometimes for hours, I listened to her ramble on, moving from one topic to the next, dropping her tidbits of wisdom with the grace and generosity of a loving mother feeding her newborns in the nest. She lectured authoritatively, like a professor in the school of hard knocks. When she got too despondent or waved a tattered flag of lifelong regrets, her loyal employee of fifty years, Trevor Washington, would just shake his head and say, "You c'mon now, Mrs. Westington. None of that doom and gloom talk or you'll scare the poor girl outta here."

Most of the time she ignored him or dismissed him with a short wave of her hand.

And the only other person who lived in the old vineyard home, her fourteen-year-old granddaughter, Echo, was deaf, and in many ways a birdlike creature herself, hovering in her private corners waiting for a song she would never hear sung.

Mrs. Westington had invited me to move in and live with them to help her with Echo and be Echo's companion. Echo's mother, Mrs. Westington's daughter, Rhona, had left Echo here more than ten years ago and Echo was without any brother or sister, any friends or any parent. I couldn't imagine a lonelier person than Echo, who had already been locked away within the four walls of silence.

"My daughter named her Echo when the doctor said her baby was deaf. 'It'll be like hearing yourself whenever you talk to her. It's a perfect name for her,' she told me when I complained," Mrs. Westington said. "Truth is, I kinda like her name now."

"It's different. I like it, too," I told her.

"I knew you would. I knew you would be a good

friend to her, too. She should have a friend. Goodness knows, that poor girl longs for a real companion."

What I soon realized, however, was that Mrs. Westington needed me as much as Echo did. She was brimful of wisdom and a lifetime of experiences she desperately had to share with someone she loved. I like that. I like the feeling of being important to someone and loved. Even when Daddy and Mama and my older sister, Brenda, and I were all still together, I didn't feel as needed as I felt here in the old house and vineyard property in northern California.

A wrong turn onto a dead-end road brought me to this place and to these people. After my mother's death, which wasn't all that long after my father's secret fatal illness, I had gone to live with Brenda and her lover, Celia. Both attended college in Memphis, where Brenda had won an athletic scholarship. Like my parents, I ignored any thoughts about Brenda's being gay. I had no doubts that my parents knew it to be true but kept it locked in their hearts. I was afraid to ask any questions, afraid that the same questions might someday be asked of me, afraid that on the back of my neck I would feel the breeze of all that whispering.

My deep unhappiness after Mama's passing and then a traumatic sexual incident with Celia sent me fleeing to my uncle Palaver, my mother's brother, for emotional asylum. Before I came here to Mrs. Westington's home, I had been living and traveling for months with my uncle. He was a magician and an excellent ventriloquist who mainly went from theater to theater in his motor home to perform. I soon realized that he suffered from serious alcoholism brought on by his own deep sorrow over the loss of his beloved companion, the African American woman called Destiny. She had been part of his act, but more important, a big part of his life.

One night after I had been with him a while, he died in the rear of his motor home, lying beside the replica of Destiny, a life-size doll he employed in his show after her passing. Even though I feared it would happen because I witnessed how much he drank and how often, it was still a horrible shock to find him dead in his bed, his arms around the naked doll. From the smile on his face, I was positive he died convinced he had found her again.

Mrs. Westington believed all this was meant to be, was fated, especially my arrival here, and I must say she persuaded me. I felt delivered, guided, and directed to this place. Mrs. Westington's theory was that our loved ones who have passed away remain with us for a time and have an influence on our lives.

"They do their best to watch over us and lead us to happiness," she said. "But only if they were good people," she added. "How good they were determines how long they can be with us to protect us. That's what the Bible really means when we read, 'The sins of the father are visited on the heads of his sons.' If he was a sinner, then his sons have no guardian angel, you see, and no one to protect and insulate them against the weight of all those sins and their consequences. In that sense, they suffer. Your mama and your papa must have been good people. They're still watching over you."

I liked that. I liked her interpretation of Scripture. However, Mrs. Westington was really not a Bible-thumping, religion-driven woman. In fact, she often went into tirades about the corruption of the clergy and the troubles in the world that religions visited on each other. She said it would take a tow truck to get her to church and she'd dig ditches with her heels all the way. She was very opinionated and very confident of all her opinions. When she went into one of her diatribes, she often made me laugh. Sometimes, she wanted to, but sometimes, I could see she was surprised herself at my smile.

"I'm serious, girl," she'd say, and widen her eyes, often followed by a quick, hard tap with her cane. That long, old hickory stick with its pearl handle was something Trevor Washington had made for her. She told me he made it, "Two seconds after I began to wobble."

"Oh, I know you're serious, Mrs. Westington," I told her, and she grunted with skepticism. "I do and I'm not laughing at you!" I insisted.

I didn't want to upset her. She'd been so kind to me. She helped me with my uncle's funeral arrangements and supported me during the whole ordeal. Brenda, now a professional athlete, was off to Germany for a basketball tournament the day after Uncle Palaver died. It all fell on my head. I knew she thought my problems were my own making. I shouldn't have run away after she had found her girlfriend, Celia, with me, but that wasn't my fault and I couldn't stand the dark cloud of Brenda's anger hovering over me. I couldn't stomach the thought of living with her while she despised me. I felt like a lead weight on her ankles anyway. Having the responsibility for a young teenage sister just when she was developing her own promising athletic career was a burden she surely would rather unload.

Even so, even after all that, when Mrs. Westington had asked me to move in, I was nervous and undecided. After all, she, Trevor, and Echo were complete strangers to me and I had been on the property less than a day. I quickly saw, however, that when Mrs. Westington made up her mind about something, she went forward "whole hog," as she would say, even though it was something she had not pondered long.

"No one should be impulsive and fall between the devil and the deep blue sea, but we don't live long enough to waste time," she lectured at dinner, where most of her lectures took place. "When you reach my age, you realize that even more. Your heart is like one of them parking meters. God puts a few coins in and you tick away, but that expired sign is climbing and old man Death is getting ready to give me a ticket. I can see his grumpy old face forming in the fog just outside the windows of my very soul."

The expression on her face, the way she focused her eyes, put the jitters in me. It was as if Death was there at the table and she really did see him.

"How do you know Death is a man?" Trevor asked her with an impish smile in his eyes.

"I've been introduced to him enough times to know," she snapped back at him. "And don't you start giving me some of that superstitious nonsense your great-aunt stuck in your head, Trevor Washington, superstitions passed down from your Southern slave ancestors. You probably wasted a ton of salt all these years throwing a pinch here and a pinch there over your shoulder, and I know you won't kill a spider.

Don't deny it!" she added quickly, and pointed her right forefinger at him.

"If it works, don't complain," he muttered undaunted. "I've seen you walk around a ladder to avoid going under it."

"That's because you leave the darn thing right in a person's path."

It was entertaining watching the two of them go at it. I felt sorry for Echo, who wasn't able to hear. When I mastered signing, I often translated their loving bickering for her and she would laugh with me.

"Until you came here," Mrs. Westington told me one day not long after I had moved in, "the sound of that girl's laughter was as rare as a birdsong in winter."

I quickly realized that in a home in which the young person was deaf, silence ruled the day. There was rarely any music and signing had replaced the sound of voices. Mrs. Westington had gotten into the habit of talking aloud to herself and for the first few days, I was confused by it. I wasn't sure if she was speaking to me or to herself, or even to someone else who I hadn't realized had entered. After a while she did it less and less if I was within earshot, but I suspected she still did it when she was alone and needed the comfort and society of only her own voice.

In the short time I had lived with Uncle Palaver and had traveled with him to help with his magic and ventriloquist's road show, I had begun to understand how painful and frightening loneliness could be. It helped me appreciate why he had invented his life-size replica Destiny doll. She had real human hair, long eyelashes, full lips, and she was soft in places where a woman should be soft. He had kept Destiny's clothing and shoes and he would dress the doll in them. He even sprayed the doll with Destiny's perfume. Instead of talking to himself, he would talk to her, to the memory of her, to the illusion and image of her he cherished in his mind. He had died with that image in his eyes and a smile on his lips. I think now that he deliberately drank himself to death so that he could join her. Behind those dying eyes he saw her and saw himself holding her hand, hearing her voice, guiding him safely through the darkness to a world in which their love shone brightly.

Maybe the dead haunt us as well as guard us, I thought. They don't haunt us like ghosts in an old house; they haunt us from within ourselves. We encourage it, even seek it. How many nights had I lain awake talking to Mama or Daddy and hearing them talk? Have respect for the dead, we've been taught. We should also have respect for the bereaved, for the suffering bereaved. And now I would have poor Uncle Palaver to mourn as well. I think the reason why I liked Mrs. Westington so much was she seemed to understand all this and even appreciate it.

"Your uncle was a truly troubled soul," she told me when I described what it was like living with him in the motor home and seeing how he related to his doll. "The only peace he found was probably when he was in front of those audiences you described. It doesn't surprise me he chose magic and illusion. It was a way out of this world, a way to stop the pain in his heart. Just don't go thinking that's the way to solve all your problems and follow in his footsteps, April. It's as good as putting your head in the sand."

Of course, I knew what she meant. I still had all of his magic paraphernalia. Nothing had been moved or touched, and when I moved in, besides my Mr. Panda teddy bear that my father had given me years ago, I brought in some of Uncle Palaver's tricks with me. It gave me the feeling he was still there. Under his tutelage, I had mastered many of the illusions and tricks, and also had become an amateur ventriloquist myself. Eventually, I would use Destiny and perform for Echo and Tyler Monahan, her tutor, who would become mine as well.

When I had run away from Brenda, I had run away from school, too. I was not yet eighteen and I wanted to get my high school equivalency. I had no idea what I would do with my life, but I knew I was at a great disadvantage without the diploma. As Mrs. Westington would say, "You have fewer roads to travel and in this world you need to have every direction available to you."

But this and much more was all to come at the end of the new journey I had begun.

Mrs. Westington said that even if you sit in one place your whole life, you still make many trips down many different roads.

"And the grave is just a way station, just a place to wait for the next train. It's why I don't visit cemeteries. The dead have all gone on their way, all the ones I loved. But they'll always be here," she said, gently tapping her long, boney right forefinger against her temple. "They'll always be here. I hear their voices, even their footsteps."

When she said things like that, we'd all be quiet, Trevor, me, and especially Echo, who saw our thoughtfulness and even though she was deaf, heard our silence.

The four of us looked out at that advancing night from the front porch. We were not like most people when it came to the approaching darkness.

We thought about it.

1

Amnesia

Filtered through the sheer white cotton curtains, the sudden sun snapped my eyelids open. For a long moment, I lay there staring up at the center ceiling light fixture, an oversized silver blue lantern with four small bulbs. My thoughts and memories spun like milk and coffee that were stirred vigorously, all of it mixing into a cup of confusion.

Where was I? How did I get here? Had all that happened since Daddy deserted us been only a dream, a long, sticky nightmare against which I had struggled and battled into the morning? If that were only true, I thought. If I really had awakened to a second chance, how would I change my life? What would I do differently? I was afraid to think about any of it. What if I did something that would bring it all back?

It didn't surprise me that I was plagued by indecision. Every significant choice I had made, especially recently, seemed to have taken me into deeper shadows, deeper bewilderment and pandemonium. I was dangerously close to becoming inert, terrified of moving in any direction.

Lying there and struggling to remember it all, I realized how much I wanted to become an amnesiac. Forgetting was so temptingly luxurious. Yes, how wonderful it would be if today really was the first day of my life, I thought. Daddy wouldn't have died of a brain tumor he had kept secret from us. Mama wouldn't have become so depressed she had to overdose on sleeping pills. My sister, Brenda, wouldn't hate me for being unable to reject her girlfriend Celia's advances, and I wouldn't have had to watch Uncle Palaver drink himself to death. Surely that was enough to drive anyone willingly into a state of amnesia.

I took a deep breath and sat up slowly. My nightgown was a little snug under my arms. Mrs. Westington had insisted I use whatever of her daughter Rhona's clothing I could fit into, which really wasn't much more than this pink nightgown I now wore. The closet was filled with what looked like relatively unworn garments, pretty one-piece dresses, skirts, and blouses I could only dream of wearing. I was still a good twenty pounds overweight and hated the sight of myself undressed. The roll of fat around my waist made it look like I had swallowed a small inner tube. When I was younger, I used to wonder if I could poke myself with a pin and let the fat out as I could let the air out of a balloon. I came close to trying it.

Despite my weight, I did hold up every pretty garment Rhona had left behind and dream of what I would look like if I could actually fit into each. When I sifted through the closet, I realized Rhona had left a considerable wardrobe. A few skirts and blouses actually still had sales tags hanging on them. There were at least two-dozen pairs of shoes. However, when she had abandoned her responsibilities nearly ten years ago, she had left more than just her clothing and other material possessions behind. According to Mrs. Westington, Rhona had deserted her deaf daughter, Echo, without a good-bye, without a promise to return. She hadn't even left a note for her to read someday explaining why she had left her!

"She gave that girl nothing but her name. When she left, it was as if that daughter of mine turned into a puff of smoke," Mrs. Westington said, and snapped her fingers. She sat in her favorite chair and talked about Rhona. While she did, she fixed her eyes on the wall behind me as if she could see it all projected and running like a home movie.

"She was always unhappy, always complaining. She told me she had to get away and have some fun with her life. She couldn't stomach being responsible for a child, especially a disabled one. One day she was gone, just like that. I should have expected it. She never cared a tinker's damn about anything that wasn't solely for her own pleasure. I swear that girl was born without a conscience. The good angels must have been on vacation when I gave birth. She was my daughter and I did what I could bringing her up, but you'd have to dig deeply into the well of stinginess to find someone more self-centered."

Even though I'd been here in the old vineyard

mansion barely three days, I could sense the pain in Mrs. Westington's heart whenever she mentioned Rhona. She tried to put on a hard shell and pretend she couldn't care much less about her daughter, but the way she shifted those dark gray eyes nervously and tightened her thin fingers around the pearl head of her brown walking stick at the slightest reference to Rhona told me she still suffered sharp pangs in her heart from the great disappointment. She couldn't simply write her off and forget her as she claimed, waving her hand and declaring, "It's as if she never was, far as I'm concerned. Never was."

Trevor Washington said, "Asking a parent to deny her own child is like asking a flower to deny the rain. Mrs. Westington can pretend all she wants, but it can't happen. Blood's blood. It can't be ignored no matter what you do."

He whispered this to me after one of Mrs. Westington's tirades about her ungrateful daughter, but I was positive Mrs. Westington had heard him. It didn't take me long to see that she didn't miss much going on around her, despite her age and fragile appearance.

I was surprised her loyal employee would say anything negative or critical about her to me, but right from the beginning, Trevor was willing to take me into his confidence. Perhaps he was desperate for company, desperate for someone who not only could hear but was willing to listen. After all, he had no family of his own and was working for an elderly lady and a deaf fourteen-year-old girl. Loneliness had found a home in his world, too.

Mrs. Westington told me about his tragedy. "He lost his young wife to a raging bone cancer that gobbled her up like some monster with metal teeth. That poor beautiful girl withered like one of his grapes on the vine and that tore his heart to shreds. There's a line in the Bible that fits him," she said. " 'If you should die, I will hate all womankind.'

"That in a nutshell is the story of Trevor Washington. The man married himself to this land and this family with the dedication of a monk. And I'm not flattered by it. I'm saddened by it," she said.

"He has no other family?" I asked.

"He has some elderly aunts and some cousins, and his mother is still alive."

"She is?"

"She's ninety-three and lives in a nursing home in Phoenix, Arizona. He visits her regularly, but he says she's in that limbo between life and death where she doesn't remember anything, including him and his visits. Of course, he goes anyway."

After Mrs. Westington's husband died or as she says, "kicked the bucket," she closed the vineyard. She knew Trevor had to manufacture most of the work he did, but she would never let him go. The old three-story house was large enough to require him to provide regular maintenance and I knew he had a pet project: farming a small portion of the once fruitful and vibrant vineyard, and then processing his harvest into Chardonnay wine. I understood that he grew enough grapes to produce 50 to a 150 cases of the Chardonnay that had built the Westingtons' their small fortune. The remainder of the property was overgrown.

Although the house still had its original charm and style, all of the furnishings looked worn and tired. It was truly as if it had aged alongside Mrs. Westington. Frayed sofas, worn rugs, a cracked figurine on a rickety looking pedestal, all of it, like her, nevertheless still had character. Giving anything away or throwing anything out would be like deserting old friends. Right from the moment I set foot in the home, Mrs. Westington would nod at something and tell me its history and why it was still important to her. This was a present; that was something she had bought on a trip East or a vacation. I imagined she recited these anecdotes to anyone who entered so as to justify why someone with her bank account wouldn't replenish, restore, or buy new and more fashionable things.

"Because people today treat their possessions with such disdain, they treat each other likewise," she declared before I could even think of asking such questions. "People who have no respect for what their ancestors left them have no respect for themselves. You don't get tired of things that had meaning," she lectured.

However, the bedroom I was using had been Rhona's and the furnishings were newer than most everything else in the house. I was sleeping in a beautiful white and pink canopy bed. The matching dresser, armoire, and vanity table had the same pink swirls in them and there was a soft, milk white area rug surrounding the bed. The only blemish was a deep yellow stain Mrs. Westington said was Rhona's fault. She had spilled wine and not told anyone about it.

Curious about the daughter who had lived here and then run off, deserting her own flesh and blood, I did search the dresser drawers and the closet for clues, but I discovered nothing that would tell me why. I found packs of old cigarettes she had probably kept hidden and some grains of what I knew was pot. Mrs. Westington had taken down posters of rock stars and scantily clad male models and shoved all of it to the rear of the closet. I found some jewelry in the vanity table drawer, but none of it looked expensive. Most of the makeup was dried out and the colognes smelled too old to be used.

The most surprising thing I found was a dildo. I knew what it was because my sister's lover, Celia, had one on the small night dresser next to her and Brenda's bed. She called it Mr. Feelgood. Brenda would get furious with her if she talked about it in front of me, but nevertheless, she once had a birthday party for it and put it in the center of a cake. Of course, I wondered now if most women, heterosexual or homosexual, used them. I quickly put it back where I found it, buried under a pile of *Playgirl* magazines deep at the rear of Rhona's closet.

I wondered why Mrs. Westington hadn't gone through this room and at least had her cleaning lady, Lourdes, throw out some of this. Had she been living with the hope that her daughter would have a surge of remorse and return? Even after all these years? Mrs. Westington didn't strike me as someone who permitted herself any illusions, but all of us, even someone like her, cling to that life preserver called hope.

As I became more awake, I remembered that today was the day Echo's tutor, Tyler Monahan, was coming. Mrs. Westington told me he had been on a trip and had returned. He worked with Echo weekdays for five hours a day. Mrs. Westington explained that he had been a teacher in a school for the disabled in Los

Angeles and had returned to the nearby town of Healdsburg to help his mother, Lee Monahan, with their chocolate wine sauce business after his father had died suddenly of heart failure. That was nearly two years ago. Up until then, Echo's education had been basically catch as catch can, the instructors being those teachers at a relatively close school for disabled children. None of them were willing to devote as much time as Tyler Monahan did, or with any regularity, and Mrs. Westington was unwilling to have Echo attend the special school and sleep away from home.

Although she never came right out and said it, Mrs. Westington had lost her daughter to bad influences and she was afraid of something similar happening to Echo, who because of her disability, was perhaps more vulnerable. According to Mrs. Westington, whatever bad genes Rhona had inherited from her father, Echo could have also inherited, and then there was the mystery of who her father was, too.

"He couldn't have been much," Mrs. Westington insisted. "Not if he was with Rhona. He probably doesn't even know he has a child, which is for the best, I'm sure."

I really didn't know how long I would remain here, but Mrs. Westington wanted me at least to stay long enough to have Tyler tutor me so I could pass the high school equivalency exam. She convinced me I was of some real help for her with Echo, which made me feel a little better about taking so much from her. Of course, I knew I had to develop the methods to communicate with Echo. In just the few days I had been here, I had already begun to learn a little signing on my own. Trevor was fairly good at it and so was Mrs. Westington, although she seemed to be able to communicate with Echo just as well through a look or a gesture. For example, even though Echo couldn't hear it, if she saw Mrs. Westington tap her cane, Echo understood her grandmother wanted her to do something promptly.

What amazed me about Echo was how conscious she was of other people's hearing ability. I realized it again this morning when not five minutes after I had awoken, I heard a knock on my bedroom door. I cried, "Come in." The door didn't open. I heard knocking again and I realized it was Echo, so I got out of bed and opened the door. She was standing there, already dressed, smiling at me and signing good morning. I signed back and combined some of my own gestures with words, telling her I would shower and dress quickly so we could go down to breakfast. She was very good at reading lips and understanding my little mime shows.

Right from the first time I set eyes on her, I thought she was a cute girl who had the potential to grow into a very attractive young woman. Her curly black hair had been poorly cut too short. It looked like a bowl had been placed around her head, so I suspected her grandmother had done it, but Echo had striking Kelly green eyes, a sweet, small nose that was turned up slightly, full lips, and a slightly cleft chin. She didn't wear a bra. Maybe she didn't even own one, but her breasts clearly looked firm and already quite shapely. She was developing a very nice figure, a figure I, obviously twenty or so pounds overweight, envied.

I turned and hurried to the bathroom to shower and dress. While she waited for me, she looked at some of the posters and pictures of Uncle Palaver I had lying about the vanity table. She was amused to see Mr. Panda on my bed. I wrote out his name for her and told her it had been a present from my father. She held it in her hands more lovingly and looked at it more intently then, because not only had she never gotten a present from her father, she didn't know who he was and had never met him.

"Would you like to keep Mr. Panda in your room?" I asked her, and her eyes brightened. She nodded quickly. The teddy bear had always brought me comfort, I thought. Maybe it would do the same for her.

She wondered about some of my other things, especially Uncle Palaver's, which I had brought in from the motor home the night of his funeral. I promised to show her more of them later. He had left instructions for cremation and the ceremony, attended only by me, Mrs. Westington, and Trevor Washington, was very short. On our way back, I asked her if she minded my bringing the Destiny doll into the house. I felt guilty leaving the doll in the motor home, sprawled on the bed upon which Uncle Palaver had died. Living with Uncle Palaver and watching him treat his doll so reverently had obviously left an impression on me.

"Not just yet," Mrs. Westington replied. "It will take a while to get Echo to understand it all," she suggested.

How could I disagree? I was still trying to understand it all myself.

Echo took Mr. Panda to her room. I dressed quickly and when she returned, we went down to breakfast together. Mrs. Westington, who was an early riser, had already eaten her breakfast, which consisted mainly of some pieces of orange, a bowl of oatmeal, and a cup of tea with honey. Echo and I squeezed fresh orange juice and Mrs. Westington put up some eggs to boil. Echo liked them soft and so did I. The table was set and there was sliced homemade bread as well as jams and butter, and fresh fruit.

"Tyler uses my husband's old office for his tutoring," Mrs. Westington suddenly blurted. With her cane she pointed at the clock over the refrigerator. "He'll be here in less than a half hour, so don't you two dillydally."

She signed what she had said to me and Echo stopped smiling and looked serious.

"He doesn't know anything about you yet," Mrs. Westington told me. "But I'll speak to him about helping you."

"Maybe he won't want to do it," I said. I wasn't disabled and he was a specialist in working with the disabled, although I had a self-image that was probably not much better than the image a disabled person had of herself.

"Maybe he won't; maybe he will. Take a letter," she added, which was her way of telling me to remember something. "If I could read the future, I sure as hell wouldn't have made the mistakes I made. But you don't cry over spilt milk, girl. You wipe it up and start over. If you dwell on the past, you'll have no future," she concluded, nodding at her own wisdom.

"I guess you're right about that," I said, recalling my first thoughts this morning.

She raised her eyebrows. "Oh, you think so, do

you? Well, that's hopeful. My granddad used to say, 'Youth is wasted on the young. Wisdom wouldn't be so bad if it didn't come with age.' Eat up," she added, bringing us the eggs. "You want coffee or tea?"

"I'm fine with this," I said, nodding at the milk.

Echo watched me crack my eggs open carefully from the small end down and then she did the same with her eggs, imitating my every move. My father used to do it this way. He was meticulous about it and it left an impression on me. I loved imitating things he did anyway.

Echo smiled and I caught Mrs. Westington gazing at her, a warming in her eyes and softening in her lips. She realized I was looking at her and quickly turned away, banging the pot in the sink as if she was upset with herself for being caught showing warm affection.

"That cleaning girl of mine comes today. I'm sure she'll be as late as ever. No one pays much attention to time anymore," she muttered. "How I wish I was younger and stronger so I could do my own housework again. Hateful thing, age. It makes you too dependant on the kindness of others and believe me, girl, you got to dig deeply into some people to find a drop of kindness in their hearts."

She took so deep a breath, I thought she was going to keel over.

"Are you all right, Mrs. Westington?" I asked quickly.

"What? Oh, yeah fine, fine," she said, but I was sure some arrow of pain had shot through her. "It's my own fault jawing away like this. All talk and no cider," she mumbled.

Echo seemed to sense Mrs. Westington's moods from the way she held her head and shoulders. I saw how she reacted immediately, a look of worry spreading over her face. What would happen to her if something happened to Mrs. Westington? I wondered. Her mother was as good as dead to her and she didn't know her father. Seeing her vulnerability caused me to recall my own when Mama had been so sick. It was terrifying for me and I had all my senses and an older sister. Mrs. Westington was Echo's lifeline to the world, even the small and restricted world she had.

"Maybe now that I'm here, I can do the work, Mrs. Westington. I don't mind. I used to help my mother with her house chores."

"What? No, no. I wouldn't take the work away from Lourdes. She needs the money, and besides, you'll have other things to do. It will be enough if you look after your bedroom," she said, and then leaned forward to look more clearly out the kitchen window. "Just look at that foolish man toiling away out there on those grapevines. You ever see such stubbornness? He thinks if he clings onto a piece of the past, he'll get me wanting to start it all again. No matter how I tell him he's wasting his time, he's at it. Don't know why I kept him around me all these years."

I smiled to myself. Already I knew she would have a hard time surviving without Trevor Washington. When it came to him, she was all bark and no bite, although she would never admit it. I was sure it was the same for Trevor. Neither would admit how much he or she needed the other, but I could see they had grown used to each other's ways. They bobbed and swayed to keep their world in balance, each easily adjusting to the other's moods, twists, and turns.

"This bread's delicious," I said. I had smeared what looked like homemade blackberry jam over it.

"Better than that store bought stuff Trevor brings around from time to time," Mrs. Westington said. "That man would eat dog food if I didn't invite him to eat here with us."

"I probably shouldn't eat so much," I said, pushing the plate away. I had already devoured two thick pieces. "I was supposed to be losing weight. I promised my uncle I would. He had a costume for me that I never could really fit into even though we both pretended I did."

"Don't you think about any of that now. It's over and done with. You've been through enough grief and that eats away at you as it is. And don't you go on one of them newfangled diets while you're living here neither!" she warned, waving her cane. "People will say I starved you, and no one ever walked out of Loretta Westington's house hungry."

I laughed. "I doubt that will happen, Mrs. Westington. I doubt I will ever look starved."

She just grunted. She'd known me less than a week, but she knew enough not to bet on my having the discipline to trim down. Was I fat because I hated myself or did I hate myself because I was fat? It was like being caught screaming at your own screaming in an echo chamber.

As soon as we both finished eating, I cleaned up our dishes and started to wash everything.

"Just leave it for Lourdes," Mrs. Westington said.

"I pay her too much as it is for what she does around here. Most of this house isn't used. I could replace her with a new vacuum cleaner."

She didn't mean that, but for some reason, perhaps for many reasons, she was reluctant to say nice things about anyone or invest any faith in anyone. Maybe that was all related to her daughter and the way her daughter had treated her and her own daughter.

She turned to Echo and signed to her that she should get ready for her lessons. She didn't have to repeat it. Echo's face filled with brightness and expectation. She hurried off to get her books together, but mostly, I saw, to fix her hair the best she could and even sneak on a little lipstick. I didn't think Mrs. Westington had any idea how Echo was developing a crush on her tutor. When she looked at Echo, she still saw the child and not the budding adolescent. She thought her only reason for interest in Tyler was educational.

"There's proof that there are all sorts of hungers in this world," she told me, nodding after Echo. "That girl's starving for knowledge. You just watch her go at it, climbing over one obstacle after another."

"I will," I said, and then I went out to see exactly what Trevor was doing, since she had mentioned it.

He was standing in his section of grapevines, carefully plucking grapes and placing them in a basket. Even with the small section he had grown, this would take forever, I thought. He glanced at me and continued.

The September sky had a bit of a haze but the sun was raining down its rays intensely. Small beads of sweat were shining like tiny pearls on Trevor's forehead. Age hadn't diminished him much, I thought. He was still a big man who looked very powerful, with a full head of stark and thick white hair. However, despite the size of his hands and the thickness of his fingers, I noticed he worked with a surgeon's accuracy and care.

"Good morning," I said.

"Morning. Sleep a little better?"

Trevor was at breakfast the morning after Uncle Palaver's funeral, and he had seen the tossing and turning I had gone through the night before scribbled all over my face and highlighted by my drooping eyelids.

"Yes, thank you."

He paused and looked at me. "Know anything about grapes and wine?"

"Not much. I know there's red and white," I replied, and he laughed.

"Don't forget rosé. These grapes are Chardonnay grapes for white wine, which was the Westington's speciality. I didn't know much more about wine than you do when I first set foot on the property. I had just lost my job at a lumber company and that very day Mr. Frank, Frank Westington, stopped in to place an order for some lumber. He overheard me being laid off and asked me if I wanted to come work for him. He wasn't much older than I was, but he had just inherited all this and wanted to expand. He wasn't even married yet. Married Mrs. Westington five years later. Asked me to be his best man, which didn't please his younger brother, Arliss, much. By then they weren't even friends, much less brothers," he added, and plucked some more grapes.

"Why was that?"

"Oh, they got into a furious battle when their daddy left title to the house and property completely to Mr. Frank. His brother, Arliss, was a wasteful, lazy, and self-indulgent young man who thought everything was coming to him," he said, and leaned toward me to add, "That's who Rhona takes after, her uncle Arliss. Anyway, they were what Mrs. Westington called oil and water. Makes you wonder how they could have had the same daddy and mama." He looked at the house and then he leaned toward me and in a loud whisper said, "Makes you wonder if their mama didn't maybe look elsewhere once or twice. Sometimes, I thought the only thing they shared was a last name."

I watched him return to picking the grapes. He had a way of doing it very quickly even though he handled each grape as if it were a valuable jewel. Later, I would hear him call the juice "liquid gold."

"Isn't there an easier way to harvest the grapes?"

"Easier? Sure. Better? No. I hand pick them and put them into small crates to protect them from being crushed in the field. Every step of this process is precious," he emphasized.

"How come you only have this small patch going?"

He laughed and looked at the house. "She thinks it's because she's always yelling at me for wasting time on a dead cause, but the truth is the tight spacing encourages competition among the plants, yielding small clusters and berries, but more concentrated fruit. Here," he said, offering me a grape. "Taste it."

I did. "Sweet as honey. Like a fig or . . ."

"Ripe apple?"

"Yes," I said.

He nodded. "Chardonnay is one of the few grapes that don't require blending. It stands on its own." He gestured at the small vineyard. "I cloned all these vines from the best Mr. Westington had."

"Why didn't Mrs. Westington want to continue the whole vineyard and the winery?"

"It wasn't her passion. It was Mr. Frank's and there wasn't anyone to inherit it. Certainly not Mr. Arliss and surely not Rhona. She never did any chores around here and had no interest in wine except to drink it with her friends."

"How come they had only one child?"

He continued to pluck the grapes without responding, so I thought he wasn't going to answer. A breeze had picked up from the north and the cooler air felt refreshing. I saw Echo standing behind the screen door looking out at the driveway in anxious anticipation of Tyler Monahan's pending arrival.

"They had another child," Trevor suddenly replied. He worked as he spoke. "A son born after Rhona was born, but he was born with some defect in his brain stem and died a few days later. They did all they could. Mrs. Westington got so she denied the boy was ever born. Don't mention it to her. She never even gave him a name. Wouldn't do it. Mr. Frank named him after his father, Byron, but she didn't acknowledge it and she didn't attend the funeral or the burial. As far as I know, she never visited the grave either. After that, they had no more children. Closest I ever heard to why not was her saying once that she didn't need to be told twice. Don't you go mentioning any of this to her," Trevor warned me, "or you'll be one sorry young woman. Ain't nobody who hates gossip more than she does, although she'll do her fair share of it," he said with a wink.

We both turned at the sound of an automobile coming up the driveway. It was a red convertible sports car. Tyler Monahan's wavy long dark brown hair floated about his face, hiding his features. He parked in front of the house and got out quickly, a packet of books and notebooks under his arm. Echo immediately stepped out of the house to greet him, signing quickly. He signed back and almost entered the house without seeing me. He glanced our way and then he turned sharply and paused. I stared back at him almost as hard as he was staring at me. I knew from the picture of him and Echo in the living room that he had distinctly Asian characteristics. With a name like Monahan, his father had to be Irish, of course. The mixture of races had produced a strikingly handsome and interesting face.

"That's her tutor," Trevor muttered.

"Yes, I know," I said.

Tyler looked about six feet tall. He was slim and very fit looking. He wore a light blue polo shirt and jeans with blue boat shoes. I thought he was going to wave at us, but instead, he brought his hand up to brush back his hair and then he turned and hurried up the steps to join Echo. They went into the house.

Trevor glanced from them to me and then back to his grapes. "His mother comes from Hong Kong," he said, imagining my questions. "She's a very independent woman, but family means a whole lot more to her than to most. No way he'd ever desert her like

Rhona deserted Mrs. Westington and her own baby. However, Mrs. Westington ain't very fond of her," he paused to whisper. "Whenever she talks to her, she says the woman makes her feel like she suspects Mrs. Westington's got her hand in her back pocket, like she's going to steal away her son or something, as if she has secret plans to bring back the vineyard and needs his help. Stuff like that."

"Speaking of help, would you like some?" I asked.

He laughed. "That's something I ain't heard much around here. Sure." He reached down for a basket and fixed the cord that held it around my neck. "Frees up both your hands," he said. "Be gentle with them and don't just drop them hard into the basket, okay?"

"Okay," I said, and began. I felt him watching me out of the corner of his eye. The grapes were like his babies.

"That's good," he said. He looked back at the house. "Don't be surprised if she bawls you out for wasting your time."

"It's not a waste of time to me. I'd like to learn all about the wine-making process."

He shook his head. "That's something else I ain't heard much around here," he said.

"Does Echo ever help you?"

"No. I don't want to cause no problems, although I often see her sitting off to the side wishing I would ask. She knows about the winery and the process. You can't live here alongside me and not know it." He winked. "Take a letter," he said, and I laughed.

I nearly had half a basket picked when I heard the screen door open and then heard Mrs. Westington call for me. "Stop wasting time out there and come meet

Tyler Monahan," she shouted, tapping her cane. "You got more important things to do than waste your time with that foolish man, girl."

"Go on," Trevor said. "Before she skins me alive."

I took off the basket cord and carefully set the basket down.

"That man," Mrs. Westington said, glaring out at Trevor when I approached the steps. "He could talk a bee into stinging itself. Go on in and meet Tyler Monahan," she ordered, and stepped away from the door.

I entered slowly and started down the hallway to what had been Mr. Westington's office, but to my surprise, Tyler was waiting in the living room.

"In here," I heard.

I stepped in. Echo wasn't there. Tyler was standing by the window, his hands behind his back. He turned slowly and looked at me. I had no trouble understanding why Echo would have a deeply felt crush on him. A girl didn't have to be lonely or isolated to swoon before so handsome a man. He had eyes like black pearls, a firm, full, masculine mouth, and skin like smooth butter. Brenda would call him buff, and although she had little interest in men, would admire him for the respect he obviously had for his own well-being and physical fitness. His narrow waist made his chest and shoulders look bigger than they were. I doubted he had two ounces of fat on him. He made me more conscious of my own weight problem. I embraced myself and waited for him to speak. He fixed his brilliant pearl black eyes on me, scrutinizing and making me feel even more self-conscious.

"Who are you?" he asked. It sounded more like a demand, especially in his deep, baritone voice.

"My name is April Taylor." I didn't know what else to tell him exactly.

"You're not claiming to be a long, lost relative?"

"No. Mrs. Westington has asked me to stay here for a while and help her with Echo."

Why was he cross-examining me like this?

"You don't attend any school?"

"Not presently, no."

"You just want to pass a high school equivalency exam?"

"Yes."

He shook his head. "Why?"

I looked away. His policemanlike questioning brought hot tears to my eyes. I fought hard to keep them locked under my lids.

"It's a very long and painful story," I replied, not looking at him. "If it's a problem, forget about it."

"I didn't say it's a problem. We don't know yet if it is or if it isn't. It's just weird, that's all."

"Yeah, well, maybe it is, but that's the way it is right now," I told him, and glared back at him.

"I'll have to prepare some evaluation exams to see what you know and don't know, where you are in the core subjects. It's not something that can be done in a week or two. How long are you staying?"

"I'm not sure yet."

"Well, if I did all this preparation and you left, it would be a colossal waste of my time."

"I don't see myself as a waste of anyone's time."

He considered me. We heard Mrs. Westington come back into the house.

"Just a minute," he said, and went out to speak

with her in the hallway. He spoke in a whisper, but loud enough for me to hear.

"I don't understand this, Mrs. Westington. She's not related, and from the little you've told me, it looks like you've taken in a complete stranger who wanders about the country in a motor home, some sort of a gypsy girl?"

"No, no. She's nothing like that. She was living with her uncle just like I told you and he died on the road. She came here for help and she's got no one else right now. She'll be good for Echo."

"How do you know that? She might be a terrible influence on her. Echo's very vulnerable. She's had very little contact with the outside world. This girl might be the worst example for her. She just left school to go on the road with her uncle. Who knows what sort of riffraff she associated with and what sort of things she's done? She looks like . . ."

"Don't worry about it, Tyler. When you reach my age," Mrs. Westington replied, "you know who has goodness in her heart and who doesn't. Believe me, you know who you should be trusting and who you shouldn't. That poor girl's been hauled over the coals. She needs a little tender loving care. As do we all."

"I can't guarantee any success with her. I have no idea what her mental abilities are, what preparation she already has, what her reading ability especially is and . . ."

"You just do the best you can, Tyler. I'll pay you for it, of course."

"You're sure you want to do this? If she picks up

and leaves after I've put in some time, you would have wasted money."

"I'm sure."

"I can't afford to give her too much extra time. You know my mother needs me and complains about the time I spend over here as it is," he warned. "And I don't like taking any attention and time away from Echo."

"Give it what you can, Tyler," Mrs. Westington said, her voice filling with frustration and fatigue.

I heard nothing else and then he returned to the living room.

"Okay, I'll bring some testing materials tomorrow so we can evaluate you," he told me. "After that I'll be able to see if there is any way of successfully dealing with you."

"Thank you," I said, even though "dealing with me" wasn't exactly how I wanted it put.

"What kind of work were you doing with your uncle on the road?" he asked.

"I was helping him with his magic and ventriloquist act. He was a well-known magician. Maybe you've heard of him, the Amazing Palaver?"

"No, I never heard of him. I don't follow road acts," he said, twisting his mouth as if I had asked him about a stripper or something. "So you just ran off to live with him and put your high school education on hold?"

"Something like that," I said.

"You left in the middle of a semester?"

"Yes."

He looked at me and shook his head as if I was absolutely impossible to understand. Maybe I was.

"Okay. I've got to get to Echo." He started out.

"Can I watch?" I asked.

"Watch? Watch what?" He had a way of grimacing that made me think he had something that tasted horrible on his lips.

"How you teach her. I'd like to see what you do so that maybe I could help, too, maybe help her with her work when you're not here."

He widened his smirk, drawing those almost too perfect lips deeply into their corners.

"I'm not sure I want you to do that. You could confuse her if you don't teach her correctly and that could damage what I do and put her behind."

"That's why I'd better watch you, to see the right way to communicate with her," I countered quickly.

"Do you know anything about signing, anything at all about how to communicate with a deaf person?"

"No. I mean, a tiny bit. I'll learn," I added quickly.

He thought a moment. "All right. You can come along, but just stay in the background, watch, and listen," he decided with obvious reluctance and walked out. I hurried after him.

Was it me? Was there something about me that annoyed boys? Was I that distasteful, ugly, and fat?

Echo was sitting patiently in front of the desk. She smiled at me when I appeared behind Tyler. He moved his chair around deliberately so that she would have her back to me and then he began signing quickly, so quickly I couldn't understand anything. Whatever he told her caused her to turn and look at me curiously. Then he tapped her knee and she turned back to him.

"We're doing her math problems first this morning," he announced. "Just sit on the sofa there and don't do anything to distract her."

I quickly sat and he opened a textbook, pointed to something on the page, and began. Most of his communication with her was through very quick signing that I couldn't follow, so that pretty soon I felt totally left out. Finally Echo began working on problems and he sat back. He was staring at me so hard, I felt like I had food on my face.

"What?" I asked.

"I'd hate to learn that you are taking advantage of these people," he said.

"I've only been here three days," I said, fixing my eyes sharply on him the way my sister, Brenda, could fix her eyes on someone who challenged her, "but I, too, would hate to learn that anyone was taking advantage of them."

He seemed to like my reply and softened his eyes.

"What about your parents? Why would they let you leave school and travel around the country in a motor home?"

"They're both dead."

"You have no one, no other immediate family?"

"I have an older sister but she is a professional basketball player and off on a tour in Europe. After my uncle's death, I was going to go live with a cousin I hardly know, but Mrs. Westington wouldn't hear of it."

"What did your uncle die of?"

"He suffered from alcoholism," I reluctantly revealed.

"So you traveled about with a drunk?"

"It wasn't like that. He drank privately. Alcoholism is a sickness, you know."

"Do you drink, too?"

"No," I said, practically shouting. He looked skeptical. "I don't, and after I've seen what it can do to someone, I doubt I'll ever get anywhere close to that, and before you ask, I don't do drugs either."

He grimaced skeptically. "How can you just drive in here and move in with people you don't know?"

I took a deep breath. Why was this so important to him?

"Mrs. Westington was kind enough to care about me. I really am trying to be as much of a help to her and to Echo as I can be."

He stared, considering me, his face although handsome, cold and unrevealing.

"Well, I suppose if you're going to be here a while you really should learn how to sign. I'll help you with that, too, when I can," he said, relenting. "You have the ASL book here, right?"

"Yes, I've begun to study it. Thank you for agreeing to help me."

"It's for her," he countered quickly, nodding at Echo. "She certainly doesn't need an added burden."

What a strange young man, I thought. He could sound friendly one moment and unfriendly the next.

"I don't intend to be any sort of added burden nor will I make her life any more difficult," I said.

"Good intentions are not always enough."

"Maybe they're not, but they're a good start," I shot back at him.

He nodded, finally offering a small smile. "Okay. Perhaps you won't be as difficult a case as I thought. Who knows? I might even enjoy tutoring you. I might enjoy the challenge."

Did I dare smile back? Was he being sincere or sarcastic when he called me a challenge? How hard it had become to trust anyone's smile, I thought. Sometimes a smile was just another mask hiding the truth.

Neither of us had realized that while we were talking, Echo had been reading his lips. She signed something quickly and he signed back. Then they both looked at me and laughed.

"What's so funny?" I asked.

"She said she could be your tutor, too, by helping you learn signing."

"And what did you tell her that made her laugh?"

"I told her I doubted you were as good a listener as she was."

"Oh, that's very funny," I said.

"Exactly," he said, shrugging. "It's very funny."

He reported our conversation to Echo and they both laughed again. I stared at them a moment and then I laughed as well. I wasn't going to let him think he had hurt my feelings in any way. I wouldn't give him the satisfaction. That pleased Echo and he even smiled.

"I'm glad you have a sense of humor at least," he said.

And I thought perhaps we would be all right.

Perhaps.

2

Silent Conversations

I sat as quietly as I could and continued to observe how Tyler used different methods to communicate his instructions and comments to Echo. At times, he relied more on lipreading than the signing. He would speak slowly and exaggerate the formation of his lips. Only as an absolute last resort did he write something and have her read it.

While she worked quietly on problems, he wrote things in his notebook or sifted through textbooks to mark places he wanted her to read. He looked my way occasionally but said nothing. Perhaps he was hoping I would soon get bored and leave, but his patience with her and her obvious determination to please him intrigued me. At times they communicated with each other as if there were invisible wires between them. The movement of an eyebrow, the twist of a lip, or even a small nod was quickly translated and understood. It made me consider how often we speak to each other through posture and gesture. Words were almost unnecessary between them anyway, lipreading or not.

Finally however, he reached that point in his schedule when he worked on her speech.

I saw that previously he had given her a list of words to practice and now asked her to take it out of her notebook and begin. She looked back at me and he tapped her on the arm to get her to pay strict attention to him. He lifted her hand and placed her fingers on his own neck. Then he nodded at her and she began. When she spoke, he either shook his head or nodded. If he shook his head, he repeated the word and then had her do it again and again. The intensity of concentration was impressive. She not only reacted to the vibrations in his throat, but the tiniest movement in his lips.

Finally, Mrs. Westington appeared in the doorway to announce that lunch was ready.

"Thank you," Tyler said, and told Echo. He also complimented her on her work. She smiled with pride when she turned to me.

"Are deaf people more sensitive to people's expressions, gestures?" I asked him as he rose from his seat.

He looked at me as if I had made a discovery it normally took years to make.

"Yes," he said. "When you lose one sense, you compensate with the others. Blind people depend more on hearing. Deaf people on seeing, feeling. I even have her listening to music."

"How?"

"By having her place her hand on the speaker so she can sense the beat, the bass. You'll see. She can actually identify tunes."

"You're very good with her," I told him as we started out. "I can see why she's learning so well with you."

As if he was distrustful of all compliments, he searched my face before replying. "She's a very bright girl and that makes it easier, believe me. She also has an unrelenting determination to bridge that gap between herself and other people. If she had been given instruction properly during the earlier ages when she should have been instructed, she would be far ahead by now."

I wasn't deaf, but I could read his gestures and demeanor clearly. He spoke down to me as if he were sitting on some high throne of authority and intelligence, and I were some lowly commoner there to pay him respect.

"She should be in a more regular classroom situation," he continued. "I worry about her not having interaction with other young people her age."

"I think that is Mrs. Westington's concern. That's why she wants me here."

He didn't look convinced. In fact, he shook his head and smirked. "That's hardly a substitution. First of all, you're not really her age."

"She's fourteen, right? I'm only seventeen."

He stopped in the hallway, drew his head back, and lifted his chin. "You're not seriously suggesting a girl of fourteen has much in common with a girl of seventeen, are you? Especially a girl like you."

"What do you mean, a girl like me?"

"You've been on your own. Who knows what you've seen and done on the road and before? Your level of sophistication is generations away from her. C'mon, you aren't out of school that long that you have forgotten the differences between a ninth grader and an eleventh grader, especially when it comes to girls. Girls," he lectured, "move up the social ladder much faster than boys." He nodded toward Echo, who was walking on ahead of us. "She's like a boy, a boy in elementary school at best. You should be very careful about what you say to her, what you show her," he added sharply.

I nodded, but his words and the cold way in which he spoke to me made me feel more and more like an intruder. I fell behind him as we entered the dining room. Mrs. Westington had put out a nice spread of cold cuts, cheeses, breads, and a jug of homemade lemonade. There were homemade cookies as well. I watched as Echo and Tyler signed between them, holding their private little chat. Then Tyler pointed to things on the table and had her pronounce them. If she didn't do it clearly, he put her hand on his neck and repeated it, making her repeat it until she pronounced the word better.

Mrs. Westington stood by watching and listening with a smile on her thin lips. I slipped into a chair, conscious of doing anything that might distract Echo from Tyler and his constant tutoring. His way was to make everything they did together, every situation and activity, part of the learning experience. The world was her classroom. No bells rung in her school to end the session or the day, but Tyler was right about her—she had an insatiable appetite for learning.

"Echo has improved so much since Tyler came to teach her," Mrs. Westington told me.

I glanced at him, but he was busy fixing himself a sandwich and dipping into the cole slaw and potato salad.

"I'm sure she has," I said.

"He'll do wonders for you as well," she said.

Tyler looked up sharply. "Let's wait and see how she does on the evaluations, Mrs. Westington. As I told you before, I have no idea what kind of a student she was when she was in school."

"Oh, she must have been a good student. She'll do well," Mrs. Westington insisted.

Tyler ignored her, and me, for that matter. He and Echo continued their private conversations. I felt like someone who didn't know she was invisible and wondered why no one paid any attention to her. I could see that even Mrs. Westington wasn't able to follow their signing that well. They moved their hands and fingers with lightning speed. It brought back memories of Uncle Palaver humorously imitating a southerner trying to understand a New Yorker who spoke so quickly. Mrs. Westington nodded at me and shrugged to indicate she was lost when it came to following them. She returned to the kitchen.

"How long does it take to communicate that well with someone who can't hear?" I asked him.

"It takes as long as it takes," he replied dryly. "Obviously, it depends on your ability to learn yourself and, as I have said repeatedly, I have no idea what you're capable of doing and what you aren't capable of doing. It might take you weeks or you might not get proficient at it for months or maybe you'll never succeed at it. School and learning have obviously not been a priority in your life. Why should it suddenly be now?"

I felt the heat that accompanied my rising blood travel up my neck and into my face. "You don't know what has and what hasn't been a priority in my life."

He shrugged. "No, I don't. That's the point."

"Well, perhaps you'll know very soon then," I replied, and ate my sandwich. I had intended to avoid the bread and cookies, but his arrogance and his aloofness riled me up and I ate more out of frustration. He watched me reach greedily for the food. I thought he looked so smug in his evaluation of me and his expectations. He thinks I'm just some fat, lazy girl taking advantage of these people, I concluded. I couldn't say why what he thought was so important to me all of a sudden, but as much as I hated to admit it to myself, it did.

I didn't return with them to the office to watch him finish his lessons with Echo. Instead, I located the book on signing and went up to my bedroom to read it and practice before a mirror, determined to impress him the next time I saw him. I was up there so long and concentrating so hard, I didn't realize how much time had gone by nor did I hear him leave. A little while after he had, Echo came looking for me. I had left the bedroom door open and suddenly realized she was there watching me go at it in front of the mirror. I heard her laugh.

"Oh," I said, turning. "I didn't hear you come in."

How silly that sounded. I didn't hear her? Lucky Tyler wasn't present. He would surely make me feel like some sort of an idiot.

She came over to me and began to help me with some of the signs, moving my fingers so they would be more accurate in depicting words and phrases. I worked with her for a while, looking into the mirror at the both of us as we practiced. She had sweet lips and tiny freckles under the crests of her cheeks. Her face was tightening and shaping. Those high cheekbones will make her stunning one day, I thought, and looked at my own bloated cheeks. My face should be in the dictionary next to *plump,* I thought.

Echo assumed I was growing bored. She began to look again at some of Uncle Palaver's magic tricks. The ones I had brought in were collected in the corner by the windows. I showed her the self-tying handkerchief, the cut and restored string, and the coin through an elbow. It all delighted her and she asked me to do each one again. Finally, I communicated the idea that she should learn them herself. I thought she would enjoy performing them for her grandmother and especially for Tyler Monahan. She didn't seem to understand when I explained and when I referred to Mr. Monahan, even when I pronounced his name slowly so she could read it on my lips.

Why was it so easy for her to read his lips and not mine?

I flipped through the book and found the sign for tutor: both T hands with the palms facing were to be placed against my temples and then moved forward and back several times. It said to add the sign for individual, which was to open my palms and trace my body down to my hips. She finally understood and laughed. Then she signed back, but I didn't under-

stand. Frustrated, she wrote on the pad on my table:
"I call him Ty, not Mr. Monahan."

Oh, so that's it, I thought.

"He wants me to call him that," she wrote, and
smiled proudly. Having a more personal relationship
with him was obviously very important to her.

I watched her look about the room and then reverently touch things that had been her mother's. Even
something as ordinary and simple as a hairbrush intrigued and fascinated her. She fingered a strand of
hair in the bristles and I wondered what the separation had really been like for her even at that young
age. She couldn't recall her mother's voice, but I was
sure she could recall the scent of her hair, the image
of her face, and the warmth of her touch. After all, I
knew what it was like to lose your mother and cling
to such memories. Sometimes, the sound of similar
laughter, the familiar scent of a perfume or even some
familiar gesture brought back a movie full of sweet
remembrances.

Gazing about the room through Echo's eyes, I suddenly realized that there were no pictures of Rhona,
either by herself, with Mrs. Westington, or with
boyfriends or girlfriends. Surely there had been some.
Where were they? Had Mrs. Westington removed
them in a fit of anger? Did Echo have any pictures of
her mother in her room? I thumbed through the ASL
book on signing and located the word for photograph.
If I avoided writing things out and forced myself to
use sign language, I would learn it much faster.

To say photograph the right C hand was to be held
in front of the face with the thumb edge near the face
and the palm facing left. The hand was to be brought

sharply around to the open left hand and struck firmly against the left palm, which was held facing forward with the fingers pointing straight up. I pointed to the brush and then did the sign again.

She understood immediately and reached for my hand to lead me out of the bedroom down the hallway to her room. I scooped up the ASL book on sign language and followed her. Although it was smaller than the room I was in, it had a similar canopy bed and matching dressers. I saw she had placed Mr. Panda on her bed exactly as I had the teddy bear placed on mine, between the two pillows. I smiled and nodded my approval.

There was a school desk in the left corner with books and notebooks on it. I saw a few dolls on shelves and some treasured souvenirs from places she probably had visited either with her mother or with Mrs. Westington. I didn't see any pictures of her mother on the shelves, dressers, or her desk, but she opened the bottom drawer in one of her dressers, cleared away the socks, and produced a four-by-eight photograph of a pretty, dark-haired woman in an abbreviated two-piece bathing suit holding a beach ball on some beach and posing like a model.

Echo handed it to me and distinctly pronounced the word "motha."

"Mother," I repeated. Did I dare take her hand and put it on my neck to get her to say it better? Not yet, I thought. Maybe I'd do something wrong.

I gazed at the picture. "She's very pretty," I said, and then realized I wasn't facing her when I had said it. Immediately, I thumbed through the ASL book and found the sign for very pretty. I put the fingers of my right hand over my right thumb, held it just under my mouth, and then made a counterclockwise circle, ending in the same position, and pointed to the picture.

That brought a smile to her lips. I thumbed through the book again and then I put my two outstretched forefingers together, pointed to her and to the picture, and did it again, telling her she was like her mother. I meant just as pretty.

She shook her head. I nodded emphatically, but she shook her head again, this time just as emphatically as I had nodded, and then she cried, "No," and looked like she was going to burst into tears.

I hadn't meant she was like her, but just that she looked like her. Had she misunderstood?

"You look like her," I repeated, and she continued to shake her head. Language is so complicated and signing so imperfect, I thought. This could be very frustrating. From what well of tolerance did Tyler Monahan draw the patience? I was sure what he did took years and years of training. Perhaps I wasn't up to this and he was right. I would grow tired and disgusted and leave sooner than I planned. I sat there, musing about it, considering my options. How long could I last out there on my own? What would I do to earn money? Would I go back to live with Brenda?

"What's going on in here?" I heard, and turned to the doorway to see Mrs. Westington standing there. "I called for you to come down."

"Oh, I'm sorry. I didn't hear you."

Echo quickly took the photo from me and buried it again in her dresser drawer. I could see from the look in her eyes that she didn't want her grandmother to know she had that picture.

"What are you two doing?"

"Oh, nothing much," I said, standing. "She was showing me her room and I was practicing signing with her." I held up the ASL book.

Nevertheless, she looked suspicious, probably because Echo looked so frightened. Why wouldn't Mrs. Westington permit her to have pictures of her own mother? That was silly, I thought, but also thought I should keep my opinion to myself when it came to Rhona.

"Yes, well, she's been in all day. That's why I was calling for you. You should get her to go out and get some air. I always worry that the child doesn't get enough sunshine."

"Okay. Wait, let me tell her," I said, and looked into the book.

I grasped my downward opened right hand and drew it up and out of my left hand's grasp. As I did so, I brought the right fingers together and then made the O sign with my left facing the right.

She smiled and nodded.

"Very good," Mrs. Westington said.

I reached for Echo's hand and we started out of the room.

"There's a little lake in back," Mrs. Westington called to me as we continued. "She likes looking at the frogs and such. A fresh stream feeds it and sometimes there are trout. It's rare, but Trevor's pulled out a few and cooked 'em. She'll show you. There's a rowboat, too, if you want to go for a ride. She can swim, so don't worry about that. Trevor taught her. Wouldn't take her in the boat until she learned. An ounce of prevention is worth a pound of cure. Take a letter."

I nodded and we went downstairs and out. Echo had been very eager to get away. Now that we were outside, I thought about the fact that she couldn't hear any birds. It came to mind because a large crow was cawing loudly off to the right while it perched on the branch of an old oak tree. To my surprise, however, Echo pulled on my arm and pointed to the crow while she imitated its cry. It made me laugh.

"How did you know the sound?" I asked. She just stared at me, smiling.

I started to thumb through the book. Now I truly felt like some visitor to a foreign country, hurrying to find the right words. I put together a *how* and *know* and she nodded, understanding.

"Ty," she said, then put her right hand softly to her throat and repeated the crow's call.

"So, you've gone for walks with Ty and he's taught you about nature, too? That's nice," I said. She didn't read my lips and I didn't sign anything. I was really speaking my thoughts. "He's making you aware of much more than just math, science, social studies, and English. No wonder you have a crush on him. I wonder if he's aware of it. To me, he looks like he'd be oblivious to that sort of thing."

Beside a deaf person, I could safely voice my thoughts. I could talk to myself aloud, rattle on and on, and not worry that she would tell him anything I had said.

She wasn't quiet, however. As we walked, she tugged on my hand frequently and pointed out things. One was the inside of a dead tree where bees had created a hive. I never would have seen it if she hadn't shown it to me. She was like a tour guide, anxious that I not miss a thing, whether it be birds, squirrels, rabbits, or the frame of an old hammock on the rear patio. Everything excited her in her small world. Her hands went everywhere, her fingers moving quickly.

I have to learn this signing thoroughly and quickly, I thought. The faster I did so, the less lonely she would be, and in fact, the less I would be as well. More important perhaps, Tyler Monahan wouldn't have as firm control over both of us.

We paused at the lake, where there was a small dock and a rowboat tied to it. I gathered from her words and her signing that she had come here often when she was little, sometimes with her mother, and many times with Trevor Washington, who took her fishing. She had learned to pronounce his name very well, with only a little exaggeration with the vowels, so it came out "Tre . . . voooor."

Then she acted out a little scene with lots of grimacing that was meant to tell me that she didn't like catching anything because she felt sorry for the fish immediately after hooking it. Reading her gestures and expressions was like unraveling one riddle after another for me, each one giving me more and more insight into what her life had been like with primarily only her grandmother and Trevor for companions.

She sat on the dock with her feet dangling over and just above the water. I sat beside her and we were quiet, both watching the insects circling in a frenzy. Occasionally we would see a fish pop to the surface to feast on something. The surface of the water was their dining table, I thought.

The sun had fallen just below the tree line in the west so that the shadows deepened and sprawled slowly and lazily over the pond, which was really quite large. To the left it went around a bend of trees. I thought it was the golden moment of the day, when everything paused for a while to enjoy the mere fact of its existence, the fact that it had lived through another wonderful twenty-four hours or so. I certainly felt that way.

I indicated the rowboat and she nodded excitedly. We got into it carefully and I asked her if she wanted to row. She was anxious to do so. She did very well, too. As we glided along, I closed my eyes and thought about how peaceful it was here, and how easy to be contented, even if only for a short while. Inside, my body felt like it was winding down, relaxing and loosening. I think I actually drifted asleep for a few minutes, because when I opened my eyes, I realized we were already around the bend. I hadn't meant for us to go that far and so I sat up quickly and indicated that she should turn around. She shook her head and pointed to the far shore. Obviously, she wanted to show me something.

She rowed with determination. I gazed over her shoulder and searched for anything significant. All I saw was a large rock. She brought the boat close to it and reached out with her hand to guide us right up against it. Then she smiled at me and nodded at the rock.

"Ty and me," she said. She pronounced it almost perfectly and patted the rock.

"Ty and you? What are you talking about?" I stood up carefully and made my way to her side to look at the rock.

There, carved with a pocketknife or something,

was a heart, and inside it was clearly scraped "Ty and Me." I stared at it and then looked at her.

"Who did this?" I asked her. I mimed carving into the rock. "Who?"

"Ty," she said.

Maybe he was trying to demonstrate something, I thought. But what? Carving a heart? A young girl's emotions are not toys. He was just arrogant enough to have done something like this.

I felt her eyes on me. She began to sign and gesture. At first I didn't understand what she wanted to know. She became more emphatic and I soon realized she was asking me if I had or ever had a boyfriend. She made me laugh with her gestures to show holding hands, kissing, and then putting her hands together and tilting her head as she flicked her eyelids.

"Yes, yes, I understand," I said, glanced at the carved heart, and then sat across from her. A boyfriend? What should I tell her?

I thought about Peter Smoke, the Indian boy I had met while I was going to school in Memphis. He had been my instructor in chess club and had taught me a lot about his Indian beliefs, especially the medicine wheel. We had started to have a romantic relationship. He was really the closest I had come to having a real boyfriend, but when he misinterpreted my intentions, it hadn't ended well. He's probably forgotten all about me by now, I thought. It was certainly not a relationship I could claim.

I shook my head. "No, no boyfriend, I'm afraid."

She looked surprised but also suspicious. Was I telling her the truth? Why not? she wanted to know, as if every girl my age had to have been or always was in a romance.

"Because I'm too fat," I said. She shook her head, not understanding, so I bloated my cheeks and held my arms out beside my hips.

She looked thoughtful and then smiled and pointed to herself. "Ty," she said.

I started to shake my head and made some silly attempt to explain he was too old for her. "He can't be your boyfriend," I insisted, shaking my head harder.

She laughed and pointed to the rock again. "Ty and me," she said.

I continued to shake my head.

And then she pursed her lips and mimed embracing him, closed her eyes, and made the sound of a kiss.

"He kissed you?" I asked, pointing at her.

She nodded.

"No, he didn't. Not like that," I told her, but she nodded more emphatically, her eyes wide. She pointed at the rock and went through the mime of kissing again. I picked up the ASL book and thumbed the pages to find the word *here*.

Your two hands were to be held out, palms up, and you moved the right to the right and the left to the left, back and forth.

She nodded. "Yes, yes," she said, and repeated the signing. She pointed down, made a rowing gesture, and then signed the kiss again.

It was clear to me what she was saying: "He kissed me right here at the rock after he drew this heart and put our names in it."

Did that all happen as she described? Was it possible? He was the one who had told Mrs. Westington Echo was too vulnerable and I could be a bad influence. He had seemed to be sincerely protective of her and yet how could he justify carving this in the rock and then kissing her like that? Was he taking advantage of her?

I tilted my head skeptically, but she kept nodding. Then she embraced herself and turned from side to side. Perhaps he had only comforted her, I thought, and she had misinterpreted it. Perhaps she was very sad and he had tried to reassure her.

"Ty?" I asked, and imitated her motion. She nodded, then rose and stepped closer to me, kneeling down in the boat. "What?" I said.

She took my right hand and brought it to her stomach. "What are you saying? I don't understand."

Smiling, she slowly ran my hand up and over her breasts. I pulled it back quickly, the firmness of her nipple sending an electric shock up my arm. Visions of my sister's girlfriend touching me, wanting me to touch her, came surging out of my memory and over my eyes.

"NO!" I cried, shaking my head emphatically. "That's not nice."

She tilted her head and looked up at me. Then she shrugged and returned to her bench seat. Instinctively, I looked back in the direction of the house to see if Mrs. Westington or perhaps Trevor had witnessed what had just occurred.

"Back," I indicated. "Go back, Echo." I gestured vigorously, almost in a panic.

She started to row, looking as if she might burst into tears.

"You don't just do that with a boy," I tried to explain. "It leads to other things."

How stupid I sound, I thought, me giving advice to a young, deaf girl.

She stared, her face soaked in confusion. I returned to my ASL book and as quickly as I could, put together some thoughts. She paused and watched me. The word for body was easy. I placed my hand against my chest and then removed it and placed it a bit lower. I pointed to her. And then I told her that her body was sacred, precious, and should be protected.

With a troubled face, she watched me put together words and sentences to tell her she was too young to do these things yet. I told her girls her age, my age, could have babies and then what would we do?

I could see I wasn't doing that good a job of explaining why I was so upset with her, so I promised I would sit down and write more of an explanation later.

As she turned the rowboat, I gazed back at the rock and then thought about what she had told me. What did it all mean? Was this really something Tyler Monahan had done and if it were so, shouldn't Mrs. Westington know about it? She was so proud and appreciative of all he had done with Echo. Here I am, after only three days, telling her something that would destroy it all.

Echo continued to look at me sadly as she rowed. She's so innocent, I thought. Maybe I was coming on too strong. I smiled back at her so she wouldn't feel bad. I told her everything would be all right and I was not angry at her. Her face brightened again. As soon as we reached the dock and stepped out of the row-

boat, I indicated we should continue our walk on
around the property, but what she had shown me and
had told me through her gestures and few words continued to haunt me. Would I dare ask Tyler Monahan
about it?

When we came to the motor home, parked off to
the side behind the house, I stopped and stared at the
bright letters painted on the side: The Amazing
Palaver. It spread such a layer of heaviness over my
heart. I was actually anxious for it to be taken away.
We were waiting for the attorney to tell us how we
should deal with it, as well as all of Uncle Palaver's
other possessions. All these legal actions had to be
woven through the convoluted halls of justice. I
imagined I was lost in some file cabinet in some
judge's office.

Echo was full of curiosity. She tugged at my arm.
Her hands were moving a mile a minute. I laughed at
her exuberance. What she really wanted was to go inside the motor home. She had been told about my living in it with Uncle Palaver and traveling about to
perform. I was sure she wondered how someone
could live in it as he or she would live in a home. I
was hesitant, but she was begging. I was reluctant to
go in there and stir my own emotions and memories,
but I didn't have the heart to refuse her, especially
after how I had reacted to what she had done at the
pond.

I opened the motor home door and we stepped up
and into it. She went immediately to the driver's seat
to toy with the steering wheel. She was like any other
teenager, I thought, intrigued with the idea of driving,
especially something as big as this. She turned the

wheel, imagining herself on the highway. Finally, she rose and went into the living room.

I hadn't done anything with the vehicle since we had arrived. Just looking at the things Uncle Palaver had left out before he had died saddened me. Now that I was inside with her, I felt embarrassed about the mess. I started to clean up and soon, she was helping. We washed the glasses and plates and silverware and put it all in the cabinets. Then I showed her where I had slept and she wanted to climb up and try lying on the bunk. It struck her funny and we both laughed. She pretended to be asleep and be comfortable.

Wouldn't it be wonderful if we could just drive off together and live on some magical road that took us only to happy, joyful places? I thought. I'd become Uncle Palaver and she would see the world. How easy it was to dream. Fantasy was catching, infectious, especially in here where I had harbored so many fantasies of my own.

I continued to straighten up the inside of the vehicle, picking up papers, closing up the garbage. For a few moments, it was as if Uncle Palaver was still alive and he and I were back on the road, parked in some lot, preparing for another show. I actually missed that life, as short as it had been. I went into a reverie, recalling some of the places and events, the crowds that had given him such applause. I didn't realize I was crying either, until the tears dripped off my chin. It snapped me out of it, but when I looked about, Echo wasn't with me. Where was she?

I turned and saw her at the rear of the motor home. She was standing there with her hands over her ears as though someone was screaming. It confused me for a moment until I realized she was standing in Uncle Palaver's doorway and she was looking in at the Destiny doll.

"Echo! Come away from there!" I shouted, but of course she couldn't hear me. I hurried to her and tugged her arm.

Her face was full of confusion, fear, and astonishment. The doll was so lifelike that I was sure for a few moments at least, she thought she was looking at a real woman naked. She shook her head. Why was she lying in the bed like that? Why hadn't she been covered or dressed? How would I begin to explain?

She didn't wait; she turned away and quickly hurried out of the motor home. I gazed in at Destiny. I should have left this door locked, I thought, or thrown something over her. How could I have forgotten? Her glassy eyes seemed to focus on me accusingly. I had left her here, deserted her. She had been so precious to Uncle Palaver and I had left her.

I sighed and closed the door. By the time I stepped out of the motor home, Echo was around the house, hurrying to go back inside, fleeing from what surely had been a most shocking sight. Mrs. Westington is going to be upset with me, I thought. She didn't want me to expose Echo to the doll just yet. She'll surely want me to leave now. Once Tyler Monahan heard about it, he would say, "See, I told you she'd be a bad influence." Mrs. Westington would have no other choice but to ask me to leave.

Resolved to it, I headed back to the house.

Apparently, however, Echo hadn't stopped to tell her grandmother what she had just seen. Instead, she had gone directly up to her room. Mrs. Westington stepped out of the kitchen when I entered.

"Did you two have a nice walk and go rowing on the pond?"

"Yes, Ma'am," I said.

"I know it's terrible that I don't get that child out and about more. Maybe now that you're here, we'll do it. I'll have Trevor take us for a ride this weekend. We'll go to a nice restaurant for lunch and shop. I need some things myself. I have a roast chicken cooking. Hope you have an appetite."

"That's been my problem. I always have an appetite," I said.

"Well thank your lucky stars you do. A good appetite means a healthy soul. Where's Echo?"

"She came in ahead of me. I guess she went on up to her room."

"Oh, did she? Well, maybe she's a little tired. Tyler works her hard and long when he's at it. He just loves that girl. He's determined to bring her up to speed. I'm sure he will. He'll do the same for you," she added.

Maybe, I thought, maybe not, but I smiled and nodded.

"I'll just go and wash up and come down to help you," I said.

"No rush now. I'm fine. I've been feeding people for quite a long time without much help."

She stared at me. It was on the tip of my tongue to confess, to tell her what had just happened, but I didn't do it.

"You look like the cat's got your tongue. Anything wrong?"

My chance to come clean, I thought, but I didn't do it. I didn't want to risk losing her and this home. I shook my head and hurried up the stairs.

You're a coward, April Taylor, I told myself. You run away from everything, even yourself.

I went directly to Echo's room. The door was open. When I looked in, I saw her hovered over the novel Tyler had given her to read. I sat beside her and she looked up at me. Her face was still a little peaked from her fright and her hands were trembling. I took them into mine, squeezed them gently to comfort her, and smiled at her. Then I reached for a pen and some paper.

Here we go, I thought, and began to write about my uncle, his dear assistant, Destiny, and the doll. I gave it to her in small doses, explaining why my uncle had the doll made and what its purpose was in the show.

She continued to look skeptical and wrote, "But isn't it a real lady?"

Again and again, I told her no but she still looked skeptical. I apologized for not warning her about Destiny. I explained how I hadn't gone into the motor home since I had gotten my things out of it and some of the magic tricks, and how I had forgotten about her in the bedroom. Again, I emphasized how the doll was part of the magic show, helped do tricks, and was used like a puppet, a ventriloquist's doll. Being deaf, her knowledge of that was nil and I had a difficult time explaining it.

Nevertheless, I promised to show how the doll worked someday and that seemed to calm her, although she still looked quite confused.

Exhausted, I went to my room and prepared for dinner. As soon as I was downstairs, Trevor caught me in the hallway while Mrs. Westington was in the kitchen. He pulled me aside to whisper.

"Something happen with Echo?" he asked. "I saw her running into the house earlier."

I told him what had occurred and I also told him quickly that I hadn't revealed it to Mrs. Westington.

"Oh, that doll," he said. I recalled how he had reacted when he saw Destiny for the first time the day I had driven up to the house.

"I don't think Mrs. Westington is going to be happy about it," I said. "It was my fault. I had better explain."

"For now, let it be," he advised.

Mrs. Westington saw us whispering and looked at us suspiciously, but she didn't ask any questions.

At dinner Trevor and I talked more about the winery, how it had been so successful and why his grapes were so special. He went into a long lecture about methods of cultivating. Mrs. Westington put on a grouchy face and complained about his wasting my time now and not just his own, but I could see she enjoyed my enthusiasm. Echo struggled to be part of our conversation, but neither I nor Trevor remembered to explain everything as we went along. I, of course, had a limited ability with signing. Every once in a while, I did what I could to keep her in the discussion, and then I suddenly got a great idea from watching her struggle to keep up with us.

However, I thought it was a terrific idea, but Tyler Monahan thought it further proved that I was too weird to be around Echo.

When he arrived the next day, I greeted him with, "I want to learn like a deaf person."

He froze in the hallway and pulled in the corners of his mouth. Then he tilted his head and said, "What?"

"I thought if I was deaf, I would be forced to learn how to communicate through signing. It would put the same pressure on me that a person really deaf has on her, and perhaps I'll learn faster."

"Oh, is that so? And how do you intend on becoming deaf, pop your eardrums or something?"

"Wax," I said.

"Wax?"

"Yes, I'm going to fill my ears with wax. My uncle Palaver was once part of a circus act that required him to assist the man who was shot out of a cannon. He told me he filled his ears with melted wax to keep himself from going deaf and he couldn't hear a thing and that they had to tap him on the shoulder to get his attention."

Tyler shook his head. "Let me understand this. You not only want me to tutor you for the high school equivalency exam. You want me to do it through signing, lipreading, and all the other techniques I use on Echo?"

"Exactly," I said.

"You're crazier than I thought," he replied. I smiled. "It won't work," he insisted.

"We'll see," I said. I had spent hours and hours the night before on the ASL book even after Echo and I had practiced for hours. I wasn't proficient yet, but I had come a long way and I was determined he would have a better impression of me and my abilities.

"Look, if you think I'm going to waste my time just to amuse you, you're—"

"I'll be right back," I interrupted before he could warn and threaten me, and I went upstairs and filled my ears with the candle wax I had already melted and prepared in a cup. I tested myself by banging a brush on the vanity counter and then by running water. It was very difficult to hear anything. With the ASL book under my arm, I returned to the office, where Tyler was already instructing Echo. He looked up suspiciously, and then he produced a packet of tests he obviously wanted me to take.

"This will help me evaluate you," he said. I knew he had said it, but I responded with the signing for "I can't hear you."

He squinted and I turned my head so he could see the wax in my ears. Then he raised his eyes to the ceiling. I saw an impish light come into his eyes. When he looked at me again, he signed, "Let's have breakfast."

I shook my head at him and signed back, "We already ate breakfast."

His eyes widened with surprise. I stepped forward and indicated the tests. "For me?" I signed.

He nodded. I took them and sat.

"What do I start with?" I signed.

"Math," he signed back.

"I hate math," I told him.

"Then that's what you should start with," he replied, signing quickly, almost too quickly. "What is your favorite subject?" he asked. I got thrown by the word favorite for a moment and then figured it out.

"English," I said.

He nodded gently, his eyes bright with his surprise and admiration for what I had already achieved.

Echo had been watching us the whole time. She started to smile, looked at Tyler, who was staring at me now with a lot more respect, and then she looked back at me.

Her smile slowly weakened until it was gone. She looked at Tyler and then at me again. I think she was afraid my initials might get carved into that heart scratched into the rock.

And maybe she thought that was the reason I had warned her against being too intimate with him or any boy?

Of course, I told myself it wasn't.

I looked at Tyler Monahan flipping through the pages of a book. He was a handsome young man, so self-assured.

Maybe what I had seen in Echo's eyes was really in my own, I thought.

And if a young, innocent girl could see it so clearly, he surely would.

3

Distractions

The tests Tyler gave me took hours and although I wouldn't admit it to him, the wax in my ears made them very itchy inside. Every once in a while, I caught him looking at me with some suspicion in his eyes. I was sure that in his mind I was simply pulling off a stunt to win Mrs. Westington's affections even more. When I saw Mrs. Westington in the door to announce lunch, I signed back at her that I was going to skip lunch and continue doing the tests. She looked confused and turned to Tyler. He told her about the wax in my ears and she came over to me quickly to look.

"I want to learn like Echo learns," I explained when she opened her mouth in amazement. "I want to be dependent upon the same means she is. It will help me develop the ability to communicate with her faster and better."

She looked at Tyler, who shrugged, lifted his arms, and shook his head with a look that said, "I don't understand her." They went off to lunch, but Mrs. Westington wouldn't hear of me not eating anything. She brought in a turkey sandwich and a glass of lemonade and put it on the desk. I thanked her. I could see her go off muttering to herself.

I was so involved in the tests, I didn't notice how much time had gone by without Tyler and Echo returning to the office. Either hoping to defeat me or trying to get me to give up on my own, he had presented me with a great deal of work that included math problems, science questions, social studies questions, and pages and pages of grammar exams. By the time I was finished, it was nearly time for him to leave for the day. I closed the test booklet and looked about, puzzled, but before I got up to leave, Tyler appeared without Echo. I looked at him curiously. He seemed very upset.

"What's wrong?" I asked. "Where's Echo? Something the matter with her?"

"You'd better scrape that wax out of your ears right now," he wrote on a pad.

"Why?"

"I want to talk to you about what you told Echo," he added. "And also about what you showed her." Of course I knew he meant Destiny.

I asked him where Echo was and he told me she was upstairs in her room working on some assignments he had given her.

"I'll be waiting for you outside," he told me. He tried to keep his emotions under a tight, firm face, but his rage swirled about in the dark pools of his eyes.

I went into the bathroom and began to remove the wax using hot water and a toothpick very carefully. I didn't get it all out, but I knew Tyler was waiting impatiently for me on the front porch.

"Let's take a walk," he said sharply the moment I appeared.

He charged down the steps.

Trevor was continuing his harvesting of his grapes and watched us walk off toward the pond. We went quite a way before Tyler spoke and when he did, he nearly shouted, blurting, "I knew you were going to create more problems and make things more difficult for me, as if it wasn't hard enough for me as it is. I just knew it!"

"What's that supposed to mean? What problems?"

He kept walking, paused, changed direction, and continued like someone caught in a great state of confusion.

"Can you please stand still and tell me what this is all about? What problems have I caused you?"

Finally, he stopped and turned to me. "You wanted to help her with her schoolwork," he said, shaking her head. "You wanted to learn how to communicate with her quickly. You put on this whole show about simulating a deaf person's condition so you'd be forced to learn like she does. You did some job on Mrs. Westington when you told her your sad, sad story. Poor April Taylor, an orphan dumped on their doorstep," he said, mimicking someone who felt terrible for me.

"What did I do to get you so upset?" I screamed.

"What did you do? I'll tell you what you did. First chance you get, what do you talk about with Echo? Her math problems? No. English homework? No. Social studies? No. What then? Boyfriends, kissing, petting, making babies! Her brain is so full of that stuff, she can't concentrate on anything I tell her to do. And she's asking me questions that would embarrass a prostitute!"

"I didn't tell her anything a girl her age shouldn't know, things girls younger than her know."

"Who told you to tell her anything?"

"Why do you want to keep her so socially innocent and ignorant?" I fired back, my eyes small with accusations. "Why would you want that?"

Instead of answering, he ignored me and continued with his assault. "And then you show her that . . . naked doll, a life-size, naked doll with . . . with pubic hair? How could you do that?" he asked, grimacing. "Did you get some sort of sick pleasure out of watching how she reacted?"

"You don't understand what happened."

"Right, I don't understand. At least you're smart enough to realize that. My advice to you is to just pick up and leave. Get into that motor home, drive off, and go live with one of your own relatives, the first ones who'll take you in."

"Oh, you're such a goody-goody, so protective of poor Echo, so worried I would corrupt her, while you go and carve your initials in a heart in that rock with her and get her to think you're going to be her boyfriend."

"Rock?"

"For your information, she showed me how you touched her, too! In places you shouldn't have! I've been thinking about telling Mrs. Westington, only I didn't want to start a whole mess after being here so short a time. If anyone has created unnecessary problems, it's you, not me, Tyler Monahan!"

His face brightened as the blood rushed into his cheeks. "What rock? What sort of touching? What are you talking about?" he demanded, stepping up to me, his chest swelling, his hands on his hips.

I nodded at the pond. "The rock that sticks up on the other side of the pond. She brought me there and showed it to me. After that she showed me how and where you touched her."

He stared at me, his black pearl eyes losing some of their rage. Then he gazed out at the pond and turned back to me. "You're lying."

"Oh, I'm lying. What are you going to do, claim it's my imagination? Maybe we can't bring Mrs. Westington out there, but I could tell Trevor to go look if you need it confirmed."

"Show it to me," he said.

"Why, you don't know where it is?"

"For your information, I don't."

I hesitated. Could he be telling the truth or did he just want to get me into that boat? I began to imagine all sorts of things. If I got into that rowboat with him, he might try to drown me.

"Just as I thought," he said at my continued hesitation. He folded his arms under his chest and stood back firmly. "You're making it up. You're sick, as sick as the uncle who had that doll in his motor home."

"No, you're the one who's sick," I said. "I'll prove it, too," I added, and marched down to the dock. Now he was the one hesitating. "Well, are you coming to see what I know or are you going to run back into the house and tell Mrs. Westington a bunch of lies?"

After a moment, he unfolded his arms and walked down to the dock. I got into the rowboat first. He looked back at the house and then he got into it.

"I'll row," I said. "I don't want you to strain yourself."

He squeezed his forehead and narrowed his eyes as I set out, my eyes fixed firmly on him.

"For your information, not that I care, I didn't realize Echo understood half of what I told her about boys and making babies. I was planning on writing out most of it tonight. She's nearly fifteen years old and she should know a great deal more about her own body and sex and everything, only who is going to teach it to her, Mrs. Westington? I doubt it. You? I don't see any books on health education."

"That's not what I'm here for."

"Yeah," I said, smirking. "That's not what you're here for. Oh, no."

"It isn't and I already told you, I thought she should be in an environment with other girls her own age. Not that you couldn't teach her about sex from firsthand experiences, I'm sure."

"Oh, you're so damn smug. You think you know everything about everybody."

He didn't respond. He turned away and looked out over the pond.

"What are you trying to do, think of some clever Chinese proverb?"

He started to swell with anger and then he just shook his head.

I rowed hard and quickly, bringing us up beside the rock. Then I reached out, stopped the rowboat, and looked at him. "Here it is. Like you didn't know."

He rose, wobbling a bit, and crossed to where I had indicated on the rock. He studied it a moment and then surprised me by laughing.

"What's so funny?" How could he laugh?

"It's pretty easy to figure out that I didn't do this."

"Oh, really? And why is it so easy, Mr. Big Shot?"

"It's easy because it says 'Ty and me.' I don't think I would have written 'Ty and me,' even though you believe I'm too much in love with myself. Also, look at how crudely this heart is drawn. It's not carved so much as scratched. Anyway, why would I put something indelibly into this rock for anyone to see if I was trying to be surreptitious?"

"Sur what?"

"Sneaky, hidden. Pass a high school equivalency exam," he muttered.

I squeezed my eyebrows together and studied the heart in the rock. Of course he was right about it saying "Ty and me." Why hadn't I realized it?

He sat and folded his hands over his lap. I returned to my seat and for a moment neither of us spoke. The boat rocked gently in the breeze and my pounding heart slowed down.

"Look," he said in a much calmer tone of voice, "what we have here is an adolescent fantasy. It's not uncommon or even unexpected, especially with a girl so isolated. Don't you think I'm aware of all that? I do the best I can. That's why I want to bring her up to a level where she could enter a structured school environment quickly and have more normal experiences."

"That's all I want for her as well," I said.

"It's hardly normal to bring her to that motor home and show her a nude sex doll."

"It's not a sex doll and I didn't show it to her. She wanted to go into the motor home to see it and I forgot about my uncle's doll."

"Naked on a bed? That's just so sick. You're uncle must have been so perverted beside being a drunk."

"He was not! You're so arrogant. You don't know what you're talking about."

"Maybe I don't, but I wonder if you do either. I can only imagine what it was like for you to be living under those circumstances and traveling about with someone like that."

"Nothing ugly happened!" I cried, and then I really did begin to cry. "He taught me magic tricks and I helped him with his act. He was my only close relative. He loved me and he was alone, too. I had nowhere else to go!"

As inscrutable as Tyler tried to be with me, his face couldn't help but soften with some compassion.

"Look, I admit I don't know your whole story. All I know is what I've been told by Mrs. Westington and what Echo described to me earlier. I'm sorry if I'm jumping to too many conclusions, but you're guilty of the same sort of impulsive judgments," he said, nodding at the rock.

I flicked the tears off my cheeks. Then I took a deep breath. This was a big mess. I wasn't here a week and already there was great turmoil. Does it just follow me wherever I go? Will it always?

"Well, what do we do now?" I asked him.

"Declare a truce," he said. "You want me to row us back?"

"No, I can do it," I said, grabbing the oars before he could. He shrugged and then leaned back.

"I don't mind being spoiled."

"Very funny."

He looked at me with somewhat more trusting eyes. "Did you complete the evaluation exams?"

"Yes."

"I'll pick them up and go over them tonight. I don't give the equivalency exam, you know. You have to schedule that at the public school. I'll help you arrange for it when I think you're ready, if you're ever ready."

"I'll be ready."

"So, if you don't mind telling me, why didn't you remain living with your sister? Even though she's off on tournaments, you could have stayed with her. She would be considered your legal guardian, I'm sure, and at least you could have remained in school and had something of a normal life."

I continued to row.

"Why did you run away to live with your uncle?"

I hesitated to say anything. I continued to row, with him staring at me.

"You don't have to tell me anything," he added in a tone of voice that meant precisely the opposite.

"I couldn't get along with her roommate!" I exclaimed.

"Oh? Why not?"

"She was too demanding."

"Demanding? In what way?"

"In a sexual way, if you have to know," I said. "And my sister was upset about it. I knew that somehow it would end up being my fault."

"What do you mean exactly? What did she do?"

he asked, his face full of interest and curiosity now.

"I don't want to go into detail, Tyler. She wanted to have sexual relations with me."

"Really? Did she just ask or what?"

"No, she did more than just ask. I said I don't like talking about it. It was very, very disturbing at the time and it's painful to think about it now."

He nodded, thinking. "Why would your sister be angry at you for something like that? You would think she . . ."

He thought again and then he nodded softly. "Oh," he said. "You mean your sister and this other woman were . . ."

"Yes."

"Man, you did have a screwed up family. A lesbian sister, an uncle in love with a doll, and who knows what else."

"My family wasn't screwed up! Not everyone marches to the same drummer. I'd think you'd understand that, being you're so intelligent."

He shrugged. "What about you? Are you a lesbian?" he asked with as much emotion a doctor might show when he asked if I had an ache in my ear. "Is that why your sister's lover made a pass at you?"

"I don't think so," I said. "Just because one person in your family is gay, it doesn't mean you have to be."

"So why do you say you don't think so? Don't you know for sure? Are you attracted more to girls than boys?"

"I'd rather not talk about all that."

"Well, have you had boyfriends?" he pursued.

"It's not really any of your business," I said.

He didn't look angry about my reaction. He just looked pensive, again like some doctor reviewing symptoms. I rowed on, biting down on my lower lip and sucking back my tears. Talking about it only brought back my painful separation from Brenda and the only family I knew.

"How did your parents die? An accident?"

"No, my father had an inoperable brain tumor and my mother fell into a deep depression and overdosed on sleeping pills."

"Wow. I guess Mrs. Westington was right. You have been dragged over the coals."

"I'm not looking for any sympathy," I said. I wanted to add "especially from you," but I held that back.

"That's good. Old Chinese proverb say 'He who feels sorry for himself can demand an apology from no one.'"

"What's that mean?" I asked, grimacing.

He shrugged. "I'm not sure. I got it in a fortune cookie." He held his expression for a moment and then he burst out laughing. The expression of surprise on my face made him laugh harder.

Finally, I started to laugh myself. I was laughing through tears and it was like sunshine on a rainy day.

"Do me a favor," he said when we docked the row-boat.

"What?"

"Show me that doll. I'm curious about it and how Echo described it."

I looked at him suspiciously.

"I just want to see how a doll could upset her so

much and understand how you and your uncle used it in the show. If it makes you uncomfortable to do it, I understand."

"No, it's all right," I said. "I shouldn't have left Destiny like that anyway."

"Destiny? The doll has a name?"

"Yes. That was her real name."

"Real name? I don't get it."

"She was a real person. I'll show you pictures of her in the motor home."

"So a doll was made of a real person. Why?"

"You'll understand when you see it and the other things," I said.

"Everything all right?" Trevor called to us from the small vineyard as we walked toward the motor home. I knew he was really calling only to me.

"Yes, thank you, Trevor," I shouted back.

Tyler waved to him but said nothing, and Trevor didn't wave back. He barely nodded.

"As Mrs. Westington would say, the jury's still out as far as his opinion of me," he said as we continued. "That's all right. It's good that he's so protective of them." He glanced at me. "Looks like he's getting to be just as protective of you."

"Believe me, I don't mind," I said. "I haven't had anyone protective of me for a long, long time."

"I guess not," he said, and then paused when we reached the motor home. "There's a car, too."

"Yes, that was my car. Uncle Palaver hitched it on after I found him."

He studied me and the way I was looking at the vehicle. "It's hard for you to go in there, I bet."

"Yes."

"We don't have to do it. It's really not that important."

"No, I've got to do something with Destiny. Now is as good a time as any. C'mon," I said, and led him to the door. "Have you ever been in one of these before?"

"No," he replied. After we went up the steps, opened the door, and entered, he said, "Pretty neat."

"Yes. This part can be expanded after the motor home is parked."

I led him down to Uncle Palaver's bedroom. He stood gaping at the Destiny doll. I hurried to the dresser that contained her clothes and began to dress the doll.

"There's a picture of them together, the real Destiny and my uncle," I said, nodding at the framed picture on the wall to his right. He looked at it and then back at the doll.

It was embarrassing for me to put on her panties and her bra with him watching, but it was how Uncle Palaver had dressed her. I worked as quickly as I could.

"That is one lifelike doll. Can I touch it?" he asked. I nodded and watched him touch Destiny's arm. "Feels just like real skin. And those breasts and nipples. Who made it, a plastic surgeon?"

"I don't know."

"There are even fingernails and hairs. No wonder the kid was so confused. Why did your uncle have this made?"

"My uncle was very much in love with Destiny and it was so painful for him to lose her. He found someone who would do all this detail."

"Even pubic hair. You didn't need that much detail for the show, did you?"

"No, but it didn't hurt that she looked this real." I turned the doll over and undid the cabinet that held the batteries. "These have to be replaced," I said, taking the dead ones out.

"What can you make it do?"

"Using the transmitter, we, I mean I, can move her arms and legs, hands and fingers. Her head and even her eyes shift. But the most important thing is her mouth. We, my uncle mainly, could do an exciting ventriloquist act with her making her mouth move. Her comments related to the tricks and he had tricks he could do that often would involve the doll holding something. There are other things, too, things he used in his act."

"This must have been very expensive to create."

"I don't know," I said, completing the dressing of Destiny by zipping up the skirt and buttoning the blouse. "He never told me how much she cost to make. I don't think the money mattered to him."

"Well, at least now I can understand why Echo still believes it's a real person lying there."

"After she saw this, she ran out. I followed her into the house and spent time with her, writing out an explanation as best I could."

"She just told me about the doll and how she had discovered it. Her description made it all sound quite kinky and strange."

"I'm sure it did."

"We'll have to show it to her again and explain."

"Mrs. Westington might not like it," I said. "She

didn't want me to show it to her. I'm sure she wanted me to leave all that out."

"So she doesn't know she's seen it?"

"I didn't tell her when I should have," I confessed.

"Hmm, well, maybe that's for the best right now. I'll speak to her about it later, when I think it's okay. I'll make sure she knows you didn't mean anything bad."

"Thank you," I said.

He nodded, still unable to keep his eyes off Destiny. Finally, he realized it.

"Let's go get your exam papers. I've got to be heading home. I'm already a good half hour late and my mother gets very upset."

"What do you do for her?"

"It's for us, our business. I oversee the manufacturing of our chocolate wine sauce and manage the retail outlet. I mean, we have enough help, but we like to keep control over everything. I'll bring some around for you to taste," he offered.

"I'd like that."

After I dressed Destiny, I carried her out and put her in Uncle Palaver's chair. Then I went back and closed the bedroom door.

"What are you going to do with all this?"

"I'm just waiting for our attorney to let me know. I imagine we'll sell the motor home quickly. I won't sell the car, of course. That's mine. I need to discuss it all with my sister, too."

"Where is she right now?"

"She's still in Europe. She should be calling me soon."

"That's good," he said. He glanced back at Destiny

and shook his head. "Man, that does look real. Even the teeth look like real teeth."

"Yes," I said. "I admit she does look alive." I still had trouble calling Destiny "it."

We left the motor home and returned to the house. Trevor had finished his harvesting in the vineyard for the day and was not around.

"For now," Tyler said before we entered the house, "I wouldn't say anything to Echo about what you've learned and all concerning the rock, et cetera."

"I won't. She'll be too embarrassed. But what are you going to do about it, about her crush on you?"

"As I said, hopefully convince Mrs. Westington to register her in the school soon. Once she meets other people, other teachers, she'll be fine. I can't tutor her too much longer anyway. My mother needs me more at the plant and store. She's not well herself and she has been trying to get me to stop doing this."

"Oh, I'm sorry."

"Don't mention it to Mrs. Westington yet. I don't want to upset or frighten her about it."

"I won't," I told him.

We went inside and he retrieved my exam papers, glancing quickly at them.

"Um, not so bad. We'll see. I'll be back tomorrow, same time," he said.

"Thank you. I'm sorry about before," I said. "Accusing you of things and all that."

"No, it's not your fault. It's not anyone's fault or at least any of our faults. If Echo had a decent mother, this might have all turned out differently for her and for Mrs. Westington."

"Someone once told me you have to deal with the hand you're given," I said.

He smiled. "Sounds to me like an old Chinese proverb."

My laughter followed him out. For a moment I just stood there in the foyer. Then I heard Mrs. Westington tap her cane. I turned and saw her peering at me from the doorway of the kitchen.

"Well now, this is the latest that boy's stayed here. He's going to catch hell and walk the plank when he gets home." She smiled. "I guess you're getting along then."

"We'll see, Mrs. Westington. I did the best I can on the tests."

"That's all anyone can do, the best she can. Come on in here and let me show you the right way to prepare a meat loaf. One of these days, you'll be winning a man through his stomach," she added, and disappeared into the kitchen.

Would I? I wondered. Would I ever have any semblance of a normal life? Any real relationships?

Working beside Mrs. Westington in her kitchen recalled the many times I worked beside my mother. Just as Mama had told me about her life as a child, Mrs. Westington told me about working in the kitchen beside her own mother. The affection and the love between her and her mother was as palpable to me as the affection and love I had shared with mine. I enjoyed hearing her stories, but when she talked about happier times with her family, she reminded me of my own and that brought tears to my eyes and a heaviness to my heart. When would nice things, happy things, stand on their own for me and not resurrect memories that only brought back pain? Would it be like this for me forever and ever?

I hid my sadness from Mrs. Westington and together we prepared the dinner. She let me set the table and then I went to freshen up.

If Echo was still upset about confronting the Destiny doll, she didn't show it at dinner, nor had she mentioned it to Mrs. Westington. Trevor Washington, on the other hand, looked suspicious and troubled to me whenever he glanced my way. When he invited me to look at the wine-processing equipment and storage facility after dinner, I quickly accepted.

"Can't you think of a better way to waste her time?" Mrs. Westington quipped.

"No, Ma'am," he said, and winked at me.

Echo wanted to go along as well. With an impish smile on his face, Trevor invited Mrs. Westington to join us.

"Might jolt your memory a bit, Mrs. Westington," he added.

"If I ever want my memory jolted, I'll put my hand in an electric socket," she told him, and he laughed.

Although she complained about it, I could see her look of satisfaction when Echo and I followed Trevor out to the plant.

"As I told you, Echo knows a lot more about the wine-making process than Mrs. Westington thinks," Trevor told me. "She's too full of curiosity to be ignored."

The building the plant was housed in was immaculate. I could see how proud of it Trevor was.

"After we separate the stems from the grape berries," he began, "the skins are broken to free the juice. The mixture of juice, skins, seeds, and pulp is called must."

We followed him about as he explained. Every once in a while, I glanced at Echo and saw she was doing an odd thing. She was signing to herself, thinking aloud, and what she was doing was repeating what Trevor was telling me, but repeating it from memory.

Tyler's right about her, I thought. She is very bright and she's not being permitted to develop as she should. She's like a bird kept in too small a cage to exercise her ability to fly. Do I dare try to convince Mrs. Westington of this, convince her to put Echo in a real school? Once she entered, there would be no reason for me to stay. It was selfish to think that, but I couldn't help it.

"And as you can see here," Trevor went on, "yeast converts sugar to alcohol and carbon dioxide. The clear white is separated from spent yeast cells and other solids after fermenting. White wine should be fermented at cooler temperatures than red and white wines are consumed when they are relatively young so they retain fresh and fruity aromas and flavors."

He looked at me. I had been watching Echo. "I'm giving a test on this later," he said.

"Oh, I'm sorry, Trevor. I really did hear everything you said."

"Right. Here," he said, walking to a stack of cases and pulling a bottle out of the top one. "I'll give you a taste of a finished product."

He uncorked it and then poured a little in a glass. He did the same for Echo. I was surprised.

"It's all right. Mrs. Westington lets her have a little now and then."

We both tasted it. I hadn't drunk much wine in my life, but I thought it tasted very good and told him so.

"Yeah, well, there was a time when pride in all this was waving over this property like a flag," he said sadly. He glanced at Echo and then turned back to me. "Everything all right between you and that tutor fellow?"

"Yes," I said.

"You just be careful about how much you invest in him," he warned.

"Invest? What do you mean? Invest of what?"

"Of yourself," he said. "A good relationship, like this wine, needs a hospitable environment and time to age properly."

I smiled. "Okay."

"I got no right to advise anyone about relationships with other people. Been living like a hermit too many years, but sometimes, what's true and right is as clear as the liquid gold."

I agreed with him and thanked him for his concern. Afterward, I again worked with Echo on signing. She had endless energy when it came to her need and desire to communicate. I was happy that she was distracted and involved so much in our work that she didn't ask me any more questions about Destiny, boyfriends, or sex. She appeared to have forgotten my promise to write it out and I didn't remind her. I didn't want to hear any more about her love for Tyler or what she perceived as his love for her.

Mrs. Westington was sitting in her chair and knitting while we worked anyway. She looked very pleased with how well Echo and I were getting along.

Was this a good time to bring up her need to be in a real school environment? I was gathering the courage to do so when the phone rang.

"Now, it better not be one of those people trying to sell me something," she complained, and went to the phone in the kitchen. A little more than ten minutes later, she returned, her face ashen, but her lips trembling red with anger. I wondered if it had been Tyler telling her how his mother wanted him to stop tutoring Echo. She gazed at Echo, who was busy correcting the way I held my arm and fingers for the word *day*.

"Something wrong, Mrs. Westington?" I asked.

She took a deep breath, closing her eyes and pulling back her shoulders. "That," she said, "was my daughter. After all these years, my daughter."

"Rhona? How is she?" I asked.

"How is she? I'll tell you how she is. She's in a Mexican jail because she was caught crossing the border with drugs in her car, so they confiscated her car and she's in a pretty kettle of fish. My first reaction is not to give a picayune and let her fry in her own fire."

She settled in her chair, looking stunned. "Of course, her father would rant and rave and then make sure she was taken care of, and if I did any less, he'd probably rise from the grave. She's the way she is because he spoiled her—spared the rod and spoiled the child.

"Well, I can't very well leave her down there. I know what sort of things go on in those places and even she doesn't deserve that. Maybe she does," she added after a moment, "but I don't have cold enough of a heart to let it happen. I called my attorney and got him on it. He'll pay off whoever has to be paid off to get her out. Where she'll go and what she'll do is anyone's guess, but don't be surprised if she shows up outside this door finally. The only reason someone like her comes home is because no one else will take her in."

"You took me in," I reminded her.

"That's a different story. You're a legitimate person in need. No matter what I do to help her, she'll only go bad again and again. She's the rotten apple who spoils the bunch, believe me.

"Oh well, maybe she won't come here. Maybe she'll use what I gave her to go on another fling. It's like paying off the devil to keep him from your door. I can't imagine what would have happened to that poor child if she had not deserted her," she added, nodding at Echo, who fortunately wasn't paying any attention to what was being discussed. "She'd have dragged her through the muck."

"I'm sorry about all your trouble, Mrs. Westington."

"Yeah, well, grin and bear it, my grandmother would say." She sighed. "I'm suddenly very tired myself."

She started to rise and I could see she had suffered an emotional shock that added age to her old bones instantly. I got up quickly to help her.

"Thank you, dear. You two go on to bed. I'll just clean up a bit," she said. "It's not good to lay down your head when it's so full of agitation. You'll spin around like a top for hours. Of course," she said, smiling at me, "you already know all that."

I watched her amble off and then I turned to Echo, who was staring up at me, concerned. She quickly signed, asking if her grandmother was sick.

"Just tired," I signed back. The words and the gestures came like a true second language. I smiled at how quickly I had drawn them out of the well of knowledge I had just acquired over the past few days. Echo smiled as well. She could see how happy I was about it.

I reached out for her. She took my hand and we went upstairs together, she to surely dream about Tyler. I wouldn't be all that surprised to find him wandering about in my night musings as well, I thought.

He returned right on time the following day. Worried about my test results, I held my breath when I saw him drive up. I was finishing up the grape harvest with Trevor. Tyler looked my way and waved emphatically, beckoning me to meet him.

"Go on," Trevor said. "You won't be no good to me itching to get over there as soon as you can."

I handed him my basket of grapes and hurried to join Tyler as he approached the house.

"All right," he said. "I'll confess I thought you'd do very poorly on all this, but you really surprised me. You must have been a decent student."

"Decent but not terrific."

"Good enough," he insisted. "I think we can get you past the high school equivalency all right." He indicated a bag of books. "These are yours. We'll start on it right away. There's a bottle of our chocolate wine sauce in there for you to taste as well."

"Thanks," I said, taking it all.

We heard Echo call to him and turned to see she had come out on the porch.

"How is she?" he asked. "Any more talk about . . . ?"

"She hasn't said a word about any of it, especially Destiny. I think it's still frightening to her."

"Don't worry about it. I have some ideas about how to handle all this. For now, let's forget about all that and get to work."

One of the first things he did when he entered the house was seek out Mrs. Westington to tell her how well I did on the evaluation tests.

"You don't have to tell me. I knew that girl was good material," she told him.

I was surprised at how much work Tyler had already done in regard to my test preparations. He had developed a structured series of lessons in every subject.

"We'll work it as close to the actual school experience as we can," he explained. "You'll read the work, do the exercises, and then we'll go over them together to be sure you understand it all."

Echo watched us, clearly annoyed about the time he was devoting to me. She interrupted us continually with questions we both knew she didn't have to ask. He exchanged a knowing look with me and directed himself more to her.

"I'm glad you're not filling your ears with wax today," he whispered. "Although, I'll admit now, it wasn't a terrible idea. In fact," he confessed, "we did similar things in school to prepare for teaching the disabled."

It felt good to get compliments from him. My self-respect was like a crumbled house of cards. It would take a lot of patience and glue to build it up again. I bore down on the assignments, motivated more than ever to do well. Time flew by. Mrs. Westington called us to lunch and at lunch Tyler was more chatty, directing himself to me now almost as much as he did to Echo. He asked me questions about Memphis, about my earlier life, and about the shows Uncle Palaver and I did on the road. Wisely, he included Echo in everything, relating my answers to her. I could see she was torn between wanting me as a friend and wanting all of Tyler's attention as well.

We returned to our work, but halfway through the afternoon, Tyler surprised me with a bag.

"What's this?" I asked, and looked in to see the batteries I would need to install in Destiny.

"I thought it might be a good idea to visit the motor home and show Echo how you get the doll to perform."

"Really?"

"Sure," he said. "That's the fastest way to get her to understand."

"Shouldn't we tell Mrs. Westington first?"

"We'll do it after so she doesn't worry about it," he said. "For now it will be our little secret. I'm curious about it myself. I want to see how good you are as a performer."

"I wasn't the performer. It was my uncle."

"But you said you were part of the show and knew how to do some of the tricks. That will help relax Echo, too."

"Okay," I said, although if there was one thing I had already learned in my short lifetime, it was that keeping secrets from people you loved and respected was a recipe for trouble.

"Good. Let's go."

"Now?" I asked.

"It's as good a time as any and everyone deserves a break from work, especially if you consider how intensely we go at it," he said.

He turned to Echo and signed quickly, explaining what he wanted us to do. She looked pleased.

"What did you tell her?" I asked.

"Just that you were going to put on a show for us in the motor home and surprise us."

This was all happening so fast and seemed too good to be true. The three of us getting along so well was a hope and a dream. Shell-shocked from one disappointment after another, I was still nervous and skeptical. How radically Tyler's attitude toward me had changed.

"Are you sure it's all right?" I asked, desperate for more and more assurance.

"Don't worry," he added. "She trusts me."

Yes, I thought, she does.

But should I?

4

Magic Show

Mrs. Westington was asleep in her easy chair when we left the house to go to Uncle Palaver's motor home. Trevor Washington was on the roof of the winery plant doing some repairs. I didn't think he saw us because he was concentrating hard on his work. Echo looked nervous as we approached the vehicle, but Tyler continually reassured her, telling her we were going to have fun.

When we entered the motor home, Echo stood off to the rear and stared at Destiny, now seated in Uncle Palaver's chair facing the sofa. Turning it over, I lifted the blouse in the back to show her the battery compartment. She drew closer gingerly and watched as I inserted the new ones. She was even more curious now and sat on the sofa to wait for me to complete the installation and preparations.

Tyler sat beside her. "We're ready for our magic show," he said.

I wasn't sure what I should do first. Without Uncle Palaver, it felt strange to do anything involving Destiny. It was almost as if I believed she wouldn't perform for me the way she had performed for him, but I thought of the easiest trick I knew using her. I straightened her up on the seat, or at least, that was what it looked like I was doing.

"Do you have a quarter on you?" I asked Tyler. He dug into his pocket and produced one.

"Okay," I said. "My uncle would ask Destiny for a quarter and she would shake her head, no. He would then ask someone in the audience and . . ."

"Don't tell us about it. Do it just as your uncle did it," Tyler said.

Echo's eyes were wide, looking from him to me to the Destiny doll.

"Okay. Destiny, would you have a quarter I can borrow?"

Tyler signed what I said so Echo would understand. Using the transmitter in my pocket, I triggered her head to shake a no and as rusty as I was, threw my voice through her to say it as well.

Echo jumped in her seat when Destiny opened her mouth. Tyler took her hand and assured her it was just a trick. She sat back, but she didn't relax. Her eyes were glued to Destiny.

"That's pretty good," Tyler said. "You made her voice so different, even I was thrown for a moment."

"Uncle Palaver was so good at that, sometimes he drank a glass of water while throwing his voice. Don't ask me how."

I took his quarter and then placed it in my palm and showed it to Echo. This part of the trick was easy for me. I had practiced it and practiced it so many times while Uncle Palaver and I rode for hours from one destination to another. I told Echo to put out her hand and open it. Then I put the quarter into her palm and closed her fingers around it.

"Don't open your hand," I said. I signed "don't open" to be sure she understood, otherwise the trick would be ruined.

Then I turned to Destiny. "Are you sure you have no quarter for me?" I asked her, with Tyler signing to Echo. Destiny shook her head again and I triggered her right arm to come up slowly and then opened her hand. Echo held on to Tyler, but he was just as mesmerized as she was by Destiny's lifelike movements. They both leaned to see that there was a quarter in her hand. The next part was simple. I opened Echo's hand and there was no quarter in hers.

"Holy smokes, how did you do that?" Tyler asked, very much impressed.

"A real magician never tells," I said.

The truth was when I had straightened up Destiny in the chair, I had placed the quarter in her hand and closed it. When I had put it in Echo's hand, I had plucked it out as I closed her fingers. I had that quarter hidden in my own hand.

"Uncle Palaver would have a funny dialogue with her now, accusing her of hoarding money. She'd deny it and then he would reach under her chin and lo and behold," I said, opening my hand to reveal the other quarter, "he'd find another."

Echo laughed and clapped her hands in delight.

Tyler nodded, looking very impressed. "You're fast," he said. "I'm not going to play cards with you. That's for sure." He looked sincerely impressed with me, which encouraged me to continue.

"This is a magic quarter," I announced, holding up one of the quarters. Tyler told Echo.

I was ready to perform the simple straight pin and quarter trick. I had already placed the straight pin in my hand, hidden between my first two fingers. I showed him his quarter again and he turned it over and studied it a moment before handing it back. "Just an ordinary quarter?" I asked.

"So?"

I placed the coin over the straight pin and after I pretended to run my other hand magically over the coin, I then raised the coin to a standing position, raising the straight pin along with it. It looked perfectly balanced on its edge. It was simply leaning against the straight pin. Keeping the pressure on the pin balanced the coin and made it seem as if it stood in midair.

Echo clapped her hands in delight. I told her to wave her hand over the quarter the way I did. She did so hesitantly and, when I released the pressure on the pin, the coin began a slow falling back onto my fingers. I then handed the quarter back to Tyler.

"Thanks for use of your magical coin, Mr. Monahan," Destiny said, nodding her head. He looked from me to her and laughed.

"You're terrific."

"It's all very basic stuff," I said. "My uncle was something to watch. People would swear he performed miracles. He really was on television, too, you know."

"I bet." He looked around the motor home and then at Destiny. He turned to Echo and signed, "See, I told you it would be fun. April is a very good magician, isn't she?"

She nodded and smiled at me.

"I guess now we can tell Mrs. Westington everything," Tyler said. "She'll understand and she won't be upset, especially after she hears from Echo about the doll and your magic show."

"Yes, you're right," I said. He was clever to have us do all this first. I was angry at myself for suspecting him of any other motives.

He looked at Destiny. "Are you going to sell her, too, when the attorney says it's all right to do so?"

"Oh, no, I can't do that," I replied quickly.

"It might be hard explaining that doll to everyone when you cart her about in your car," he said. "Especially when they see how realistically created she is."

"I don't care. I can't give her away or sell her to anyone," I said, surprised myself at how much panic was in my voice when I said it.

"It's just a doll, April."

"I know, but it was my uncle Palaver's most cherished possession. It has meaning no one else can appreciate."

He thought a moment and nodded. "Okay. Let's see if Mrs. Westington will let you bring her into the house."

"It's not that important yet," I said. "When I have to sell off the motor home, I'll think about her. As silly as it might sound to you," I added, looking at Destiny, "this is the only home she has ever known."

He looked at me with a slight smile on his face

and then he nodded. I was sure my reactions amused him.

Afterward, we walked back to the house to continue our lessons.

"Where have you been?" Mrs. Westington asked. When we entered, it woke her.

"We'll let Echo tell you," Tyler said, and told her to do so.

She began excitedly. Most of it Mrs. Westington didn't understand or follow, but she did get the main idea.

"You put on a show for them?" she asked me. "Using that doll?"

"As best I could," I said.

"When I heard April's story, I thought it would be the best way to explain that doll to Echo," Tyler added. "She saw it in action and understood its real purpose."

"Hmm," Mrs. Westington said. "Well, I guess it all worked out for the best then. You can bring it into the house whenever you want," she told me.

I thanked her and we all returned to our work until it was Tyler's time to go home. Echo was always very disappointed when the clock struck that hour. To get her off her sadness, he gave her one more thing to do, asking her to have it ready for him when next he returned and making it sound like it was very important to him. That was enough to get her started immediately. He could ask her to dig a ditch all night and she would do it for him, I thought. He kept talking to me about my own assignments and preparation for the high school equivalency exam, so I walked out with him.

"I'm glad this is turning out better than I had expected," he said. There was almost nothing else he could have said that would have made me feel as good. "I only hope I can be here long enough to help you."

After we left the house, I walked with him to his car. The late afternoon sun was threading its rays through the tops of the trees that surrounded the pond. A light, golden layer like the icing on a cake made the water glimmer.

"It looks like a pond of Chardonnay," I said, nodding at the water.

Tyler laughed. "I guess Trevor Washington and his winery are having an influence on you."

"It is interesting. I imagine this was once a very beautiful vineyard."

"Probably. My mother remembers it in its heyday. I don't." He got into his sports car and looked up at me before starting the engine. "Aren't you bored here? There's not much for you to do except prepare for your exam and help Trevor. They don't even have cable television. Their set is still attached to an old-fashioned antenna."

"I haven't had time to think about it," I said, "with my uncle's death and all that followed."

"Yes, I guess that's true." He started the engine. "Well, maybe one night, I'll show you around the area."

"Really?"

He shrugged. "See you. Spend some more time on those algebraic equations."

I watched him drive off. He waved just before turning at the bottom of the driveway, the sound of his car engine reverberating over the street and dying away like thunder in the distance. It was then that I realized my heart was thumping, and it was then that I vowed to myself I would go on a serious diet and begin to once again do the exercises Brenda had once designed for me.

It was as if thinking about her brought her back. As soon as I entered the house, Mrs. Westington told me Brenda was on the telephone, calling me from Europe. I hurried to take the receiver.

"Why are you still there?" she demanded as soon as I said hello. "Why didn't you go to Cousin Pete's? I called him and he said he knew nothing about you or Uncle Palaver's death. You never even called him. I felt so stupid."

"Mrs. Westington invited me to stay here and help her with her granddaughter, who's deaf and lives here alone. She's nearly fifteen, but she's very immature. She's hired her granddaughter's tutor to coach me for the high school equivalency exam as well and I'm helping with the small vineyard and wine-making," I said, all in one breath. Brenda was so quiet, I thought we had lost the connection. "Did you hear me?"

"Yes, but if you had gone to live with Cousin Pete, you could be in a regular school, April. I don't understand how you could simply take up with strangers like that."

"Once you meet Mrs. Westington, you'll understand. This is a big house. It was once a famous thriving vineyard and winery and . . ."

"I've got another few weeks in Europe and then I'm coming back to live in Seattle," she said over my words, as if they had no importance.

"Seattle?"

"Yes. I was calling to tell you I've been offered a position on a professional basketball team in Seattle and I've taken it. Now that I know you're still there, I'll keep in touch. I'm going to stopover in San Francisco for a few hours, and I don't think you're far from there, right?"

"No, I'm not."

"Then we'll meet and talk about all this then, April. I'll let you know my exact schedule. Afterward, I'll be on the road with the team a great deal, but you can come to live with me once I'm set up in Seattle."

"Just you?" I asked.

"For now," she replied honestly.

"We'll talk when you're in San Francisco," I said.

"Are you really all right?"

"Yes."

"Okay. I'll call you," she promised. "Take care of yourself."

"You, too."

I couldn't help crying softly. Just hearing her voice brought back so much so quickly it took my breath away. Mrs. Westington saw me wiping away the tears.

"Why don't you go up and take a little rest. Take a warm bath and relax. I know that boy overworked you."

"No, he didn't," I said.

She raised her eyebrows at how quickly I had come to Tyler's defense. It embarrassed me, too.

"I mean, he's just trying to get me to make up for all this time lost. I didn't do any schoolwork when I was on the road with my uncle."

"Uh-huh," she said. She tried to hide a smile from me and went to busy herself with dinner preparations. I hurried out and up to my room. My head was swirling with confusion. Yes, I would like to be with Brenda again, I thought. She was my only family, despite what had occurred, but the life she proposed for me sounded so tentative and so lonely, and not so much different from the way it had been in Memphis. Surely it wouldn't be long before she'd find someone, a new companion, and I would be shoved to the back of the bus again. I longed to be independent, despite my age. I didn't want her to be my legal guardian. If someone like Tyler Monahan proposed to me, I'd accept in a heartbeat.

Was that even a remote possibility or was I just as immature as Echo when it came to my fantasies?

I gazed at myself in the mirror. Was I such a lost cause? Couldn't I lose weight, make myself attractive, have a young man seriously consider me, fall in love with me? Wasn't I capable of loving a man? In a true sense, I suppose if I wanted to be honest, I would admit that I wasn't much more sophisticated about it all than Echo was. If Tyler Monahan only knew the truth about me when it came to my experiences with boys, I thought, he'd be quite surprised.

I returned to the closet, where Rhona's pretty and sexy clothing hung like a tantalizing promise, daring me to turn it into a reality. I vowed then and there to get up earlier every morning and jog just as Brenda used to do. I had to develop an attitude. I had to hate the body I was in and swear to myself I would get out of it. Brenda once told me to conjure up a vision of myself as I would like to see myself and whenever I looked into a mirror, I should be unsatisfied until I saw that vision reflected back.

"Focus," she urged. "Become a monomaniac. Think only of that goal and twist and turn everything to service it. Focus, focus, focus," she chanted at me.

I know it annoyed and even disgusted her that I could never do it. I would try to do it for a while and then drift back to my self-destructive ways.

"You're a lost cause," she would tell me. "Don't ask me for anymore help or advice. I don't like wasting my time and energy on someone who really doesn't care about helping herself."

I couldn't call it tough love because her face was really filled with disdain. The tough was there but not the love, and it was no act for my benefit. I often thought she wished I wasn't related to her, and in school I saw the way she would ignore me, pretending I wasn't around. If she didn't see or hear from me all that day, it wouldn't bother her a bit. In fact, she preferred it. She had a joke she used often. "We had a different mailman when April was born."

Her attitude about me often made me wonder if Daddy had the same thoughts when he looked at me. I was caught in a maddening cycle. The more depressed I became about myself, the more I abused myself, and the abuse continued to make me distasteful to myself.

It's got to end, I thought. I need self-discipline. To punctuate my conclusions, I dropped to the floor and began to go through a battery of exercises Brenda had once designed for me: leg lifts, sit-ups, trunk twists, even jogging in place until my heart was pounding and I was sweating so much, my body was slippery. Then I took a shower, instead of a bath, and I scrubbed at my rolls of fat so hard, someone would think I was trying to shave them off.

Tired, but surprisingly happy about it, I dressed and went down to dinner, determined to push away the delicious but fattening foods Mrs. Westington had prepared. She would be upset, but I would stand my ground. She was sure to see the determination in my face and retreat.

However, instead of being upset with me, Mrs. Westington had an amused look on her face when I limited my portion of mashed potatoes to a teaspoon and I took no bread and butter. I ate only the chicken and vegetables and drank a glass of water. Once in a while I caught her and Trevor exchanging glances. I absolutely refused to eat any dessert, especially her homemade blackberry pie with a scoop of vanilla ice cream. I was dying to have it, but I slammed down the lid hard on my gluttony.

"Aren't you feeling all right, dear?" Mrs. Westington asked me. "You're not eating very much."

"I'm fine. I have to lose weight," I said. "My sister reminded me when we spoke," I added, even though she hadn't.

"Oh. Well, your sister is looking after your best interests, I'm sure," she said. I thought I saw her wink at Trevor.

Echo appeared to be mimicking my eating, however, and that did annoy Mrs. Westington. I quickly signed to her that I had to lose weight. She didn't. She remembered I had told her I had no boyfriend because I was too fat.

"You want a boyfriend now?" she asked me through her signing.

"No," I told her. "I just want to like myself."

She looked skeptical and then she ate normally.

That night, after dinner, while Echo was doing her homework, I returned to the motor home by myself. I stepped in quietly, flicked on the light switch, and closed the door behind me. Then I went into the living room and sat on the sofa across from Destiny. Now that Mrs. Westington had given me permission to do so, I decided I would take her into the house and up to my room after all. I couldn't help thinking she was lonely, but maybe I was just projecting my own loneliness. Any day now, our attorney would be calling to tell me to get the motor home ready for auction anyway. I'd have to come here and pack away all that was inside, the linens, dishes, books, and mementos that had belonged to Uncle Palaver. I had to decide what of that I wanted to keep and what I wanted to give away or sell.

To me it looked like Destiny was sitting there anticipating something very dramatic would be done with her. I imagined the doll missing Uncle Palaver. I was thinking like a little girl who talked to her doll as if the doll were alive. As children we could pretend and no one would think it was anything but cute, but at a certain age, all make-believe had to stop abruptly or else we'd be considered abnormal. And yet we all talk to ourselves as if there were someone else there, as if we were two people, chastising ourselves for doing something stupid, complimenting ourselves for doing something good. We need to talk to ourselves, don't we? I thought. The doll just made it easier in a real way.

"It's time to go," I told Destiny. "Time to leave. Uncle Palaver's never coming back. We're alone in the world, you and I. We have only each other now. I can't imagine Brenda liking my bringing you into her home, but I promise, I won't go anywhere without you."

I fought the temptation to throw my voice and have Destiny reply to me just the way Uncle Palaver often did. If I did that, I would surely scare myself, I thought, and sighed deeply. I looked around. I really had to begin organizing things in here. Maybe tomorrow I'd ask Trevor to give me some of the cartons he had for the cases of wine and I would label everything after I had packed it away.

I looked at my watch. Carrying Destiny back to the house and up the stairs to my bedroom would be quite a sight. I wanted Echo to be asleep and even Mrs. Westington to be in her room. I'll just wait, I thought. I was going to turn on the little television set and rose to do so, when I heard a gentle tapping at the motor home door.

It surprised me.

"Who could that be?" I asked Destiny.

I rose and opened the door to see Tyler Monahan standing there.

"Hi," he said.

"What are you doing back here?" I asked.

He showed me a videotape. "I thought you could use this. It's a tape I forgot I had, a tape of sign instruction. It will make it easier and quicker for you to learn," he said.

"Oh. Thanks." I didn't move and he didn't move. "How did you know I was here?"

"I asked for you at the house and Mrs. Westington said she thought you had gone out for a walk. I saw the lights on in the mobile home."

"How did you get away from work?"

"We're closed for inventory. I forgot," he said. He started to look annoyed at my questions and then gazed past me. "What are you doing here anyway?"

"I've got to get started on packing. I was just thinking about everything. The call could come any day to put the motor home up for auction and I'll have to get everything personal out of it."

He nodded and just stood there. I realized how silly it was talking to each other over the small stairway.

"Come on in if you want," I said. I backed away and he came in, closing the door behind him. He glanced at Destiny.

"I still can't get over that doll. You do wonders with it," he said, then looked about. "I meant to ask you where you slept when you traveled with your uncle. On the sofa?"

"No, up there," I said, nodding at the bunk above the driver's seat.

"Oh. I guess you couldn't toss and turn too much," he said, looking up at it.

"I'm not a light sleeper, but I never fell out. Would you like something to drink? I know we still have some sodas in the refrigerator." I went to it and looked. "Cokes and ginger ales."

"No, that's all right, thanks," he said. He placed the videotape on the coffee table and looked again at Destiny. "It's funny, but it seems like her eyes move with you as you move about."

"I know."

"I never saw anything like it. Those lips look soft."

"They are. As you saw, she's soft wherever she is supposed to be," I said.

He looked like he wanted to see for himself, but I didn't give him permission to touch her. He hovered about her, looking at her ears, her fingers.

"She has pierced ears, too?"

"Yes. Occasionally, Uncle Palaver put earrings on her, depending upon the outfits, the show. You can take her pulse if you want," I said. It had always intrigued me.

"What? Take her pulse? You're kidding."

I shook my head and he brought his fingers to her wrist slowly. His eyes widened.

"How . . ."

"Something electrical run by the batteries to simulate a heartbeat. Stagehands used to get a real kick out of it, but they couldn't touch her when Uncle Palaver was around."

"What was the point of having that?"

I didn't answer. I knew the point. The more she resembled the real Destiny, the happier Uncle Palaver could be. I wouldn't even begin to tell him other things, like when he gave her a bath or brushed her teeth, things I had seen him do, but never mentioned to him or asked him about for fear of embarrassing him. In those earlier days when I was with him, I had one fear and that was I would upset him too much and he would send me back to Brenda or leave me on some street corner in some village.

Tyler sat on the sofa and shook his head at Destiny.

Then he looked up at me as though he just remembered I was there, too.

"So where did you live before you went to live with your sister in Memphis?" he asked.

"A small community called Hickory about ninety miles from Memphis. My father was an attorney there. Where did you go to college?"

"California State, Northridge," he said.

"Did you always want to do this kind of work?"

"No."

"What made you go into it then?"

"My mother has a sister who had a child born deaf. My uncle was embarrassed by him."

"Why?"

"He saw him as an indication of his own personal, manly failure. He had produced an imperfect child. He did nothing to help the boy, refused to spend money on special instructors or a special school. He had only the most basic help. My uncle even forbade my aunt from practicing signing with him, especially in front of other people. I remember thinking the child was like a bird with a broken wing, never able to fly. He was growing up wild, sort of like Helen Keller, in a way. You know about her?"

"Sure."

"Anyway, as a hobby almost, I studied signing and whenever I could, whenever my uncle wasn't around, I practiced it with my nephew and slowly began to teach him things. My aunt knew I was doing it, but said nothing, hoping my uncle would never find out. My nephew was almost as hungry for knowledge as Echo is and learned rapidly. His mental development improved almost geometrically and he slowly began to develop social skills as well. By the time my uncle found out what I was doing, his son had become an honor roll student. It all took him by surprise and he could do nothing but accept the compliments. I knew then that I had a special gift for this and this was what I wanted to do with my life."

"What a wonderful story. How lucky you are."

"Yes," he said. He looked pensive and then a bit sad. I thought that was because he missed the work he had done.

"Couldn't your mother have found someone else to help her and leave you working at the school in Los Angeles?" I asked.

"No," he said sharply. "It's a family business. She needs me."

"It can't be more important than what you were doing."

He looked up at me. His eyes told me he agreed, but he shook his head. "Family," he said, "is more important."

"It seems selfish to me," I told him, refusing to be quiet about it.

He looked away. "I didn't exactly tell you the truth about Echo," he said after a moment of silence, during which I thought he was just going to get up and leave because I was so opinionated.

"What do you mean?"

"I mean, I told you the truth about the rock, but she pushes herself on me in ways."

"Pushes herself?"

"Physically, deliberately pressing her breasts against me, that sort of thing. I stop her, of course, but she's getting more and more aggressive about it and she is becoming a woman. It makes me uncomfortable."

"She's going to be very pretty," I said.

"Yes. This is why I have to stop tutoring her and why I was so upset when Mrs. Westington brought you into their home to be her companion."

"Why? What did I have to do with it?"

"I thought it would prevent her even longer from permitting Echo to go to school. You're nice and you'd probably be a good companion, but it's not what she needs."

"Oh. You're probably right about that," I admitted.

"I won't leave before I help you," he promised. "You should get a high school diploma. You can't do much in this world without that at least and you might want to go on with your education."

"I don't know what I want. I just know I don't want to be me," I said, and he raised his eyebrows.

"Why would you say that?"

"Why? Look at me! Beside what's happened to me and my family, I'm not someone anyone would care about. I'm just a blob with eyes and a mouth."

"That's not true. Just lose some weight. Big deal. You have a very pretty face," he said.

"Thank you, but I'm not fishing for a compliment."

"I'm not biting on the hook," he replied quickly, and we both laughed.

He looked about the motor home again. "What a great little clubhouse this would make, huh?"

"I suppose."

"Well, until it gets carted off, maybe we'll use it. It could be our classroom once in a while."

"Really?"

"Why not?"

"Okay. Oh. I have to get the generator charged, run the engine."

"I'll help you organize things and pack, too, if you like."

"Thank you, but what about your mother and the time you're already spending here and . . ."

"Don't worry about that." He looked at Destiny again and then turned to me. "Did your uncle dress her in a costume for the show?"

"Oh, yes." I rose and went to the closet. "Here are two," I said, showing him. "They belonged to the real Destiny."

"So the doll is exactly her height, weight, measurements, everything?"

"As far as I know, yes," I said.

He stared at her and nodded. Then he looked up at me. "Did you have a costume in the show?"

"I did but my weight went up and down so much that I wore it only when I had lost weight. Now, as you can see, I've gained it all back."

"Let's see the costume you wore."

I squinted and felt the folds form in my forehead. "It's nothing," I said.

"Come on," he urged. "Don't be bashful."

I turned to the closet, hung up Destiny's outfits, and took out mine. He rose and took it from my hands to hold up in front of me.

"Doesn't look like you can't fit in it."

"I can't. My bulging waist will show."

It really wasn't much more than an abbreviated one-piece bathing suit in bright colors. The back was open almost below my waist. The bodice had cups that lifted my breasts and made them look even larger, deepening my cleavage. There were secret pockets where I kept coins and other things used in some of the tricks Uncle Palaver performed.

"Put it on. Let me see."

"No. I'll be embarrassed."

"Destiny," he said, turning to the doll. "Should she do it? What do you think? There," he said quickly. "She nodded."

"Oh, she did not."

"I saw her do it. Go ahead. Put it on."

I thought about it a moment and then walked back into Uncle Palaver's bedroom to change into it. I didn't look great, but I didn't look as bad as I thought I would. When I stepped out, Tyler turned and widened his eyes.

"You look very good," he said. I was sucking in my stomach. "Turn around."

I did and he whistled.

"My legs look like they belong on a baby elephant."

"They're not that bad. You don't have to lose all that much, April, and I'm not simply trying to make you feel good. You've known me long enough to know I'm brutally honest when I have to be."

I stared at him, not knowing what to say. He stepped up to me, pouring his eyes into mine. He brought his lips closer and closer. I was afraid to move, afraid I was dreaming and I would wake up. His kiss was so soft, I wasn't sure it had even occurred. He put his hands on my waist and gently pulled me into him before he kissed me again, this time holding his lips on mine while he moved his hands up to the straps of my costume and slowly pealed them off my shoulders and down my arm.

Was this really happening? I asked myself. Was I going to let it happen?

He didn't say anything. He stepped back slightly and continued to lower my costume. My breasts fell free. He stared at me a moment and then he touched my nipples as if he were examining them first. He kissed me again, but he did nothing more. It was as if he wasn't sure what came next or if he should do anything more.

I looked up at him, anticipating. He looked like he had just snapped out of a coma.

"I'm sorry," he said, his lips trembling. In fact, his whole face looked like it was in an earthquake. "I'm sorry. I . . . I have to get home."

He turned and hurried out of the motor home. I stood frozen and confused, not only at what he had done, but how quickly my own heart had begun to pound and how excited I had become. I wanted him to do more. Why didn't he try? I felt like I was drowning in disappointment.

My eyes fell to Destiny. I didn't remember turning her head my way, but that's the way it was. He must have done it while I was changing, I thought.

I had to sit and get myself calmed down before I took off the costume and put on my clothes. I decided to leave the videotape in the motor home to watch it there, and for now, because I was still trembling and confused, I decided to leave Destiny where she was.

I started back to the house in the darkness, my mind still reeling in confusion. Should I be happy about what had happened? Did my body turn him off finally? Should I be sad? Were the feelings I felt different from the feelings I had felt when Celia had touched me?

How would I ever fall asleep tonight? I paused for a moment and looked to the rear of the house where Trevor Washington had his own private quarters. His television set spilled a glow over the side of the house and onto the small patch of grass. How lonely his life was, I thought. How was he able to contend with that loneliness? Was his work enough? It hadn't been for Uncle Palaver. Trevor seemed so contented, accepting. Would I end up like that, alone into my senior years?

Rather than feel elated and excited by what had just occurred between me and Tyler in the motor home, I now felt frightened. I'll be rejected all my life, I thought. Why was I born?

Mrs. Westington had gone to bed and I imagined Echo was asleep. I stopped by her room and looked in and saw her in her bed, her eyes closed. Was she dreaming of Tyler? It occurred to me that in the darkness, she was truly alone. She couldn't hear me and she couldn't see me. I could stand by her bed and tell her things she would never know. Despite how terrible I felt about myself, I felt sorrier for her. I stood by her bed and looked down at her sleeping so softly.

"You've never heard the sound of your own name and your own voice," I told her. "It is truly as if you have been locked away in your own body. I'm sorry for you, Echo. I really am."

She continued sleeping and breathing regularly.

"Who's worse off?" I asked her. "You or me?"

I went to my room and prepared for bed. For a

while after I had crawled into my bed, I just lay there staring up at the darkness wondering if Mrs. Westington was right about my parents watching over me from the great beyond. What did they see, feel? What could they do to help me, if I could do so little, it seemed, to help myself?

We're all disabled in this house, I thought. Maybe that was why I was so comfortable living here, why I was so quick to accept Mrs. Westington's invitation. She was cutoff from her only child and struggling with her granddaughter. Echo was so dependent upon everyone around her, in danger of being cut off and left to drift. Trevor worked on a patch of a vineyard to cling to what had given him meaning in his life. His survival was so tightly entwined with those grapes. They would die with him and he would die without them.

And then there was me, a tiny voice trapped in a body it despised. I closed my eyes and dreamed I was a snake anxious to slither out of its skin.

I was tired when I woke up. I knew I had spent the night tossing and turning, twisting out of the grip of one nightmare after another. I barely had the energy to get up and get dressed, much less go for the morning jog I had planned to take daily. If Brenda was here, she'd be shaking her head and muttering about me, I thought. At least, I ate little at breakfast, which displeased Mrs. Westington.

"You're taking this weight thing too far," she said. "A body needs nourishment."

I ate a little more just to satisfy her. She tapped her cane in frustration.

"We don't really need enemies," she said. "We do

plenty of damage to ourselves without them, thank you. Take a letter."

Echo ate slowly, her eyes shifting constantly from her grandmother to me. She's deaf, I thought, but she senses people's moods and feelings with a sensitivity that might be greater than the sensitivity of people who hear.

"Are you all right?" she signed.

I nodded and gave her my best smile, but her eyes told me she could see right through it, maybe down to my very dark and lonely soul.

I couldn't help being nervous about Tyler's arrival. He was returning for his final lessons of the week. Weekends, he had told me, were particularly busy in his retail outlet and he had to spend most of the day in the store. They sold more than just the wine sauce they made. There were jams and honey and all sorts of wine-related kitchen and dishware items, as well as souvenirs and books about the valley. He'd revealed that Echo had never been to his store.

When he arrived, he looked at me without any sign in his expression that he felt either good or bad about what had occurred in the motor home. In fact, he didn't act in any way differently from how he had acted previously. It was truly as if nothing had happened between us and it had all been my imagination. He had never come to the motor home. I actually planned on returning to see if the videotape was there so I could confirm it had all not been an invention of my desperate imagination.

He went directly to the assignments. In fact, for most of the day, the only things we discussed were associated with the work. I had difficulty with some

of the math and he concentrated on it until he was
satisfied I understood. At lunch, he began a discussion with Mrs. Westington about Echo's future and he
used me to support his points. It was clear to me the
time when he was going to leave was drawing closer
and closer.

"She's doing fine, Mrs. Westington, but she's not
getting a fully rounded education as she would if she
were in a classroom with other girls and boys her age.
April is really the first companion she's had anywhere near her age, but April will be the first to tell
you, she should be with more young people."

He looked at me and I nodded.

"It's true, Mrs. Westington. She needs to build
self-confidence for her social interactions later on in
life."

"Everyone's always rushing to grow up in this
world today," Mrs. Westington said. "Take a letter. You
young people don't realize what you have when you're
young. You're so anxious to get older and take on all
those responsibilities. She's got time for all that."

"It's worse to drop someone into the adult world
without preparation," Tyler insisted. "She won't know
how to meet and greet strangers. She won't—"

"Oh, fiddlesticks," Mrs. Westington said. She became very uncomfortable.

He saw it and stopped talking about it until she left
the room. Then he turned to me immediately. Finally,
I thought, finally he's going to talk about what had
happened between us. I was waiting for either an
apology or an explanation for his running out like
that. Instead, he continued to talk about Echo.

"Mrs. Westington's not a young woman. If that girl

gets left alone in this world, she'll be practically a social invalid. You know what her mother is like. Even if they find her and tell her what's happened, she'd probably put Echo into an institution. Keep working on Mrs. Westington," he said. "She likes you very much and will listen more to you, perhaps."

I promised I would. I waited for him to talk about us, but he did what he always did when he ended the day's session: he gave Echo something to do that would distract her from his leaving. I followed him out, my arms folded, my head down, my heart thumping so hard, I was sure he could hear it or feel the vibrations that traveled from it, down through my legs and into the floor of the porch itself.

He stepped off the porch, glanced back at me, and headed toward the pond. I hurried after him. It was a cloudy day and it looked like raindrops were hanging at the bellies of the darker clouds, minutes away from dropping. The wind had come up from the west and trees were nodding, the leaves rustling. A ripple moved over the surface of the water.

He paused and turned to me. Finally, finally we were going to have a special, intimate conversation.

"I didn't want to say this in front of Mrs. Westington, of course, but I think you should let her know that you're not going to stay here indefinitely. As I told you last night, she'll use you as a reason not to permit Echo from leaving, just as she's used me, and as I stressed last night, my time here is coming to an end soon. Once you pass your equivalency exam, you'll think about moving on, too, won't you?"

"I guess," I said. Tears were coming into my eyes. How could he simply ignore what had happened, pre-

tend it never had happened? And here was stupid,
gullible me actually expecting so much more, expecting him to ask me out on a date.

"You should. You can't have much of a future lingering here unless you want to work beside Trevor
Washington in a miniature vineyard."

I became suspicious. Why would any boy ignore
what had happened between us?

"You don't have a girlfriend here, do you?"

"No," he said. "Between my work here and all that
I have to do at our store and plant, I haven't had
much time to socialize since I returned."

"Did you have a girlfriend back in Los Angeles? Is
she coming here?"

"I had no one special," he said quickly. "We're not
talking about me," he added a little sharply. "We're
talking about them and about you." His tone and cutting words were equivalent to a slap in the face.

"You're right," I said. "I might leave soon, sooner
than anyone thinks."

"Oh?"

"My sister is returning to the States soon. She's
taken a position with a professional basketball team
in Seattle," I told him. "I might go back to living with
her."

"What about her lover?"

"They're not together anymore."

"Oh." He thought a moment. My response had
given him pause. "Well, then that might work out for
you."

"I'll see. We're going to meet when she stops in
San Francisco."

"Good. Well, I'm happy we had this little talk,"

he said. "Stay on that math. It's your weakest area."

He turned toward his car. The first drops began, splashing over my face.

"You'd better hurry up inside. Going to be a downpour!" he called back. He started to run and got into his car.

I stood there, permitting the rain to fall on me. He beeped his horn and started away. I watched him go and then, perhaps to drive away my disappointment more than lose any weight, I started to run after his car, ignoring the rain and not really being able to tell the difference between it and my own tears anyway.

Maybe, I thought, I should just keep on running. Or maybe, I should go back, pack my things, and leave in my car right now. Our attorney can look after the motor home. Just like Mrs. Westington's daughter, Rhona, I'd disappear like a puff of smoke. That's all I really was anyway, just a puff of smoke. Yes, I should leave, I thought.

The only real companion I had was a doll anyway.

5

Before and After

When I returned to the house, I was literally soaked to the skin and quite exhausted. I stood in the entryway holding my side and catching my breath. Sometimes, when I watched Brenda train and go through her exercises, I thought she was punishing her body for disappointing her during the most recent game or contest. I couldn't imagine how she could enjoy driving herself into pain and fatigue, but right now, I felt good punishing myself, perhaps for being so naive and so hopeful.

"What are you doing?" Mrs. Westington cried when she set eyes on me. "How did you get so wet? That's a cold rain out there, girl. Let's get you into a hot bath right away before you come down with pneumonia."

Echo came up beside her and stared at me, confused. She signed, "What happened?"

I signed back that I had gone running and got caught in the rain. I slipped off my sneakers and pealed off my soaked socks.

"Give me that," Mrs. Westington ordered. I handed her the socks. "Go on up and get out of those wet clothes. Start running the tub. Lordy dee."

Like a puppy at my heels, Echo followed me upstairs. I mumbled to myself with her behind me.

"You don't have to worry about me stealing your boyfriend, Echo. He couldn't care less whether I stayed or left this place. All he seems to care about is his mother and their business."

As soon as I got to my bedroom, I began to strip off my clothes. Echo stepped into the bathroom to run the tub for me. She signed to me quickly, telling me to hurry up before I got sick.

"I won't get sick," I said. "I'm not made of paper and even if I did get sick and die, it wouldn't make all that much difference to anyone."

She didn't understand all that I had said, but she understood enough from my dark expression of unhappiness to look confused. "What's wrong?" she signed.

"What's wrong? What's wrong? Look at me!" I told her.

She tilted her head and shook it to indicate she still didn't understand my outburst. I was standing there in my bra and panties.

"Why should I look at you?" she asked. "What should I see?" She raised her hands.

Of course, I thought, how could she possibly understand the frustrations I felt? She lived like a girl in a plastic bubble. Her only real windows on the world were the novels she read, the little bit of television she watched without hearing a thing, and whatever Mrs. Westington, Trevor, or Tyler told her. None of them could tell her about a young girl's disappointments in herself and in the people she trusted. She had yet to understand her own disappointments, especially the full meaning of what her own mother had done to her.

She stood there looking so unaware, so innocent, so lost to reality, I thought. I should be giving her lessons in real life whenever I could.

"Take off your clothes," I ordered. "Go on, do it."

She stared at me, looked at the bath, and then shrugged and began to undress. When she was down to her panties, I took her hand and pulled her abruptly next to me. Standing side by side, we looked at ourselves in the full-length mirror on the back of the bathroom door. There I was with my tree trunk thighs and no waist standing in contrast to this beautifully developing young girl with curves and soft places I dreamed of having. We could be models for a before and after advertisement.

"See?" I signed, and seized the roll of fat around my waist and patted my bulging belly. "See?"

She still looked confused. I put my hand on her waist and on her belly. I pointed at her budding, perky breasts. "You're already pretty," I told her. "I'll never be."

She insisted I would and I told her not to worry about me.

"Just worry about yourself. I'm not worth anyone worrying over." She looked like she was going to cry. "It's all right. It's okay," I signed. "I don't care anymore."

I really didn't care anymore. I took off my bra and panties and stepped into the hot tub. She came over and spilled in some bubbly bath powder. I lowered myself into the water, tempted to just keep going until my head was underneath so I could keep it there and end my agony. Echo stepped around the tub, took a washcloth, and began to wash the back of my neck and my back for me. Despite my desire to feel bad and suffer, it did feel good. The hot bath, the delicate scent of the bath powder, and her soft touch relaxed me.

"I'm sorry I'm being so miserable," I muttered with my back to her, "but I can't help it. The love of your life kissed me last night. He did a little more and I thought maybe I could have a boyfriend, but he opened his eyes and I guess what he saw disgusted him so much he ran for his life. He's probably had nightmares about it and is trying to forget that it ever really happened."

She heard nothing, of course. She washed down my shoulders. I closed my eyes and sat forward. She was doing a good job of massaging my neck. I continued to relax and just drift. I remembered when I was a little girl, I used to do this for my mother. She would moan with exaggerated pleasure. I was so serious, concerned I would miss a spot on her back or her neck. Why can't I return to that? Why can't I be a little girl forever and ever and not worry about being pretty or too fat and never finding love?

If only there was this time machine that you could activate when you were absolutely positive you were the happiest you could be and your family was the happiest they could be. You would push a button and time would stand still, freeze forever and ever. No one would grow older and nothing would ever change.

Other girls my age were probably fantasizing about boys or becoming movie stars or singing stars, but here I was fantasizing about being a little girl again. Something's very wrong with me, I thought. I'm a lost cause and I'm not even a lost cause for anyone else. There was no one else. I'm a lost cause for myself.

I lowered my head to my hands.

Echo leaned in to dip the washcloth into the bath water, and when she did, her breasts grazed over my back. A myriad of sexual imagery flowed over my eyes—Celia caressing me and bringing her lips to my neck, Peter Smoke's kiss and touch, Uncle Palaver, naked beside his naked Destiny, Tyler lowering my costume and touching my nipples. I moaned, longing for the warmth of a loving embrace, anyone's loving embrace.

I reached up and held Echo's hand for a moment. She remained leaning over me, confused, I was sure. I was about to bring it to my lips, to run her hand over my cheeks.

"What in blazes is that girl doing?" I heard Mrs. Westington say. I let go of Echo's hand quickly and looked up to see Mrs. Westington standing in the bathroom doorway, a cup of piping hot herbal tea in her hands. She signed at Echo, asking her why she was almost naked.

"She just didn't want to get her clothing wet," I said quickly.

"Get your clothes on!" she ordered Echo. She put down the teacup and tapped her cane. She signed as well, saying, "Get dressed."

Echo moved quickly to her clothing. Mrs. Westington watched her and shook her head.

"I'm sorry," I said. "I didn't ask her to wash my back. She wanted to do it." That wasn't a lie, I thought. It just wasn't the whole truth.

"That child has no modesty. Never did. She used to run around naked when she was five and six and even seven. I'd find she took off her clothes because this itched her or that bothered her. Just lucky we live out here with only a few birds and rabbits. People would think I was raising a wild animal. Anyway, I have some tea and honey here for you. Drink it before it gets too cool," she told me, and handed the cup to me.

"Thank you," I said.

Echo stood by looking remorseful.

"Go on," Mrs. Westington told her, and waved her hand at the door. She signed and spoke. "Leave April to finish her bath, get dressed and into bed before she gets sick." She punctuated it with another tap of her cane.

Echo glanced at me and with her head down, left the room. I felt sorry for her. It was my fault. I couldn't move a foot right or a foot left without causing someone trouble.

"I swear," Mrs. Westington said, looking down at me sitting in the tub, "the older I get, the more I'm amazed at the things people do to themselves. You don't know enough to come in out of the cold rain. I swear."

How was I going to explain it? I sipped the tea instead and looked down, afraid now that she would say, "You're too much trouble. You should leave."

She said nothing more, however. She left me sipping the tea as I sat in the tub. After a few more minutes, I put it down, stepped out of the water, and dried myself quickly. I wasn't getting sick, but I felt tired and emotionally drained. I shouldn't have done what I had done with Echo, I thought. There was no reason to make her feel bad about my own problems. Perhaps I wouldn't be as good for her as Mrs. Westington had hoped I would be. Tyler was right. I'm not a proper companion. Maybe I really should be out of here as soon as possible. Even if I was afraid of living with Brenda again, I had little other choice but to leave. I belonged nowhere. That's why I was so content traveling from place to place with Uncle Palaver. Home was wherever we were that moment. We were two lost souls, drifting so that we didn't stay in one place long enough to see what other people had and then feel sorry for ourselves.

I crawled into bed, wishing I was crawling into my own coffin. I'd reach up and close the lid on myself. When I finally fell asleep, the darkness in my heart was as deep as the darkness outside.

Hours later, I was woken by the movement of the mattress and the lifting of my blanket. For a moment, I thought I was still dreaming or perhaps one of the loving dead souls, perhaps my parents, had come to me to reassure me, but when I turned, I realized it was Echo crawling into my bed to lie beside me. I quickly sat up and turned on the lamp on the night table.

"What's wrong?" I asked, seeing the terrible twisted expression on her face.

"I had a bad dream," she signed back. She then put both her hands side by side, the fingers together, facing her heart, opening and closing them quickly over her heart. With the expression on her face, I remembered that meant she was frightened. She continued the sign until I put my hand out to stop her.

I looked at my door. Had Mrs. Westington heard her come into my room? Would she burst in on us at any moment, confused and upset? I thought I should quickly tell Echo to return to her own bed before we were both in trouble, but one more look at her face told me I couldn't just throw her out. She did look terrified.

"What was your dream?" I asked.

She shook her head. She didn't want to talk about it, but I could feel her trembling still. I wondered if she had ever crawled in beside Mrs. Westington after she had a bad dream. I couldn't imagine it. Mrs. Westington was too afraid to show affection. She didn't even like me catching her looking at Echo and smiling to herself. How alone and frightened Echo must have been all her young life to never have anyone to comfort her. How many, many times I recalled snuggling up beside my own mother or between her and my father when I was little. At least I always had that.

What was I going to tell her now? That it wasn't right for her to be in my bed? How would she understand that, and why wasn't it right for her to do it anyway? Didn't girlfriends sleep together in one or the other's bed? I was never close enough with any of my school friends to be invited over and do so, but I knew others did.

"Okay," I told her. "You can stay with me, but you have to go back to your room as soon as it's morning."

She nodded and cuddled closer, putting her arm over my waist and bringing her head to my pillow. I kept my back to her. Many mornings I had looked in on Brenda and Celia and seen them so entwined, still asleep, clinging to each other as if their nights were free falls through the darkness. Sometimes, Celia's lips were still touching Brenda's neck. Her mouth was slightly open with her lips looking as if they were caught forever in an endless kiss. I had never been that close to my sister and I couldn't help but be jealous.

I could feel Echo's body soften and relax in the comfort of being beside me. I lay there with my eyes open, intrigued with the way my own body was reacting to the feel of her breasts against my back, her leg touching mine, her breath on my neck. She moaned almost as soon as she fell asleep and then drew herself even closer to me. My body tingled and a wave of warm, erotic excitement traveled up my legs and settled in the pocket of my sex. It frightened and yet intrigued me. Should I be having these feelings? Do all girls who sleep together experience them? Does it mean anything?

I tried to move away from her, but she held on firmly in her sleep. Images in a slow, syrupy way began to flow under my closed eyelids. I felt Tyler's fingers on my nipples again. I saw myself beside Echo gazing in the mirror at our bodies. The excite-

ment began to grow stronger inside me. This wasn't
the first time I had experienced this, but with Echo
beside me, I was embarrassed by my own oncoming
sexual crescendo. I tried to hold my breath, to slow
my heart, to think of something else, but it was relentless, my heart now like a parade drum pounding a
march to accompany the promenade of sexual images. She had pressed herself closer to me and when
she moved, I suddenly thought she might be having
an erotic experience as well.

What about that? I wondered. She was old enough
now. She had her period. She read about people being
in love. She surely had sexual fantasies about Tyler.
Although she had wanted to talk about all this, I had
been avoiding it. How could I, with my little experience, give her any sensible advice anyway? I was still
unsure about myself.

Many times I was tempted to ask Brenda how she
first knew she was a lesbian. When she found herself
attracted to another woman, did she know if she was
bisexual or simply attracted to a friend? Did she
know what she was from a very early age? I knew she
never had a conversation about it with our mother and
certainly not with our father. Was there someone with
whom she would have such a discussion? I couldn't
remember anyone with whom Brenda was that close.
She certainly wasn't close to any other relative.
Maybe she had formal discussions with the school
nurse.

After I had discovered what she was and whom
she loved, I read about lesbianism whenever I could. I
knew that some women, just like some men, didn't
discover these things about themselves until they

were in their forties or fifties, and all that time, they had been living heterosexual lives. Some were even married. What a shocking revelation that must have been for their partners! Could such a thing happen to me? Would I find some young man, think I was in love, marry him, and then discover I was just like Brenda? What if I had children? What happens then? Do they hate me, find themselves embarrassed at the sight or the mere mention of me? What sort of fate was that?

Right now, I wasn't really worried about such an event, of course. I didn't think I'd ever have a partner, male or female. The only one who would be shocked by my discoveries about myself would be me.

All these thoughts and feelings blossomed out of Echo's merely coming to my bed to get some comfort. She was years younger emotionally than her chronological age. She was like an eight-year-old when it came to something like this. But even adults get terrible nightmares and reach for someone in the night to reassure them. Mama once told me even Daddy had stunning nightmares and looked for the comfort of her embrace.

"We're all children at heart in one way or another," she explained when she had to reassure me after a terrible dream. "Don't be ashamed."

Ashamed? It was far too late for that. My nights are going to be filled with endless nightmares, I thought, and I'd have no one to embrace but myself. Maybe that was why I couldn't help enjoying the fact that Echo had come to me for such comfort, despite the way I was reacting to her body pressed against mine. It was all pure and good, truly innocent, wasn't it?

Pull yourself away and end it, a voice inside me urged. You're not capable of innocence.

Relax, another voice persuaded. Let it come and let it pass. Don't deny yourself any pleasure. Fate certainly doesn't deny you any pain.

I'm not sure Echo was aware of what happened to me next, but once again I couldn't stop myself. When it was over, I held my breath and listened to see if she had awoken. She was still breathing softly, regularly. I curled my body tighter and squeezed the pillow against my face so firmly, I almost smothered myself. All I wanted to do was sleep and forget, drive these troubling thoughts and questions into the darkness. For so many of us, sleep is truly a mercy. Finally, it was granted to me.

I woke when I felt a hand on my forehead. Mrs. Westington was standing there looking at me. The first thing I thought was she has found Echo in my bed with me and is very angry, but when I turned and looked, I discovered Echo was gone. I stared at the empty place beside me. Was she here or did I fantasize it? Neither answer would make me feel any better, I thought.

"Well, you don't feel like you have any fever," Mrs. Westington said. "How are you feeling, dear? I worried about you all night."

"I'm okay," I said. "Thank you."

"I can't imagine you running in that weather, especially wearing what you were wearing. Well, you're lucky. No sore throat?"

"No."

"That's good. You be more careful from now on. Young people think they're immortal. Take a letter.

The Grim Reaper enjoys collecting the souls of children the most. But no more dark talk," she quickly vowed. "Since you're fine, we'll go ahead with our plans to go shopping. Right after breakfast, Trevor will drive us in the old station wagon," she said. "He's up early this morning cleaning it out. It's filthy from his silly vineyard. We'll go to one of those malls," she continued. "I want you to help me pick out some new clothing for Echo. She's growing out of everything, and it's long overdue she get herself a couple of bras. I realized that last night. She needs some new shoes, too. Can you do that?"

"Of course. I'd be happy to help," I said. "Not that I'm any sort of expert when it comes to clothing."

"None of you young people are that. What children wear these days would make Casanova blush. Torn jeans, blouses you can see right through, panties that are no bigger than rubber bands, rings in belly buttons and noses. I don't want her in any of that," she said. "We'll go to good stores."

"Okay," I said, but I didn't know what she meant by good stores. She had probably not done too much shopping recently. She's sure to be shocked by what's in fashion, I thought.

She looked at me. "You sure you're feeling okay?"

"Yes, I'm fine." I couldn't help wondering about Echo. Was she still upset, afraid?

"You look down in the dumps this morning. I want you to pick out something nice for yourself, too, when we get to the mall. Some pretty new dress or blouse and skirt, maybe, and new shoes, as well," she said.

"You don't need to do that for me, Mrs. Westington. You've done enough."

"What I don't need is for someone to tell me what I need and don't need to do," she retorted, pulling her shoulders up. "I got money buried in cans all over this place. If I don't spend it, I'll forget where it is."

"No, you won't," I said, laughing.

"Now, that's better. A smile puts sunshine into your face. Plant one there and happiness will bloom."

"Okay, Mrs. Westington," I said. If someone as old as she was with what she's been through could still be jolly, I had no right to sing the blues in her home, I thought.

"Well now, get dressed," she said. "You can bet Echo didn't forget about our shopping excursion. She's already dressed and downstairs."

"She is?"

"She's out there helping Trevor clean up the station wagon, in fact."

Up and dressed? I thought. When did she leave my room? Did I really imagine it all?

I got out of bed, washed and dressed as quickly as I could. When I stepped into the dining room, I found Echo and Trevor seated and eating breakfast. Echo looked up at me and smiled, signing about our trip and telling me we were going to have lunch in a restaurant. I looked at Trevor and at Mrs. Westington. I wanted to ask Echo about her having a nightmare and coming to my bed, but I was afraid to do so in front of them. When we're alone I'll ask her, I thought, and left it at that.

Echo's excitement recalled my memories of my trips with my parents and Brenda when I was much younger. At fifteen I was already hanging out in malls and making trips on my own, of course, but before that, every family excursion was an adventure, a holiday, no matter how short.

After Echo and I helped clear the table and do the breakfast dishes, we got into the station wagon. Her excitement was so infectious she made me feel like it was my first trip away from home as well. Because of her confinement at the vineyard, Echo's face was filled with wonder at almost everything she saw. It brought home Tyler's concern that she be permitted to go to a school where she would be with other kids her age and have most of the experiences a girl her age should have. She had a thirst for knowledge, for information, and was moving quickly ahead in her schoolwork, but she was, as Tyler described, socially retarded.

"You stay close to April," Mrs. Westington warned her when we reached the mall. "Don't you go wandering off. She could do that," she told me. "She gets fascinated with something and forgets where she is."

"She needs to be out and about more, Mrs. Westington," I said gently. "She's too old to be on any sort of leash."

"Yes, well, that's what we'll do now, now that you're here with us," she told me.

But I won't be all that much longer, I thought to myself. I didn't like reminding her, but I could see that I had to leave soon. Brenda would be coming home and making plans for us, for me. I had to get on with my life, whatever life that would be.

At the mall I helped pick out some new clothes for Echo, clothing I knew was in style for girls her age. As I anticipated, Mrs. Westington was critical of almost everything, but reluctantly relented when she saw how pleased Echo was with the selections. We bought her bras and new panties, socks and new nightgowns as well. While we shopped, Trevor went off to get himself some things in the hardware store he said he needed.

At Mrs. Westington's continued insistence, I finally relented and chose a new black skirt and a blouse. I hated having to buy anything in the sizes I needed now but I remembered Brenda once saying to wear black because it hides your weight the best. It had been a long time since I had bought anything for myself, actually. The last time was just before my mother had died and my mother never admitted to me or perhaps even to herself that I was a little tank. She hated when I chose things in black.

Echo's attention went from the clothing to the kids moving through the mall. She was fascinated by both the girls and the boys and asked me questions continually about them. How old were they? What did they do in the mall? Do they all know each other? We saw them in the music stores listening to their favorite artists on earphones. Of course, Echo wanted to know what they were doing and I explained that supposedly that was how they decided whether or not to buy an album.

"Most just go there to hang out and listen and don't even buy anything," I told her.

She looked at them again, watching how they shared what they heard, and for a moment I thought of a poor homeless girl standing outside a restaurant gazing in at people enjoying wonderful dinners. It was a world she wasn't to know, but a world she envied. I felt so sorry for her and for a while, I stopped feeling so sorry for myself. After all, I could fix my problems. She couldn't. She could only learn how to live with hers.

Suddenly, surprising us both, Tyler Monahan stepped around a large display in the music store. Echo's face lit up. Mrs. Westington didn't notice him because she had met another elderly lady whom she knew and they were having a long catch up conversation.

Tyler turned in our direction. The first question that came to my mind was how could he be here? I thought he was desperately needed at his mother's retail outlet on weekends. There was no doubt in my mind that he had seen us, but he didn't wave or smile or walk toward us. He turned instead and hurriedly headed out of the store. Echo panicked at the realization he was not going to greet us. As clearly as she could pronounce it, she shouted his name.

I knew he had heard. Other people near him had turned in our direction, but he kept walking away. Echo looked at me with desperation.

"We'll be right back, Mrs. Westington," I called to her. She glanced at us, but her friend kept talking.

"Don't get lost!" she cried.

I took Echo's hand and we started after Tyler. He was walking very quickly and not looking back. I started to shout for him again when he stopped at a woman's shoe store just as an Asian woman stepped out. I stopped walking. He spoke with her and she turned our way.

His mother was a good three to four inches shorter than he was. She had her hair cut stylishly short and she wore what looked to me to be an elegant light blue designer suit. We were too far away to see much more detail, but I was sure I saw her shake her head slightly. She then turned abruptly in the opposite direction. Tyler glanced back at us. I thought he was finally going to acknowledge us and greet us, but his mother called to him and he spun around quickly and hurried to join her.

"Ty!" Echo shouted.

They rounded the corner and were gone.

Echo looked at me, her face full of confusion.

"He must have had to get right back to his store," I signed and spoke. I didn't do all that good a job of signing the ideas, but she understood enough.

She looked after him again. How cruel, I thought, no matter what he thought of me or what his reasons could be. He couldn't help but see how excited Echo was at the sight of him. Even if he really did have to get back to their business, why wouldn't he take a few minutes out to explain that at least? What, did his mother have a leash around his neck or something? It made me furious.

This is all going to end badly, I thought. I just have to have a heart to heart conversation with Mrs. Westington. I turned Echo around, but she kept looking back hopefully as we returned to the part of the mall where her grandmother had been talking to an old friend. Trevor Washington had already joined her when we arrived.

"Where did you two go?" she asked.

I glanced at Trevor, hoping he hadn't seen us, and then I told her I just wanted to show Echo the Nature store.

"Oh, well maybe we should go there and get her something," she suggested.

"Actually, we're both hungry," I claimed.

"Oh?" She looked at Echo. I knew she could see the unhappiness in her face. I had been with her a short time and already I knew how to read her moods and feelings. Mrs. Westington looked at me as well. I'm not good at lying or covering things up either, I thought. She knew it, but she played along.

"Okay, let's go have something to eat," she said.

We went to a restaurant in the mall. I ordered a salad. Echo was still upset about Tyler, but the excitement of eating in a restaurant overtook that for the moment. She wanted a cheeseburger and a Coke, which was something she never had at the house, of course. Afterward, we bought her a chocolate frozen yogurt. I could see that if I didn't order one as well, she'd be upset, so I did, but when neither of them were looking, I dumped it in a garbage can. Buying myself new clothes reinforced my determination to diet. I'm going to shed pounds, I vowed. I didn't need Brenda on my back or Tyler Monahan's attention to get me to do it, either.

Laden down with packages and bags, we returned to the station wagon.

"You wanna drive?" Trevor asked me. It took me by surprise, but I could see Echo thought it was amusing and even exciting. I looked at Mrs. Westington.

"The man's getting lazy," she said, glaring at him. "Just don't go speeding," she warned.

As we headed home, our route took us through

Healdsburg and we went by what Trevor told me was Tyler Monahan's retail outlet. I slowed down, tempted to pull over and have us all go in. He couldn't ignore us then, I thought.

"Maybe we should stop by and say hello," I suggested. "I'd like to see their store."

"It's nothing," Mrs. Westington said quickly. "It's just another shop with overly priced things for tourists. I'd never buy anything there."

I drove on, glancing in the rearview mirror at Echo, who sat staring out. How confusing the world was to her, trapped in silences she couldn't understand. We who could hear and hear well had difficulty with silences as it was. No matter how well I could sign, no matter how well she could read my lips, there were so many things lost between us. Interpret Tyler Monahan's look and silence for her? I couldn't do it for myself.

I knew when we arrived home, Mrs. Westington would interrogate me about Echo's sadness, but as it turned out, she didn't have a chance. There was another surprise awaiting her, awaiting us all.

When we turned up the driveway, we saw an old van that looked like it had been tie-dyed, a leftover from the sixties flower people days. One of the rear lights was battered and broken. The bumper was tied on with wires and the rear windows were so caked and clouded with dirt and grime, no one could possibly look out of them.

"Who's this now?" Mrs. Westington asked as we pulled alongside the van.

There was no one standing outside and from what we could see, no one in the van.

"I hope it's not someone coming to sample wine or buy one of your cases," she told Trevor. "Word gets out there's a restricted amount of a wine around here and everyone starts inquiring. Nothing sells like hard to get," she remarked.

"I haven't told a new soul about our wine. I just have my regular customers and there's not enough of our wine to expand the sales."

"Not our wine. Your wine, Mr. Vineyard," she told him.

He started to laugh.

The sight of the strange van brought some life back into Echo's face. We were all very curious. When we stepped out of the station wagon, we peered into the van and saw what looked like makeshift beds in the rear. The front seat and passenger seat were torn, the stuffing pouring out. There were empty beer bottles scattered about and wrappers from food as well as some clothing. On the dashboard was a paper plate with what looked to be the remnants of a pizza.

"It must be driven by hogs," Mrs. Westington said. She looked about. "Where are these people? Why are they on my property? Maybe we should call the police immediately," she told Trevor.

He nodded and started toward the front steps and then stopped, holding up his hand.

"What?" Mrs. Westington asked.

He turned slowly to us. "The door's been opened. It wasn't closed completely," he said.

"Good grief, we're being burglarized!" Mrs. Westington cried, and pulled Echo to her. "Stay back, girl," she told me, and I retreated a few steps.

Trevor went to the corner of the house and got a thick-handled rake he had there.

"Be careful," Mrs. Westington said. "Maybe we should just drive down to the nearest phone."

"I'm fine," he said. "Stay back."

He walked up the stairs slowly and then carefully opened the door and peered in, listening. When he turned back to us, he looked confused.

"Whoever's in there has the television on," he said in a loud whisper.

"Make themselves at home, why don't they?" Mrs. Westington said.

Trevor held his arm out to remind us to keep back and then he entered the house. We waited, listening, but my thumping heart was so loud in my ears, I didn't think I'd hear a thing. It seemed like minutes but was only seconds.

"Who the hell are you?" we heard him shout. I stepped back, terrified. Mrs. Westington embraced Echo tighter. She was totally confused and as frightened as I was. We heard a man's voice and then Trevor cried, "Well, I'll be damned!"

A few moments later, he appeared in the doorway. Before he could say a word, a woman wearing a red, white, and blue bandanna came out from behind him. There was a tattoo of a blue dahlia on her right cheek and a string of what looked like small seashells around her neck, falling down the valley between her ample breasts. She wore what looked like an Arab woman's black robe. She was barefoot. Her hair was long and stringy, the strands raining down limply over her ears to her neck.

Before she even spoke, I knew who she was.

"Hi, Mom," she said.

I guess it's a day for disappointments and night-mares, I thought. Now Mrs. Westington was about to have one of her own.

6

Mama Comes Home

"**W**ell, ain't this a pretty kettle of fish," Mrs. Westington said. She glanced at Echo and then relaxed her embrace. "You probably don't remember who that is, Echo. It almost takes a divining rod for me to determine her identity, but that there is your mother or what passes for her," she said.

"Now let's not start out on the wrong foot, Mom," Rhona said.

"We've been on the wrong foot for some time, Rhona. Too late to get off that," Mrs. Westington said.

"Hi, Echo," Rhona said. "I wouldn't have recognized you. You've grown so. Don't you want to give me a kiss and a hug?" She held out her arms.

Echo stared up at her, unmoving, her hand tightly clasping Mrs. Westington's. Did her own mother forget her daughter was deaf?

A tall, thin man with a grubby beard stepped up

beside Rhona. He was wearing a white button down shirt that looked like it had last been washed ten years ago and a pair of torn, ragged jeans with black sandals. His toes were so dirty, it was hard to tell where they were and where the straps of the sandals were. The strands of his dull brown hair resembled broken springs shooting off in every direction. When he smiled, his thin lips practically disappeared, producing a dull slice above his slightly protruding cleft chin. His neck looked like it needed a good scrubbing.

"This is Skeeter," Rhona said, lowering her arms.

"Hi there," he said, saluting quickly at Mrs. Westington. I glanced at her. She looked like she had just swallowed some sour milk. "You have a very nice house and great property. Love this old door. Oak, isn't it?"

"Skeeter? Didn't your parents give you a real name?" she asked.

I laughed to myself. Mrs. Westington wasn't one to hold back her thoughts and criticisms, even when she faced a complete stranger.

"Well, my real name is Sanford Bickers, but I never saw myself as a Sanford."

"Everyone knows him as Skeeter, Mom. No one knows him as Sanford."

"Then you two have something in common. You're both running away from yourselves," Mrs. Westington told her.

"I never knew you to be inhospitable, Ma," Rhona said.

Mrs. Westington looked at her askance.

"You're happy to see me at least, aren't you,

Trevor?" Rhona asked him, her voice sweet and syrupy.

Trevor's eyes shifted quickly to Mrs. Westington and then he looked away.

"All right, Rhona," Mrs. Westington said sharply, "to what do we owe the pleasure of this visit by you and Mr. Skeeter?"

"I've just been through hell, Mom. Skeeter helped me a great deal. I would have thought you would be a little more considerate since you knew what I've been through," Rhona whined.

"I'm sorry to say it, Rhona, but I doubt very much you're through with hell," Mrs. Westington said. She turned to Echo and me. "Let's get our things inside and up to your rooms, girls," she told me. I signed quickly to Echo, who was just standing there and gaping at Rhona.

"Who is she?" Rhona asked, nodding at me.

"This is April Taylor. She's been helping me with Echo. You can thank her properly later," Mrs. Westington told her.

"Is she staying in my room? I see it's being used."

"Your room? You gave up that room and a lot more years ago, Rhona."

"Well, where are Skeeter and I going to stay?"

"Who says you're staying?" Mrs. Westington retorted, and urged Echo and me to get our things again. I moved quickly, taking it all out of the station wagon. I glanced at Rhona, who had folded her arms petulantly under her breasts and stepped to the side, glaring at her mother. Skeeter kept a small smile on his face. They watched us enter the house and then followed.

"Now listen to me, Mom," Rhona began. "Please."

Ignoring her, Mrs. Westington turned to Trevor and nodded at the living room. "Would you be so kind as to turn that television set off, Trevor? We don't need the noise right now. Seems we have enough static already."

"Yes, ma'am," he said, glanced at Rhona, and then went into the living room to do it.

"Go on up, April. Help Echo put her things away, please."

"Okay," I said. I looked at Rhona again. Her eyes were inflamed with indignation and resentment and it looked like it was all directed at me, as if I were the cause of all her lifelong problems.

Trevor stepped back into the hallway. "I've got something waiting on me back at the winery," he told Mrs. Westington, nodded at Rhona, and hurried out.

I gestured to Echo for us to go up the stairs.

"Wait a minute," Rhona said, reaching for Echo, who couldn't take her eyes off her. "Don't you want to say hello to your mother, Echo? Give her a proper greeting?"

"You forget the little signing you knew?" Mrs. Westington asked her.

"She knows what I'm saying."

"I doubt that," Mrs. Westington told her. "I'm not deaf and I don't know what you're saying."

Rhona held out her arms, again expecting Echo to come to her for an embrace. Echo looked at Mrs. Westington and then she turned and started up the stairs with her boxes and bags.

"Echo! Echo, you listen to me."

"Lordy Dee. Did you forget the child is deaf?"

Mrs. Westington asked her. "She doesn't recognize you, probably. She was barely out of infancy when you deserted her."

"Look, Mom. I came here because I need you to help us and since you helped me get past my recent troubles, I thought you would have a different attitude, especially when you hear and see how I would like to make things right and to do the right things from now on."

"Mending fences, are you?"

"Yes."

"Turning a new leaf, are you?"

"Yes, Mom," she said in a tired voice.

"With Mr. Skeeter?"

"Can we sit down and talk like two adults, please?" Rhona pleaded.

"Two? Are you saying Mr. Skeeter or you ain't adult?"

"Mom?"

"I'll make some tea," Mrs. Westington relented. "You can use the guest room at the end of the hall upstairs. It's clean. My girl cleans it once a week no matter if anyone uses it or not, so don't mess it up so it looks like that pig pen you're driving out there. Put on some decent clothing, clean yourselves up so you're both fit to be in the same room with decent people, come down to the living room and I'll let you get down to brass tacks."

"Brass tacks?" Skeeter asked, smiling widely and looking at Rhona.

"Mom has a colorful way of speaking. We already brought our things to that room, seeing mine was messed up."

"Messed up? It's twice as neat as your best day in it."

"Okay, Mom. Just come on," she told Skeeter, and headed for the stairs.

I had been climbing slowly so as to hear their conversation. I sped up behind Echo and continued toward her room with her to help her put away her new things. I could see she was quite stunned with her mother's unexpected appearance.

"That's my mother," she signed to me as soon as we entered her room and she had put her bags and boxes down on the bed.

"I know."

"She looks different," she told me.

"People change. You haven't seen her in a long time," I said. "Let's put your things away."

I began to hang up clothes for her and she began to put things in her dresser drawers. She was full of questions, of course. Her hands were moving too quickly for me to follow, so she began to write.

"Is my mother staying here now?"

"I don't know."

"Who is that man? Is he my father?"

Again, I wrote, "I don't know. I don't think he's your father, however. I think she met him long after you were born, Echo."

"I don't like him," she wrote, and I laughed.

"I don't think your grandmother is particularly fond of him either."

She thought a moment and then wrote, "Why didn't Tyler say hello to us?"

"He was in a big rush. As I explained to you, something must have happened at their business," I told her. She thought about my answer and for the moment that seemed to suffice.

I was going to ask her about her nightmare last night and her coming to my bed, but on second thought, I decided she had been through enough turmoil already today. It could wait for a time when we had a quiet moment together. I told her I was going to put my new things away.

When I entered my room, I found Rhona there, rifling through her closet, tossing garments onto the bed. She turned as soon as she realized I was standing there.

"These are my things," she said. "I'm not taking anything that belongs to you."

"I know."

She stared at me a moment and then turned to me completely, her hands on her hips. "Who are you anyway? How come you're living here?" she demanded.

I began to explain, describing how I arrived at the vineyard after Uncle Palaver's death. I told her who he had been and what we had done together.

"So that's why there's a motor home and a car back there. My mother just took you in?"

"Yes," I said.

"What about the rest of your own family?"

I told her about Brenda, about my parents.

"This is ridiculous. Now she's turning this place into an orphanage," she said. Her eyes narrowed with suspicion again. "Did you touch any of my things, my clothing?"

"Your mother wanted me to wear one of the nightgowns, but other than that, I . . ."

"I don't know why I even asked. You couldn't possibly fit into anything of mine anyway, but I assure you I don't intend to let you just take over my possessions," she warned. "My advice to you is to find another elderly old lady to take advantage of."

"I am not taking advantage of anyone."

"Right. I've been on the road myself, you know. I know what's what. I'm sure it wasn't hard for you to pull the wool over the eyes of an old lady and a deaf girl, and Trevor Washington's head isn't exactly filled with lightbulbs."

She scooped up a pile of her clothing and started out of the room. She paused at the doorway and turned to me, her face flushed with fury. "Now that I'm back, I can assure you that you're not going to stay here," she said. "I intend to take back custody of my daughter and get what's rightfully mine. If you know what's good for you, you'll just get out now before there is any more unpleasantness."

She walked out of the room. My heart was pounding and tears had come to my eyes. I put away the clothes Mrs. Westington had bought for me and then I sat by the window, looking toward the motor home and thinking. I did have some money, Uncle Palaver's cash still in the motor home. I could leave. Brenda was probably right. I should just return to a regular high school and graduate. The equivalency exam wasn't going to work out anyway with Tyler behaving as he was. Mrs. Westington would say "the writing's on the wall." He'll be giving notice any day now and be gone. I should be gone along with him.

And then I thought how deserted and alone both Echo and Mrs. Westington were going to feel. Would Rhona and that man remain here? I had no right to interfere, of course, but I didn't have to be a fortune-teller to see what Echo's future would be like if Rhona did take custody of her again and Mrs. Westington was unable to prevent it. Who knows where Rhona would put Echo? How lost and alone she would be. No, I thought. Mrs. Westington needs an ally now more than ever and Echo needs a friend. Trevor Washington, as devoted to her and Echo as he was, wasn't enough. It seemed to me I had to stay. It would be totally ungrateful for me to just up and leave right now when they needed me the most.

I heard Rhona in the hallway talking to Echo. She was probably returning to the bedroom for more of her things, and she had stopped at Echo's room.

"I really can't get over how you've grown," I heard her say. "And fortunately for you, you look more like me than your father, whoever he was." She followed that with a thin laugh.

I stepped up to the doorway and saw her enter Echo's room. The door to the guest bedroom was open and Skeeter came out of the bathroom with a towel wrapped around his waist. I saw he had the tattoo of what looked like a dragon wrapped around a mermaid across his chest. He paused and looked out, catching me looking at him. Then he turned and unwrapped the towel from his waist, exposing his rear end, which looked like it had tattoos on each side of his buttocks as well. I stepped back into my bedroom quickly.

Rhona came in behind me and walked directly to the closet again. She picked out some other garments, sifted through the boxes of shoes, and then went to the dresser drawers. She didn't look at me at all.

"I can fit into all of this. I haven't gained a pound since I left here," she muttered. "I don't know how some women get so plump and lose all their appeal to men. Being fat makes you asexual, you know," she added, finally turning to me. "Skeeter came up with that in one of his poems. 'Your sex sank into your fat like a foot in quicksand.' Men don't like fat women, of course, and even women who like women wouldn't look at them. So where are you? In lard limbo, that's where. How old are you anyway?" she asked. "Were you always overweight?"

"I don't think it's necessary for you to know any more about me."

"You're right about that, since you'll be going now that I've returned."

"I'll go when Mrs. Westington tells me to go."

"She will. Don't worry." She saw my new black skirt and plucked it off the hanger. Then she held it up in front of herself. "I could get in this with you, I think." She laughed and tossed it at me. "Pack," she said.

Tears came to my eyes, but I drove them back. Brenda would make mush out of her, I thought, and stepped forward.

"I said I'd leave when Mrs. Westington asks me to leave."

"My mother is an old lady. She waited too long to have me and now she's too old for all this."

"She didn't wait long enough," I fired back at her. "She should have waited for menopause."

"Oh, you're a wise guy, too." She piled some undergarments together and smiled. "Did you see how Echo looked at me? It won't be long. She'll want me

with her, want to be with me. It's only natural.
Skeeter happens to know how to use deaf people's
signing language, too. He was a street performer, a
mime. He's very educated even though he hasn't been
to college. He's smarter than most college graduates
anyway. He'll have Mother eating out of his hand
soon. You'll see. He's a charmer."

"Yeah, I could see it the moment I set eyes on his
filthy hair and clothing. Won me right over," I said
dryly. Brenda would have loved that one.

"Skeeter is like a chameleon. He can adjust to
whatever he has to in order to succeed."

"Yeah, he looks very successful."

"He happens to be. You can't judge a book by its
cover."

"What cover? I'd say he's down to his last pages,
chewed and stained."

She glared at me a moment and then she laughed,
shook her head, gathered her things, and left the bedroom. I stood there, trembling, but keeping it under
control and undetected. Then I went to see how Echo
was. She was sitting on her bed, staring down at the
photograph of her mother she had shown me. She
looked up at me when I stepped near her. Her eyes
were glazed over with tears. She smiled, however.

"My mother has come home," she signed.

My heart sank.

Rhona was right to be confident. I had forgotten
how desperately we all need our mothers, no matter
how terrible they seem to be to us. It wasn't that difficult to imagine a young Echo searching the house for
her mother after she had left, waiting at the doorway
for her to return, looking for her at the sight of any

approaching car, waiting for her in the night. Neither I nor her grandmother could ever imagine the dreams she had, the silent prayers of hope she had recited to herself and maybe still did.

And I had no idea what sort of promises Rhona had just made to her. I didn't know what to say. I smiled weakly and she took back the picture and this time, instead of putting it under her clothing in a drawer, she put it on the dresser top in front of and against another picture of herself. She was obviously no longer afraid of her grandmother knowing she had the picture and getting angry about it.

For now, however, she wanted to talk about Tyler again, about the mall and the kids she had seen. Since she now knew I could drive, she wanted to know if I would take her in the car to see Tyler's store. He had promised to do that one day but had not. I didn't have any trouble imagining why. She thought it would be a wonderful surprise if we just walked into the store.

I couldn't say I wouldn't want to do that, but I hesitated to make any promises. Too often in my life promises turned out to be as far away as rainbows, beautiful for a moment and then gone. They might not be forgotten, but they were gone.

"We'll see," I told her. She was still trusting enough to take that as a promise, nevertheless.

I looked up when I heard footsteps in the hallway. Both Rhona and Skeeter stopped at Echo's doorway. Skeeter had his hair brushed and tied back in a ponytail and was now cleanly shaven. He was wearing a relatively clean looking dark blue shirt and a pair of slacks that were wrinkled, but were nicer than his jeans, of course. He wore slightly scuffed black shoes and socks and some sort of turquoise wristband.

Rhona had put on one of her old "new" dresses, a light pink one-piece tied at the waist. She had washed off the tattoo on her cheek and had her hair brushed back neatly and pinned, clearly showing a pair of gold teardrop earrings. I noticed she was wearing one of the newer pair of flats that matched her dress.

"What are you doing in her room?" Rhona asked in a demanding tone of voice.

"We're practicing communication skills," I said.

"Is that all you're practicing?" Skeeter asked.

"What's that mean?"

He laughed. "C'mon, Rhona. We have more important things to do right now."

Rhona started away and then stopped. "Wait a minute," she told him, and walked into the room right to the dresser. She looked at the picture of herself, picked it up, and smiled at Echo, who was staring up at her like an idolizing rock fan at her favorite performer.

"What's that?" Skeeter asked, coming in, too.

"It's me when I was just eighteen." She showed it to him. "I don't look much different, do I?"

"Not that I can tell," he said, which was just what she wanted to hear.

She knelt down and looked at Echo. "I'm glad you kept this, sweetheart," she told her, and then she embraced her and kissed her cheek.

Slowly, Echo brought her hand to her cheek as if she wanted to be sure she had really just felt a kiss from her mother. Rhona laughed, put the picture back on the dresser, turned to me with a sly, confident smile on her face, and then walked out of the room with Skeeter.

When I looked back at Echo, I saw she was crying and I knew it was possible to break a child's heart many, many times. She had too much hope to be cynical and distrusting or rather, she had too great a need to believe and be loved.

I talked her into going out for a walk with me and we started down the stairs. I paused when we reached the bottom because I could clearly hear the conversation among Rhona, Skeeter, and Mrs. Westington in the living room. I gestured for us to be silent and we stood there, me listening. Echo appeared to understand I was eavesdropping. She lowered herself slowly to the last step on the stairway and waited patiently.

"We just need this chance, Ma," I heard Rhona say. "The money we need is not a big deal to you, but to us it will mean a whole new start, and that's what you would like for me, isn't it? A new start?"

"If it was a real start that had any chance of making sense, I'd be for it, yes."

"This is a real start, Mrs. Westington," Skeeter said. "I've been working construction on and off for twenty or so years now. I know the business."

"You know it from a laborer's point of view, not an entrepreneur's point of view, and as my husband would say, that's a horse of a different color."

"He wouldn't say that, Ma," Rhona told her. "He'd be willing to stake us."

"As a home developer? Please, spare me," Mrs. Westington said.

"We've been studying how to do this for some

time now. You buy an old property no one really wants, so you get it for a song," Skeeter said. "Sometimes, you can find a foreclosure, too. Then you go in there and you rip it up and rebuild it with the best materials and modern appliances and you can literally double or even triple your investment. You'll end up making money on this deal, not losing it, Mrs. Westington. And at the same time, you'll be helping Rhona get a foundation upon which to build a new life for her and her daughter."

"Her daughter? You leave that girl here for nearly ten years with nary a phone call, a letter, and then you return with this fantasy and expect all that has washed under the bridge to be forgotten?"

"I know I was a bad mother, but—"

"Bad mother? First you have to be any sort of a mother to be good or bad. You abandoned ship, girl, and you never cared to know if the ship sank or not."

"I was too young to have a child," Rhona whined. "I wasn't mature enough or responsible enough, but that's all changed now, Ma."

"The only change I see is you put on some weight."

"I did not! I just compared myself to the picture Echo has of me when I was eighteen and even Skeeter says he can't see any difference."

"What picture?"

"The one she has on her dresser. She hasn't forgotten me. She still loves and needs me."

Mrs. Westington was quiet. Echo's secret was a little betrayal in her eyes, I was sure, but she had to understand and not be upset about it.

"I'll think about it," she relented.

"Thanks, Ma. That's all we hoped you would do."

"I doubt that. If you're going to stay here a while, you check your lies at the door, girl."

"I'm sorry, Ma. I'll behave. I promise. Skeeter and I will start looking for a good potential property right away, won't we, Skeeter."

"Tomorrow morning, first thing," he said.

"I said I'd think about it. I didn't say I would do it," Mrs. Westington reminded them.

"Some of the money you have belongs to me anyway, Ma. Daddy wouldn't have just left me out of it all, I'm sure."

"Oh, are you? Well, I have some terrible news for you, Rhona. You never took any interest in this place, in the winery and in our business, but the truth of it was I was the one in charge of all that. Your father was a good talker, loved to be out there in the fields with Trevor, but when it came to finances, he was lazy and indifferent. He even came to me for his daily spending money. I was the one who set up the will and the estate with my lawyers and my accountant and he signed everything I told him to sign, so don't think for a moment you can come here threatening me with legal actions of any kind. You'll be sorrily disappointed."

"I'm not threatening you, Ma. I'm grateful for what you just did for us, I mean me, and what happened to me woke me up. That's why I decided it was time for me to take on my responsibilities and why I returned."

"We'll see," Mrs. Westington said.

"I see that there is still some wine being made here."

"That's not me; it's Trevor's doing and I don't approve of the waste of time. It's a hobby for him, more than anything else," she admitted. "We don't make any real money on it, so don't get your hopes up about it."

"Oh, we're not looking to do anything with the winery. I just thought it would be interesting for Skeeter to see, right, Skeeter?"

"Absolutely. I love good wine."

"Yes, I imagine you're a real sommelier," Mrs. Westington said.

"What?"

"Never mind. I'm tired and need some rest," Mrs. Westington said. "We took Echo shopping at a mall today to get her some clothes and other things she needed, things children normally have mothers for."

"You've done wonders with her, Ma. Don't think I don't appreciate it."

"I didn't do anything for you."

"She's so big," Rhona continued, ignoring her. "She's becoming beautiful, too. She looks a lot like you did when you were her age."

"You know what I think of false flattery, girl."

"I mean it, Ma. I'll show you some pictures of my mother when she was young and you decide, Skeeter. Are the albums still in Dad's old office?"

"I'm surprised you remember where anything is in this house," Mrs. Westington said, her voice sounding tired, defeated.

"I'm different, Ma. You'll see."

"That's true. I'll see," Mrs. Westington concluded.

I waited just a moment or two too long before I turned to Echo to signal we were leaving. Rhona stepped out and saw me in the hallway. She smiled coldly.

"Spying on us, were you?"

"No. We're on our way out for a walk," I said quickly.

"Sure you were. I know you. I know your kind, and do you want to know why I know you?" she asked, stepping toward me. "I'll tell you why. Because once I was just like you, a parasite. C'mon, Skeeter," she said, turning to him before I could respond or react. "Let's get our other stuff out of the van. We're moving in."

They stepped forward and then she saw Echo at the stairway. "Oh, Echo, sweetie," she cried. "Skeeter, ask her if she wants to help us bring in our things?"

"I'm not sure I remember it all that well, Rhona. Let's see," he said, and started to sign. He was able to say, "You want to carry . . ." He started fumbling for other words, but Echo was smart enough to realize what he meant. She looked at Rhona, who was smiling at her and holding her hand, and she nodded quickly.

"Great," Rhona said, putting her arm around her. "Come with us. You don't want to waste your time on a walk with her."

Rhona looked back at me triumphantly as she took Echo out the door with her, her arm around her shoulders.

"You don't want to mess with her," Skeeter told me as he followed. "She can be a viper."

I watched them leave and then I looked in on Mrs. Westington. She was in her soft chair, her head back, her eyes closed, asleep. She looked years older to me. It was all foreboding, frightening. I hurried out the rear door of the house and then around toward the motor home. In more than one way now, it had become my true sanctuary. I knew I'd be comfortable in there beside Destiny.

As soon as I entered, I sat across from the doll and just as Uncle Palaver would do, I started a conversation.

"You can't imagine what a horrid thing has happened, Destiny. Rhona has returned with her so-called boyfriend and she's trying to win Echo away from Mrs. Westington and force Mrs. Westington to give her money, money she'll surely waste. I don't know what I can do about it."

"You can stop whining for one thing," I heard. I looked up. Did I just do that, think it and throw my voice through Destiny? It was more like something Brenda would say. You don't let someone like Rhona push you around, she would surely tell me. She's really a coward at heart. Stand up to her and she'll back away so fast, it will leave a back draft.

"Yes," I told Destiny. "I bet she really is a cowardly person. I'm not sure about Skeeter. He's not much better, but I think he's a sly, conniving sort of person. He's probably egging her on in all this. I saw how big his eyes were when he saw the house and the property. I should talk with Trevor," I continued. "He should know what just happened."

To me it looked like Destiny was smiling. Those soft lips were pulling in a little.

"We'll make them disappear," she said. "One way or another."

She didn't really say it, of course. I had thrown my voice through her again, but it was comforting. I must surely be having a feeling close to what Uncle Palaver felt when he carried on his conversations with the doll. For now, the illusion was enough. I didn't feel as alone. Did that make me terrible, weird, strange, or was it just normal for someone as frightened and alone as I was, as Uncle Palaver had been?

I gazed back at the house through the motor home window and saw Trevor Washington's light on in his apartment at the rear. I hadn't thought of him until now. Why was he so eager to get away when Rhonda and Skeeter showed up? I thought about it for a moment and then I rose, looked down at Destiny, who, as Tyler had said, seemed to follow your every move, and then I left the motor home and walked to Trevor's apartment entrance. I knocked and a moment later, he opened the door. To me he looked more tired and troubled than I had ever seen him.

"I hope you don't mind," I said, "but I wanted to tell you what Rhona said to me and what she's threatening to do."

His eyes widened. "What she said to you, huh?"

"Yes."

"Come on in," he said, stepping back.

All he had was what would be known as a studio apartment, a living room with a pull-out bed and a small kitchen. There was a table barely big enough for two. Had he lived in this little place all these years and not been unhappy?

"It ain't much," he said, seeing how I looked around at everything. "Just a place to rest my tired bones every night." He turned off his small television set. "You want something to drink? I got some soda, some juice, whatever."

"No, I'm fine, thank you."

"Well, take a seat," he said, nodding at the small sofa. He sat in his well-worn big cushion chair.

I saw the picture of a pretty African American woman on the dresser.

"That was your wife?"

"Charlie Mae, yes," he said. "Angels decided she was more than I deserved. She's gone, but I know she's still here," he said. I didn't need an explanation. "So, tell me about Miss Rhona. What poison came off that tongue?"

"She wants me out. She says she's going to take back custody of Echo and she's pretending to be a loving mother now. She and that man Skeeter want Mrs. Westington to give them money to buy old houses for him to fix up and sell."

"Oh, so that's their game. Might as well go over to the toilet, drop it in, and flush," he said.

"I think that's what Mrs. Westington thinks, too, but I'm worried Rhona and Skeeter will use Echo to blackmail her."

"No doubt," he said, nodding. "Rhona knows how to blackmail people real well."

"Oh?"

"She's probably going to tell you one day soon, so I might as well tell you myself," he said. "She wanted money to run off with and of course, Mrs. Westington wouldn't give her a penny, so she come to me."

"Why would you give her any money?"

"I wouldn't, but she sat right where you're sitting now and began to unbutton her blouse. She didn't wear a bra. Half the time, she didn't wear panties, neither. I don't know how many men she brought up here at night, but the list is probably a good half of the male population.

"Anyhow, she threatened to claim I tried to rape her. To make her point, she dug her own fingernails into her shoulder and tore down the skin right to her breast. She didn't wince. She sat there smiling and tearing her skin and her blouse. She said she wasn't going to run to her mother, either. She was going to get into her car and drive right to town and go to the police on me. I had no doubt she would do it.

"Anyway, I gave her all the money I had here, which was considerable because I didn't do much investing. She knew I had it. My guess was she spied on me through the windows and saw me counting it or something. She knew my hiding spots and she probably would have stolen it if she could get in, but I never forgot to lock the door and windows.

"The way I saw it, it was good riddance anyway. She was aggravating Mrs. Westington to death with her antics. I thought, of all the possible investments I could have made, this one was the best because it rid us of Rhona.

"Of course, I felt sorry for Echo. She was a mite of a thing and didn't know how bad Rhona was. I justified it by telling myself the child was better off without her. But I know a child never can forget or disown her own mother and be happy about it. And then there was my guilt over making it possible for Rhona to leave Mrs. Westington like that.

"One day, she turned to me and with those eyes of hers burning into me the way she can make them burn, she asked me where I thought Rhona got the money to take off like she had. I had little chance of getting away with any sort of a lie, so I upped and told her the whole story. Of course, she bawled me out for it, but she also admitted she understood why I would be afraid. 'My daughter's an expert when it comes to lying and cheating,' she said. 'She could make John the Baptist look like a serial rapist.'

"Still, I felt bad about keeping everything secret all that time. Grapes are sure a helluva lot easier to raise than children," he concluded.

"Well, what should I do now? Should I leave?"

"That's up to you, of course, but I think Mrs. West-ington would rather you stayed on. She's quite a bit older than she was when Rhona ran off, but she's still got lots of grit. I'll do whatever I can, too.

"I won't kid you about it," he added. "Rhona's pretty resourceful. I don't know where you've been and what you've seen in your short life, April, but you're about to learn how low-down someone can get. When that girl gets buried, there'll be black weeds sprouting all around her grave and every animal in the world will steer clear. Birds won't even fly over the tombstone."

I nodded. "I'm not going to run away," I said. "I've done enough of that."

"Maybe so. Echo's sure found a friend in you."

"Thanks, Trevor," I said, rising.

"Nothing to thank me for."

"Yes there is. Thanks for trusting me with the painful truth."

He smiled.

I walked to the door. "We're not getting pushed around anymore," I vowed.

"Yes, ma'am. If you say so," he told me, and I walked out.

Where did I get all the courage? I wondered. I looked at the motor home. The light was on. Had I left it on? I guess so, I thought. I'd better go turn it off. The batteries are weak enough as it is.

I hurried back, opened the door, and started up the short stairway only to stop dead in my tracks. My mouth hung open stupidly.

Sitting where I had been sitting, across from Destiny, was Tyler Monahan.

7

Kissing a Fool

"**W**hat are you doing in here?" I asked.

"When I drove up, I saw the light on and thought you were in here," he said. "I was just about to leave to see if you were in the house. I was hoping to see you without Echo knowing I was here."

"Why do you want to see me now? You weren't very interested in seeing me earlier," I said, unable to keep the note of anger out of my voice.

"I know. I felt bad about what happened today. I felt bad about it all, actually," he said.

"You should. Echo was heartbroken and couldn't understand why you would simply ignore her." I wanted to add, "and so was I," but I didn't.

"That's why I came here. I wanted to talk to you about . . . about it all," he said. He did look repentant.

I retreated a step to close the door and then I walked into the motor home and sat just to the right

of Destiny. It occurred to me that we were both staring directly at him. From the way he looked from her
to me and smiled, I could see he was thinking about
it, too.

"What's so funny?"

"You and the doll have the same expression on
your faces," he said.

"What's that supposed to mean? I'm just another
doll in your eyes?"

"No, no, nothing like that." He looked very nervous. "Whose van is that out front?"

"That's Mrs. Westington's daughter, Rhona, and
her boyfriend, Skeeter."

"Really? You mean, after all these years, Echo's
mother has returned to her home and family?"

"If you want to call it that. She didn't return because she missed her daughter. They want to get their
hands on Mrs. Westington's money."

He nodded. "Nevertheless, she's come home," he
said. "I think it was Robert Frost who wrote 'Home is
the place where when you go there, they have to take
you in.'"

"I don't think Mrs. Westington is anxious to do
that."

"Yes, but she will," he said confidently. "It's easier
for a child to run away than for a mother to turn her
out or him out, for that matter."

He was probably right. That inevitable outcome
depressed me, but I didn't see as I could do much
about it.

"Why didn't you at least wave to us in the mall
today?" I asked, returning to the reason for his appearance. "And don't claim you didn't see us."

"I saw you."

"So?"

"I've already told you how upset my mother's been at how much time I spend here, spend on Echo. She doesn't know anything about you and what work I've been doing with you."

"So? I still don't really understand why she's so upset about your working with Echo. You're doing what you were trained to do, what you were educated to do. Isn't she proud of that?"

"She would rather I help out in our business right now. She thinks Mrs. Westington should be sending Echo to a special school and I shouldn't be taking on all this responsibility. She thinks I'm too involved with their family matters."

"Well, Mrs. Westington will send her to a school, eventually." I raised my hands and smirked. "This is your excuse for not saying hello, for ignoring us?"

"I just didn't want to create any more tension. It wasn't the right time to introduce you and Echo to her. She thinks Echo was brought to the mall deliberately to see me. She thought you were all following me."

"What? That's ridiculous. How would we know you were there? As I recall, you said you had to work in the store and you wouldn't have time for us on the weekend."

"My mother's not thinking straight about this at the moment. It'll be all right, once I finish here, which I have to do very soon, actually sooner than I had planned."

"It'll be all right? Is that what you think? I'm happy for you."

"I just meant—"

"Look, Tyler, this all sounds stupid to me. You're not a child. Just stand up to her."

"It's not a matter of that. It's a matter of respect," he said.

"Right." I looked down at the control for Destiny and slipped it into my hand. "What do you think, Destiny?" I asked the doll, and threw my voice to have her speak

"We have a mama's boy here," Destiny said.

"Very funny. An obedient son is not a mama's boy, April. My mother comes from a different world and she hasn't lost her tradition and her sense of what she was taught is right and is wrong. It's how I was brought up," he explained. "Our first duty is to our parents. We don't desert them because they're old or sick and we respect their wisdom."

"You should be telling Echo all this, not me. Why come to me with these explanations and excuses, anyway?" I asked.

He looked away and then he sat forward, his head down. "It's not only what happened in the mall. I'm ashamed about how I behaved here with you. I shouldn't have done what I did."

"I didn't mind it," I confessed with a nonchalance that brought his eyes up sharply. "Look, I know exactly what happened here, Tyler. You don't even have to try to explain it or make up something."

"You do?"

"You just looked at me and got disgusted. I told you I didn't want to get into that costume. I knew what I would look like in it."

"Oh no, it wasn't you at all."

"What?"

"I mean, it wasn't solely because of you. It's me," he said. "You were very honest about yourself and told me some intimate things. I appreciate that, but it makes me feel deceitful."

"Deceitful? Why?"

"I haven't told you the truth about myself, April. The truth is not only don't I have a girlfriend here or in Los Angeles, I've never had a girlfriend. I've never been out on a real date, in fact."

I squinted, skeptical. "You've never been on a date? This is what you want me to believe?"

"I'm not lying. You have your personal and emotional problems and I have mine."

I thought a moment and it was as if a lightbulb went on in my head. "You don't mean . . . are you saying you're gay?"

Was this why he was so interested in why I had left Brenda and run to Uncle Palaver, why he pursued me for details about Celia?

"I guess I'm saying I don't know. I'm not sure if I'm gay or just afraid, insecure. It's how I am, how I've always been. Sometimes, I think I'm asexual, like an amoeba."

"Well, as you asked me, are you attracted to boys or aren't you? Are you more comfortable being with boys?" I repeated like a prosecutor.

"No, but I know I'm not as aggressive or as interested in girls as I should be, as other men my age are, as in fact my friends were when I was in high school and in college. They tried to include me in everything, parties, trips, but eventually they gave up on me and so did most of the girls."

I studied him. Who would ever think a man as good-looking as he was would have trouble with women? On the other hand, his look was different and there were probably many girls and women who thought of him as Asiatic and therefore not for them. Maybe this was why he had a complex, felt insecure. Suddenly, instead of being angry at him, I was feeling sorry for him and I was thinking he and I were more alike than he might think.

"You were never close with any girl, ever?"

"No, not really. I mean, I studied with them, things like that, but when it came to socializing, going out on dates, I went into retreat. There was a girl once who I knew liked me very much. She tried to develop a romance between us, but I didn't respond the way I should have and she just became angry at me, the way you were, I'm sure. Anyway, I decided I would come here to tell you about it so you wouldn't feel that it was your fault. I came to apologize. I'll fix it with Echo, too. I'll have to prepare her for my ending the tutoring."

"She won't understand. No matter what you tell her, she's going to think it's her fault somehow and she's going to be heartbroken."

"I hope you'll help me with her and prevent that. She thinks of you now as her best friend in the world."

I sighed deeply and shook my head. "I know, and I regret it now."

"Why?"

"I don't know how much longer I'll be here, Tyler. Rhona is determined to get me out. She's already threatened me."

"What does Mrs. Westington say about that?"

"She doesn't know how bad things could get and I don't know if I will be able to stay around here any longer anyway. I promised Trevor I would try, but it's really not my business or my right to come between a mother and her daughter. Anyway, I have my own troubles."

"I'm sorry to hear that," he said.

"Is it really important to you that I stay?"

"Yes, important for Echo especially. Will you?"

"We'll see. As I told Trevor, I'll try."

"I'll help you if I can," he promised. "It could be that Rhona will get quickly discouraged once she sees how big a responsibility Echo is and take off again anyway."

"I don't know as I would count too heavily on that, Tyler. As you have pointed out, Mrs. Westington is not a young woman. I think Rhona came here because she realizes it and wants to be sure she has control of everything, the property, the money. If Mrs. Westington should leave it all to Echo, Rhona will have a mother's authority. What could I possibly do to help or prevent any of that? What can you do?"

"Well, don't make any quick decisions about it," he said. "I'll return on Monday. Please."

I looked at him. He really did seem to want me to stay. Was it only to make things easier for him or was there some interest in me, enough to keep him thinking about me?

"I tell you what," I said. "I'll promise to stay as long as you do."

He thought a moment and then nodded. "Okay."

"Is that a firm promise?"

"Yes."

"Destiny, do you believe him?"

"Give him the test," I made her say.

Tyler laughed. "What test?"

"Test of truth," I said. I stood up and went to the cabinet under the television set to get a deck of cards. Then I handed it to him. "Pick a card and whisper what you've chosen into Destiny's ear."

"What?"

"Just do it."

He started to pluck one out of the deck.

"No, this is the honor system. Don't pull it out. Just pick it and tell her."

"Tell her?"

"That's right. Whisper it in her ear. Go on."

I took the deck back and went into the kitchen. He laughed, rose, and whispered into Destiny's ear. Then I returned and knelt down to put my ear to her lips. Her lips moved and then I turned and plucked a card from the deck.

"Was this it?"

He looked from the card to Destiny to me. "How could you do that?"

"A good magician . . ."

"Never tells, but you've got to tell me or I'll go crazy."

"It's better you believe it was simply magic," I said, and started away, but he grabbed my wrist and pulled me back so roughly I nearly fell over him.

"In a minute I'll give you magic you won't forget, if you don't talk."

"I must warn you. I'm trained to endure all sorts of torture to keep the great secrets," I said.

He stood up. "Is that so?" He smiled and then he started to tickle me and I squirmed to get away. He held on and we both fell back on the sofa. He held me down and started to blow in my ear. I screamed and he stopped. "Are you going to talk?"

I shook my head.

Then he poked the tip of his tongue into my ear and I squealed. He held himself inches from my face. We were both very silent. I'm not like Brenda, I thought. I'm not. I want him to kiss me. I really do. I raised my lips toward his. He didn't move and then he brought his to mine.

"I'm a stumbling fool when it comes to this," he said.

"So am I," I whispered, and he kissed me again. I moved more to the left to make room for him on the sofa. It occurred to me as he slid down beside me that we were truly like two young teenagers making an initial foray into the sexual jungle. A man his age really should have more sophistication, I thought. He wasn't lying to me about his inexperience and lack of romantic involvement. Could I be the first girl he's ever gone this far with?

He fingered the buttons on my blouse awkwardly. Should I help him? I wondered. Would he be embarrassed, insulted, and once again turn away from me? I waited with my eyes closed until he finally had it all done. Then I let him lift me so he could take off my blouse and begin to fumble now with the fastener of my bra. It was easier and in moments, he had my breast cupped in his hand, his lips to my nipple. I

moaned and sank back on the sofa. He started to undo
the button of my jeans and gently pull them down. I
felt his fingers move under the elastic of my panties
and then I let him lift my legs to slide my panties
lower and lower.

"I do like you, April," he said. "I do, I do," he
chanted. I heard him undoing his pants. I am going to
do this, I thought, almost solely to prove to myself I
wanted it as much as I was proving it to him and letting him prove himself to me.

And then I turned slightly to my right and looked
at Destiny.

"Wait," I said, but I said it through her. "Wait."

Tyler stopped, a confused smile on his face.
"What?"

"Are you prepared? Are you ready for this?"

My lips didn't move. He turned and looked at Destiny and then back at me. "What are you doing?"

"She's right," I said. "We have to be careful. I
don't want to get pregnant. That would be horrible
right now. Are you prepared?"

He thought a moment and shook his head.

"Then let's wait until you are, Tyler. Please," I said.

He nodded and sat back with a dazed look on his
face. I saw his eyebrows rise and fall with the ebb
and flow of his thoughts as he gazed at Destiny. The
foggy look lifted away from his face and left behind
his thoughtful, more intelligent expression. He turned
to me.

"You're right, of course, but why did you throw
your voice through the doll to say it?" He smiled at
me, but it was a smile of confusion and even a little
annoyance.

"I don't know. I just . . . it seemed to be what she would say."

"She? She? It's a doll, April."

"I meant, what she would say if she were really sitting there."

"You think we would do this in front of someone?"

"You know what I mean, Tyler."

He thought and then he glanced at Destiny and buckled up his pants. I started to dress as well.

"Tell me this. Did you enjoy being with a male, with me?" he asked.

"Of course I did. I wouldn't have gone this far if I didn't, and you already know I was upset and disappointed the first time because you ran out," I told him.

That seemed to satisfy him. "I'd better get home," he said, rising.

"Can you come back tomorrow?"

"I don't know. I have chores to do at our plant."

"On Sunday?"

"I can do what I have to do better when there's no one else there. I'll try. I'll call you," he said. "We could meet here again, but it would be better . . ."

"If Echo didn't know. I know," I said.

"Until I had a chance to explain things to her and make sure she was all right."

"Okay."

He glanced at Destiny and then he looked at me and smiled. "C'mon, tell me how you did that card trick. I promise I'll never tell another living soul."

"Why do you want to ruin the magic?"

"I find my magic in reality, not in illusion," he replied. "It's healthier."

He's right, I thought.

"All right, I'll tell you. Hand me the control," I said, pointing to it on the seat beside Destiny. He did. "There's a tape recorder inside Destiny's head. I just push this button on the control," I said, showing it to him. "Destiny's ear is the microphone. When you whispered the card in her ear, it was recorded and I just played it back through her mouth by pushing the button again."

"Wow," he said, looking at Destiny. "What else can this doll do?"

"That's for me to know and you to find out. For one thing, she just stopped us from going too far without protection."

"Yeah, right," he said, shaking his head. "She stopped us. I gotta go before I end up throwing my voice through her, too." He stepped forward and kissed me quickly on the lips. I watched him go down the short stairway and out the door.

I turned to Destiny. "Should I be happy or sad?" I asked her.

She said nothing, of course.

It was too soon to know.

I turned off the lights this time and left the motor home. Before going any farther, I stopped and looked at my car. It had been so long since I had driven it. Maybe I'll take Echo for a ride tomorrow, I thought. Maybe we'll look Tyler's mother in the face so she can't ignore our existence or at least Echo's. Tyler might be upset about it, but maybe his mother would see how sweet Echo is and she wouldn't be so against Tyler's helping her. Once in a while, it's good to think positively and be optimistic, whether it has a chance to come true or not.

Once in a while.

When I rounded the corner of the house, I immediately saw the van was gone. I was relieved at that. I wasn't looking forward to confronting Rhona so quickly again. The house was very quiet when I stepped in, but then I heard the rattle of a pan in the kitchen and I headed for it.

It wasn't hard to see Mrs. Westington was upset.

"Where is everyone?" I asked.

She stopped working, took a breath, and turned to me. "My daughter has decided to take her daughter to a restaurant for dinner tonight. She says it's about time they got to know each other. Can you imagine? It's about time? Ten years? There's enough water under that bridge to fill an ocean. But," she said after another deep sigh, "I guess a child always has a right and a need to know her mother, even if that mother is as irresponsible and as selfish as Rhona."

She looked at me as if she just realized she wasn't talking to herself aloud.

"I've prepared a nice chicken salad for the two of us. Do you want a baked potato as well? It won't take long."

"No, the salad is quite enough for me."

"Determined to lose weight now, are you?"

"Yes, I am," I said. I wondered if I should say any more about Rhona, about her wanting me out. I decided for now I would just ignore it and see what I could do to help Tyler with Echo. "Let me help with the table," I said, but she told me everything was already done.

"I had to keep myself busy so I wouldn't be nervous about Echo going off with Rhona in that junk heap."

I helped her bring the food into the dining room and we sat at the table, just the two of us. I watched her nibble at her food. Lifting a fork seemed to be a great effort for her.

To me it seemed as if a strange thing had happened with Rhona's return: Mrs. Westington, instead of finding any pleasure and hope in this reunion, grew older instantly because of it. Rhona was like a dark storm aggravating Mrs. Westington's arthritis, invading her very bones. She moved slower, looked much more fatigued and simply overwhelmed.

I was sure that for a time early on in her marriage and life with Mr. Westington, the world was joyful and bright. The vineyard prospered. They had friends and parties. Their home and property glistened with success. Her beauty was nourished by the happiness and she blossomed. Before Rhona became their problem child, there were waves and waves of laughter rolling over this house and family. Neighbors and other people who knew them or of them were envious. Many wondered why it was some people were so successful and so lucky. Why weren't they as blessed as the Westingtons?

And then Mrs. Westington's life took a dark turn. The death of their newborn, the battle with her brother-in-law, the growing discipline problems with a rebellious Rhona, and eventually Mr. Westington's death sent her spiraling down a long, seemingly endless hole of pain and disappointment. The burdens grew. Echo was enough of a responsibility and a weight for young, healthy parents, much less an older woman, a widow deserted by her daughter.

Nevertheless, her spirit was too strong, her determination too fixed, to permit her to surrender. She made do with what she had and she continued, assuming the role of mother again, but this time far more protective than she had been with Rhona. In a real sense Echo suffered for her mother's sins because she was being stifled, kept in this cocoon her grandmother had lovingly woven around her. Mrs. Westington saw hope and promise in Tyler Monahan's successes with Echo, and I, in my small way, looked like I would contribute in the areas that were still deficient. She truly believed I had been brought here not for myself so much as for her granddaughter's best interests. There was new hope.

And then Rhona returned and the prospects of what she had brought along with her—not only in Skeeter, but in her new determination to get what she believed was hers, including control of Echo—was a new weight on the frail shoulders of this heroic old lady I quickly had come to love.

More than ever, I was determined to help her.

"I guess," she said, "I might just have to give them the money."

"She doesn't have the legal right to make demands on you," I offered.

"I don't have faith in the courts. I've seen too much injustice signed, sealed, and delivered by greedy lawyers. Rhona gets one of them legal criminals working for her and we could be knocked into a cocked hat. An old lady, who's already lived long past her due date with the Grim Reaper, and an old black man won't suffice as a substitute family."

"But you have!" I insisted. "You've been more than a grandmother. You've been a real mother and you're providing for her and you've protected and taken care of her."

"I couldn't have done otherwise. No one would have expected less, but it's not enough to guarantee they'd agree with us. No, we'll have to face the music one way or the other eventually, I'm afraid. Best we can hope for is putting it off as long as we can. Maybe, just maybe she's grown up some, too."

I looked down. I was happy she included me by saying "we," but I had no false hope about Rhona having changed for the better. Just the little I had seen of her had already sickened me. I didn't have the heart to disagree, however.

"You just make sure Echo is okay," she continued. "If you see something bad happening, come right to me. Don't be afraid and don't hesitate. I'm happier than ever that I have you here to do all this with me."

I nodded, tears building in my eyes.

"You're a sweet child," she said. "Your parents were lucky folks and I'm sure you were lucky to have them, too. But you see how unjust things are with their being gone too early? We can't depend on the right things always happening on their own. We have to do our best to ensure they do and that's all we can do. I think you already know all that."

"Yes, Ma'am."

"Eat up. I know you won't have any of my home-made apple pie."

"Maybe just a small piece," I said, relenting.

"I don't put all that much sugar in it like store-bought pies."

"I know. Thank you."

She smiled and we finished eating silently, both of us lost for a while in the hopes and the dreams that gave us reason to go on.

I enjoyed the pie, helped clean up, and then went up to my room. As the hours marched by and I didn't hear Rhona, Skeeter, and Echo return, I knew Mrs. Westington was probably growing more and more agitated. I hadn't heard her come up to bed either, so I went downstairs and found her dozing in her chair in the living room with the television set on but the audio almost too low to hear. The moment I entered, her eyes snapped open.

"Are they back?"

"No, not yet," I said. She looked at the clock. It was close to eleven.

"Where could they have taken that child this late?"

I had no answer, but I saw she wasn't about to get up and go to sleep, so I sat on the sofa.

"You don't have to wait up with me, April."

"It's all right. I won't fall asleep knowing you're down here worried."

"If my daughter had one ounce of your decency, I wouldn't be worried."

I wondered if I should reveal what Tyler had told me about his having to stop tutoring Echo very soon. It seemed like a flood of bad news. Maybe wait a little longer, I thought. Maybe he would change his mind anyway.

I gazed at the television.

"You can make that louder or change the channel if you want. Half the time I fall asleep watching it. My eyes get tired and most of what I see seems silly."

I reached for the remote just as the headlights of the van ran a ray of light over the walls. We both turned to look out the windows.

"Finally," she said, rising.

We both went to the doorway of the living room. We could hear Rhona's loud peal of laughter. Skeeter was making some strange sound, imitating something that resembled an elephant. The door opened and they entered with Echo, who looked like she had been asleep, probably in the van. Her eyes were droopy and she barely had enough energy to smile when she saw us.

"Where have you been with her?" Mrs. Westington demanded immediately.

Even though a good five or six feet separated us from them, I could smell the odor of whiskey. Skeeter swayed a little, holding on to his dumb grin. Rhona wavered, her hands on Echo's shoulders.

"What are you getting yourself in an uproar about, Ma? We just stopped at one of my old hangouts and I met some of my old friends, friends I haven't seen for ten years."

"And what did Echo do all that time you were in a bar? Don't tell me you took her in, too."

"No. She stayed in the van and actually took a nap on our bedding."

"You let that girl sleep on that lice-infested filthy old mattress you had in that van?"

"Don't exaggerate, Ma. It just looks dirty. It's not. It's old."

"And well used," Skeeter added with a laugh.

"Yes, well used," Rhona agreed.

"Come here," Mrs. Westington beckoned to Echo. She moved quickly to her and Mrs. Westington looked through her hair. "She'll need a good bath and shampoo."

"That's disgusting, Ma. We're not dirty slobs."

"Until someone invents a better way to describe you two, I'll stick with that," Mrs. Westington said. "This is no hour to bring home this girl. She has to get her sleep."

"It's Saturday night, for chrissakes," Rhona said. "Are you still living in those dark ages?"

"I'm still a responsible person, if that's what you mean, yes."

"I don't expect to frustrate the girl the way you frustrated me, Ma. Here I was locked up in this house while my friends were out there having fun all the time. You have to trust the people you love and not expect they'll do something terrible all the time."

"In your case, Rhona, you exceeded my expectations," Mrs. Westington said, and turned Echo toward the stairs. She signed and told her she would help her take a bath and get to bed.

Rhona and Skeeter watched them start up the stairs and then Rhona turned and glared viciously at me.

"Did you work her up into this mood?" she asked.

"I just came down myself, surprised you weren't back yet."

"Oh, so you let her know you were surprised. Very convenient. I'm warning you, I'm not going to let you turn her against us," Rhona said, stepping toward me.

"I don't have to do that. You do it so well your-self," I replied and, even though I was trembling, glared back at her and then turned and followed Mrs. Westington and Echo up the stairs.

"Bitch," I heard Rhona call after me.

"Easy," Skeeter told her.

I glanced back and saw him whispering in her ear. She nodded and smiled and then they turned and went into the living room. I looked in on Mrs. Westington and Echo, who was already in the bathtub, the water running.

"Come here," she said, bringing me over to the tub. "Just look."

She pulled some strands of Echo's hair apart and I could see the bugs.

"This is what wants to turn a new leaf and be a mother. Lord, give me the strength." She poured the shampoo into Echo's hair and began to scrub.

"I can do that for you, Mrs. Westington. Please. Let me," I said.

She thought a moment and then stepped back. I shampooed Echo's hair and rinsed it with the shower hose. Mrs. Westington stood by with a towel and wrapped her as soon as she stepped up and out of the tub.

"Let's get this child to bed," she said. She told me where to find her pajamas. Echo put them on and got into bed. She still looked confused, dazed. Mrs. West-ington arranged her blanket and gave her a kiss. "I'm going to sleep," she told me. She started out.

"Are you all right?" I signed to Echo.

Through her fatigue, she smiled and then brought her hands out from under the blanket to tell me.

"I had dinner with my mother. And she said she was sorry she left me," Echo told me. "She said she would never leave me again. Never."

Her happiness not only disappointed me, it frightened me. She was being set up for a great fall. I was positive, but I dared not contradict her or Rhona directly.

"People say things sometimes and forget," I told her.

"No," she said, and shook her head vehemently. "She won't forget. She promised."

All I could do was smile and nod. I kissed her on the forehead and told her to sleep tight. She nodded and hugged Mr. Panda to her.

When I stepped out into the hallway, I could hear Rhona's and Skeeter's laughter below. They had put on some music, not caring how loud it was and if it would disturb me or Mrs. Westington. I thought I heard the sound of something being knocked over, too. Their laughter stopped and then I heard Rhona moan. Skeeter laughed and Rhona cried out passionately. They're probably making love right on the living room floor, I thought. For a moment I was tempted to go look. I went into my room instead and closed the door.

I stood there in the darkness, trembling. How horrid all this had become. How sorry I felt for Mrs. Westington. I was sure she would be having a troubled sleep tonight.

"Uncle Palaver," I whispered, "you taught me how

to make coins and cards disappear. You even showed me how you could make me disappear after I crawled into your magic box on the stage. But you forgot to show me how to make a horrid person disappear."

That's a bit of magic I'll have to learn on my own, I thought, and went to bed dreaming that somehow, maybe through Destiny, I would find the way.

8

Caught Naked

Rhona and Skeeter didn't come down for breakfast. They made lots of noise going up the stairway very late at night, completely inconsiderate of Mrs. Westington and me, especially me. I heard Skeeter growl at my door, in fact, because he woke me and then I heard them both laughing. If Mrs. Westington heard anything, she didn't mention it. In the morning Echo kept looking for her mother to come down and even asked me if I thought she should go up to see if she was awake.

"They went to bed very late," I told her. "Let them sleep." Let them sleep forever, I thought. Maybe that was mean, but I couldn't help it.

Just as I sat down to have breakfast with Echo and Mrs. Westington, the phone rang. She told me it was

Tyler Monahan calling for me. Echo didn't know it was Tyler and I wasn't about to tell her.

"How are things today?" Tyler asked. I told him what had happened the night before with Echo and how upset Mrs. Westington had been and still was.

"I guess this wouldn't be a good time to bring up my leaving," he said.

"No, it wouldn't, Tyler."

"Can you meet me tonight in your motor home after Echo goes to sleep?" he asked, confirming his promise to return.

Excitement trickled through me like a low voltage shock. I knew why he wanted to meet, of course, and it wasn't to improve my academic skills for the equivalency exam.

"I suppose," I said.

"And could we turn that doll around?"

I laughed. "You're the one who keeps saying it's just a doll, Tyler."

"That's not just a doll," he said.

"Okay. I'll put her in the bedroom."

"No, maybe leave her out of the bedroom. That's the one place I don't want her to be," he said. I could feel myself blush. "One other thing. I think it might be better if I parked on the road and walked to the motor home. No need to let anyone else there know I'm around."

"Okay," I said, although I wasn't comfortable with us sneaking about the property. Was he trying to keep all this secret from the people here or from his mother?

"I'll be there about nine-thirty, waiting for you," he said.

Mrs. Westington looked curious about the phone call, but she didn't ask me anything after I hung up and I didn't volunteer anything. It's better to say nothing rather than lie, I thought, and returned to the breakfast table to join Echo. Trevor hadn't shown up for dinner the night before and had not come to breakfast either. I imagined he just didn't want to see much of Rhona. As it turned out, he wouldn't have risked it this particular morning. She and Skeeter didn't come downstairs until nearly noon.

When they finally appeared, they were both dressed to go out, Rhona wearing one of her old dresses and a light blue leather jacket I had wished would fit me, and Skeeter in a relatively clean-looking pair of jeans, a blue shirt, and a jean jacket with all sorts of emblems with silly things written on them like *Down with Milk*. Mrs. Westington was in the kitchen. Echo and I were in the living room reading and working on some of her English grammar problems in preparation for her tutoring session the next day.

"Don't bother making any breakfast for us, Ma," Rhona called to Mrs. Westington from the hallway. "Skeeter and I are going to eat at the Mars Hotel in Healdsburg and then look at some properties we found out about last night. We'll see you later. Maybe Echo wants to go," she added.

"That girl needs to do her homework for tomorrow's lessons," Mrs. Westington replied quickly.

"Oh. Well, we don't want to interrupt that now, do we, Skeeter?"

"Absolutely not. Maybe we'll take her to a movie or something tonight."

"A movie? How do you expect her to enjoy a movie if she can't hear a word?"

"People used to go to silent movies, Ma," Rhona said. "You probably did," she added, and they both laughed.

"Silent movies were made differently," I offered from the doorway of the living room. "They had written words and the actors performed differently."

"Who said that?" she cried, pretending it was a voice from out of the blue. She turned and looked at me. "Oh, you're still here?" She turned her back on me and then marched to the front door. "C'mon, Skeeter, we have work to do," she called back to him.

He smiled licentiously at me and moved his tongue over his lower lip. Then he laughed and joined her at the door. They both laughed at something he whispered and then they walked out. I looked back at Echo. She hadn't realized they had come down and I wasn't about to tell her.

A short while after they had left, Trevor came in to see how things were and Mrs. Westington gave him an earful about the night before. He listened, shook his head sympathetically, and urged her not to let herself get too upset. She told him all about their request for money and why.

"I got a very bad feeling about those two," he told me when Mrs. Westington went upstairs. "I don't think they're here for the real estate business prospects they claim. Before they left yesterday, two men drove up and spoke with that Skeeter fellow, and both looked like they had been dragged out of a swamp. My guess is they need money, but not to buy old houses to fix up. They have serious debts with bad people."

"What are we going to do?" I asked him.

"Nothing right now. All I got to go on is a feeling, but you watch and wait long enough and the rat comes out."

"To me it already has," I said.

He nodded and went out to the winery. Meanwhile, Echo, impatient now, went looking for her mother and discovered she was gone. A look of panic came over her when she found out they had left. Her hands were flying about like small birds trying to draw diagrams in the air. "Where were they? When did they leave? When were they coming back?"

"They have business here and had an appointment," I told her. Maybe I was passing on a lie as Trevor thought, but I didn't want her worrying. I saw she couldn't concentrate on our work. She was constantly thinking about her mother, looking out the window for her and Skeeter's return, so I asked Mrs. Westington if it would be all right to take Echo for a ride. "We'll return to the mall," I told her. "I need some other things and Echo enjoyed it so."

She thought a moment and nodded. "It would be good to keep her mind off you know who," she said, reading my mind. "And I know you're responsible and trustworthy enough to look after her."

When I told Echo, she was bright and happy again. This would actually be the first trip she had ever taken without her grandmother and Trevor Washington. I unhooked my car from Uncle Palaver's motor home and brought it around to the front of the house.

"Where you headed?" Trevor asked. I told him and explained why.

"Can't blame the girl, I guess," he said. "After you lose someone you love or someone who loves you, you'd forgive them all their sins and imperfections if you could have them back. You'd even make a deal with the devil."

"That's who Echo would have to speak to about her mother," I told him, and he laughed.

"Have a good time," he said, and returned to his favorite work. I realized it was work that kept him in close contact with the best memories of his life. It was truly a labor of love, and despite all the complaining Mrs. Westington voiced about it, she was happy for him, maybe even envious. I wished I could find a way to reconnect with my good memories, too, reconnect without all the baggage of sadness that accompanied them.

I honked the horn and Mrs. Westington brought Echo out. She had helped her choose one of her new skirt and blouse outfits and she did look pretty. It was a partly sunny day with high brisk winds smearing the clouds over the blue sky so that they thinned out and spread like tattered white cloth toward the southwest. Sunlight brought a brightness to her face the way it would open a flower.

Echo got into the car. She was very excited now, the short trip truly a major adventure in her eyes because it was just the two of us. She watched me drive and then told me Tyler had promised that soon he would teach her how to drive so she could be ready for her driving test when she was of age. She showed me some of the signing related to driving that he had already taught her, such as the signs for right and left turn, speeding up and slowing down. Wasn't it wrong to make such promises to her knowing he was inevitably going to leave much sooner than she ever imagined he would? I made a mental note to ask him about that later.

By the time we arrived at the mall, school had ended for the day and many of the students were already gathering at their favorite mall stores, pizza hangouts, and the arcade. I took Echo directly to the shoe store first to buy myself a new pair of running shoes. I remembered all the things Brenda had told me about good running shoes and sought them out. Afterward, I bought Echo a bread pretzel and a soda and just had a diet soda myself. She was intrigued by the other girls her age and couldn't take her eyes off them while they flirted with boys and giggled. The worst wallflower wasn't as outside of teenage society as poor Echo was, I thought. I should know. I had been one.

Once again, she was fascinated by the kids in the music store listening to music and riffling through CDs. To my surprise she wanted to go in. I had no idea what we would do there, but I agreed. She went to the racks and, watching how the others were doing it, began to sift through them, picking one out and reading about the artist or the band as if she was really thinking of buying it. I stood by smiling to myself until, imitating the others, she put a CD on a player and then put a pair of earphones on herself, too. How sad, I thought. If my heart were made of glass, it would have shattered in my chest.

When I tried to sign to her, she turned her back on me quickly so the others couldn't see and discover she was deaf. She nearly pulled it off, too, but she caught the eye of a boy about a year or so older than she was and he sauntered over to her. He smiled at her and began to talk about the music she was playing. I could see her desperately trying to read his lips, but her fear of speaking poorly and his slightly turned head made it impossible for her to go on with her fantasy much longer. I saw the confusion in his face and so did she. She turned to me quickly in desperation and I had no idea what to do or say.

Instead, I moved in quickly and took the earphones off, stepping between her and the boy.

"What are you listening to?" I asked her, and put on the earphones. I grimaced. "You think this is good?" I asked the boy.

He glanced at Echo and then at me, his face filling with annoyance.

"I wasn't talking to you," he said. "I was talking to her." He then sidestepped to ignore me and asked Echo who she was and where she went to school. He wanted to know why he hadn't seen her before. Was she a new student?

I tried to prompt her, but she was too nervous to pick up the signals and he immediately caught her looking at me instead of at him.

"What the hell's going on?" he asked, his suspicions building.

"Nothing. Bug off," I said. I signed to Echo that we should leave quickly.

He caught my hand movements and his eyes widened.

"What are you doing?" He looked at her and then at me. "She can't hear?"

"That's right, smart ass," I said.

"Then why was she . . . what are you, both nuts?" He shook his head and backed away as if we could infect him with some strange new disease.

I hurriedly put away the CD and seized Echo's arm to turn her toward the door. The boy was already describing us to his friends, who all looked our way. I heard their laughter. Echo looked back and saw their faces of ridicule. Her face quickly fell into an expression of total embarrassment. For her it was truly as if she had been caught naked. I tried to walk us down the mall corridor faster, but it was too late. The small group of teenagers decided we were to be their entertainment for the afternoon. We were too unusual to be ignored and a great alternative to their ordinary mall activities. They charged out of the music store behind us, a small clump of kids, laughing and hooting, which only attracted more attention and more of their friends.

No matter where we went, they tagged along, anxious to catch me signing to Echo, who by this time was so frightened and confused, she was trembling. I searched desperately for the nearest exit and directed her to it, hoping that when they saw we were leaving, they would get bored and return to their own interests. But they were probably bored with themselves, I thought, for they weren't discouraged. By now there were nearly twenty or so of them following us and the scene was attracting everyone's attention, store clerks, adult customers, and security guards. Like nails to a magnet, other teenagers joined the moving mob.

Because we left the mall from a different exit, I

was momentarily confused about where I had parked.
I started in one direction and then another, Echo now
clinging to my arm with a sickening desperation. We
couldn't shake off the hooting and jeering kids. One
of the younger, bolder girls behind us ran to catch up
and stepped in front of us.

"Why was she listening to music if she's deaf?"
she asked with a wide grin on her face. She practically screamed the question so the others would hear.
I tried to ignore her, but she followed alongside and
repeated the question, punctuating it with a louder
"Huh? Well? Huh?"

Finally, I stopped and turned on her. The others
drew closer.

"You're a very cruel person, you know that," I
said.

"Cruel? You're weird. Why did you bring her to a
music store?"

"Because she's never been to one!" I screamed at
her. She took a step back. "She's your age and she's
never heard music. She didn't even see a music store
until recently and she wishes with all her heart she
could be like you and be like them," I said, gesturing
at the group behind us. "She was pretending, all
right? She was just pretending that she didn't have
any disabilities at all."

"I still think that's stupid," the girl replied, angry
now that I had made her retreat.

"That's because you're stupid. It's a shoe that fits
and fits well," I said. "Now just leave us alone. Go
back to your own deafness."

"Huh? My own deafness? What's that supposed to
mean?"

"Figure it out," I said, and moved Echo forward.

"You're weird! Nuts! Freaks!" the girl shouted after us. A chorus of "Freaks" followed.

For the first time, I thought Echo was better off being deaf.

I couldn't wait to get us back into my car and drive off. I had a fear they would get into cars and follow us, but I didn't see any automobiles rushing out after us, so I finally relaxed. Echo looked as if she had retreated into a very private, dark place. She was curled up in her seat, her head down. I had no idea where I should take her now. I simply continued driving until we reached Healdsburg. I drove into the town and, seeing an arts and crafts fair in the square, pulled into a parking spot and asked Echo if she would like to walk about the booths and see the things people were selling. She looked very timid and still frightened, but I urged her to go, hoping to show her good things and wipe away the bad experience we just had. Hesitantly, she got out of the car with me and we began walking through the square looking at the pottery, the paintings, and the handcrafted jewelry. I stopped when I saw a collection of dream catchers.

It brought back memories of Peter Smoke, the Indian boy I had met in school when I lived with Brenda in Memphis. He had given me a dream catcher, but I had left it behind when I fled Brenda's home.

"What is it?" Echo wanted to know.

I couldn't think of all the signs for the words I needed, so I borrowed a pen from the handicraft artist and wrote it all out on a slip of paper for her, just the way I remembered Peter Smoke had told me about it.

*The Indians believe that the night air is
filled with dreams both good and bad. The
dream catcher, when hung over or near
your bed swinging freely in the air,
catches the dreams as they flow by. The
good dreams know how to pass through
the dream catcher, slipping through the
outer holes and sliding down the soft
feathers so gently that many times the
sleeper does not know that he or she is
dreaming. The bad dreams, not knowing
the way, get tangled in the dream catcher
and perish as soon as the sun comes up in
the morning.*

She read the note and smiled with incredulity.

"Really? Does it work?" she wanted to know.

I nodded and then I bought her one.

"We'll hang it over your bed and you won't have anymore nightmares," I told her.

She blushed. I imagined she was thinking about the night she crawled in beside me. I thought about it, too. Was there any difference between the sexual excitement I had felt then and the excitement I had felt with Tyler? There were still questions about myself I desperately needed to answer, and I knew I wouldn't find the answers in books or magazines or even talking with more experienced women. These were answers that had to be discovered by myself within myself.

We continued through the arts and crafts festival, pausing to watch an artist create a sculpture out of clay, another painting someone's caricature, and another showing how she had woven beautiful blankets. There was a booth where you could have your picture taken and put on a mug. Echo thought that was terrific, so I had both our pictures taken and put on mugs.

"We'll drink from them tonight," I told her when they were completed.

She was smiling widely again, laughing and enjoying herself. Thank goodness for the fair, I thought as we reached the other side of the displays. I was turning her so we could make our way back when I caught sight of Skeeter and Rhona coming out of a tavern at the corner of a side street. Afraid Echo would see them or they would see us, I quickly moved to block her from view. When I glanced back, I saw that two dark-haired men, both stout and rough looking, had followed Rhona and Skeeter and were now facing Skeeter and speaking to him with large, threatening gestures. They were backing him up, one stabbing him repeatedly with his finger in Skeeter's shoulder. I hurried us along the path of booths, telling Echo we had better get home before her grandmother got worried.

As soon as we were home, Echo couldn't wait to tell her grandmother about the fair. She mentioned nothing about the mall and neither did I. She went, instead, into a long explanation about the dream catcher and the mugs.

"It's very nice of you to buy all that for her," Mrs. Westington told me. "Let me reimburse you."

"No, please. They're my gifts to her."

"That's very nice of you."

The house was filled with the wonderful aromas of

all the food she had been making while we were
away.

"Something smells delicious," I said.

"I decided to think of this as a form of Thanksgiv-
ing," she said. "Maybe if I change my attitude, things
will be better. Maybe, just maybe, that girl's been
turned around enough to set her eyes on a decent life
for herself here. I fixed a turkey, my special garlic
mashed potatoes, cranberries, and asparagus, which
used to be Rhona's favorite vegetable. I took out one
of the pies I had frozen as well, the apple. We'll put
some ice cream on it, too. Rhona used to love that."

She explained it all to Echo and then she asked us
to help set the table. I saw that Trevor was definitely
going to be at this dinner, which made me happy.
Echo considered it all to be a big party, a celebration
and confirmation that her mother was back for good.
I decided not to say anything about what I had seen
back at Healdsburg. I really didn't know what it was
all about anyway, and for the time being I saw no reason not to hitch a ride on Mrs. Westington's train of
hope. I was just so happy she could get herself to be
optimistic after all that had happened.

To Mrs. Westington's deep disappointment, however, Rhona and Skeeter did not return, nor did they
call to say when they would be back. Trevor, dressed
in what were obviously some of his nicest clothing,
arrived at dinnertime. He saw from the look on my
face that all was not well.

"Just sit yourself down, Trevor," Mrs. Westington
told him. "We won't be waiting dinner on anyone
who doesn't have the decency to call."

Nevertheless, I saw how she procrastinated and

tried to delay the actual start of the meal. Finally, at nearly seven-thirty with no word from Rhona, she decided to begin, and Echo and I helped her bring out the food. Rhona and Skeeter's empty place settings were difficult to ignore. Hoping to change the mood, Trevor raved about the food and so did I.

"I'm past the age where I need compliments," Mrs. Westington said.

"You need compliments till the day you die," Trevor countered. "Everyone needs a pat on the back now and then."

"Well, I won't hear of it," she said. "And I don't need to be treated like a disappointed child. I was a fool to harbor any expectations and waste my energy."

"You mean, you didn't do this dinner for me, April, and Echo?" Trevor teased.

She gave him a look that could sink a battleship and he roared with laughter.

"I have a madman on my property," she told me.

Actually, I thought Mrs. Westington was more depressed because of Echo's disappointment than because of her own. Such an elaborate and joyous family dinner as the one Echo had envisioned with her mother present was probably a dream. She nibbled on her food and had to be continually pressed to eat more.

"I wish that girl wouldn't have come back," Mrs. Westington finally muttered. "She's only made matters worse by giving the child hope."

After dinner Mrs. Westington permitted Echo to do more of the cleanup than usual. Trevor waited in the living room to challenge Echo to a game of checkers, something they often played in the evening. She played, but she kept looking toward the windows, hoping for headlights to indicate her mother's arrival. It didn't happen and she finally grew tired enough to go upstairs to bed. The sadness brought on fatigue as well. Trevor and I looked at each other. Now that I had the chance, I told him what I had witnessed in Healdsburg.

"There's the distinct possibility they're gone," he whispered. "Run away."

"I hope so," I said. Looking at Echo's face, I felt cruel for saying it, but every instinct in me told me that I wasn't wrong to have that hope.

I followed Echo up because I saw in Mrs. Westington's face that she would like me to do so to be sure Echo didn't burst into tears and cry herself to sleep. One of the most moving things I saw and probably would ever see was when I stood off to the side and watched Echo signing her bedtime prayer. She did it slowly enough for me to understand she was praying more for her mother than for herself.

After she crawled into bed, I hung her dream catcher and she smiled. Of course, she wanted to know why her mother had not come home.

I explained that to be fair to her, she didn't know her grandmother had made such a wonderful dinner.

"If she had called, she would have known," she correctly reminded me.

I nodded and, struggling for some excuse, came up with the idea that she probably had met many of her old friends again and wanted to renew her friendships and catch up on the news. For now, Echo accepted that. She gazed up at the dream catcher again and closed her eyes with an expression of comfort and self-assurance on her face. She hugged Mr. Panda, too. I watched her for a while and then I went downstairs. Trevor had gone to his own quarters. Mrs. Westington was alone. She was listening to music and knitting.

"I do it just to keep the arthritis at bay," she told me. There was still a half hour to go before I would meet Tyler at the motor home, so I sat with her. She was quiet, but then she suddenly put the knitting down and turned to me. "I know I'm not long for this world, April. My daughter's unexpected visit has brought home clearly what that means."

"Now, Mrs. Westington . . ."

"No, no false hopes, no promises, no head in the sand any longer. I can't have Echo left in the lurch and I certainly can't have her at the mercy of her selfish mother. I want to talk to Tyler about getting Echo placed in one of those schools quickly and then I'm going to talk to my lawyer about future custody, the money I have in trust, all of it. I'd like you to help me with it all."

"Of course I will," I said.

"Thank you." She lifted the knitting and fixed her eyes on me. "So don't go thinking about picking up and leaving," she added.

I laughed. Either I wore my heart on my sleeve and had a face that was made of glass with my thoughts printed on the inside or she was just a good mind reader.

"Like I told you," she said, "your coming here was meant to be."

"Maybe so," I said, thinking about everything, especially Tyler parking his car in the shadows on the road and making his way through the darkness to meet me in the motor home.

"If you want, turn on the televison."

"No. I'm fine. I'm going over to the motor home," I said. "I still have things to pack. I'll be getting rid of it any day now."

That was no lie.

She nodded and then stopped knitting. "You never did bring that doll into the house."

"No, but I guess I will, if it's still all right."

"Considering what else has been brought here," she said, smirking, "there's no reason not to. I'd much rather have that doll around than that Mr. Skeeter."

"Yes," I said, smiling. "So would I."

I left her knitting, but sinking deeper and deeper into her own thoughts and worries. They were written in the darkening lines on her face and I was truly very concerned about her.

When I stepped outside, I saw that a heavily over-cast sky had thickened the darkness. There was just enough of a glow from the house lights to outline the way to the motor home. Tyler had chosen a good night to arrive unseen, I thought. I saw that he hadn't put on any lights in the motor home either, but as I drew closer, I did see he had lit one of the candles we had in the kitchen. The light flickered in the windows. He was being so careful. A veil of secrecy had been cast like a net over the motor home and both of us. It made what we were about to do seem even more forbidden.

I opened the door slowly and entered, closing it softly behind me. I realized I was tiptoeing, too.

When I looked into the living room, I saw Destiny silhouetted in the shadows, but I didn't see Tyler. For a moment I had the chilling idea that Destiny had lit the candle.

"Tyler?"

"Back here," I heard. He was in Uncle Palaver's bedroom.

"You could have put on the lights," I said.

"I thought you had to conserve the batteries."

"Yes, I suppose."

I took the candle and made my way back and found him lying on the bed, his hands behind his head.

"Hey," he said.

"Hey."

"I see Rhona's van isn't there. Did they leave for good?"

"We don't know. They didn't call or return for dinner. I took Echo for a ride earlier to the mall and then to the fair in Healdsburg."

"You were there today? We had some of our product for sale at one of the booths."

"Yes, and while I was there I saw Rhona and Skeeter come out of a tavern. Two men looked like they were threatening him. Maybe because of that, they ran off. When I got back here, I found Mrs. Westington had prepared a big dinner as a sort of celebration."

"Why? Celebrating what?"

"She was hoping that somehow Rhona would change if she made her feel more at home, I guess. She's very, very depressed now. She wants to talk to you about getting Echo into the school and then she wants to set things up with her attorney, trusts, stuff like that. She's thinks the Grim Reaper has been peering in her window."

"Well, I hope not, but she's wise to want to do all that. I'll help with the school."

He sat up. "What does this mean? You're going to leave?"

"Not until it's all arranged. I promised her."

"Good," he said. "Well, in an ironic way, Rhona did us all a favor. She convinced Mrs. Westington to do the right things with Echo and I won't have to quit tutoring to force her to do it. That will make my mother happy, too."

"That's nice," I said dryly, still not appreciating why his mother was so against his tutoring a deaf child, since that was his life's work.

"You okay? You want to put on the lights?"

"No, this is fine," I said. Actually, it made me feel better to be more in the darkness than the light when it came to being with him like this.

"Destiny eyed me coming in," he said. I could see his smile. "But I told her I had your permission and she relaxed."

"Right," I said, laughing.

He patted the bed. "You okay with this? Being in here?" he asked when I hesitated.

"Yes. It's fine," I said, and sat.

"I thought about you a lot today," he said.

"Did you?"

"Yes. Actually, I couldn't get you out of my mind and couldn't wait to get here."

"Where did you tell your mother you were going tonight?"

"Just out. Don't worry about it," he said sharply.

I wanted to ask him if he didn't think he was a little old to be sneaking around his mother, but I didn't want to ruin the moment or get him angry.

"Echo's so upset about her mother," I told him. "It's heartbreaking to see."

"We'll help her later," he said. "Let's not think about all that now." He reached out for my hand and to turn me more toward him. "Let's just think about this." He brought his lips to mine and we kissed. It was a long, lingering kiss, almost too long. I had to take a deep breath.

"Sorry," he said. "I'm a little overanxious."

"It's okay."

He kissed me again, softer, and then he held me for a moment, brushing his lips over my cheek and then down to my neck. I moaned softly and lay back. I let him start undressing me. He wasn't as awkward about it this time and he paused periodically to kiss me again on the lips, the neck, and then my naked breasts.

"One second," he said, rose, and went to the bedroom door. "I'm not taking any chances on that doll," he told me, and closed the door.

I laughed. In the shadows he undressed and then he prepared and returned to me. I'm going to make love, I thought. I'm going to make love with a man willingly. It was funny, but before we began, I couldn't help wondering if Brenda had ever tried to be with a man and if that was when she'd been convinced she'd rather be with a woman.

There was no doubt in my mind that this was Tyler's first time, too. Once again, he was somewhat awkward and clumsy, not sure of whether or not he was hurting me or not. He got excited quickly and it all seemed to be over before it had really begun. I felt terribly disappointed. He realized it and kept apologizing.

"Just wait," he said. "Give me a few minutes. I'll be better. It will be better."

I didn't know what to say. I wasn't that sure about how it was supposed to be anyway. He lay next to me, talking, telling me about how much he had looked forward to tonight and being with me, but I couldn't help feeling he was trying desperately to keep me interested in him and in us.

"You must think I'm such a fool," he said. He sounded very angry now and I wasn't sure he was directing all that anger at himself.

"No, it's all right."

"Sure."

"Really," I said. "I'm fine."

"Maybe we should have the doll in here," he suddenly suggested.

"What?"

"I don't know. Maybe it adds something."

"That's a silly idea, Tyler. Really."

"I'll be right back," he said, rising. He went into the bathroom and a few minutes later, he returned. "Let's do it by the book this time," he said.

Had he really studied up on it, read a book on lovemaking with directions and diagrams?

He sprawled over me, this time not bothering so much to kiss me. Instead, he lifted my legs and fit himself comfortably in between them.

"I'll be better," he said. "I'll be better."

He entered me slower and then we began to make love quite differently, with less of a frantic sense. I closed my eyes and he leaned down to kiss me.

"Yes," he said. "Yes, this is better. Tell me. Tell me," he insisted, as if he had to be reassured.

"It's better," I said quickly.

And it was.

I wasn't afraid so much of being like Brenda as I was of not knowing if I was or if I wasn't. My fear was I would be in some sort of sexual limbo, never attracted to anyone, never attractive to anyone.

Celia, in an intimate moment, once told me she had been with men in her youth. "I was just never able to develop any sort of romantic relationship with any and after a while, I saw them as human dildos," she added. It was early on during my time with her and Brenda, and I was actually embarrassed to hear these things. I certainly didn't know what to say. She followed it with her short but melodic little laugh and never spoke of it again. I said nothing about it to Brenda.

I thought about it now, however, and wondered if what Tyler and I had just done meant we would have a romantic relationship. Even though it had been better the second time, so much of what happened seemed mechanical. He sat back on the bed, still naked, and said nothing. In the glimmer light of the candle, I thought he looked very content with himself. He was almost gloating.

"Neither of us are ever going to forget this," he said, "for the rest of our lives. I read somewhere that sexual experiences are the most permanently and deeply embedded memories a person can have. I can't imagine someone saying he can't remember having been with this woman or that or when, can you?"

"I guess not," I said.

"Anyway, I'm glad I came up here tonight."

That was the closest he came to saying anything romantic even though he might have planned to say more because a moment later, we heard a rap on the bedroom window. I turned and looked to see Rhona's and Skeeter's laughing faces and somewhere within my chest, my heart bobbed like an apple in a pot.

"Jesus!" Tyler cried. He hurriedly covered himself, but a moment later, their faces were gone.

"Who the hell was that? Was that Rhona and her boyfriend?"

"Yes," I said, and quickly began to dress myself. "They must have seen the candlelight flickering in the window."

"Damn," he muttered, hurrying to get his clothes on, too. "Who knows how much they saw? Who knows how long they were standing there?"

"What's the difference what they saw and didn't? I don't care about them," I told him.

"Yes, but they could talk, gossip about us," he said. "Damn."

Was he worried about me, us, or that his mother might find out he had snuck up here to be with me? I wondered.

"Take it easy," I said.

He shoved on his shoes and zipped up his pants. "I'd better go," he said, hurrying. "I'll see you tomorrow morning."

He opened the bedroom door and started for the front, practically charging out of the motor home.

"Tyler!" I called to him.

He paused in the dark. "Yes?"

"You could at least say goodnight before you run out of here."

"Oh. Right. Sorry. Good night," he offered, glanced at Destiny, and left.

I blew out the candle.

I was suddenly more comfortable in total darkness.

9

Dream Catcher

I delayed returning to the house. Despite what I had told Tyler about not caring what Rhona and Skeeter thought, I wanted to avoid them and their gleeful dirty smiles for as long as possible. What I didn't anticipate, however, was their eagerness to tell Mrs. Westington what they had just seen. She was still up and waiting for them in the living room, I imagined to bawl them out for not calling or letting her know what they were doing. But if that was what she wanted to do, she never got the chance to voice her complaint, or if she began, Rhona quickly interrupted and used me to change the subject.

When I finally walked in, Mrs. Westington was still seated in her chair. They had gone up to bed. She raised her eyes and turned to me. It took only one look at her face to see and understand what they had done.

"Did Rhona tell me the truth just now? Were you with Tyler Monahan over at your uncle's motor home tonight?"

"Yes," I said, my eyes down.

"Was it a coincidence or did you and he plan to meet there?"

"We planned it," I said.

"I see. Well, you both have a right to do what you want," she said. "As far as I knew, you were going over there to organize your things. I knew nothing about Tyler and Rhona was happy to see the surprise on my face. I just don't like it looking like something dirty or sneaky."

I felt so terrible adding to the weight of her troubles and worries.

"I'm sorry. I didn't mean it to be either. Tyler was more concerned about anyone knowing than I was," I added, and immediately felt like a tattletale trying to get herself out of trouble by blaming most of it on someone who was with her at the time.

"Uh-huh. Knowing his mother, that doesn't surprise me," she said. She sighed deeply and stood. "I was hoping there would be trust between us."

"There is. I'm sorry," I said, this time nearly shedding tears.

"Rhona just loves jumping all over something like this, not that she has a right to poke an accusing finger at anyone else ever. You just can't give her the opportunity. She was always like that, eager to point to someone else's weaknesses or troubles as a way of diminishing her own. I didn't bring her up that way. She inherited it from some ancestor who was probably hanged as a witch in Salem or more probably one

of those who hanged poor women who were accused.
I was never like most mothers, lying to herself about
her own child. Never trust her, no matter what she
tells you, April."

"I know."

"Well, we'd best go to sleep. Contrary to what I
had hoped, it looks like we'll be needing all our
strength for the days to come," she said. "Good
night."

"Good night and I'm really sorry this happened."

She lifted her hand but continued on. I watched her
walk out of the living room. She climbed the stairs as
if she was climbing Mount Everest. Without even
knowing her that well, I hated Rhona more than I had
ever hated anyone for what she had done, but I hated
myself even more tonight for giving her the opportunity to add to Mrs. Westington's grief and worry.

I barely slept, anticipating the coming of morning
and whatever else Rhona and Skeeter would do. My
conscience was like a hammer pounding at me,
pointing out that after all Mrs. Westington had done
and wanted to do for me, I had only made her life
and Echo's life more difficult. A number of times
during the night, I actually thought to get up, get
dressed, take my things, and sneak off before morning came. I truly felt like I didn't belong anywhere.
Finally, maybe only an hour or so before the sunlight
washed way the darkness, I fell into an exhaustion
and slept.

Echo shook me awake to tell me her mother had
come home. She had peaked through the slightly
open bedroom door and seen her in bed.

"And the dream catcher worked!" she declared

with excitement in her face as she signed. "I didn't have any nightmares."

I should have bought one for myself, too, I thought, but said nothing. I told her how happy I was for her. Full of new energy and hope, she urged me to hurry along while she went on to help her grandmother with breakfast. I moved like a zombie, but got washed and dressed and went downstairs. Mrs. Westington still looked troubled and tired to me, but neither of us said anything more about the events from the night before. What should have been a wondrous, memorable experience for me had become troublesome and embarrassing. Would I ever have a satisfying romantic experience?

After breakfast I waited outside to greet Tyler before he entered the house so I could warn him about what had happened. With all her work to be done spread out on the desk, Echo was in the office eagerly waiting for him. Trevor had gone to buy some supplies he needed at the lumber company, and Rhona and Skeeter were sleeping late as usual. The moment I saw Tyler's sports car turn into the driveway, I hurried to meet him.

"What?" he said, seeing the look on my face. I told him what Rhona had done and how Mrs. Westington was disappointed in our sneaking around the property.

"I'm sure she made me look disgusting to Mrs. Westington," he said, as if he were the only one in the motor home. "I was afraid that would happen," he added, walking toward the house. "I almost didn't come back to tutor."

"Didn't come back to tutor? Why not? Echo has

nothing to do with what you and I did last night and what happened because of it."

He paused at the steps and turned to me. "Let's pretend it didn't happen," he said.

"What?"

"It's better if we do that." He continued up the steps to the front door. "Better if we put it out of mind."

"But . . . you said we'd never forget."

He turned. "We won't, but we don't have to acknowledge it in front of anyone else. This way it's just our word against Rhona's."

"But I already told Mrs. Westington the truth."

"All of it?" he asked, his face twisting with shock.

"Not in detail, but I didn't say it wasn't true that you and I met at the motor home. How could I do that?"

He thought for a moment. "Just don't talk about it," he said. "No matter what."

"Don't talk about it? You mean with you as well?"

"Right. Just the way you wouldn't talk about anything else that never happened."

He entered the house and left me standing in my own cold numbness. Just the way you wouldn't talk about anything else that never happened? What did that mean, that whatever had been between us was over already? Was he ashamed of it? What about all that stuff he told me about thinking about me all day and how he couldn't get me out of his mind? He said he was so looking forward to being with me. All that had made me feel so good. How could I pretend it never happened? How could he? When we looked at each other now, would we look at each other the way

we did before last night? Had nothing changed between us even after the most intimate act?

I hurried in after him. I knew Mrs. Westington
wouldn't bring up anything about it with him. She
was far too much of a lady. She greeted him the same
way she did every time he had arrived and he acted
the same, too. He went right to the office to begin his
work with Echo. Mrs. Westington exchanged a quick
look with me that more or less said, "Let sleeping
dogs lie," and then returned to the kitchen to prepare
a salad for lunch. She was roasting a chicken.

However, the peace we hoped to keep in the house
was broken almost the moment after Rhona and
Skeeter came down. I heard Rhona cry, "Where are
the lovers this morning?" She followed it with a
laugh. "Still in the motor home? It was rocking so
hard, Skeeter and I thought it was an earthquake.
Right, Skeeter?"

"I immediately hugged a tree," he said, and they
both laughed hard and loudly.

Mrs. Westington said nothing. She offered them
breakfast, but all they wanted, really demanded, was
a business meeting with her, as they put it.

"Since we can't use the office because the lovers
are there, let's go into the living room, Ma," Rhona
said.

I was in the office by now, too. In an attempt to
keep myself from thinking about it all, I was reviewing some of the material Tyler had given me for the
equivalency exam. He looked up from his work with
Echo when we heard Rhona's derogatory remarks
and demands.

"I knew this was going to be far more difficult

now," he said. The expression on his face convinced me he somehow blamed me.

"Maybe we should go in there, too," I suggested. "We can't let her use us to take advantage of Mrs. Westington."

"It's not our business," he replied. "You're just a guest here and I'm just the tutor. If you or I go in there, we'll only make it worse."

"But last night we said we'd help her and . . ."

"I told you to forget last night." He turned back to his work with Echo, who didn't know anything unpleasant was happening.

I slammed my book closed and got up. "You're so afraid your mother is going to find out that you don't want to do the right things anymore?"

"Stop it, April," he said without raising his eyes from the page.

"Maybe I will forget last night," I said, "but not for the reasons you have."

I spun around and left the office. I started down the hallway toward the living room and stopped. Was Tyler right? Would I make things worse for Mrs. Westington if I went in there? I wondered. Undecided, I stood in the hallway and listened.

"We found the perfect property for our business purposes, Ma, and we need one hundred thousand dollars immediately."

"One hundred thousand dollars? Are you absolutely crazy?"

"No. We can turn that into four hundred thousand in six months, can't we, Skeeter."

"No problem," he said.

"Before I'd invest in anything like this with that

kind of money, I'd have my business consultant review it completely. What paperwork do you have?"

"He won't know about this sort of thing," Rhona said.

"Oh, and you would? Please, Rhona, don't act like a child now. Adults don't make such impulsive foolish decisions."

"I'm a child? I make impulsive foolish decisions? Look at you taking in runaways and providing tutors and clothes and who knows what. You have some freeloader in our house, an orphan girl, and it's all right to give her money but deny me? Your own flesh and blood? We need this money, Ma, and we need it now."

"I told you. If you have something to show my business consultant, produce it and we'll see what he thinks."

"Oh, that's ridiculous. I'm not going through all that. I have a right to the money anyway. I'm going to see an attorney today. There'll be courts and judges and all sorts of horrors. You can avoid all this trouble for everyone if you just write the check."

"I'll do no such thing and I won't let my own daughter blackmail me," Mrs. Westington said. I could hear the shrill tone in her voice and the fatigue as well. She needs help. She'll die under such pressure, I thought. Where was Trevor? How could I just stand out there and listen?

I lurched forward and stepped into the living room. Rhona and Skeeter looked up at me.

"Did you want me to help you with lunch today, Mrs. Westington?"

"Did you want me to help you with lunch today,

Mrs. Westington?" Rhona mimicked. Then she pointed her right forefinger at me like the barrel of a pistol. "I'm going to report you to the police. You probably ran away from some institution or something and you're setting up a whorehouse in a motor home on our property."

"Rhona!" Mrs. Westington cried.

"Well, she is. Ask her to her face and bring that Chinese kid in here. Let them deny screwing in that trailer. Go on."

"That's enough," Mrs. Westington said, and stood up sharply and with more energy and strength than I had seen. "I won't have such disgusting things said in my house and especially not in my presence. If you can't behave like a decent adult, a lady, then leave."

Rhona glared at me and then turned to her mother. "We're leaving, Ma. We're going to see an attorney. I don't think you're in your right mind anymore, taking in such a tramp and exposing my daughter to such bad influences."

"What? Exposing your daughter? You accuse me of such a thing when you run off and leave her here without so much as a phone call for nearly ten years!"

"That has nothing to do with what's happening here now. You'll see. When we return, it will be different and that tramp better not be here," she said, rising. "C'mon, Skeeter."

"Now wait a minute. There doesn't have to be all this unpleasantness," Skeeter said in a calm voice. "I'm sure your mother will change her mind once she hears more about my project. It's being done all over the country these days, Mrs. Westington, and the property values here are skyrocketing. It's not a foolish plan."

"If you're so confident, then you shouldn't be opposed to giving me something to show my business consultant," Mrs. Westington replied, her thin lips now pale and trembling.

"Sure we will," he said. "There's no sense in everyone getting all worked up like this. Relax, Rhona. Let's just take it all a step at a time."

She looked at him as if he was totally crazy and then she shrugged when he narrowed his eyes. "I can wait a little while, I suppose."

"Of course, we can. We just need a little down payment in the meantime so that we can hold on to things. If it doesn't work out, we'll return the deposit, okay?"

Rhona looked up at him quickly and smiled. "Yes," she said, "exactly."

"What sort of down payment?" Mrs. Westington asked.

"I think we can manage with five thousand dollars. If Rhona here asked you for it to help her along, you'd probably give it to her anyway, wouldn't you, Mrs. Westington?" he added quickly.

"And it would probably be just as bad an investment," she replied.

Skeeter laughed. "Your mother's a tough old broad, all right. She said you were a tough lady, old school, and always unfair when it came to her, Mrs. Westington."

"Rhona thought I was unfair to ask her to brush her teeth every night," Mrs. Westington quipped.

Skeeter laughed. "Well, we're going to see an at-

torney today for this project. As Rhona says, why
don't you consider giving her the deposit money so
we can avoid any unpleasantness. No one wants that,
but if there is no other choice, no alternative . . ."

This time he sounded threatening.

"I have choices. Don't tell me I don't have
choices."

"Okay, okay, but look, Mrs. Westington, you have
enough to deal with here as it is and no one wants to
add to that. We're just trying to do something worth-
while. Surely, you don't want to prevent that. That
wouldn't be very nice, not very nice at all for you, for
Echo, and for us."

Rhona looked at him as if he was brilliant, her
hero. How could she permit her own mother to be
treated this way? Her own daughter, too?

"I'll give you the five thousand dollars," Mrs.
Westington relented, "but I warn you to not waste it,
Rhona, because if you need anything, you'll have to
take it from that money. I won't be giving you anymore until I see something substantial, some real indication that you've turned a new leaf."

Rhona was about to challenge her, but Skeeter
gave her a sign to stay calm.

"That's very kind and reasonable of you, Mrs.
Westington. Thank you," he said.

Rhona fumed but turned herself away. "I'll wait
outside," she said. "You get the check from her," she
told Skeeter. She glared at me on the way out of the
room. As she passed by, she whispered, "Your days
are numbered here, sweetie. Go off with your boyfriend or else."

Mrs. Westington went into the office to write the

check. Skeeter followed her and then he and Rhona drove off in their van, both of them laughing. I watched from the front window, fuming. I put Mrs. Westington into this difficult position, I thought. It was my fault.

"All I've done is buy some time," Mrs. Westington muttered after she returned to the living room. "I'm only surprised she didn't show up on my doorstep with some other freeloader and make trouble years ago."

"I'm sorry, Mrs. Westington."

"Don't stand there blaming yourself, April. Whether you were here or not, she'd be doing what she's doing. I have no doubts about that."

Having heard all that went on, Tyler finally decided to join us. "April told me about your plans for Echo now, Mrs. Westington," he said. "Seeing what's happening here, I think that you would be very wise to act on them quickly. I have the name of the administrator you should call at the school. I've already told him about Echo so he'll know you when you phone him."

He handed her a slip of paper with the name and number on it. Echo had followed Tyler and stood there watching us from the living room doorway. She looked like she knew we were discussing her. What sort of a traumatic experience was it going to be for her to leave the only home she knew and Tyler Monahan?

"I wouldn't be coming here all that much longer anyway," Tyler added, avoiding my eyes.

Mrs. Westington nodded. "I have a lot to do," she said. "Thank you. I'll have some lunch for us in a little while."

"Let me help you," I said quickly. At that moment I just wanted to get away from Tyler. I was so disappointed in him. He returned to the office with Echo without another comment.

I followed Mrs. Westington into the kitchen and began to get the place mats, silverware, and dishes to set out for lunch. I saw how she kept looking out the window toward the winery. I knew she wanted Trevor to join us. She would fill his ears with what had happened. He was, after all, her most trusted companion. I wondered why she wasn't close to any relative, but then again, neither was I. I had already learned why she didn't have much contact with her brother-in-law, Arliss.

"I hated to give them any money," she muttered as she worked on the salad. She was twisting and turning and knotting herself up in an argument with herself. "It's as good as opening the window and throwing it into the wind, but when it's raining and pouring, sometimes you have to do something to get yourself out from under. It's not like me to do that, to act out of desperation, but I don't like that man and I don't like what Rhona's becoming by being with him, not that I expected her to turn up here wearing wings."

"I shouldn't have done it," she suddenly decided, and slapped the counter. "What's wrong with me, knuckling under like that? I should have just thrown them out. Lawyers don't scare me. I got lawyers, too, and where are they going to get the money for lawyers anyway? Lawyers cost plenty."

"Don't run yourself down so, Mrs. Westington," I told her. "You'll just make yourself sick over it."

"Yeah, well, I really am sick over it. You know

how it is with that sort. You give them an inch and they'll take a foot. As soon as we finish lunch, I want you or Trevor to drive me to see my attorney, Randolph Wright. There's a good name for an attorney. He's always right," she said. "He'd better be when I pay him. Where's that Trevor gone?" she asked, gazing out of the window again. "The man lollygags whenever he goes to one of those huge lumber or hardware stores. To him the place is a gigantic toy store. I never could understand how or why he saw so much pleasure in screws and bolts, hammers and drills. Can't give him a better birthday present than a new power drill or a hammer. Men never grow up. They just get bigger toys. Don't know why I depend on him.

"Oh, look at me. I haven't done anything here. Cut up those tomatoes for me, would you, April?"

She sighed and shook her head, taking deeper and deeper breaths.

"Did you hear how they threatened me? All of a sudden she's worrying about bad influences on Echo, too. Was she here when the girl got measles or was she here to nurse her through coughs and colds and rashes? No, Ma'am, she wasn't.

"Now she comes waltzing in and waves the flag of motherhood as if she was the first to discover what it means. Imagine telling that Skeeter fellow that I was unfair to her while she was growing up. Truth is I would have been harder on her if my husband wasn't such a sapless tree when it came to her. He pushed all the unpleasantness and difficult parental decisions off on me. I had to be the mean one. You ever hear that expression, 'let George do it'? Well that was my husband's motto when it came to disciplining Rhona. She knew how to charm him. Men are fools. You'll see," she said, her hands fluttering about.

She didn't realize it, but she was signing some to me as well as talking. This was the angriest and most worked up I had seen her. Suddenly, she stopped and looked at the food. "Where was I?"

She spun around and went to the refrigerator to get some lettuce, celery, and olives. I cut up the tomatoes and said nothing. I felt too terrible for her and I was afraid she would hear it in my voice and feel even more terrible for herself. She took out the chicken she had in the stove and then she turned and headed for the pantry.

"I have some peas in here. Echo just loves peas. Where are those darn peas?" I heard her say. "I know they're here. I know. Oh," I heard a few moments later.

A shelf rattled and some cans fell.

"Mrs. Westington? Are you all right? What happened?" I cried, and hurried to the pantry.

There she was, sprawled on the floor, her body twisted so awkwardly that her right foot was turned in far enough for me to think her ankle was broken.

"Mrs. Westington!" I screamed. "TYLER!" I shouted. "COME QUICKLY!"

I kneeled down beside her and shook her shoulder. Her eyelids fluttered and then opened.

Tyler came charging into the kitchen. "What's going on?"

"Mrs. Westington fainted," I called back to him. He came into the pantry.

"I'm . . . fine . . . ," she said, and struggled to straighten herself.

I put my hand under her left arm and Tyler got down to get his hand under her right. We started to lift her to her feet. She didn't put any weight on her legs. They dangled.

"I just need to sit for a while," she said.

The two of us literally carried her to the chair in the kitchen. I hurried to get her a glass of cold water. Echo was standing in the doorway looking in, her body and her face locked in fear.

Mrs. Westington's face was as white as an eggshell. There was no color in her lips and her eyes were glassy. She leaned back and took the water from me, sipping it slowly. Finally some color returned to her cheeks.

"I'm all right. Just a little dizzy spell. It's too damn hot in here. Open a window," she ordered.

"They are open," I told her.

She looked at them and shook her head. "No breeze at all today. One of those days my husband calls dead air days. Called, I mean," she quickly corrected. "Cut that chicken up for us, will you, April?"

Echo was signing at her now, tears streaming down her face.

"I'm fine, child. It's nothing. Don't be upset," she signed. "Go back to your work. Go on. April and I will finish preparing the lunch. Thank you, Tyler. I'm fine."

He glanced at me with concern, nodded, and left the kitchen. Echo lingered a moment until Mrs. Westington waved at her.

"Go on. Don't make me look like a fool. You'd

think no one had ever had a dizzy spell," she muttered.

"Are you sure you're okay, Mrs. Westington?" I asked.

"In the pink," she said. "Give me another moment and we'll forget it. Go on, finish working up the salad. Oh, I found the can of peas. They're on the floor in the pantry. Please get them and heat them up. She loves them warm."

I nodded and did what she asked, keeping my eyes on her constantly. When she didn't think I was looking, she took deep breaths and rubbed her temples. I have to tell Tyler, I thought. She has to go to a doctor right away. She will surely fight it, but with his help, we'll make her do it.

I went to the door of the office and signaled him. Looking annoyed, he rose and walked over to me.

"What now?"

"We've got to get her to go to a doctor. What do you think happened to her?"

He thought a moment. "Probably a small cerebral stroke. My father started having those before his heart attack."

"Stroke? Oh no, Tyler."

"Look, it's none of my business," he said. "I told you my mother thinks I'm too involved with this family as it is. I can't go telling Mrs. Westington what she should and shouldn't do about her own health. She's certainly old enough to know what she should do."

"That's cruel, Tyler. I can't believe you're saying these things. You certainly didn't talk this way last night. What's happened to you?"

"I don't have time for this sort of hysteria, April.

I've got to finish up with Echo. She needs to master a few more things before she enters the school and is placed in the correct grade level."

"This sort of hysteria? What are you talking about? Mrs. Westington could die!"

"Of course she'll die. We'll all die someday," he said, and returned to the desk. Echo was leaning over her work and didn't watch us talking. I glared at him a moment, but he didn't look back at me. I returned to the kitchen. I don't need his help, I thought. I know what has to be done.

Mrs. Westington was sitting back with her eyes closed.

"You've got to go to your doctor immediately," I said firmly.

She opened her eyes and started to protest.

"Don't argue, Mrs. Westington. If you don't take care of yourself, Echo will be at the mercy of Rhona. You said so yourself. And you've preached to me many times about not putting my head in the sand. That's exactly what you're doing right now. Well?"

She nodded. "You're right, of course. Let's just give them lunch. I'll call my doctor."

"Let's do it right now," I insisted. "They can wait a few more minutes for lunch."

She smiled at me. "You're better than a conscience. All right. His name and number is in the file by the phone under *B* for Battie."

I quickly looked it up and called before she could come up with any other reason for delaying it. When the receptionist answered, I told her I was calling for Mrs. Westington, who had had a serious dizzy spell and fainted. Even though Mrs. Westington would deny it, I told the receptionist she was in some pain as well. She wanted me to take her to the hospital emergency room. When I mentioned that, Mrs. Westington shook her head so vehemently, I thought she would fall into another faint.

"No, please," I pleaded. "She's okay at the moment. We just want her examined and she'll be more comfortable with the doctor."

The receptionist squeezed us into an afternoon appointment between two-thirty and three. We had to tell Echo, of course, but to ease her fears, Mrs. Westington deliberately did more than she should at lunch. The entire time Tyler behaved the way he had when I first met him. He was aloof, disinterested, and only involved with Echo and her lessons. Watching him, you'd think nothing at all ever happened between us since that first day we had met and nothing had happened to Mrs. Westington right before his eyes.

"Since you're leaving for the doctor and you won't be back before the lesson normally ends," he told Mrs. Westington, "I'll cut today's work short. I'm sure you'll want to bring Echo along and not leave her here."

"Yes," Mrs. Westington told him. "That's true, although Trevor might be back by then." She thought a moment. "But I guess we should bring the child."

After I helped clear the table and cleaned the dishes and silverware to be placed in the dishwasher, I put the leftovers away and then went out to the winery because I saw the truck parked in front and realized Trevor had finally returned. He was busy replacing a small electric pump on one of his machines when I found him.

"Mrs. Westington fainted," I blurted. "She's all right now, but I'm taking her to her doctor in about an hour. She's still dizzy and I know she's having some pain."

He put his tools down and stood. "Something happened with Rhona?"

"She demanded money. There was a big argument," I said. "Mrs. Westington gave them five thousand dollars and they left, but they'll be back."

"I knew it. A bird flew in here this morning. Not a good sign, not good," he said, shaking his head.

"Tyler thinks she might have had a slight stroke."

"Very likely, very likely. She needs to do less, have less to worry about, too."

"She's agreed to place Echo in the special school. I'm going to help her with that and with the things she wants to do with her lawyer."

"That's good. I guess it was a lucky thing, your showing up here," he said, nodding at me.

"I'm not so sure of that, Trevor. The jury's still out on that one."

He smiled. "I'll clean up and come along."

"I'm sure that will make her angry. She'll say we're making too much of it and she might not go."

"Yeah, that's her, all right. You picked up on stuff fast. Okay, so if she wants me along, I'm going. You let me know."

"I will," I said.

He nodded and returned to his pump.

When I mentioned he was back and maybe we should bring him along, Mrs. Westington had the reaction I expected.

"You make a big thing of this and it becomes a big

thing," she said. "The child's terrified enough. We're just taking a ride to my doctor's office."

"Okay," I agreed quickly.

Tyler poked his head in the living room doorway and wished her good luck with the doctor.

"I'll call later about tomorrow," he said, which sounded ominous to me.

Mrs. Westington thanked him. He avoided my eyes and left without saying good-bye to me. Mrs. Westington noticed, but she said nothing about it. A short while later, the three of us got into her station wagon and I drove us to Healdsburg, where her doctor's office was located.

Despite how often we reassured Echo, she still sat in the car like someone frozen, her eyes revealing the panic in her heart. Mrs. Westington had been a spine of strength for her family. She had always been independent and dependable. Living so closely with her and being so dependent upon her had created a lifeline between Echo and her grandmother. I had come here feeling so sorry for myself and in a short time found myself feeling sorrier for them. It wasn't that discovering someone worse off than you made you feel any better; it just kept you from bemoaning your own troubles and fate.

We were fortunate in that we didn't have to wait long for Mrs. Westington to be seen by the doctor, despite his crowded patient schedule. She introduced me as her houseguest. He was Echo's doctor, too, and I could see she liked him very much. He had a good bedside manner about him. Mrs. Westington wouldn't permit me to go into the examination room with her, but I managed to tell the doctor about her fainting spell and how pale she had been. I was sure he would ask her if anything had disturbed her recently, but I was just as confident she wouldn't tell him anything. She was too proud a woman to reveal her personal problems to anyone, even her own doctor.

I was surprised when he asked the nurse to have me step into the examination room a little while later. I told Echo to wait in the lobby and continue reading magazines.

"Mrs. Westington speaks very highly of you," Doctor Battie began. "She says you're quite the mature and responsible young lady."

I looked at her, surprised. I had thought her opinion of me had gone down since my secret rendezvous with Tyler in the motor home.

"Never mind all that," she said.

"I called you in here to help me convince her that she should follow my orders."

"What are they?" I asked.

"She has to go to the hospital. I'm alarmed by her blood pressure and I want to do some other tests. I'm going to miss something here if you don't go, Loretta," he told her.

"I can't do that," she said.

"If you don't, your granddaughter could very well lose her grandmother. How would you like that?"

"You're a terrible alarmist and blackmailer, Doctor Battie," she told him.

He laughed. "Look, I can't prescribe the right medications for you or medical services if I don't know exactly what's happening, now can I? You're being unfair to me, Loretta. You're not letting me do my job properly and that will make me look bad. You want to hurt my reputation, my livelihood, my family?"

"Oh, stop it," she said. She looked away and then she turned to me. She was obviously surprised by her own physical weakness and finally a little frightened. "I'll go if you promise and swear you will not leave the house until I return. You will not let anything or anyone drive you away and you will look after Echo."

"I promise," I said quickly.

"Of course, the girl's going to be terrified. There hasn't been a day in her life that I wasn't there for her."

"We'll make her understand," Doctor Battie said.

As it turned out, he was an expert in signing, too. We brought Echo into the room and he explained it all carefully to her, reassuring her. When he asked her if it was all right to have her grandmother go to the hospital, she nodded enthusiastically.

"All right. I see I'm outnumbered here," Mrs. Westington said. "I'll go tomorrow."

"No, you'll go right now, directly," Doctor Battie said. "Whatever you need from home can be brought to you later. The quicker you get this started, the quicker it will be over, Loretta."

"Did you ever see such a man?" she asked me. "Are you all right with it?"

"Yes, of course, I am, and Trevor's there to help as well."

"When he doesn't have his nose in a clump of grapes."

"You still producing that Chardonnay?" Doctor Battie asked her.

"Not me. That foolish man I have working for me stubbornly continues."

Doctor Battie laughed and then pulled me out of the examination room and explained where I was to take Mrs. Westington. He said he would make the calls and have everything underway.

"Don't let her talk you out of it at the last moment," he warned. "She can do that and she's dangerously close to having a serious stroke, I'm afraid," he said.

It brought tears to my eyes. "I won't," I promised.

All the way to the hospital, she questioned the wisdom of what we were doing. "Leaving you alone there. I don't know. I don't know. I'm sure it's a mistake."

"We'll be fine. I'm not going to let anyone drive me out. I promise."

"You call me if there is even the slightest bit of trouble with those two," she said. "I won't go in unless you make that a promise."

"I will."

"I can tell when someone lies to me. I can smell it," she said.

"I will," I insisted, even though I wouldn't unless it was the last possible resort.

She looked at me askance and then smiled to herself. When we arrived at the hospital, there were attendants and a nurse waiting just as the doctor had promised. Of course, she thought they were making things worse, creating a bigger commotion than was necessary.

Very quickly she was behind a curtain, dressed in a hospital gown, and hooked up to machinery that would give the doctor the information he wanted. The sight of her in a hospital bed was hard for me and absolutely earth-shattering for Echo. The gown and the medical apparatus diminished her. She looked tiny and far more fragile outside of her own home, where she ruled like a queen.

"Come here," she told me, and drew me closer to the bed. "When you get back to the house, I want you to go directly to my bedroom. In my closet on the floor you'll see a brown wooden box. It has a tiny lock on it that is far from strong enough to keep Rhona or that Skeeter out of it, and inside I have some valuable jewelry and some money. Actually, a lot of money. Take it and ask Trevor to hide it somewhere for me. Be sure Rhona doesn't see it."

"I will," I said.

"Be sure," she emphasized.

The nurses began to surround us, so I told Echo to kiss her good-bye. I promised to bring her back after dinner.

"Wait," Mrs. Westington said. "I have a stew in a container in the freezer. You just have to defrost it. Echo likes the creamy corn with it and there's some apple pie left over and fresh bread in the pantry. When you heat the stew, don't make the fire too high because—"

"We'll be all right, Mrs. Westington. Don't worry. I cooked for my uncle for a long time and helped my mother, too, for years."

"Good. Good," she said. "Confound this getting old!" she cried at the nurses, as if they were somehow responsible.

I smiled at them. They were in for it, I thought,

and guided Echo out of the room, to the elevator and out of the building. I was afraid Rhona and Skeeter would be back before we got home, but they weren't. Trevor came running out of the winery to greet us when he saw Mrs. Westington wasn't with us.

"She's in the hospital," I told him quickly, and explained it all.

"Well, that's best, and good for you for making sure she did the right thing for herself. She's the last one she thinks about these days."

I then told him about the wooden box and went into the house quickly to find it and get it to him.

And I didn't do it a moment too soon. Right after the handover, Rhona and Skeeter's van appeared in the driveway. I went back inside and told Echo she could help me with dinner preparations. At least that would keep her mind off things, I hoped.

Skeeter and Rhona came bursting into the house, laughing as usual and sounding a little high on something. They stopped first in the living room to look for Mrs. Westington and then appeared in the kitchen doorway.

"Well, look at our little cook working away. Where's my mother?" Rhona demanded.

I paused and turned slowly. "Your mother had a bad dizzy spell. I took her to the doctor and he wanted her to go to the hospital for some tests. That's where she is now."

"My mother's in the hospital?"

"After dinner, I'm bringing her some of her personal things," I added, and returned to the dinner preparations.

Echo was signing at her, but Rhona ignored her

completely. "What happened exactly?" she asked, stepping into the kitchen.

"I told you. A dizzy spell."

She exchanged a look with Skeeter, who raised his eyebrows. The news appeared to sober them both quickly.

"Well now, it looks like things are going to change around here," Rhona said. She looked at Echo, who was still signing her concern for her grandmother. "Stop that. You're being annoying," Rhona told her.

"How can you yell at her like that? She's just afraid for her grandmother. She wants you to comfort her, to—"

"Don't tell me how to talk to my own daughter. What nerve! I want you out of this house tomorrow. Tomorrow, understand? Do you?" she screamed.

"No one's going anywhere unless Mrs. Westington tells them so," I heard.

And so did Rhona and Skeeter. They both turned to Trevor, who had entered the house.

"We don't want to do anything that will upset her anymore than she is, now do we?" he added, walking toward Rhona and Skeeter.

Rhona stared at him and then she smiled coldly. "Of course not," she said. She turned back to me. "Once someone sees she can't get anymore out of my mother, she'll probably hightail it out of here anyway." She stepped closer and looked at the food. "I imagine my mother prepared all that before she got sick."

"Yes, she did," I said.

"Good. Call us when dinner is ready. We're both ravishingly hungry, aren't we, Skeeter?"

"Ravishingly," he said, and they laughed again.

She glared at me one more time and then, smiling like a cat who had her prey trapped, shifted her eyes to Skeeter. He nodded and they left the kitchen and went upstairs, their laughter rolling back behind them.

She didn't notice or care that Echo was crying.

10

Mother's Little Helper

"**D**on't you worry," Trevor said after they left. "I ain't gonna let her take over here. Things are different from the way they was years ago. She doesn't have her father around to take her side. Don't let her frighten you or discourage you either."

"I won't. I made a promise to Mrs. Westington that I wouldn't leave before she returned and I intend to keep it," I said.

"Good. Food does smell good. That woman can cook," he said, looking over my shoulder.

"Just give me another fifteen minutes or so and I'll have it all ready, Trevor."

"I'll be back," he said, smiling. Then he looked at the door and said, "You come to me if she causes any trouble at all."

"I will."

I turned my attention to Echo and tried to cheer

her up. She was caught like a leaf in the wind, spinning and turning over with confusion. I had her set the table. I wasn't looking forward to eating with Skeeter and Rhona, but I didn't see any way out of it, and for the time being it was better to avoid conflict as much as possible.

"Where's our dinner?" Rhona shouted from the top of the stairway. "I told you we were hungry. What are you doing down there?"

I started to bring everything to the dining room. "Everything's ready. You can come down to the table," I replied.

"That's better," she said. "If you're going to be my mother's little helper, than you're my little helper, too, while you're here freeloading. C'mon, Skeeter," she called, and the two of them came down the stairway and walked into the dining room.

Trevor showed up immediately afterward, having changed his shirt and brushed his hair.

"Well, look how fancy the help are, Skeeter," Rhona said. "Puts us to shame."

"Sure does," Skeeter said.

They dug right into the food.

"Echo says grace first," I told them.

"How can she do that?" Rhona asked.

"Why don't you watch and see," Trevor told her, and nodded at Echo.

They paused and looked at Echo. I nodded at her, too, and she began her signing, thanking God for our blessings.

"What the hell is she saying? She could be saying she wants a new dress or something for all we know."

"I thought Skeeter could read sign language."

"A little," he said, "but I'm sorta rusty."

"Didn't you ever know how to use it?" I asked Rhona.

"No," she said. "I never had the time for that. My mother knew enough for the both of us anyway."

"Then maybe you should learn it now if you're going to stay here," I told Rhona. "I have the book for you and—"

"Oh, you're such a goody-goody all of a sudden," she replied, twisting her lips. "You have the book for me." Her face hardened. "Trying to get on my good side? Hoping I won't throw you out? Forget it. The kid belongs in a special school or something, right, Skeeter?"

"Exactly. She'd get much better help from people who do that for a living."

"Your mother is actually arranging for that soon and she has the information and—"

"Oh, she does? How convenient." She thought a moment. "How expensive is the school?"

"I don't know."

"Well, it doesn't matter what you know and what you don't. Soon, I'll be making all those decisions anyway. The writing's on the wall, as my mother would tell you. That goes for you, too, Trevor. I don't know why you remained here since the vineyard went out. All these freeloaders," she told Skeeter, who was attacking the food as though he had been starving on an island for weeks. He nodded.

"Ain't no worse freeloader than an ungrateful, irresponsible daughter coming around for money," Trevor replied.

"I would watch my tongue if I were you, man," Skeeter said.

"Would you?" Trevor responded, his eyes fixed so hard and coldly on Skeeter. "That's good, only you ain't me, man."

"Right," Skeeter said, smiling and looking at Echo. "Add that to the thank-you's you're giving God, Echo," he told her. Of course, she didn't understand. Both he and Rhona laughed.

I could see the muscles in Trevor's neck tighten. He looked poised to leap over the table at Skeeter at any moment. It was only Echo's frightened eyes that kept him from doing anything more than just glaring back and then beginning to eat. They grew bored with us anyway and started their own conversation about some of their friends and their own plans. Rhona talked as if Mrs. Westington was already dead and buried and she had inherited everything.

"There isn't much point in keeping this property any longer. It's not being used as it should be. There's probably a winery nearby that would love it and would pay a lot for it so they could expand."

"Absolutely," Skeeter said as if he was a real estate expert.

"You'd better start thinking about a retirement home for yourself," Rhona told Trevor.

He ignored her, chewed his food, and looked ahead as though they weren't there.

"So what are you trying to do here anyway?" she asked me. "And what have you already taken from my mother? You'd better let me know or eventually I'll have you arrested for stealing."

"All I've taken from her is the love you never accepted," I said.

Trevor smiled.

Her smile evaporated. "What things did she want at the hospital? I'll be bringing them to her, not you."

"She asked me to do it and I'll be doing it," I replied firmly.

Echo was signing to me, asking why her mother looked so angry.

"God, does she ever stop that?" Rhona asked, looking at her. "Looks like my mother never taught her dinner manners. All I used to hear from her was that children should be seen and not heard at the table."

"Maybe she just meant you and not all children," I suggested.

Again, Trevor smiled. Even Skeeter smiled.

"Oh, you're so smart." She leaned toward me. "I don't care what my mother told you. This isn't your family and this isn't your home and the law will be on my side when it comes down to it. You'll see." She pushed her dish away and stood up. "You'll both see," she said, turning to Trevor. "C'mon, Skeeter, I want to go to the hospital and see what exactly is happening to my mother." She stressed the "my."

"What about the apple pie? That looks good," Skeeter said, nodding at it.

"Take a piece with you, damn it," she told him.

He shrugged, cut a piece, and rose with it in his palm.

"Hey," he said to me, "if you can cook like this, you can stay." He laughed.

She glared at him and they walked out of the dining room. I saw how lost Echo was with all this. I smiled at her and told her after we cleaned up, we'd go see her grandmother.

Trevor sat back, troubled. "I told you," he said. "I knew things were not going to be good when I saw that bird fly into the building. But don't worry," he added quickly. "I'll fix it."

He was going with us to the hospital, too. We wouldn't be far behind Rhona and Skeeter. I went upstairs to change into something nicer and brush my hair. After that I went into Mrs. Westington's room to get her personal things. The moment I walked through the doorway, I stopped and gasped.

Rhona and Skeeter had practically ripped the bedroom apart in their search for money and valuables. The dresser drawers were still open, clothes sprawled. The closet was open and clothing on the floor. Every box, every cabinet had been rifled. They had even searched her bathroom and her linen closet, not bothering to put the towels and sheets back on their shelves. Echo came up behind me and pulled my arm so she could ask what had happened.

I just shook my head and started to put things away. She helped immediately and we soon had the room looking tidy again. Mrs. Westington was right on target when it came to predicting what her daughter would do, I thought. She was wise to have me hide the box of valuables and money. I gathered up her personal things that she wanted brought to the hospital and placed them all in a woolen bag that looked like something she had made for herself.

"Let's go, Echo," I told her. When we stepped out

of the house, Trevor was waiting in the station wagon. As soon as I got in, I told him what I had found in Mrs. Westington's bedroom.

"They'll be all over that house while she's away. Wouldn't surprise me to see Rhona try to sell some of the furniture. I wish I could put everything under lock and key. That Rhona . . . some child to have raised. I don't think she gave her mother a moment of happiness. Don't worry about any other mess she makes, though. Lourdes will be here tomorrow," he reminded me.

When we arrived at the hospital, I was happy to learn that Rhona and Skeeter had not gotten in yet to see her mother. The nurse informed them she was asleep and they should not disturb her. Rhona was in a pout, threatening not to sit around waiting much longer for her mother to awaken.

"I can't even get any sensible information about her. The doctor's not available and the nurses don't know anything or won't tell anything. Resting comfortably is their stock, stupid response to everything," Rhona said.

Neither Trevor nor I said anything. We sat in the small lobby on Mrs. Westington's floor and Echo began looking at magazines. I could see Rhona didn't have the patience for this. She paced a bit. Skeeter sat with his eyes closed looking like he could fall asleep in seconds. Finally Rhona nudged him and told him she wanted them to go.

"We'll come back tomorrow. This is a waste of time. If you're still here when she wakes, tell her we stopped by," she told me.

"Okay," I said. "We'll let you know how she is."

"Oh, thank you, thank you," she said with exaggeration. "C'mon, Skeeter."

He shrugged, rose, and followed her out.

"You know what I think," Trevor said. "I think when Mrs. Westington heard it was Rhona looking to see her, she told her nurses to say she was asleep."

I laughed.

As it turned out, however, he was right. Shortly after the nurse told her we were there, we were permitted to visit.

"Are she and that clown gone?" Mrs. Westington asked.

"Yes," Trevor said. "How are you feelin'?"

"How do you think I feel being locked up in here like this?" she snapped back at him.

"You're not locked up, Mrs. Westington," I said. I gave her the bag of personal items.

She grunted and looked at Echo. They communicated with sign language and then Mrs. Westington turned to me.

"You did well with the dinner, but she says Rhona's been on a tear and wrecked my room. That so?"

I looked at Trevor.

"Don't wait for his permission to tell me the truth. I ain't incapacitated yet. What did she do?"

"She's just making all sorts of wild statements and threats."

"She and that man tried to find my money and jewels, didn't they?"

"Yes, but we got it all hidden before they came home."

She nodded, pleased with herself. "They say when

you step on a pickle, you never know which way it will squirt. She's one pickle easy to predict. Always was, and you know why? Because she has only one purpose, one goal in her life: to please herself no matter what. Remember that time you found her in the garage in the back of the car with that boy, Trevor? She tried to blame Trevor afterward. No telling how low she'll get. I was a fool to think there was any change in her. You'd think a girl who had lived like she has would have learned something."

"Has the doctor been in yet?" I asked.

She smirked. "Yes, he has. He claims he needs to keep me here to try some medicines on me to see which works best and which don't."

"That's reasonable," Trevor said.

"Oh, is it? How would you like to be treated like some guinea pig?"

"Oh, that's not it," Trevor said, smiling. "No sense in him prescribing something for you that don't work."

"Ain't anyone on my side anymore?" she moaned, and signed to Echo.

Echo went to her and hugged her.

Mrs. Westington looked at me. "Better tell Tyler about this. I guess it's more important than ever she go into that school now. I kept her under my wing as long as I could, but the feathers are getting too thin."

"Now you goin' to start that gloom and doom talk again?" Trevor asked.

She narrowed her eyes when she looked at him. "Are you going to stand there and tell me you haven't seen any signs that concern you, Trevor Washington?"

He glanced at me and she caught it. She was just as keen as ever, I thought happily.

"Go on, tell me what you've been doing. Burning candles, throwing salt? What are you doing to remedy this situation?" she demanded.

"None of your business," he told her, and she laughed.

The nurse entered. "The doctor wanted us to keep her visiting hours restricted for the first few days," she said.

"Days?" Mrs. Westington cried. "I'm not here for days."

"We have to go anyway," I said. "We have lots to do."

"You don't worry none," Trevor said.

"Oh, no. I'll just lay here hunky-dory. The cook puts glue in the mash potatoes and the meat they expect you to eat must first be beaten for hours on a rock."

"I'll bring you something," I said.

"She has to watch her salt intake," the nurse said. "That's very important right now."

"Sneak it in," Mrs. Westington said loud enough for the nurse to hear. She turned to Echo and told her to be a good girl while she was away and listen to both Trevor and me. They kissed good night. I put my arm around Echo and we all left the room. Trevor's face made me nervous. He looked so worried.

"She'll be all right," I said, trying to reassure myself as much as him.

"For now," he said. "But there comes a time when time ain't on your side no more. You start to hate clocks and calendars and the only birthdays you like

are the birthdays other people have. My mama used
to say you can dam up water, you can shut out the
wind, and you could get out of the rain, but you can't
hold back that minute hand. No, sir. Don't try. Just
hang on and hope for the best.

"Now you got me doin' it," he said, laughing. "You
got me talkin' doom and gloom."

He joked about it, but I was beginning to believe
that was all I was capable of doing.

"Let's treat Echo to an ice cream," he suggested.
"Get her mind off doom and gloom."

"Okay, but I'm not having any," I said firmly.

Later, when we drove up the driveway, we were
surprised to see two other cars beside the ugly van in
front of the house.

"What's this now?" Trevor wondered aloud.

When we stopped and got out, we could hear loud
music coming from the house.

"I don't like the sound of this," Trevor said. "I'll
go in with you two."

When we entered, we realized all the noise was
coming from the living room. There were five other
people there, all drinking and smoking. I recognized
cocaine on the coffee table. A short, dark-haired
woman was just about to snort it when we appeared.
Rhona was sprawled on the sofa, her head against
Skeeter, who had a bottle of whiskey in his hand. There
was another young woman on the other side of him,
her blouse open down to her navel and her breasts
quite visible. She was smoking a joint. Two men, one
with hair as long as Skeeter's, were sprawled on the
floor. A rather heavy balding man was in Mrs. Westington's chair, his bare feet on the side of the coffee

table. There were open beer bottles, glasses, pizza boxes with pieces still in them, and a container of melting ice cream that was leaking off the table and onto the floor. No one seemed to notice or care.

"Well, look who's here, everyone, the Lonely Ranger and her trusty companion, Trevor. Trevor's been here since the first grape was discovered," Rhona said. The fat balding man laughed, but the others just held their smiles.

Skeeter kept his eyes fixed on Trevor as if he was anxious to see exactly what he would do.

"These happen to be some of my old friends," Rhona added. "Maybe you remember Billy Roche and Gretta Lockheart, Trevor. They were often here."

"I remember them," he said, nodding. "You're making some mess for Mrs. Westington," he said.

"Oh, she won't care and besides, she's not coming home tomorrow, is she? We have extra domestic help. Everyone, that girl standing there gaping at me is my daughter, Echo. Echo is deaf, so just smile at her, please.

"Besides, Trevor," she continued, "April Fool will clean up after us, won't you, April Fool? That's how she earns her room and board, cleaning up. Oh," she said, nodding at something on the other side of the coffee table, "I'm sorry, but that cup with your face on it just fell apart. You watch out when you pick up the pieces. I don't want you to cut your fingers or anything."

She laughed, but everyone else just looked at us, waiting for the response. Skeeter took another swig of his whiskey.

"Mrs. Westington asked me to look after things

while she's away," Trevor said slowly. He took a step forward. "She don't like there being strangers in her home while she's away and she don't want no parties and messes either. You tell these people to go and take their drugs and crap with them," he said.

Rhona started to sit up, but failed. Skeeter laughed and then pushed her.

"Don't tell me what to do in my own house," she said.

"This ain't your house. It's Mrs. Westington's house. Now you people leave quickly or I call the police, and I got no reason not to tell them what's on that table there," he said, nodding at the cocaine.

"Shit, Rhona," Billy Roche said, sitting up quickly. "You said we'd have no trouble crashing here tonight."

"Don't listen to him," Rhona said.

"Yeah, right. I'm about to explain myself to the Highway Patrol." Roche stood up.

The woman at the table started to brush the cocaine into a sheet of paper.

"What are you doing? Don't let him frighten you!" Rhona cried.

Trevor stepped up to the heavy man in Mrs. Westington's chair and glared down at him. "That's Mrs. Westington's chair you're in, boy, and she don't like no one else sitting in it, much less putting his dirty feet on her table."

The heavy, balding man pulled himself up quickly. "Hey, I'm getting the hell outta here. I'm on probation," he said, quickly slipping on his shoes.

"Tommy!" Rhona shouted. "Don't let him tell you what to do. He's an employee."

"You comin', Martha?" he asked the woman at the table instead of responding to Rhona. The woman got up quickly, carefully folding the paper with the cocaine in it and putting it into her purse.

The others moved toward the living room doorway. One man wobbled a bit, but put one leg in front of the other.

"You're all just a bunch of wimps!" Rhona shouted after them.

I stood back, holding Echo's hand. Rhona looked at Trevor and then groaned and fell back against Skeeter. He took another swig on his bottle.

We heard them all leave.

"You're going to be sorry you did that," Rhona threatened. "I've already met with my attorney. Things are going to change very quickly here. Start thinking about leaving."

"I better not hear you made any more trouble tonight," Trevor replied.

Skeeter looked at him, but couldn't stare him down and shifted his eyes quickly.

I told Echo we should go up to bed. She nodded, looked at the mess and at her mother, and then moved quickly to the stairway. I knew she was very frightened and I decided to invite her to sleep with me.

"I hate leaving you two in here with them," Trevor said.

"We'll be all right, Trevor," I told him.

"You come get me if you're not," he said. He glared at Skeeter and Rhona and then he left the house.

"Good riddance!" Rhona yelled after him.

As we went up the stairs, I heard her mumbling and crying to Skeeter.

"Relax," he said, loud enough for me to hear. "Time's on our side."

When we got to the top of the stairway, I heard the phone ringing and hurried into Mrs. Westington's bedroom to pick up the receiver. Echo followed me. It was Tyler.

"I'm just calling to see what happened with her," he said when I said hello.

I told him about Mrs. Westington and then about Rhona and the mess they had made with the friends they had over.

"That's a bad situation there," Tyler said. "My advice to you is to get out."

"Get out? But how can I do that? I can't leave them like this, with Mrs. Westington in the hospital. We'll talk about it tomorrow, okay?"

"I'm not coming back tomorrow or the day after or the day after that," he said. "I promised my mother. I'm finished up there, April."

"But I thought you were going to wait until we had Echo established at least. I thought—"

"Rhona stopped in our store today."

"What?"

"Rhona stopped in our store today. She told my mother what she saw you and I doing. My mother thinks that's the only reason I wanted to go there."

"Oh, my God. Rhona's such a lowlife."

"Yeah, well, she did it. She only wants to make trouble and get rid of you. My mother was very upset, so I told her it wasn't true."

"I know. Put it out of mind. Like it never happened."

"I'm sorry, but she was too upset. I told her Rhona was lying. I convinced her when I told her that you . . ."

"What?" I demanded when he hesitated.

"Don't like to be with boys. I had to do it," he added quickly. "I told her what happened to you with your sister's girlfriend and I said you liked it."

"You said what?"

"I had to do it," he repeated.

He had to do it? I couldn't speak.

"You don't need me to help you anymore anyway. Just contact any school about the equivalency exam and get yourself scheduled, if you want. You should pass."

"How could you do that, say that? What I told you about Celia was something I hadn't told anyone. Not even Mrs. Westington knew those sort of details about my feelings."

"I'm sorry. It was a way to get my mother to believe me. It doesn't matter anyway what she believes about you."

"But how can you just stop coming here?"

"I'm sorry," he said. I began to hate the sound of the word.

"But what am I going to tell Echo? Tyler, you can't just not come."

"Just tell her I have to help my mother."

"Why can't you tell her?"

"I can't," he cried. "Just do it!" he said, and hung up.

I held the receiver in my hand and against my ear as if his words were still reverberating. I knew Echo was standing right behind me and I didn't want her to see the tears streaking down my cheeks. I sucked in my breath and with my back to her, I wiped my tears away. Then I hung up the phone and slowly turned to her, smiling.

She was worried it had been the hospital and something about her grandmother.

"No, no," I assured her. "It was . . . Tyler."

"Ty? What did he want?" she signed.

I thought a moment and then, keeping my smile, I told her he called to see how her grandmother was, but also to say he was having problems at his business and he wouldn't be coming around for a while.

"When will he come?" she wanted to know.

"Soon," I said. "I'll work with you until he does," I said.

She stared at me. "You're lying," she signed. "You're lying!"

She turned and ran out.

"Echo!" I cried.

I heard Rhona's laughter on the stairway.

"April Fool, don't you know she's deaf?" she screamed, and laughed even harder.

I followed Echo into her room to reassure her. She sat on her bed, staring down at the floor, refusing to look at my signing or my lips. Her whole world was in free fall, a mad state of turmoil with Mrs. Westington in the hospital, her mother behaving badly, and now Tyler Monahan refusing to return. I was all she had and I wasn't much, I thought.

Rhona paused at the doorway as she and Skeeter made their way to the guest room.

"Look at them. How pathetic. I want you out of my room tomorrow, April Fool. You move into the guest room until you leave, which won't be much longer, understand? I don't know why I stood for you being in there in the first place."

I didn't answer. I sat quietly, waiting for her to pass.

"C'mon," Skeeter told her. "I'm tired of all this crap. We got a lot to do tomorrow."

"Yeah, we got a lot to do and everything we do moves you closer to being thrown out," she told me. She lingered there. Echo looked up at her. "Don't think you can turn her against me either. She's my daughter no matter what."

"Rhona!"

"All right, damn it, hold your water." She turned back to me. "You'll be sorry. You'll all be sorry," she said, and walked on.

Echo looked at me for some explanation.

How do you sign *she's drunk*? I wondered, and just improvised with gestures showing drinking and wobbling and spinning my eyes. It brought a smile to her face.

"C'mon," I told her. "You can sleep with me tonight. Bring Mr. Panda."

She liked that idea and followed me out. We both got ready for bed. I closed the bedroom door, but there was no way to lock it. For a moment I considered putting the vanity table chair up against it, but decided that was too much and I didn't want to frighten Echo any more than necessary.

Before she got into bed with me, she ran back to her room. I thought she was going for her pajamas, but instead, she returned with the dream catcher.

"Good idea," I told her. If there was any night we needed it, I thought, it was tonight.

She got undressed and into bed and I did the same.

I saw her signing her prayer, which included her grandmother and then something about her mother. Then she turned over and went to sleep. I lay there staring into the darkness slightly brightened by the starlight coming through the windows. I heard Rhona's laugh and then her curses and eventually, what sounded like her sobbing.

Skeeter doesn't have it as good as he thinks being with her, I thought. She'll bring him bigger and bigger problems. The question was how big would the problems be that she would bring to us.

A few hours later, I had the first indication when I realized the bedroom door had been opened and Rhona was standing at the foot of my bed. She was naked and had a glass of water in her hand. Her disheveled hair flew wildly about her face masked in the darkness. There was just a small glitter of light caught in her eyes. She looked ghoulish, ghostly, the shadow of Death itself in some female form.

"What the hell is going on here?" she demanded. Echo didn't see her there and was in a deep sleep.

"What do you want?"

"Why isn't she in her own bed?"

"She's frightened with her grandmother in the hospital and you getting drunk and having drunken drug addict friends here messing up the house, which she has seen only respected and kept neat and clean."

"Is that the truth?"

"Look in the mirror," I replied. I was frightened, too, perhaps as frightened as Echo was, but Brenda always taught me never to show fear. Fear slows you down, weakens you, she said. The opponent gets stronger. Swallow it back, cover it up, hate it.

"You'd better be out of this room tomorrow or else," she threatened. "And don't go running to my mother for help, either. You make her sicker with your lies and stories, and I'll have you arrested. She might really have a stroke then," she added. "You'll be responsible."

She stepped closer and more into the illumination. I could see her cold, calculating smile, her teeth like a mouth of ice. She was right, of course. I wouldn't tell Mrs. Westington about any of this or she would insist on coming right home. For now, I was trapped. We were trapped. I said nothing. She took a drink of her water, turned and walked out, leaving the bedroom door opened.

I waited until I heard her go into the guest room and then I rose to close my door. I didn't feel safe with it open, but I knew it didn't provide much security even when it was closed. Rhona could return. She could bring Skeeter with her. Things could get very nasty and Echo wouldn't understand. If only we had enrolled her in her school before Rhona had returned, I thought. I would have been gone by then as well and none of this ugliness would have mattered to me. I would flee my disappointment with Tyler as well, leave it behind like some piece of rotten fruit, just another bad experience to forget. I had an arm's length list of them. What difference did one more make?

Thinking like a runaway as usual, aren't you, April? Thinking like a coward? I asked myself. When are you going to stand pat and battle the demons, face the challenges? Or are you always going to be in flight, hiding in shadows, hovering in some dark corner, shivering like some terrified bunny whenever there is any sort of conflict or disappointment in your life?

I didn't have an answer for myself.

I didn't close my eyes much before morning either. I listened and stared at the door, challenged by the urge to get up and run out of it, down the stairs, and away at the moment I heard Skeeter or Rhona in the hallway.

Echo moaned in her sleep, but it wasn't a moan of fear. It was more like a baby's moan. She had Mr. Panda clutched in her arms and she looked years younger than she really was. I touched my teddy bear, a father's gift that now gave comfort to us both. My trembling stopped. My heartbeat slowed and my body softened and relaxed just like hers had. We were like two children who had wrapped the promise of protection around ourselves and found the security to open ourselves to sleep.

Trevor was there first thing in the morning to be sure we were all right. Echo had a hard time waking up. I rose, dressed, and went down to make us some breakfast before she had even opened her eyes. There were no sounds coming from the guest bedroom. I was sure Skeeter and Rhona were in their morning comas as usual and I was glad for that. Trevor took one look at Echo's sleepy face when she came down and asked about the evening.

"She was just overwhelmed by everything," I told him. "Nothing more happened. I had her sleep with me."

Just then Mrs. Westington's cleaning lady, Lourdes, arrived. She walked in as usual, but stopped dead in her tracks when she saw the mess in the living room.

"Let me speak to her," Trevor said, and went over to her. He spoke some Spanish and told her Mrs. Westington was in the hospital, her daughter was here with her boyfriend, and they had some messy friends over the night before. She went right to work and he returned to speak with me.

"I was thinking that for now it be best we don't tell Mrs. Westington about any of this," Trevor said. I nodded. "We'll deal with it."

"I'm taking Echo over to the hospital right after breakfast. We'll stay there as long as we can so that we'll be there whenever Rhona shows up," I explained. I had been thinking about it. "That way, I might be able to make sure she doesn't irritate her too much."

"Fat chance," Trevor said. "She just has to appear and it's an irritation, but it's a good idea. I have some things to look after here and then I'll pop over, too."

Feeling more optimistic because we had a strategy, I was able to get Echo into a better mood, too. Trevor returned to the winery and Echo and I ate our breakfast. I was surprised, however, when Skeeter appeared without Rhona. He wore only a pair of jeans, no shoes and no shirt.

"Smelled the coffee," he said, and poured himself a cup. He sat back at the table and smiled at Echo. Anyone could see she was afraid of smiling too enthusiastically back, but she was sweet and innocent and in desperate need of love and affection, like a puppy that had been lifted away from its mother and siblings and dropped in some strange new place.

"Cute kid," Skeeter told me. "Shame about her hearing. Rhona never mentioned it. She just told me she had a kid back here so it came as a surprise to me."

"What kind of woman would be like that, forget to mention her daughter was deaf?" I asked.

Skeeter shrugged, a slight smile on his face. Men like him were very difficult to understand. I wasn't all that experienced when it came to men or even women for that matter, but while traveling with Uncle Palaver, I had met men that reminded me of Skeeter, men who worked the odd jobs at the theaters and other places, who hung on to the small incomes to survive, but perhaps more to justify why they weren't doing anything substantial with their lives. Why worry about it now? They could basically pay their rent, have what they wanted to eat and wear, and work out some entertainment for themselves. They lived on some shelf of mere existence as if they really believed they would live forever and sometime in the future, they would do something significant. Years could go by and they could miss opportunities after opportunities, but they were carefree and nonchalant about it. Sometimes, I wondered if they weren't right and the rest of us, intense, determined, focused, were somehow missing out on something important.

"Rhona's been through a lot more than you can imagine," Skeeter said. "When I met her, she was close to cashing in. She had been betrayed, abused, and neglected by almost everyone she had trusted. She wasn't going to come back here, you know. She told me about her mother, this place, and I talked her into it. Don't make it difficult, any more difficult than it has to be for her.

"Besides," he said, leaning forward to rip a piece of bread and just smear it across the butter as if he were dipping it in gravy, "you should really move on and get on with your own life. You can't just stop somewhere and become part of someone else's family."

"You're doing it," I retorted quickly.

"Well, I'm with Rhona. We'll probably get married, maybe have another kid. The old lady isn't going to last much longer. You know," he continued after chewing and swallowing the bread, "homes, farms, land, stores, whatever, are not much different from seats in a movie. You're there for your time and then you get up and leave and someone else is there."

"That's not true. Families pass their homes and property down."

He shrugged again. "That's my point. Rhona's time has come for this. What she does with it is her decision. It certainly has nothing to do with you. Go hook up with one of your relatives, meet some guy and have your own time."

"I don't desert people."

"Yeah, you do," he said, gulping the rest of his coffee. He poured more in the cup. "We all do. I'll take this up to Rhona and see if I can get her engine started." He smiled at Echo again and left us.

In the wake of the silence he left behind, I thought Trevor Washington was right. It was a bad, bad sign, that bird flying into the barn.

11

White Lies

Doctor Battie was with Mrs. Westington when Echo and I arrived at the hospital. We had to wait in the lobby, but the moment he stepped out of the room, I leaped to my feet to talk to him in the corridor. He wrote some instructions for one of the nurses to carry out on Mrs. Westington and then turned to me. I didn't like the look on his face.

"I haven't been able to get that blood pressure down yet," he said. "I know she has a lot of tension, a lot on her mind, but we've got to get her calm and relaxed and I've got to get the right prescription. Don't say or do anything that would make her worry, okay?"

"I won't, but did she tell you her daughter has returned and what's happening?"

"A little. I know she's upset about it. Can you have . . . what's her name, Rhona?"

"Yes, Rhona."

"Rhona call me. They'll page me if she calls while I'm still making rounds in the hospital and I'll speak with her."

"Good," I said, although I wasn't optimistic about it doing any good. I think he saw it in my face.

"Let's just work on keeping her comfortable and calm. I need a few more days."

"Okay," I said.

He looked at Echo. "How is she doing with all this?"

"Not great," I said honestly.

"Well, it's a traumatic time and probably not the best time to get her enrolled in the school, but we should do it soon," he said. The way he emphasized *soon* put a chill in my heart.

"Yes, thank you," I said. He patted my arm and walked on to his next patient.

Echo looked to me for some information. I signed that the doctor said her grandmother was doing well, but he still needed some time to work on getting her the proper medicine. She nodded with relief. We lie to each other so much, I thought. A good deal of the time, we either tell half-truths to protect and insulate the other person or tell outright lies to avoid conflicts we know would be inevitable and hurt everyone. We even lie to ourselves for the very same reasons.

I took her into her grandmother's room. Mrs. Westington was sitting up and spooning some soup into her mouth. She put the spoon down quickly.

"Did you bring me anything to eat?"

"No," I said, laughing, happy she had an appetite.

"The doctor would be furious and he was right there in the hallway when we arrived."

"Fiddlesticks. Eating this food is making me sicker than anything you would have brought me from home. Taste this soup. I swear they use it as dishwater."

"There's probably not a grain of salt in it," I said.

"I never worried about what I ate and I made it this far in good health." She pouted a moment and then smiled at Echo. "How's my doll?" she asked her.

Echo rushed to her for a hug. She held on to her just a little too long.

Mrs. Westington looked at me sharply. "What happened at my home last night?"

I shook my head.

"You want me to get it out of the child? I can do that," she threatened.

"Mrs. Westington, are you going to do everything you can to keep yourself sick and in this place? I need you to get well and get home. Echo needs you. Even Trevor needs you. Why can't you just be a cooperative patient for just a short while, long enough for the doctor to get you stabilized and on your way home? What sort of an example are you setting for Echo? You'll only make all this harder on everyone," I lectured.

I held my breath. Was she going to fly off the bed at me, tell me to mind my own business, tell me to get out of her house? She nodded slowly and leaned back on her pillow.

"Well, now, I see you're no longer the little girl full of self-pity who first arrived on my doorstep. Where did you get all this grit?"

"I got it from you," I said. "So don't make it a wasted gift."

She laughed. "So you're telling me you and Trevor have things under control?"

"We do," I said firmly. "Echo's fine, too."

"I see. Where is that daughter of mine? I half expected her to be standing here at the bedside with a pen and paper for me to write out my last will and testament when I opened my eyes this morning."

"Give her time," I said, and she laughed again.

"I'm afraid she's going to be in for a shock. I called my attorney, Randy Wright, yesterday and he's overhauling my papers. Most everything I have is in Echo's name and a trust has been established with a trustee. There's something in there for Trevor, of course, and a little something for you."

"Me?"

"Just in case. Everyone needs a little boost."

"What about Rhona?"

"What about her? You heard her and that Skeeter threatened me with lawsuits and the like. I thought I'd better start taking defensive actions as soon as I could, and I wasn't going to let a little thing like this hospital stay prevent it."

"Doctor Battie will be upset you're doing all this."

"Oh, it's nothing. A lawyer does the work. I read it and sign it. For now, however, I think it would be best if we kept this to ourselves," she said.

We heard a knock and I turned to see Trevor.

"How we doin' today?" he asked.

"How does it look like we're doing? I'm still chained to this bed, aren't I? I'm still here. Where have you been? Like I have to ask," she added. "Delivering cases of wine, I imagine."

"You imagine correctly," he said. "And your grapes are still the most cherished in the valley."

"They're not my grapes. My grapes died years ago on the vine, along with a lot of other things," she said. "How's my house?"

He glanced at me.

"Don't wait to see what she told me and didn't tell me! Is it still in one piece?"

"Everything's just fine, Mrs. Westington," Trevor said.

She looked from him to me and back to him.

"Look at the two of you, with faces that could be billboards advertising terrible liars."

Trevor laughed and Echo, even though she didn't follow most of what had been said, laughed as well. Before we could talk about it anymore, there was another knock on Mrs. Westington's door and my jaw unhinged at the sight of Tyler Monahan. He had a bouquet of red roses in his hand. Echo's face lit up like a neon sign. Even Trevor, who I knew distrusted him from the start, smiled.

"I hope I'm not interrupting," Tyler said. "I just wanted to stop by and see how you were doing, Mrs. Westington."

"Interrupting? What could you be interrupting? Nothing's doing here. I'm practically in solitary confinement. In the soup as they say. I really should say dishwater."

"These are for you," he said, approaching. "To cheer up the room."

"Thank you, Tyler. Lord knows, this room could use a ton of roses to cheer it up. Trevor, please take those dead weeds out of the vase on the windowsill and put these in, would you?"

"Right," Trevor said, and went to work on it.

Tyler glanced at me and then back at Mrs. Westington. "So how are you doing? How long will you be in here?"

"Until hell freezes over, it seems. My doctor is rolling the dice with different medications to see which one sticks. If I survive it, he'll let me out," she replied.

"That's not the way it is, Mrs. Westington, and you know it," I said.

Echo was signing to Tyler, trying to get his full attention, asking him when he was coming back. "What she should do with the work he had given her?" "How would she know what to study next?" He gave her a quick, "We'll worry about it later, after your grandmother is well," reply, and her arms floated down like two small kites that had lost their lift of wind.

"What I really stopped in to say, Mrs. Westington, is I would be glad to help you with the arrangements for Echo while you're stuck in here. I thought about it and realized I could be of assistance in that regard."

"Oh, that's kindly of you, Tyler, but I think I'll wait on that until I'm out. It's not going to be easy for her and I'd like to be right there with her."

He nodded. "I understand. I just wanted you to know I would be glad to do whatever else I can. I assume you've been told that I have to end my tutoring," he added, glancing at me.

"No. No one bothered telling me, but I'm not surprised at all this secrecy."

"Things have become harder for my mother at the store and the plant. I must devote more time to it."

"I see," she said. "Well, then we'll make enrolling Echo in that school a priority as soon as I'm out."

"Good. I really can't stay long. I'm just on my way to do some errands for my mother and took a detour to see you."

"Thank you for coming and for the flowers, Tyler."

"You're welcome, Mrs. Westington. I always liked working for you and being in your home."

"And you're welcome back anytime," she said.

He looked at me again, but all I did was glare at him. I didn't care how uncomfortable it made him. He nodded, said good-bye to Echo, telling her to be a good girl, and then hurried out.

"Well now," Mrs. Westington said as soon as he was gone. "What other bad news are you hiding from me?"

"Nothing," I said quickly. "I didn't think it mattered to tell you that right away."

"At least the boy has a conscience."

"The jury's still out on that," I muttered, and she looked at me.

Trevor laughed and then she did, too.

To my surprise, Rhona did not come to the hospital all day. Trevor left to return to his deliveries. Echo dozed off out of boredom a few times, as did Mrs. Westington. It took me a while to get over Tyler's unexpected appearance, but I finally calmed myself and went down to the hospital store to buy magazines for Echo and myself. We had lunch with Mrs. Westington and then she insisted we go home.

"This is no place to keep her anyway," she told me. "Just let her go home and stay busy and keep her away from her mother as much as possible."

"I'll try," I promised. I signed to Echo that we'd return in the morning and to say good-bye for now. She did and we left.

I knew where the school was that Echo would attend. I thought it might be beneficial to show it to her. She didn't mind the riding around with me anyway. I knew she wasn't anxious to return to the house. Her mother's behavior the night before had disturbed and frightened her. Being out and about with me made her feel older, more mature as well. I didn't tell her we were going to the school or mention it until we drew close to it.

From the outside, it looked like any other public high school. It was a long, rust-colored brick building with a decent-sized front lawn and a parking lot off to the right. At first Echo didn't think anything of it. Then we both caught sight of a young woman using sign language with a girl about Echo's age. The other girl signed back and they continued to stroll around the north side of the building.

Echo turned to me and asked about it. I explained that it was a special school for kids her age who had hearing and seeing disabilities. Behind the school itself was a dormitory for the students.

"You mean you sleep here, too?" she asked.

I nodded and she looked at it again. I didn't think it would be harmful to drive in and look around, but when I did, she immediately asked me why I was doing it.

"Wouldn't you like to go to school here?" I asked

her. "You could be with other young people your age."

She stared out at the buildings for a moment. The way her eyes narrowed and widened told me she was thinking deeply about it all. Suddenly, she turned and just stared at me.

"What?" I asked her, smiling.

"My grandmother is not coming home?" she asked.

I nodded, emphatically. "Yes, she is."

I saw she didn't believe me. I never thought that bringing her here might make her think that. I should have waited before doing this. I should have waited for Mrs. Westington to explain it first.

"You're just . . . older." I signed "bigger" and she smirked and looked at the building, sadness seeping into her face from every angle.

I can't do anything right, I thought. Why don't I just do what Tyler said and leave?

A side door opened and two boys stepped out, both signing to each other. One, who looked to me to be maybe sixteen, had meticulously styled ebony hair. He had a lean, swimmer's build and even from across the parking lot looked handsome. He was about to turn toward the rear of the building with his friend when he saw us and stopped. Echo was staring at him and he realized it. I saw him smile and sign hello. She gasped and sat back like someone discovered peeping. He laughed and then joined his friend.

"Who was that?" she wanted to know.

I shrugged. "A boy who goes to school here," I said.

She strained to look around the building and follow the two boys, but they were gone.

"Let's get home," I said. "I have to make dinner."

She nodded, but she nearly twisted her head fully around to look back as we drove down the drive and turned right to head back home. Maybe I didn't do such a bad thing, I thought, rather hoped.

The dirty old van was parked in front, so I knew Skeeter and Rhona were there. I wondered why she hadn't gone to the hospital to at least make a show of caring about her mother's health. The two of them were in the living room watching television. Skeeter had a can of beer in hand. Rhona was smoking a cigarette. They both looked up when we entered.

"The doctor would like you to call him," I said immediately. "His name is Doctor Battie and the number is in the kitchen pinned to the wall by the phone."

"How is she?" Skeeter asked.

"Just call the doctor," I said.

Rhona looked at us as if she was contemplating how she would perform the murder. Echo started signing, but Rhona turned away without acknowledging her.

"You're out of my room. Whatever you had in it has been moved to the guest room," Rhona said. And then as nonchalantly as she had said that, she added, "I've decided you can stay awhile longer. I'm going to need your assistance with my mother after all."

"What does that mean?" I asked.

Skeeter smiled at her and looked at the television set.

"We had a phone call while you were at the hospital," she said. I didn't like the way she was smiling at me with such gleeful confidence. Echo had stopped trying to get her to respond and stood by, confused about being ignored. I instinctively put my arm around her shoulders.

"Look at that, Skeeter," she said, nudging him, and he turned back to us. "Can't keep her hands off her."

He laughed.

"What's that supposed to mean?" I asked, but with the speed of a reflexive action, took my arm away from Echo.

"That phone call I mentioned? It was Mrs. Monahan looking for her son. She was worried he had come back here. He had promised her he was finished tutoring Echo and he wouldn't have anything more to do with this situation. Of course, I told her he wasn't here and then, like most mothers, she went into this frenzied defense of her son, calling me a liar for telling her the story about you two.

"I wouldn't let her get away with calling me a liar, especially after what we saw with our own eyes, right, Skeeter?"

"Exactly," he said, more interested in the television program he was watching.

"I laid into her and then you know what she told me? I think you do," she said before I could offer any response. She laughed. "You're quite a little sexual tramp, aren't you? But it runs in the family, huh? A gay sister? Her lover and you having lesbian sex? You're a walking tabloid magazine. I don't think my mother knows the gritty little details, does she? I couldn't imagine her tolerating you around here, especially around Echo, if she did. She'd say something like lie down with dogs and you get up with fleas."

Tears seeped into my eyes. I pressed my lips together to hold back the ache and the sobs that were rising like bubbles to the surface. I didn't know what to say, how to respond. Tyler's betrayal of my intimate secret in order to calm his mother's concerns left me with few options for defense.

"Naturally, I was very surprised. We both were, right, Skeeter?"

"Shocked," he said, nodding, but turning back to the television set.

"And then I thought, so that's why she's always in Echo's room and why she had Echo sleep with her!"

"That's not true!" I cried.

She shrugged. "Hey, I don't knock anyone's sexual preferences. I would have to admit that I experimented with same partner sex on occasion or participated in a . . .what do they call it, Skeeter?"

"What? Oh, ménage à trois."

"Right, ménage a tra la la or whatever. However," she said, losing her self-satisfied grin, "when it comes to some tramp coming here and seducing my innocent, deaf daughter—"

"That's all a lie," I cried.

"Maybe. But I'm sure I could get that Tyler to testify that you told him those things and with Skeeter and I adding what we saw here, I think the police or whoever would believe us or find it interesting enough to investigate, don't you? Would Echo there deny being in your bed?"

For a moment it felt as if all the air had been sucked out of my body and I couldn't breathe in any new air. My face was hot with the blood that had rushed up through my neck. I looked at Echo, whose eyes were full of questions and confusion.

"Don't worry," Rhona said. "I'm not going to do it unless I absolutely have to do it. It would probably devastate poor little Echo there to be dragged into a police station and asked all sorts of questions about her body, your body, stuff like that."

"You're disgusting," I said.

"Me? I don't go around telling boys I just met how I slept with my sister's girlfriend."

"I didn't say that!"

"You said enough. I doubt that Tyler would have made it all up, don't you, Skeeter?"

"No," he said, half listening. "I mean yes," he added, unsure of what she wanted. She glared at him and then turned back to me.

"Do you deny that you have a gay sister? Will she deny it if she is asked by the police?"

Words choked in my throat like cars on a highway smashing into each other.

"You get the point. I think we understand each other a little better. Now, let's get back to what I said at the beginning. I'll let you stay here a while longer, but you have got to help me with my mother. I want you to convince her to sign over the money that belongs to me anyway. We had the paperwork prepared for us and all she has to do is sign a power of attorney document. You can convince her that once that's done, we'll be on our merry way, right, Skeeter?"

"Sure," he said. "We'll make like a tree and leaf."

"In the meantime, tell that cleaning girl to go home. She's annoying. I don't like the way she looks at me and she's in my face too much. She acts like she owns the place and has the nerve to complain about the mess she had to clean up in here. Tell her my mother told you to send her home. *Do it!*" she screamed. I couldn't help but wince and even jump back. "Then get dinner started. We saw steaks in the freezer. Both of us like them medium. Don't over-cook them. And Trevor is not invited. You tell him not to come to dinner here. Go on. Do what I say," she ordered.

"Mrs. Westington isn't going to believe you," I offered, finally responding with some defense.

"Oh, really? You actually want me to go to the hospital and put on a scene about my daughter being sexually assaulted by some transient girl my mother stupidly took in to live with us? Because I will do it and you know I will," she said firmly, her eyes fixed on me with such evil and hate, I didn't doubt her for a moment. "How will her doctor like that? Who the hell do you think people will blame for my mother's bad health and maybe death? Me? Her daughter just trying to protect her own poor, deaf child? Or you, a runaway with no home, no school, nothing but a history of disgusting behavior?"

I felt my body soften in defeat.

"She won't listen to me. You're wasting time having me ask her to sign those papers," I said weakly. After what Mrs. Westington had told me she had done with her lawyer already, it was pointless to go up there and try to convince her of anything, I thought, but I couldn't tell Rhona about that.

"Maybe, maybe not. She seems to have taken to you and in the condition she is in right now, there's a good chance she'll listen. Look," she continued, softening her tone, "you'll have prevented all sorts of horrible unpleasantness if you get her to do it. Think of it that way. Think of how you're protecting everyone. You'll be a regular heroine, won't she, Skeeter?"

He looked at me and smiled. "You know," he said, "girls who like girls more than boys always intrigued me. Is it because you're afraid of men or is the sex somehow better?"

Rhona smiled.

Echo was signing now, asking me why we were standing there and what were all these words, some of which she had caught by reading lips. Why were her mother and I arguing so much? I had to get her away, to protect her, to ironically do what Rhona said, look after her.

"It's a fair question, April," Rhona said. "You've been with both now. Which do you prefer?"

"You're both disgusting," I said.

They laughed and their laughter confused poor Echo even more.

"Get going," Rhona said. "You have a lot to do."

I turned Echo away and led her to the stairway. She was full of questions for me, but I told her to go up and change to help me prepare dinner. I said I would tell her more later. She did it, but she didn't like it. Meanwhile, I went to Lourdes, who was working in the kitchen, and told her I had just come from visiting Mrs. Westington in the hospital and she wanted me to tell her to leave. She didn't believe me and insisted she finish up in the kitchen. I explained that Mrs. Westington's daughter was in charge now and she wanted me to do the cleaning. I saw how it hurt Lourdes's feelings, but reluctantly she finally obeyed and left, mumbling in Spanish.

I took out the steaks and got potatoes out of the pantry, some canned vegetables, and then began to prepare a salad with what was left in the refrigerator. I kept looking through the window toward Trevor's vineyard and winery, anticipating his arrival. How was I going to tell him what was happening? I wondered. If I didn't say it right, he would get enraged and come at Rhona and Skeeter. Then she might just do what she threatened and I would have made everything ten times as bad.

All I've done is brought hardship and horror to this house and family, I thought. Maybe it wasn't my loving dead souls who delivered me here after all. Maybe it was something darker, something very evil. My anger and rage toward Tyler was greater than ever. Because of what he had told his mother, I was now in this predicament. All of us were ensnared, Echo, Trevor, Mrs. Westington, and me. Trust no one but yourself from now on, I thought, if there would be a now on. Right now, disaster loomed over this house like a gigantic bruised cloud threatening to drop a cold, hard rain.

Echo came down and I immediately got her busy peeling potatoes and then setting the table, which I told her would be set only for four. Of course, she wanted to know why not five, but instead of answering, I said, "Just do it." I hated being so hard, but I had no explanations I could give her and I was tired of searching high and low for acceptable lies. Silence, I thought, was finally a better choice after all when it came to her.

Soon after I heard Trevor's truck pull into the driveway and park by the winery. He got out and carried some boxes into the building. I rehearsed my story and prayed that I could be convincing enough to keep him from getting too upset and causing trouble. I took a deep breath, told Echo I would be right back, and then walked out, pausing near the living room.

"How's our dinner coming?" Rhona asked.

"It's coming," I said.

"Good. After dinner you can return to the hospital to see my mother. I'll give you the papers for her to sign. You'll leave Echo here," she added. "I don't like her going back and forth to a hospital. Kids can catch something, right, Skeeter?"

He laughed. "Yeah, like a sexually transmitted disease."

They both laughed. I bit down hard on my lower lip and went out to speak with Trevor.

"They giving you trouble?" he asked the moment I appeared in the winery doorway.

"No, but I think they're getting very bored here," I replied.

"Very likely."

"It's probably best to just avoid confrontations. I don't think they'll hang around much longer."

He nodded.

"I mean, if they make more trouble or we get into fights with them, Mrs. Westington will just get so upset and that won't help her get better."

"Uh-huh," he said, scrutinizing me with eyes that went over my face like a fine-tooth comb. "They ask you to come over here and tell me to stay away?"

I looked up.

"It's all right," he said. "I know they just making things miserable for you and Echo over there. I'll stay out of their faces until they go or unless you need me. All you gotta do is holler my way, understand?"

"Yes."

"The truth is she's blood and I ain't and the courts and law will side with her against me and you anyway. We just got to do what's best for Echo and Mrs. Westington right now. Sometimes going around a fire is better than confronting it head on. It'll burn itself out and those two will surely burn themselves out eventually."

"I know you're right, Trevor."

"I'm here if you need me," he emphasized.

"Okay. Thanks," I said, and returned to the house, grateful for Trevor's understanding.

Skeeter and Rhona had gone upstairs. I looked in on Echo, who had put on her grandmother's apron and was preparing the salad. Stepping into her grandmother's shoes made her feel closer to her, I imagined. I complimented her on her work and told her I was going upstairs to wash and change for dinner. When I got to the top of the stairway, I went to what had been my room, not thinking or remembering what Rhona had said she had done.

I opened the door and confronted them both naked, making love on the bed, Rhona's legs wrapped around Skeeter's waist. The bed was shaking and rocking with his thrusts. The sight was so surprising and shocking, I didn't move or speak. Rhona looked around Skeeter's arm and smiled at me. He saw she was looking my way and turned his head.

"This is how normal people do it," she said.

"Come on in and watch if you want," Skeeter said, not pausing for a moment.

I gasped, backed out, and closed the door. My heart was pounding. They were both laughing loudly. I turned and ran to the guest room, where my things had been tossed over the bed and the floor. I shut the door behind me quickly and caught my breath. They're like two animals, I thought, and yet I couldn't deny to myself that I had been intrigued and fascinated by the sight. Did that make me as bad as they were? I shook myself as would a dog shaking off water, trying to get rid of my mixed feelings and disgust. Then I picked up my things, hung up my clothing, and put my other clothes in drawers. I gathered all the tricks and the posters that they had scattered about and put them together in a corner. After that, I went to the bathroom in the hallway, locked the door behind me, and took a quick shower.

Echo was sitting at the kitchen table when I went down, still feeling dizzy and stunned by what I had seen. I did my best to hide my nervousness from her and put up the steaks. I sautéed some onions and mushrooms to go with them. The aroma traveled through the house and up the stairs. Soon, I heard their voices and laughter as they descended.

"Sex stimulates the appetite," Skeeter said, poking his head into the kitchen. "I hope you made enough."

"If she didn't, we'll eat her portion," Rhona told him. They went into the dining room and sat like two people who believed everyone else existed to serve and honor them. I started Echo on bringing in the water, bread and butter, and the salads. Not realizing all that was happening around her, she was simply trying to impress her mother with her work and looked desperately for a compliment. None came. Just as before, Rhona and Skeeter behaved as if they were the only ones there or we were invisible. Echo's signs went unnoticed except by me.

"Couldn't you at least tell her she did a good job on the salad?" I asked.

"Sure," Skeeter said. He turned to Echo, pointed to the salad, smiled, and circled his mouth.

She looked at me to explain and I properly signed what he meant. She was really looking for Rhona's reaction, but Rhona was busy eating, her head down. How could someone carry a child in her body and ignore her existence like this? I wondered.

"Don't overcook those steaks!" she warned me when she noticed I was staring at her.

I hurried back into the kitchen. I had forgotten them and they were no longer medium. I put them on a serving dish nevertheless and brought them into the dining room. As soon as I placed the dish on the table, Skeeter stabbed a steak with his fork and put it on his plate. Rhona served herself slowly. He cut his and smiled.

"Very tasty," he said.

She cut hers and grimaced. "Overcooked!" she cried, and flipped the steak at me. I shifted my body to avoid it and it went sailing into the doorway and slid over the floor. "Make another one and stand there watching it cook this time," she ordered.

"Hey, I would have eaten that," Skeeter said.

"Take hers if you're still hungry. She doesn't have time to eat and she doesn't need anything. She can live off her fat for weeks," Rhona said.

I looked at Echo. Her mouth was open and she was in a state of shock and fear. She was actually trembling.

"Look what you're doing to her," I said.

"Not me, honey, you. If you had cooked that steak right, this wouldn't have happened, so don't blame me. Blame yourself. Go on. I'm not waiting forever."

Echo couldn't eat after that. I saw she was having trouble swallowing anything she put in her mouth.

"You could wait until my meat is cooked, Skeeter," Rhona cried.

He paused and looked at me. I hurried back into the kitchen and took out another steak. Cooking them right from the freezer usually made them tougher, but what choice did I have? I couldn't marinate it as my mother had taught me. I waited and continually tested it.

"What's taking so long?" Rhona cried. "You're not overcooking it again, are you?"

"No. I'm watching it," I told her. Echo was just sitting there staring down at her plate.

"What's wrong with her? Why isn't she finishing her food?"

"You frightened her," I said.

"Oh, what a sensitive baby. If that frightened her, she had better not set foot out of this house. There's a lot more frightening stuff going on out there."

I wanted to say I had been out there and there was nothing more frightening than her, but I bit my lower lip and returned to the stove. When I thought it was medium, I brought it in and stood by while she cut it and considered it.

"That's more like it," she said.

I noticed that Skeeter had taken my steak. I
didn't care. Like Echo, I had lost my appetite as
well. See, I told myself, even in this there's a silver
lining. The longer you're around Rhona, the more
weight you'll lose. I signed to Echo that if she
wanted to leave, she could. She nodded and started
to get up.

"Where does she think she's going? I'm not finished eating. Tell her to stay until everyone is done.
That's impolite," Rhona said. "Tell her!"

I did and Echo sank back into her chair, only
glancing at her mother. Skeeter was eating like it was
truly going to be his last meal on earth.

"You're such a slob, Skeeter," Rhona told him. He
grinned from ear to ear, his lips greasy and some
meat on his chin. "I lost my appetite," Rhona said,
shoving the plate away from her. He eyed her meat.
"You're not going to eat that, too, are you?"

He shrugged.

"See what a pig I'm with?" she told me. "Clean
up. I want you off to the hospital with the paperwork
in twenty minutes," she said. "Tell her she can leave
the table, too. She's making me nervous sitting there
like that."

I started to sign, but Echo picked up on Rhona's
lips and was up and out of her chair before I finished.
She ran upstairs to her room.

"My mother's done some terrible job with her,"
Rhona quipped. "She doesn't belong here, but I don't
see why she has to go to one of those very expensive
places. They can do just so much for her and after a
while, it doesn't matter where she is."

"How do you know that?" I asked.

She spun around on me. "Don't you get snotty with me or I won't even give you a chance to get out of here gracefully. Just be grateful I am and do what I tell you," she said.

Skeeter burped and pushed himself back.

"Are you finally finished?" she asked him.

"For now," he said, and looked at me. "What's for dessert?"

"There's a piece of apple pie left over."

"Just bring it out before you go," he said. "I'm a little full at the moment."

"You're such a slob," she told him again, and he laughed.

"Don't let that fool you," he said to me. "You saw how she loves me. I have the scratch marks on my rear end to prove it." I felt heat move into my face, picked up dishes, turned, and hurried into the kitchen with his laughter resounding. Sex had been turned into a weapon they could use freely against me.

Before I left for the hospital, I made sure Echo was all right. She was lying on her bed, embracing Mr. Panda. Of course, she wanted to know why her mother was being so mean and why she had thrown her steak at me.

I told her Rhona had drunk too much whiskey and was drunk and not to worry about it.

"Just stay away from her tonight," I said. "She'll be better tomorrow."

"No, she won't," she replied. "She'll never be better."

I couldn't disagree and Rhona was shouting for me below.

"I'll be right back," I told her. "I need to do some

errands. Just do your work and I'll look it over and help you with anything you get wrong."

"Why? Ty isn't coming back?"

"He'll come back," I said, but she simply waved off my signing as would someone wave off annoying flies and then turned away from me.

I was crying inside for her, but I couldn't stay any longer and help her feel better. Her world was in chaos and I was sure she felt she was spinning like a top in outer space. There was nothing to stop it.

I turned and walked to the door. Just before I left, I noticed something was different. What? I wondered, and then my gaze fell on the pile of torn picture pieces.

She had torn up the old picture of Rhona, the mother she had once known and had lost forever.

12

Bats in the Belfry

I took the paperwork from Rhona.

"She won't listen to me," I insisted. "I'm just a guest here. I don't have a right to tell her what to do with her money."

"She'll listen if you tell her we're promising to leave. I saw the way she looks at you. You're more than just a guest here. You've become her daughter. You've replaced me. I'm not jealous or upset about it. Better you than me be stuck here. Just do it and do it well, sweetie, or you know what news bulletins will be released," she threatened.

I left the house and walked to my car. Trevor must have been watching the front door all evening, I thought, because the moment I appeared, he came hurrying out of the winery to meet me.

"What's happening? Is everything all right? Where

are you going? Where's Echo?" He fired his questions at me without taking a breath.

"I'm going to see Mrs. Westington. Echo's up in her room."

"And?" he said, seeing the papers in my hand. "What's all that?"

"Rhona believes Mrs. Westington will listen to me and sign this power of attorney giving her rights to money."

"Why doesn't she go to see her mother herself and ask?"

"Mrs. Westington has already told her no. Actually, she's already called her attorney to prevent Rhona from doing anything, but Rhona doesn't know that yet."

"You shouldn't have agreed to show those papers to her," he said.

"I was going to see her anyway. I'm just humoring Rhona. Like you said, sometimes it's better to go around a fire and let it burn itself out."

"Yeah, but I don't like it," he said, looking at the house. "She's a lot different, meaner, sneakier. I can't even imagine the places she's been and the things she's done. Sending you to do this makes me suspicious."

"Don't worry, Trevor. When they finally realize they won't get anything more, they'll leave," I told him.

He looked at me, thought a moment, and then shook his head. "I don't like it," he said, and walked back to the winery.

How I wished I could tell him the real reason I was doing all this, how Rhona was blackmailing me, how

Tyler had made it all possible for her, but I was afraid of seeing it all blow up into a bigger mess that would hurt all of us, especially Echo. Swallowing back the truth, I got into my car and drove to the hospital.

When I arrived, Mrs. Westington was making a scene with the nurse, complaining about the food and demanding they send the cook up to her so she could instruct him or her in how to prepare chicken so it tasted like something other than cardboard. The nurse was just trying to get her to calm down. She looked to me for help.

"Please stop this," I said. "Immediately."

Mrs. Westington widened her eyes, blew air through her lips, and fell back on her pillow with her arms folded under her breasts, pouting like a child. Uncle Palaver told me when people get older, they act more and more like children. He called it the second childhood. That was what I thought I was witnessing at the moment.

The nurse thanked me and left.

"You know they make you sicker in hospitals, don't you?" Mrs. Westington quickly began in her own defense before I could say another word. "They feed you slop. They wake you at all hours of the night to see if you're alive or give you some pill. They don't want me walking about either. They've turned me into an invalid!"

"You promised you would behave. All you're doing is prolonging everything."

I shook my head and she looked away a moment and then sat back.

"Where's Echo?"

"She was tired and I thought you were right about

this not being a good place for her. She's in her room, doing her lessons."

She looked at me askance, her eyes two slits of suspicion. "What's that in your hands?" she asked.

"Your daughter asked me to bring this to you to consider. She and Skeeter promise they'll be leaving immediately if you do this," I said. "I didn't tell them anything about what you've been doing with your attorney."

"What is it exactly?"

"A power of attorney document so they can get money."

"You know where you can put that," she said. Then she stared a moment and added, "How did they get you to bring that to me? They threatened you?"

"No, they just asked me to be their spokesman," I lied.

"Spokesman? That girl's got bats in the belfry. She could send the governor here to see me and I wouldn't change my mind. What made her think you could do it for her? How come she's not coming here herself?"

I thought I would try the same logic on Mrs. Westington that I used with Trevor.

"I think they're getting bored and want to leave," I said. "All Skeeter is doing is eating and drinking and watching television. Rhona is getting tired of it."

"Very likely. She had the attention span of a four-year-old when she left. I don't imagine it's improved."

She leaned over to her side table, opened a drawer, and took out a pen. "Hand those papers to me," she said.

Was she going to sign? I gave them to her and she wrote a tremendous "NO" over each sheet.

"There. Even Rhona might understand that response. You let me know immediately if she gives you any trouble, April. I'm depending on you," she said, which only made me feel worse. "How did dinner go?"

I sat and described what I had made and how Skeeter had attacked the food. That amused her at least. Of course, I left out anything about Rhona throwing the steak, complaining, and frightening Echo.

"I'm truly sorry about Tyler Monahan leaving us, leaving you before you took your test," she said when I finished describing the evening.

"I think I'll do all right on the test when I take it anyway," I said.

She nodded and smiled. "That's what I like to see and hear, optimism coming out of your mouth. I'm no fool at my age. I know after we get Echo established that you have to move on, maybe join up with your sister again. Whatever. You have to take care of business, start your own life on the right track, April. You don't belong in an old house with only an old lady and an old man vainly trying to resurrect a dead dream. You deserve to go off and pursue your own dreams and not be stuck in the mud with ours. You promise me you'll do that, April. I'm not saying you can't stay in touch, but you promise."

"I promise, Mrs. Westington."

"Good, good." She closed her eyes. "Something they're giving me makes me tired early. I'll lay into that doctor when he shows up tomorrow morning."

"They're just trying to keep you calm and get your pressure lower."

"Yeah, well, you'd think a woman my age wouldn't have so much pressure in her anymore." She smiled. "Take care of my baby until I bust out of here."

"I will," I said.

She lay back on her pillow. She fought to stay awake, but in moments, fell asleep. I rose slowly, quietly, fixed her blanket, and then picked up the papers and left. I had a great temptation to just keep driving. Fear of Rhona, especially when she saw what her mother had done to her legal papers, made me shiver. Of course, I was more afraid of how she would treat Echo and how frightened Echo would be if I didn't return.

Both Rhona and Skeeter were waiting for me in the living room.

"Get your rear end in here!" Rhona called the moment I opened the front door.

I took a deep breath and entered.

"Turn that off, Skeeter," she ordered, and he clicked off the television set. "Well? What happened? Did she sign? Did you convince her?"

I shook my head. "She said she gave you as much as she intended to give you," I said. "I couldn't change her mind. I tried. I told her you were planning on leaving, but she was adamant."

"Adamant? Listen to her. Adamant. What did you do, buy a dictionary before you came back?" She looked at the papers in my hand. "What did she do to them?"

She leaped up and seized them. Her face filled

with rage. "Look at this, Skeeter," she said, throwing the papers at him. He picked one up and looked at it and then he laughed.

"I don't think that's so funny, Skeeter."

He shook his head. "She's your mother."

"Thanks for reminding me." She turned back to me. "You didn't do a very good job of convincing her if she had the nerve to do something like that."

"I tried," I said. "Believe me, I would love for you to get your money and leave."

"Oh, you would, would you? Why? You think you'll inherit the rest of it if I go?"

"No. I'm not staying here forever," I said.

"Oh, that's for sure. Matter of fact since you failed in your mission and I don't need you anymore, you should leave tomorrow."

"I'll leave when Mrs. Westington comes home," I said. "And don't try to threaten me with all those nasty things you intend to spread about me. I promised her and I would rather keep my promise than anything."

"Oh, how sweet. Hear that, Skeeter? She promised my mother she would stay."

"That is sweet," Skeeter said. "So, tell me, April. Speaking of being sweet, you never answered me before. Why do you like girls more than boys?" He rose from the sofa. "Maybe, I can help change your mind about that," he said, taking a step toward me. "If you just give me the chance, I—"

"Get away from me!" I cried, and ran out of the room and back to the front door. I charged out of the house, his lustful smile and laughter chasing me.

Trevor was standing in the driveway near his truck.

I stopped and quickly got hold of myself. If he found out what was happening, he'd rush into that house and have it out with Skeeter for sure, I thought.

"What happened?" he asked.

"Nothing. Of course, Mrs. Westington wouldn't sign their papers and I told them. They're upset, but it doesn't matter. They'll leave soon."

"How was she doing?"

"Complaining as usual," I told him. I didn't tell him how tired she looked and was.

"That's good. How's Echo?"

"She's okay. She's asleep. Who knows? Now that they see they can't get anywhere with Mrs. Westington, maybe they'll leave tomorrow."

"I hope so. Okay," he said. "You know where I am if you need me."

"Thank you, Trevor."

He headed for his apartment. I walked on to the motor home, debating as to whether or not I should simply move in there with Echo until Mrs. Westington returned. I was tempted to sleep there tonight. Right at the moment, it seemed far more comfortable and secure.

I went in and sat across from Destiny.

"We'll be leaving here soon," I told her. When I looked about the motor home, it seemed suddenly very depressing to me, not only because Uncle Palaver was gone, but because of what had occurred here between Tyler and me. Places, like people, can upset you, I thought. Memories cling to them like flies on fly paper.

I was surprised by a sudden knock on the motor home door.

"Who is it?" I asked after I got up and went to the short stairway.

"It's me," Trevor said.

I opened the door quickly. Now it was my turn to read unhappiness quickly in his face. His eyes were gazing down, his shoulders slumped.

"I just had a phone call. My mother's passed on," he said. "I got to go down to Phoenix and make arrangements."

"Oh, I'm sorry, Trevor."

"She's had one foot in the grave for some time now. I feel bad leaving you with this mess."

"I'll be fine. Mrs. Westington will be home soon anyway and it will all be over. Don't you worry about us. Go do what you have to do."

"I'll be staying with a cousin of mine. Here," he said, handing me a slip of paper. "This is the telephone number. Don't hesitate to call me if you need to. We got some relatives coming over from Houston, my mother's younger sister and her son, so I'll be away two, three days maybe."

"Just go and do what you have to do, Trevor. Is there anything you need done at the winery?"

"No, that'll keep," he said. "I'll be leaving in a few minutes. I've got to drive to San Francisco and catch a plane. There's a flight I can make early in the morning. You'll explain it all to Mrs. Westington for me, okay?"

"Of course, Trevor. Don't worry about us," I emphasized. He nodded and walked way.

I closed the door and sat across from Destiny again.

"You put on a good act for Trevor," Destiny said.

"It was nice of you to do it, but you know deep inside that you're very frightened about being in that house with those two with Trevor gone."

"You know. You're right," I said. "It's time you came out of here, Destiny," I muttered. "I shouldn't be alone." I picked up the doll control and then I lifted her out of the chair and carried her out of the motor home. Of course, I was anticipating Skeeter and Rhona making fun of the life-size doll, but that didn't matter to me now. Nothing they said mattered to me.

Fortunately, however, they were already upstairs and in their room when I entered with Destiny. I carried her up to the guest room and placed her in a chair in the corner. Then I put the control on the night table by the bed. I didn't want to admit it to myself, but I needed her company more than ever now, even though I knew she was only a doll. Having her here helped me feel close to Uncle Palaver again. She was part of the little family I had.

I left to check on Echo. She had gotten into her pajamas and fallen asleep with Mr. Panda cradled in her arms. The small lamp on her night table was still on, so I turned it off and then returned to the guest room.

"I'm going to change these sheets and pillowcases, Destiny," I said. "I certainly don't want to sleep on what they slept on."

"You should," I had her say. I know it was crazy to throw my thoughts through her, but it gave me the feeling of having company, a companion. My situation was like a magical key opening the door to understanding my uncle even more. With Mrs. Westington in the hospital and Trevor leaving, I did feel alone, maybe as lost and alone as Uncle Palaver had felt.

"You should change into one of your own night-gowns," Destiny remarked.

"Good idea."

I found one I had brought in from the motor home and then I fetched a different blanket from the linen closet and got into bed.

"It's more comfortable than the bunk in the motor home, but not as nice as the bed I first had here," I told Destiny. Then I reached for her control and had her nod.

"I bet," she said. "I used to wonder how you slept up in those cramped quarters."

"It was all right. I felt safe being with Uncle Palaver."

"Me, too," she said. I turned her head from side to side. "This isn't such a bad room. It's sort of quaint, old-fashioned. It has character."

"That's what Mrs. Westington says."

"How wise she is," Destiny said, nodding. It was almost as if she was doing it all before I pressed the right buttons. My imagination is running away with me, I thought. It was like mounting a magical horse and galloping out of the shadowy reach of loneliness.

"I guess I'll go to sleep." I reached up and turned off the small lamp on the night stand, but I kept the control for Destiny beside me. I just liked knowing it was there, knowing she was there watching over me as my mother would when I was very young and had a childhood illness, a fever or a rash.

For a while I just lay there looking into the dark-ness. This won't last much longer, I thought. I was

confident what I had told Trevor would come true.
Rhona will find out how Mrs. Westington had gotten
her attorney to stop her from getting anything and
she'll give up and leave. She certainly wasn't interested in her child or bearing any responsibilities for
her, and with Echo attending a special school soon,
she won't have even a phony excuse to remain.
Skeeter was surely going to grow bored as well.

Doctor Battie would find the right medicine for
Mrs. Westington soon and she'd be coming home.
There wasn't much more that Rhona could do then. I
wanted to shout at her what she had said to me, "The
writing's on the wall." Her days were numbered, re-
duced to hours, not mine.

But then I thought about what Mrs. Westington
had said to me in the hospital. Of course, she was
right. I did have to start thinking of myself and my
future. Brenda would surely be calling me any day
now and we'd meet and talk about our lives together,
her future and mine. Despite all that had happened
since we had last seen each other and what had happened immediately before I left, I was anxious to re-
unite with her. After all, we were still sisters and as
Trevor was fond of saying, blood was telling and
strong. We couldn't deny who we were to each other.
The truth was I actually missed her, even missed her
criticisms of me as much as anything.

I was a changed person. She would see that immediately. Beside becoming more mature, I was more
determined to stop neglecting myself. I'd lose these
pounds and gradually gain more self-respect. Brenda
would appreciate that. I was sure we would get along
better than we ever had.

These thoughts filled my aching heart with renewed hope. Mrs. Westington was right about the ne-
cessity of being optimistic. If you saw only the dark
side of everything, you'd be blinded by the light of
any promise and your savings account of expectations would be bankrupt. I can get us through all this,
I thought, as I turned on my side and cuddled up with
the blanket I had taken from Mrs. Westington's linen
closet. It had the scent of lilac and it made me feel
good.

I can survive it all and I can help both Echo and
Trevor get through it as well. We'll be fine. The
morning would bring light and no matter what Rhona
said or whatever tantrum she pulled, I would be
strong and ignore it. She'd get frustrated and give up
on terrorizing me, too. Mrs. Westington was right.
Rhona didn't have the attention span for it.

I welcomed sleep. I needed sleep so I could restore
myself, my strength and my grit, as Mrs. Westington
would call it. I wanted to be as confident and as trusting in the future as the birds who were sleeping in the
darkness out there. We'll be fine, I sang to myself as I
would a lullaby. We'll be fine and safe again.

I did fall asleep quickly, much more quickly than I
had expected, because it was only minutes later that I
woke when the mattress dipped beside me and the
blanket was lifted away. The smell of whiskey curled
under my nostrils before any other odor. My body
froze; my throat tightened. I was terrified of turning
around. It was as if I was trying to get out of a nightmare and if I turned, I would fall deeper into it.

I felt something wet and warm on my neck and realized it was a tongue licking me.

"Hi, April," Skeeter whispered.

He shoved his left hand under my left side and brought his right hand over my waist, lifting the nightgown up, his palms moving across my breasts. Then he pulled the nightgown so hard, it brought my arms up and he slipped it off me. I cried out, but he put his hand over my mouth and brought his lips next to my ear.

"Nobody who wants to hear you can hear you," he whispered. "Don't waste your breath."

"Stop," I moaned.

"Naw, you don't mean that," he said, his hands moving down over my hips and between my legs.

I tried wresting myself out of his grasp, but he was too strong. The shock of feeling his hard sex moving between my thighs froze me for a moment.

"Hey, you like that?" he asked.

"No, please, let me go."

"You fascinate me, April. You're the youngest bi-sexual girl I know. Rhona thinks you just haven't had a real man yet. That Chinese boy is a wimp. I think she's right. You'll thank me for this. I'll help you make up your mind."

I squirmed and tried pushing him away, but he put his weight against me and I was barely able to move.

"You don't want to keep fighting me like this, April. It takes away from the experience, the plea-sure."

"Get off me!"

"Hey, if I get off you, I'll have to go elsewhere and Rhona is asleep," he said. "Where do you think I might go? Huh?"

It had the effect of a knife made of ice cutting toward my heart. Was he saying he would go into Echo's room?

"All the young women here need the experience, don't you agree?"

"No."

"Sure you do. Who's it going to be first?"

"You're horrible."

"You don't know that yet, April. I might be very, very good. You saw how I was with Rhona. Don't tell me you didn't think about it, want it, too. Rhona said you were standing there and watching us for quite a while."

"I was not! And I don't want you. You're disgusting," I said.

He laughed.

"Stop!" I cried, trying to elbow him away.

"Take it easy. You're about to have the experience of your life and if you're a good girl, I'll help you with Rhona and keep her from driving you out of here, but you have to be a good girl," he said. "Hmm, lots here to grab onto. That's nice," he continued, his hand all over my sides, my stomach, working on turning me around. I tried to fight it, but he was too strong and he threw his leg over me as he turned me, pushing me down until I was on my back, looking up at him. He sat on my legs and in the starlight coming through the window, I could see his tormenting smile.

I swung at him and he grabbed my right wrist and twisted it hard.

"You're hurting me!" I cried.

"Makes it more exciting," he said, and didn't let up on his grip. "Rhona likes that, too. Now what we're going to do here is be very cooperative. I don't like forcing myself on a girl. I like feeling I'm wanted."

"Well, you're not. Get off me."

He twisted my wrist again and I cried out in pain.

"I can break your wrist in half, you know."

"I thought you don't like forcing yourself on someone."

"I don't, so don't make me do it. I want you to pull your legs apart slowly, see, and then I want you to put your feet flat on the bed and lift your bottom a bit so I have no trouble fitting in neatly. Got it?"

He slipped off me, but held onto my wrist. I tried pulling it free, but he was far too strong. In the process, my left hand hit Destiny's control and I remembered it was there. He hadn't noticed her sitting across from us, facing the bed. Somewhere in the deepest, darkest places in my mind, I realized that she wouldn't like this and that she would help me. Where I found the power, I do not know, but it came back to me; all the skill Uncle Palaver had taught me returned.

"What do you think you're doing?" Destiny asked in her deeper voice.

Skeeter stopped moving but held on to my wrist. "What?" he muttered, looking at me.

"If you don't get off her this instant, I'll call the police."

I saw he couldn't understand how I could speak and not move my lips.

"Get off her! Get off her this minute!"

Very confused now, he turned ever so slowly and looked at Destiny. Just then I pressed the control and had her lift her right arm, turning her hand so that her forefinger pointed right at him. It took him by total surprise.

"Who the hell are you?" he screamed, and twisting back, fell off the bed. He scampered quickly to his feet.

"Get out of here! Now!" Destiny cried, nodding her head, "or we'll call the police."

He backed up, looked at me. "Who is that?"

"I'll tell you who I am. I'm your worst nightmare if you're not out of here in a split second," she told him. I turned her torso in his direction. His eyes widened and he sputtered and then turned and left the room.

I leaped off the bed and shut the door the moment he was out of the room. Then I brought a chair to it and wedged it under the handle so it couldn't be opened. My heart was pounding so hard, it sounded like there was a drummer in the room. I pressed my ear to the door to listen for him.

Out in the hall, he gathered his wits about him and turned back to my room. I heard his footsteps and I moaned. He hit the door with his fist so hard, it bounced against my temple. I stepped back and watched him try to open the door against the chair.

"What the hell is that? Who is that? Open this door!" he screamed.

"What's going on, Skeeter?" I heard Rhona ask in a sleepy voice, probably from her bedroom. "What are you doing?"

"She's got someone in there with her, some black woman," he said.

"What?"

"There's someone in the room."

"Who?"

"I don't know. It looked like a black woman."

"A black woman? You're crazy and you're drunk," she said.

"I'm telling you . . ."

"What are you doing in there, anyway, Skeeter? God, you're pathetic."

"I was just . . . having some fun."

"Fun? You call that fun. Come on back to bed. We have a lot to do tomorrow. You know you have to talk to Billy and Lester. That five thousand isn't going to make them happy."

"But . . . I'm telling you someone is in her room."

"Now? This time of night she has a black woman visiting her? You're drunk and you're seeing things."

"I'm not drunk. I heard her and I saw her sitting there. Go look for yourself."

I listened hard, my heart still pounding. Rhona came to the door and tried it.

"What is this? Open this door immediately, April. Do you hear me?"

"He tried to rape me!" I cried.

"Is there someone in the room with you?"

"Yes," I said.

"Who is it?"

"Destiny and she saw it all. She'll tell the police if you don't leave me alone," I said.

"Destiny? What the . . . open this door," she demanded, and shook it hard. "Do you want me to have Skeeter break it down? He can do that and you'll have to explain it to my mother."

"Leave me alone. I'm calling Trevor if you don't

go away," I said. They didn't know his mother had died and he was gone.

She stopped shaking the door.

"I'm telling you she has someone in there," Skeeter insisted, his voice high and frantic.

"Good for her. I'm going back to bed, Skeeter. I'm not in the mood to start dealing with Trevor and all this in the middle of the night. Who cares about her?"

"But—"

"Will you stop. I'm tired, dammit."

I held my breath and listened. I heard Rhona walk away and then I saw Skeeter's face in the cracked opening.

"Tell your friend I'll be waiting for her in the morning," he said. He pulled back and returned to their bedroom. I closed the door completely, but left the chair there. I stood waiting for a while to be sure he wasn't coming back. I could hear them arguing in their room. Rhona was mad at him for going into my bedroom. He kept saying it wasn't a big deal. Finally, they were quiet.

How fortunate for Echo that she couldn't hear what went on tonight. What a frightening experience it would have been for her, too, I thought, and returned to my bed. I was still shaking so hard, my teeth were clicking like an old typewriter. I had held my breath so long, my chest ached. I looked at Destiny.

"Thank you," I said, and put on my nightgown again. I sat there for a moment just catching my breath and then I realized that in the morning Skeeter would be charging in here looking for her. Who knew what he would do when he discovered he had been frightened by a trick mannequin? In a rage he might damage or destroy her, I thought. Fear of that kept me awake. I had to think of something.

A good half hour or so later, I got out of bed as quietly as I could and took the chair away from the door. I opened it slowly, inches at a time, to keep the squeaking of the hinges down to a minimum. Then I lifted Destiny from the chair and, moving almost in slow motion, carried her out and into Echo's room.

She was fast asleep and of course wouldn't hear anything. I went to her closet and, first putting Destiny down softly on the floor, opened the sliding door. Then I pulled the clothes forward to make some room and as carefully and surgically perfect as I could, inserted her in the corner of the closet.

"Just for a little while," I whispered, and slid the clothing back to cover her.

I closed the closet door and tiptoed over the floor. It creaked, and I stopped often to listen and be sure neither Rhona nor Skeeter heard. They were in a dead sleep finally, thankfully, so I made my way back to my room. I got into bed. I was so exhausted, nervous, and frightened that I couldn't fall asleep for the longest time. I did just before morning and I was in a dead sleep, dead to the world. Echo had to shake me hard to get me to open my eyes.

Her first question was, "Will Grandma be coming home today?"

I told her I didn't know, that we'd see when we got to the hospital.

She told me she was hungry and she would start breakfast for us. I nodded, groggy and achy. My eyelids wouldn't stay open. She shook me again to tell me she would bring up a cup of coffee for me. I smiled at her, but closed my eyes again and in an instant, fell back asleep.

The next time she shook me, she had a cup of coffee in hand. I thanked her and pulled myself up to a sitting position. She wanted to know if I wanted scrambled eggs. She liked making them. I said yes, even though eating anything was the furthest thing from my thoughts. She turned excitedly and hurried out and down to the kitchen. I sipped some coffee and sat there with my eyes closed.

"Where the hell is she?" I heard next and woke up again. I had fallen asleep sitting up. I looked at Skeeter. He was in his underwear, his hair falling around his face, his eyes bloodshot.

"Huh?"

"Where's who?" I said.

"Very funny." He looked around the room and went directly to the closet, shoving the door open. "Where'd she go? Is she still in the house? Downstairs?"

"No," I said. "No one else is here."

"Skeeter!" we heard Rhona shout. "Get the bitch to bring me a cup of coffee."

He stared at me. "Who was she? Is she related to Trevor, a sister or a girlfriend? I'm going to go ask him."

"I wouldn't tell Trevor that you came into my room last night," I said. "That might not go over so well for you."

Where I found the courage, I do not know, but I did know I had to put on a good act or I would be at his mercy. He pointed his right forefinger at me, but he didn't say anything for a moment. Then he nodded and smiled.

"Too bad. She ruined a good time for you. I could have drilled you into ecstasy."

"I'd rather have root canal work," I muttered, and his smile slid off his face.

"You heard her. Get her a cup of coffee," he said, glanced around the room again, his eyes full of confusion, and then turned and left.

I rose and got dressed as fast as I could. Echo had my scrambled eggs ready. I told her I had to bring her mother a cup of coffee and she insisted on doing it so my eggs wouldn't get cold. I didn't see how I could stop her, so I let her go up, but I waited at the foot of the stairway. I could hear them clearly.

"There's not enough sugar in it," Rhona complained. "Skeeter, tell her."

"I don't remember how to say that," he said.

"Damn it, why didn't April bring it up? Get April. Go downstairs and get April," she shouted at Echo.

I hurried into the kitchen, grabbed the sugar bowl and a spoon, and ran up the stairs. As I expected, Echo was standing there confused and unsure of what to do next

Skeeter was in bed beside Rhona, who was sitting up naked. I went to her quickly.

"How much more do you want?"

"A teaspoonful. Why did you send her up here? She's worthless doing these things."

"She wanted to do something for you," I said. Of course I knew she really wanted to do it for me.

"If she wants to do something for me, tell her to

tell her grandmother to give me the money I need. Yeah, maybe if she tells her, she'll do it. What do you think, Skeeter?"

"I think we're just going to have to wait around for her to die," he said bitterly.

It was on the tip of my tongue to spurt out the news that Mrs. Westington was already in the process of preventing them from getting their hands on her money.

"Make us some eggs, over easy, and some toast with my mother's jam and more coffee. You want anything else, Skeeter?"

"Yeah, but I'll get it some other time," he said, smiling licentiously at me.

"You and your one-track mind," Rhona said.

"You like going down that track, so don't complain."

She laughed.

I urged Echo out of the room and we went downstairs to prepare their breakfast. The faster I did what they wanted, the faster I could get us out of here, I thought. I didn't want to be around Skeeter any longer than I had to and I was really worrying about Echo now.

I started on their eggs. Echo wanted to do it so I could eat, but I had lost any appetite. I told her to eat them and promised to let her make me some after I finished with her mother and Skeeter. She wasn't happy about it, but she sat and started to eat.

Just as I broke the first set of eggs, the phone rang. I was in such deep thought and full of so much worry, it stunned me. It was as if it had rung in my heart. I stared at the receiver, too frightened to lift it. Before I got to it, Rhona had picked it up in her room. I lifted the receiver to listen in nevertheless.

"Hello," Rhona said.

"Hello, this is Doctor Battie. To whom am I speaking?"

"Rhona Westington, Mrs. Westington's daughter."

"I'm glad I reached you. Didn't you get my message to have you call me?"

"Message? No," she replied in outright lie. I was about to contradict her, but thought it better to simply remain undetected on the line. "I haven't been feeling well myself. I've been up there a few times but the nurses don't tell me anything and you weren't around. How is my mother today?"

"I'm afraid Mrs. Westington has had a bit of a setback," Doctor Battie said.

I held my breath. Setback?

"What? Why? Is she dead?" Rhona asked quickly.

"No, but she has had what we call a cardiac event. It looks like she's a candidate for a pacemaker, but I don't want her to have any procedures until we stabilize her blood pressure. I'm getting close to doing that."

"What do you mean, she had a cardiac event? What happened to her?"

"She has a heart block. The block effects the heart's electrical activity but the cardiologist believes that the pacemaker will help a great deal."

I felt like I was going to melt into a pool of shock and disappointment.

"Oh, really?" She certainly sounded disappointed. "Is that expensive?"

"It's not the expense. Her insurance will handle it

well, but she won't agree to our setting it up until she speaks with your houseguest."

"Houseguest?"

"April. I'm afraid I don't recall her last name or even if Mrs. Westington told me."

"Let me get this straight, Doctor. My mother won't agree to do what she has to do unless she first speaks to April?"

"Yes. Is she there? Do you know if she's coming up here to visit soon?"

I was about to speak, but Rhona said, "Let me go look for her."

I hung up the phone as quietly as I could and walked out of the kitchen, pretending to be busy with setting the table for their breakfast. Echo looked at me quizzically. I just smiled back, nodded at the table, and then waited in the hallway.

"Hey, April," I heard Skeeter call.

I walked to the foot of the stairway. "What is it?" I asked.

He was still dressed only in his underwear and had already started down the stairs. "Come up here," he said.

"Why?" I demanded. I could pick up the phone down in the kitchen just as easily. Why didn't he just tell me to do so?

He moved quickly until he had his right hand on my neck, his fingers squeezing like vice grips sending incredible pain into the back of my head. With his other hand, he grabbed my wrist and pulled me so I would go forward up the stairway.

"Ow!" I screamed. "You're really hurting me. I'll go up. Stop it," I said.

I stepped up, but he kept his grip on the back of my neck. What did they want to do, listen to what I said to the doctor? When we reached the top, he shoved me hard to the left instead of toward Rhona's room as I was expecting.

"What are you doing?" I cried.

He put his left hand over my mouth and grabbed my hair with his right hand, forcing me to walk toward Mrs. Westington's bedroom.

As we passed Rhona's room, I could see her standing by the night table, holding her hand over the mouth of the receiver and looking out at us. I tried to resist, but Skeeter had a very firm grip on my face and my hair felt like it was being ripped out of my skull in clumps.

What were they doing?

"Oh, Doctor Battie," Rhona said, loud enough for me to hear, "I'm sorry I took so long, but I've just learned that April has left. Yes, she went off to meet her sister and live with her. She's no longer here.

"But tell my mother I'll be up to see her as soon as I get dressed."

I tried to shout, but Skeeter's fingers pressed down on my tongue and made me gag. I squirmed and twisted to get out of his grasp.

Rhona hung up the receiver.

"No!" I finally managed.

"Yes," he said. He lifted me and carried me into Mrs. Westington's bedroom, and he shut the door behind us.

13

Bound and Gagged

Skeeter dropped me to my knees hard and then pushed me to the floor with his foot.

"Stay down," he said, keeping his foot pressed on my lower back. "Don't you move."

"What are you doing?" I screamed.

"Don't move. So where's your friend now, huh?" he asked, his foot twisting on me. "I don't know what the hell that was about, but I know I was right. There was someone here, but don't think she's going to help you now."

He went over to the telephone and tore the wire out of its socket. Then he brought the wire to me and twisted my arms behind my back, wrapping the wire around my wrists and tying them tightly. I cried out in pain, tears coming into my eyes. I gasped, trying to catch my breath.

"Don't start shouting for that Trevor, either," he warned.

"You don't have to worry about him," I heard Rhona say from the doorway. "His truck's gone. He's off somewhere already."

"Oh, really? That was thoughtful of him," Skeeter said.

"What do you think you're doing?" I cried, still on my stomach on the floor because Skeeter had his knee on my buttocks. "Why did you lie to the doctor about my leaving?"

Rhona walked into the bedroom. I turned my head and looked at her feet and then up at her.

"You should have left when I told you to leave. Now you're going to be cooperative whether you like it or not." She smiled. "My mother ever tell you how she locked me up once for nearly three days? I got into trouble with the police when I was a little more than eleven, and she was so angry and embarrassed she decided to show me what it would be like to be in prison or something. I guess she thought the prison would be in a Third World country. She dug up one of her antiques, a chamber pot, and gave me a roll of toilet paper, water, and that was it. Nice mother, huh?"

"You probably deserved it," I said, squirming. The wire was tied so tightly, I was afraid it was shutting off the blood to my hands. Skeeter took his knee off me and stood up. I turned on my side.

"Sure I deserved it, April. Just like you deserve this."

"You'll both get into serious trouble for this. You'd better let me go."

"As soon as I get what I want, we'll let you go,"
Rhona stated. "In fact, we'll kick you out the door
and if you go running to the police or anyone, we'll
tell them how we caught you in bed with Echo doing
all sorts of ungodly things." She turned to Skeeter,
who was looking down at me with a satisfied, in-
sanely sadistic smile on his face.

"Yeah. I'm sure Rhona can come up with them,
too," he said.

"Never mind all that, Skeeter. You take her car and
drive it to Bill. Tell him to keep it there for us and explain about the money. When Trevor comes back
from wherever he is today, I'll tell him she left to go
live with her sister. We'll tell Echo the same thing,"
she added. "She won't see her or of course hear her."

"Very good plan, Rhona," Skeeter said, smiling
with admiration, as if she had come up with a cure
for cancer.

"Get a sock or something and gag her so she can't
shout loud enough for Trevor to hear her."

I debated telling them the truth just so they
wouldn't gag me, but I was afraid of letting them
know how much in control they really were and giving them more confidence.

"No one's going to believe you when you tell them
I've left, least of all Mrs. Westington," I said.

"Oh, she will when I tell her what we learned from
Mrs. Monahan and how when we confronted you
with it, you just picked up and ran out of here because you were so embarrassed. She'll be so disappointed. With her health problems, I'll have an easier
time taking charge of Echo and she'll know that, too.
I'll tell her that either she'll sign what I want her to

sign or we'll leave with Echo and she'll never see nor hear from her again. What do you think she will do then? Do you think she'll be so high and mighty and write 'NO' over my papers?"

"How could you be like this to your own mother?"

"She was never much of a mother to me as far as I was concerned, so don't even go there. Now guess what I saw the other day in my mother's room. Yes, that's right," she said. "That same old chamber pot. Aren't you happy. You won't have to mess your panties."

She looked around. "Find something to tie her feet with, Skeeter, and put her in the closet and close the door. I'll bring in the chamber pot for her."

"How am I going to use that if my hands are tied?" I asked.

"No problem. Skeeter, would you be so kind as to remove her jeans and panties so she simply has to sit on the pot to pee. And do it all quickly and nothing more," she added. "I want you out of here with that car before Trevor returns."

"I'll get right on it," he said.

She smiled as if he was doing her a wonderful favor.

"We'll keep the door closed, but you're banging or knocking on anything won't help, since poor Echo couldn't hear you anyway. My advice to you is to be as cooperative as you can be, otherwise you'll make it even more difficult for yourself, understand?" she added, her eyes cold and her lips tight. She turned to Skeeter. "Gag her first," she decided. "I don't want to hear any more of her lip. I'll bring her some water when we return. I'm getting dressed and getting over to the hospital to break the news to dear old Mom," she told him, and left.

He searched one of the dresser drawers and found a pair of socks. I shook my head and tried pushing myself away from him, but he grabbled my ankles, straddled me, and then put the sock to my lips. I kept my mouth locked shut.

"Rhona's not going to like your resisting like this," he said. "She's very imaginative and clever. She can come up with worse and more painful things for you," he warned.

He grabbed my jaw between his fingers and thumb and squeezed. It was so painful, I couldn't keep up the defiance. As soon as my mouth opened a little, he shoved the sock into it and then, using a belt, he wrapped my face so I couldn't spit it out. It was hard to breathe and I began to panic.

"Relax and it won't be so bad," he said. "If you struggle, you only make it worse for yourself. I know. Something similar was once done to me by this girl I met in New Orleans, but I enjoyed it."

He began to undo my jeans. I tried to make it difficult by twisting and turning, but he sat on my ankles and then began to lower my jeans and panties together. Once he was below my knees, he rose and pulled off my shoes, and then the jeans and panties. He tossed them across the room and stood there, smiling down at me.

"I kind of like your tummy," he said. "It turns me on."

He located another belt and wrapped it around my ankles. Then he lifted me under the arms and pulled me to the closet. He took clothing out to make room

for me. I tried desperately to keep him from getting
me into the closet, but it was a useless effort with my
hands and feet bound.

"I'll be back," he said, smiling, and closed the
door.

I tried to push out the sock with my tongue. I managed to get a little more breathing space, but I
couldn't get it out far enough for me to make any
loud sound. The belt was too tight around my face.
Who would hear it anyway? I thought, and fell over
on my side. The tears from my left eye ran over the
bridge of my nose to join the tears from my right. I
squirmed and struggled against the wire around my
wrists. It loosened a bit, but not enough to get my
hands free and it hurt terribly to pull and push against
it. I had skinned off my wrists a bit and it was raw be-
neath the wires. Helpless, I stared at the little light
coming from under the closet door.

Suddenly, it was thrust open and Rhona, now
dressed, stood there with the chamber pot in her
hand.

"Here you go, sweetie. Try not to fill it up too
quickly. I'll bring your regrets to my mother. She'll
be so very disappointed."

I cried out against the gag. She shook her head and
closed the closet door. I felt horrible for myself, but
all I could think was poor Mrs. Westington. She was
liable to believe them and then she would become so
despondent. She was too proud and independent a
woman to permit herself to be bamboozled like this.
It would break her heart, but there was probably not
much she could do under the circumstances. She
wouldn't even understand why Trevor wasn't coming

around. I hadn't had a chance to tell her about his mother dying. She would feel totally deserted.

And Echo? What would she think when they told her I was gone? How lost she was going to be in just a little while and there was nothing I could do about it, do about any of it. The ironic thing was that when someone has done such terrible things to you and made you so defenseless and incapable of doing anything to help yourself, you end up hating yourself more than you do them.

Why hadn't I anticipated this or something like it? Why did I put up with them after last night? Why didn't I just take Echo and run out of here when I had the chance? I let myself get trapped like this. I am stupid and my worse enemy, and because of me, other people will suffer, people who don't deserve it. I was drowning in self-disgust.

With all my strength, I shouted and pulled against the binding on my hands and feet. My muffled scream died inside me and I collapsed with the effort. I closed my eyes and fell back, looking up at the ceiling of the closet and listening as hard as I could. By now Echo was surely running about looking for me. Would they be leaving her here? Would she see Skeeter drive my car away?

I thought I heard her calling me and then, I did hear the door of the guest bedroom open. Despite knowing she couldn't hear a sound, I cried as loud as I could. The sock muffled my screams and made them reverberate in my head. I then leaned back and struck the wall of the closet with my feet. I waited, hoping that somehow she would sense my being in here, but I heard nothing. The house became very quiet. I imagined Echo had gone out to look for Trevor. She would see he was gone as well and she would know that for now she was totally alone and had no idea why or for how long.

Frustration tied my stomach into knots and then my mind ran away with itself. I envisioned the hospital room and Rhona putting on her act, explaining why I had left. She would exaggerate every detail and certainly tread on the verge of being disgusting when she told her what Tyler had told his mother about me. If she aggravated and upset Mrs. Westington as much as I imagined she would, surely her blood pressure would go up and maybe she would even cause her to have a heart attack and die. Hopefully, the doctor and the nurses would prevent Rhona from doing that, but then how would they know what she was intending to do? All they would think was that as her daughter, Rhona had a right to speak to her mother.

I closed my eyes and, only as a way to avoid frustration and pain, willed myself to sleep. I did drift off, dreaming I was with Uncle Palaver again and we were traveling on some wide highway. The classical music he loved was playing and he was talking to me and telling me one story after another about his experiences on the road. I saw myself laughing and so happy that I was with him.

Then I thought about my mother and father and Brenda and put myself back in time to when we were all together and I was on the sidelines with my mother watching Brenda and Daddy play basketball in our driveway. Brenda was only about fourteen in the memory I had. She was trying so hard. Daddy would look to us every once in a while, impressed with her. She was so quick and wiry, he had trouble keeping up.

"Ho," he cried, holding his side. "You're killing your old man."

Mother was laughing. Daddy put his arm around Brenda's shoulders and shook her lovingly. I longed to have him do that with me and for a while, when no one paid any attention, I went out by myself to the driveway and practiced, but I was never any good. I was too awkward and clumsy and after a while, grew too discouraged to continue. I'd have to find another way to get my father to embrace me with such affection and admiration. Would I? Would I ever?

Not being able to see my watch or look outside, I had no idea how much time had passed when I woke from my sleep and dreams. I listened hard. I thought I heard Echo sobbing in her room, but then I realized, it was my own sobbing I was hearing. I had to piddle in the pot. It was awkward getting myself over it without tipping it, but I managed and then I rolled over and stared at the dark rear wall of the closet.

Finally, I heard heavy footsteps and then the closet door was opened. I turned and looked up at Rhona, who was carrying a jug of water. She smiled at me and knelt down, placing the jug on the floor to undo the belt from my face. As soon as my mouth was free, I took in large gasps of air.

"Well now, you'll be happy to know Mother is going to be very cooperative. Despite what you expected, she bought into the whole story, especially when I got into your love affair with your sister's girlfriend. She's also going to have her pacemaker put in, but not for a few days. The doctor won't do it right now. He said her blood pressure shot up again. I wonder why."

She poured a glass of water for me and brought it to my lips. I didn't want to take anything from her. I wanted to spit it into her face, but my throat felt like it was blistering from dryness. I swallowed quickly because she had no patience and was pouring it so fast. In fact, I gagged and she had to stop.

"I've been thinking," she said. "This is really a big favor I'm doing you. I'm really not going to feed you anything. You'll lose a few pounds. I'll have to keep you here a while longer. It will take until tomorrow for Mother to get what she has to get signed and then I'll return and turn you loose. If you're a good girl, that is."

"What about Echo?" I asked.

"What about her? After I'm gone and Mother comes home, if she comes home, she can put her in that school or any school that handles disabled people. Everyone will be happy, except Mother maybe.

"I see Trevor has not returned. Where is he? I don't want him coming around here looking for you or things can get even nastier."

"His mother died," I revealed. There was no point in keeping it a secret any longer. She couldn't be more confident she would succeed and I didn't want her doing anything with Echo. The news surprised her.

"Oh, really? You mean he left to go to a funeral?"

"Yes."

"That's great. Why didn't you say so before? How long is he going to be gone?"

"He said a few days."

"Now isn't that considerate of his mother, dying at this time? This all may work out after all and easily, too."

She picked up the sock to put back in my mouth.

"Wait," I said. "Trevor's not here. No one can hear me shout if I shout. Please don't put that back in my mouth. It's hard to breathe with it in my mouth."

She hesitated and then looked at me suspiciously and tilted her head. "What if you're lying to me about Trevor? What if you made all that up just so I wouldn't put this in your mouth and you could scream loud enough for him to hear you when he does return?"

"I'm not lying. Please. Call the home his mother was in if you don't believe me."

"How am I supposed to know where that is?"

"It's in Phoenix, Arizona."

"What's the name of the home?"

"I don't know, but I'm sure you can find out. He gave me his cousin's phone number. It's in my jeans. Call."

"Right. I'm really going to go through all that just to make you more comfortable, and don't you think he'd wonder why I was calling?"

"Please. I'm not lying."

She shook her head. "I can't take a chance. If he doesn't come home by evening, I might leave it out. Open up."

"No," I said.

"You want me to call Skeeter to do it? He won't just put a sock in you."

"Please," I begged. "I'm not doing anything. What could I do anyway?"

"Open up," she said, holding the sock near my lips.

I saw Skeeter step into the doorway to say to Rhona, "What are you doing? The kid's asking after you and asking all about her, I think. It's hard to tell what she's saying, but you don't want her coming up here."

"April?" Rhona said. "Am I going to do this or is Skeeter?"

I opened my mouth.

"Wider," she said, and I did it. She put the sock in and reattached the belt around my face. Then she stood up, backed out, and closed the closet door. I heard Skeeter's laugh and the two of them walk out, closing the bedroom door behind them.

My body ached so from being cramped and twisted. I moaned and rocked back and forth. Then I tried to get to my feet by pressing my back to the wall and pushing up, but my ankles were so close, I simply toppled and hit the floor hard with my shoulder. I nearly knocked over the chamber pot as well. What seemed to be a good hour or so later, the door opened and Rhona knelt down to take off the gag.

"Well now, guess what," she said. "Apparently, Trevor did tell someone about his mother, one of his wine customers who called to leave a message of sympathy. I promised to pass it along first chance I got. I'm going to give you some more water and that will be it for the day. I have my own things to take care of since you're not around to help make the meal. Echo is apparently very spoiled about what she will and won't eat. She can go hungry, too, for all I care. That will get her off her high horse quickly. Go on, sip it quickly or I won't give you any."

I drank.

"Some more please," I said when she took the glass away. She didn't even get me fresh water. She grimaced and brought it back to my lips, this time forcing me to gag on it.

"You don't want to drink too much anyway, otherwise you'll fill the chamber pot and I'm not about to empty it for you. You'll do that yourself before you leave. Hungry?"

"No," I said.

"Good. You can send me a thank you note later for all the pounds you shed." She glanced at the sock, started to reach for it, and stopped. "Since you've been so good, I'm going to leave it out of your mouth. If I hear you make a peep, I'll send Skeeter in to shove it down your throat again, understand? Well?"

"Yes," I said.

"You should say, yes, thank you. Didn't your mother teach you any manners as my mother taught me?"

"Yes, thank you," I corrected.

"Very good. See? We can be civil to each other when we try," she said, smiled and stood up. "Have a very good night. I'll give you some more water in the morning before I leave to see my attorney and get the new papers for Mother to sign. I'm asking for more than I did before because she didn't behave well and has to pay a penalty now."

I just stared up at her.

"You'll thank me, really, for all this someday. You

wouldn't want to spend your life here, believe me. Good night," she said, and closed the closet door.

The darkness defeated me. I closed my eyes and wished I would just die. After all this ended, how could I face poor Mrs. Westington knowing I had been the one who put her in this terrible position? I was sure she would hate me for it, even though she would pretend she didn't, and Trevor would be so disappointed in me as well for having hid so much from him. When it does end, I thought, I will leave. I'll get into my car and just drive away as quickly as I can. What Rhona had told Mrs. Westington concerning me might as well prove to be true.

I fell asleep on and off. One time when I woke, I felt very dizzy. It was as if my whole body was spinning in space. I was so weak and tired, I couldn't struggle much against the bindings. I could feel myself falling into a world of hallucination. There were brilliant colors flashing across my eyes, even when I opened them. The silence, the darkness, and the terribly restricted area and movement sent me wandering through all sorts of tunnels in my own mind.

I slid my body over the closet floor and put my ear to the rear wall. Was it my imagination or was someone whispering just on the other side?

"I don't like it in here," I heard. "Why did you leave me in here?"

Oh, my God, I thought, it's Destiny. I had forgotten that I had placed her in Echo's closet and closed the door. She was in much the same kind of situation as I was.

"Destiny? Is that you?"

"Yes. Where are you?"

"I'm in a closet, too. They tied me up and put me here."

"Well, how am I going to help you? How am I going to get out of here? Echo can't hear me if I shout and cry."

"I don't know," I said, sobbing. "I'm sorry. I should have thought about it more."

"Yes, you should have. Now what are we going to do?"

"I don't know."

"Stop saying that. Think."

"I'm trying," I said. "I'm so tired and my body aches in so many places."

"Stop thinking of yourself only. Just imagine what it's like for me and for Echo, too."

"I have been imagining that. It is painful to think about it. I know it's my fault. I know."

"It's not entirely your fault, but you did make it all easy for them. You should have told Trevor more. You should have confided in him. You have to learn to trust good people more and stop being so ashamed of yourself."

"I know."

Suddenly, the closet door was thrust open. The light from the bedroom blinded me for a moment. I blinked and looked up. Skeeter was standing there totally naked.

"Who the hell are you talking to?" he asked. I saw him wobble and realized he was drunk again. "Is she in here with you?" he asked, the thought occurring to him. He leaned in and pushed the clothing that remained away from me. "You're crazy," he said. "Talking to yourself."

"Please, untie me and let me out," I begged.

"Sure. And Rhona will skin me alive. You look like you're doing fine."

He stared down at me and then smiled, looked back at the doorway, and started to squat. He brought his face so close to mine, I could smell the whiskey mixed with the sweat. It turned my stomach. He moved his tongue over his lips. Panic, like two giant hands, tightened a grip around my ribs, making it harder and harder for me to breathe.

"I was thinking about last night and how disappointed you must have been," he said.

"I wasn't disappointed. I was disgusted. Just like I am right now. Get away from me."

"You just asked me to help you. You don't know what you want, do you?"

"Yes, I asked you to untie me. Nothing else."

"You know, I have this theory about lesbians. They just don't know what they're missing, never having had it. Am I right or am I right?"

He poked me in the stomach with his right forefinger and I pulled back. Then he gripped my stomach with his thumb and forefinger and squeezed until I cried out.

"Hey, shut your mouth. You wake Rhona and there'll be hell to pay," he said, and looked back at the doorway.

"Leave me alone."

"Now that would be stupid and a total waste of an opportunity for you," he said, smiling.

Instinctively, I pushed myself as far away from him as I could by twisting and turning my body, until I was against the closet wall. He reached out and seized my ankles, turning and pulling me back. I started to scream but stopped when I saw his eyes go to the sock.

"Shout again and I'll stuff that deep into your throat," he threatened.

"Please, leave me alone."

"It's against my religion to pass up an opportunity to please a young woman," he said.

He turned me more and then he lined himself up and put his arms around my thighs to lift me as he drew closer. I couldn't put up much resistence. This is going to happen, I thought. What good did it do to scream? Who would help me? All I can do is close my eyes and try to close my mind to it as well, maybe pretend to be somewhere else, somewhere pleasant and beautiful. My silence and my cessation of even the smallest resistence only encouraged him.

"That's more like it. Now you're getting the idea," he said. "This is going to be an eye-opener for you. You'll never forget it."

Where had I heard that before? I thought.

I felt his hardness move against me and looked at him, at the way he threw his head back, his eyes closed, his mouth slightly open and for a moment, only a slight moment, I was intrigued by how much pleasure he expected he would have, even without my being willing. It occurred to me that he could be doing this with anyone, that emotions, affection, love didn't matter to him. Rhona probably didn't matter all that much to him either. He was with her only because of what she promised and what he saw he could gain for himself. In the end perhaps being gay or straight didn't matter as much as whom you were

with and why you were with him or her. Everything
we did in our lives could have little or no meaning,
which was what I thought described Skeeter, or if we
truly gave ourselves, invested our trust and love in
someone else, could have deeper, lifelong meaning.

Was it too late for me? Would I be like him? Like
Rhona? Would what he was about to do to me ruin
my chances for any real happiness? Was that what he
was taking from me? Or had I already lost it along
the way during this journey that had brought me to
this horrible moment?

"NO!" I cried, despite his threat if I wasn't quiet.
"NO!" I cried for myself, my dreams and hopes, my
faith in all that was possible and good in this life.

My cry took him by surprise. He had thought I
had totally surrendered. My shout gave him pause,
which was quickly turning to anger, but before he
could do anything more, we both heard this most
horrendous and shrill scream. He turned and fell
back on his side and I had a clear view of the bedroom doorway in which Echo stood, her hands on
her ears as though she could hear her own basic, desperate howl rising out of the depths of her own fear,
instinctive and raw.

A moment later Rhona was right behind her looking in at us, her face in a rage with her eyes wide and
her lips twisted.

"Skeeter!" she shouted. "You damn idiot. You fool.
Look what you've done!"

"Huh?" he said, as if he was just awakening from a
bout of sleepwalking. He looked at me and then at
Echo, who was silent with her mouth wide open and
her hands still on her ears, her neck straining. It had

the effect of making us all feel as if we were the deaf
ones, unable to hear her.

"Now she knows April's still here and she's seen
what you're doing and what we did."

He shook his head. "I didn't . . . how could she
hear her scream?" he demanded, as if somehow he
had been cheated, as if someone had broken one of
the rules.

"Does that matter now, you fool? Why did you
come in here? Why did you have to do this? We're almost there."

"Aw," was all he could say, and waved at her. He
struggled to his feet.

Echo looked at him with confusion and terror and
then looked down at me. I tried turning myself so I
wasn't so exposed. I could just imagine how frightening a sight I was to her. Rhona seized Echo by the
shoulders and walked her deeper into the bedroom,
forcing her to sit on the bed with her back to me.

"Stay there," she said, waving her finger at Echo.
"Stay!"

"She's not a dog," I muttered.

"You shut up," Rhona said. "Why are you still
standing there like that, Skeeter? Go put something
on while I think. Go on!" she shouted, and pointed at
the doorway.

He moved quickly out of the room. There was no
doubt she had sobered him up instantly.

"Now you listen to me," Rhona began, stepping
closer to me. "This doesn't change anything, understand?" I could almost see the wheels churning in her
head as she thought and spoke. "No one's going to
believe what she tells them after we describe how you

seduced her. Of course, she would say whatever you tell her to say. Anyone would realize that. You'll just put her through a terrible, terrible ordeal."

"She's your own daughter," I said as though she had to be reminded. "You're the one putting her through a terrible, terrible ordeal, not me."

"You're going to make it worse for the both of you now," she replied, undaunted.

Skeeter returned in his underwear and a T-shirt. He stood by looking like a remorseful little boy, his head slightly bowed, waiting for Rhona to either whip him or grant him a reprieve. She looked at him, at Echo, and at me.

"All right. Here's what we'll do," she began. "You and Echo will stay in this room until we return from the hospital tomorrow. Skeeter, you'll nail that door shut, tie the handle, do whatever has to be done."

He nodded, looking happy he had been given something to do to repent.

"What about her?" he said, nodding at me. "Echo could untie her while we're away. I mean, I'll get that door shut so tight, it'll take a tank to open it, but still, they can go to that window and start screaming or something. I could nail it shut, too, I suppose, but they could break the glass and she could make a commotion."

She thought, nodded, and turned to Echo. "We'll have to tie her up, too, then, so she can't free April," she said.

"No, please don't do that to her. She's absolutely terrified as it is."

"It won't hurt her to lie still for a few hours."

"I promise. I won't shout out the window. We won't try to escape."

Rhona raised her eyebrows. "Sweetie, the last time I believed in promises, I believed in Santa Claus, and you know what that's worth," she said. "Skeeter, get something to use."

"No, don't do that," I pleaded.

Skeeter turned and ran out.

Rhona walked over to the closet, lifted her foot to push me into it, and closed the door on me.

"How can you call yourself a mother?" I screamed.

She was still right at the door. She brought her lips to the slight opening. "I never did," she said.

14

The Great Escape

I heard Echo's cries for help and her moans of confusion. She surely wondered how her mother could stand by and watch Skeeter tie her up. Trevor was wrong, I thought. Blood wasn't as telling and strong as he imagined it to be, at least for someone like Rhona, who was so selfish.

Once again I heard them talking to Echo as if she were some sort of pet.

"Stay here. Just stay here," Rhona shouted at her. "We'll be back as soon as we can to untie you."

Echo was probably too hysterical and frightened by now to have the concentration required to read lips and had no idea what she was being told. All she saw was a wild, angry woman shouting down at her, a woman she once hoped would be the mother she never really had. In her small, protected world what was happening to her was far too bizarre for her to understand.

Now that they had us both tied up, Rhona decided it wasn't necessary to nail the door shut.

"It would be something we would be forced to explain later," she realized.

I heard Skeeter agree and they left to get some sleep. I could hear Echo whimpering. Apparently, so could Rhona. She returned to the bedroom and shouted at her to be quiet. She probably put her finger to her lips and gave her some sort of threatening look as well because soon after, Echo did stop crying. In my mind's eye, I could see her shivering on the bed, her hands and feet bound. Before long, like me, she drifted into the escape of sleep.

I woke to the sounds of Skeeter and Rhona getting themselves up and ready in the morning for what they believed would be their big day. I heard Rhona come back into the room to check on Echo first.

"See? You're fine," she told her. "Just rest. Drink this water," she said.

I didn't know whether Echo did or not, but a few moments later, Rhona opened the closet door and looked down at me with the jug of water in her hand.

"If all goes as I expect it will, I'll be back to cut you loose," she said. "Don't make any more trouble, not that you could. Just don't try and you'll be out of here and on your way, wherever that is."

I said nothing and then, probably more because she didn't want anything to happen to spoil things for herself than because she felt compassion, she knelt down and poured me a glass of water, too. I took it greedily and she was a bit more patient about it.

"Actually," she said as I drank, "I expected things would have gone better than this from the very beginning of my arrival here. I was being Pollyanna like you and deluded myself enough to believe my mother would be generous and forgiving and happily give me what was mine, especially after she willingly helped me when I was in trouble in Mexico. Of course, I didn't know you were here and that she had formed this surrogate daughter relationship, leaving me out in the cold."

I stopped drinking and she took the glass away.

"That's not true," I said. "I never replaced you as her daughter."

"Don't tell me how my mother thinks. I don't think she liked me from the day I was born. She always used to tell me I cried too much. I whined too much. I demanded too much. Half the time she pushed me off on my father and made him take care of me, comfort me, entertain me. Who knows? Maybe I wasn't really her child, although I'll have to admit she was very pretty when she was my age and looked like I do now.

"She got pregnant again, hoping for something better than me, I'm sure. For the longest time, she kept it a secret that she had given birth to a boy after me. I bet she didn't even tell you that, huh? Well?"

"No," I said. "Trevor told me. The memory is too painful for her."

"Ha! Too painful? After all these years?"

"Unlike you, most women would find losing a child too traumatic to ever forget or forgive," I said, dipping into some well of wisdom I didn't know I had. She raised her eyebrows.

"Nice try, but I'll tell you what I think. I think she believed I had taken all the health possible out of her body and left the next baby deformed and inadequate. She blamed my existence for his death."

"That's so stupid," I said, and she flushed with anger, her cheeks flaming red.

"How dare you tell me I'm stupid! You didn't live here all those years and listen to her and the way she spoke to me. I could hear it in the tone of her voice. What do you think Echo's being deaf meant to her, huh? The same thing. It was somehow my fault. That's why I had to get out of here. I couldn't stand it," she said. "I couldn't stand being blamed for every disaster in the world."

"I'm sure that was something you yourself imagined," I said, though I couldn't be sure there wasn't a grain of truth in what she said. Even so, it didn't come close to justifying all the terrible things she had done and would do.

"Are we going or what?" Skeeter called from the doorway. "I'm growing old waiting."

She glared at me. "It's a waste of time to talk to you anyway," she said. "Just keep quiet."

She stood up and closed the closet door. I heard them leave the room and even descend the stairway. Then I took a deep breath. Somehow, I thought. Somehow, I've got to find a way to stop all this.

But what could I do, tied and shut away in a closet? What would Brenda do? I wondered, not that I could ever imagine her permitting herself to be in such a predicament.

"She wouldn't lie here like a dead one," I heard. Did I say that, throw my voice again?

No, she wouldn't, I thought. She wouldn't be feeling sorry for herself, moaning and groaning about how this is her own fault and how terrible the world and some people are. She wouldn't flee to the escape of constant sleep either.

I looked up at the closet doorknob. To me, with my wrists bound behind my back and my ankles bound together, it was as far a reach as the moon itself. Struggling, turning and twisting, I managed to get to my knees.

Now what? I wondered. I couldn't bring my leg forward to get on my feet, but I could move inches at a time to get myself down to the part of the closet that had some shelving for shoes in it. Then I leaned over until I was on my left side and I extended my legs. Using my hands, I pushed myself around until my feet were at the bottom shelf. Once there, I pushed hard against the shelving. My back was against the opposite wall. As I pushed, my lower back rose and I pressed my hands to the wall. It took so much effort to do that much, I had to stop to catch my breath. If I didn't have enough reason to lose weight, I had it now, I thought.

After I caught my breath, I manipulated my feet until I was finally flat-footed on the closet floor. Then I straightened and pushed along the wall behind me until I actually reached a standing position. Never did I imagine that such a simple move would seem like such a monumental accomplishment. I had a rush of excitement and renewed hope.

I slid along the wall until I was at the door and my hands were just below the door handle. I leaned over and then got to my toes and again pushed my lower back up until my fingers found the handle. For a few moments, I couldn't figure out how to manipulate it, which way to turn it, down or up. I pushed up when down didn't do anything, but I wasn't getting it up high enough apparently. My hands were down too low and I couldn't raise my arms higher. It was too awkward.

I had also not anticipated how being without any nourishment for so long would effect me when I made all this physical effort. I felt my head spin and my legs wobble. I closed my eyes and once again waited for my heart to stop pounding and my breathing to get better. Then I stood there thinking. I needed an inch or so more height. Another idea occurred to me. Sliding back along the wall, I turned and squatted enough to reach into the shelves so I could grasp a pair of high boots. I pulled them out and dropped them to the floor. What I wanted to do was stand on them.

The next part seemed to take me hours, but I slid along the wall again, shoving the boots along until I was sure I was close enough to the closet door and the handle. Because my ankles were bound, I couldn't raise my foot and step on the boots. I held my breath and leaped, turning myself slightly so that I would come down on them. It was awkward and uneven, causing me to fall hard onto my shoulder, this time even rapping my head against the closet floor.

I just lay there, exhausted, and once again feeling defeated. I screamed in frustration and then turned and, pulling my legs up, pounded at the closet door. I couldn't get my legs back enough to strike the door hard, but I did what I could and then I stopped, closed my eyes and rested. Before I could start again, I saw the handle of the closet door jiggle.

They had come back, I thought. Something had gone wrong. Who knew what they would do now, especially if they heard me making all this noise and effort to get out? I raised my feet in anticipation. I would fight with every ounce of strength. The doorknob clicked and the door opened so gradually, I thought it was being pushed by my breath.

I stared in joyful disbelief.

Echo was there. Still bound around her ankles and at the wrists, but Skeeter had not put her arms behind her. She was able to lift her arms and get her hands on that doorknob. She had managed to roll, slide, and whatever from the bed to the closet and then get to her knees and get her hands around the knob.

I wished she could hear my cry of joy. She smiled as if she had and I twisted and turned to get myself rolled out of the closet.

"You did good," I told her. She nodded. I saw how streaked with tears her face was.

What would we do now? I wondered. I turned my back to her to show her how my wrists were bound with the wire. She was able to use her hands even though her wrists were tightly bound together. She worked on the knot. It was difficult and she stopped and whined her frustration, but I kept encouraging her until finally, she made some headway and became encouraged and more determined herself. I could feel the wire loosening until finally, she was able to pull it far enough apart for me to jiggle my hands free.

I turned and hugged her and then I quickly undid her wrists. We both smiled and laughed with joy as we untied our ankles. Once again, I had to pause to catch my breath, but I wasn't going to linger long. When I stood straight this time, I felt the ache in my legs. I had to move about and limber up quickly. I put on a new pair of panties and another pair of jeans. I located my shoes where Skeeter had tossed them and then we went to the door. She was worried they were still in the house, but I had no doubt they were well on their way to putting their plan to work, which meant going to the attorney they had dug up from some legal junkyard and then rushing over to the hospital to get Mrs. Westington's signature.

One of the first things I did when we walked out and down the stairs was go to the kitchen and get some orange juice. I found some bread and smeared some jam on a slice, gobbling the food quickly. Echo was signing all sorts of questions at me: "Why did they do this to us? Were they gone? How was her grandmother? Can we go to see her? Where was Trevor?"

I made my answers as simple as I could, explaining that her mother was just after money. I told her about Trevor's mother dying and then I said we had to go see her grandmother immediately. She nodded, eager. How ironic it was that she was the one who had saved me, I thought, and then I thought back to when she had first appeared in that bedroom doorway and saw what Skeeter was trying to do to me.

"How did you know I was still here?" I signed.

She smiled and pointed up.

"Destiny," she said. She pronounced the name rather well, I thought. And then she signed, "She told me."

It was a strange and eerie moment for me. What did she mean? She couldn't hear anything, even if my voice had come through the walls.

"How?" I asked her.

"I found her in my closet," she explained. "And I knew you would never leave without her."

I smiled. Yes, I thought. Destiny did tell her. In more ways than one, Destiny had rescued me again. "Thank you, Uncle Palaver," I muttered under my breath.

"Come on," I said. "We have work to do."

It didn't occur to me until we had stepped out of the house that Skeeter had taken my car, and of course, Trevor was still away.

"Hurry," I said, and led her to the motor home. How happy I was that the legal system moved so slowly and it was still here on the property. Echo was excited about riding in it. Despite all that had been done to her and all she had seen, she still had a young girl's innocent view of the world. How sad it was to have to give that up, but eventually we all had to do it.

I started the engine and turned it around to head down the driveway. I really had no detailed plan. I thought first about going directly to the police to tell them what Skeeter and Rhona had done to us, but my first concern wasn't that. It was Mrs. Westington, so I drove as quickly as I could to the hospital. Of course, I was afraid of what it would be like confronting Rhona and Skeeter, and I was even more frightened of what effect it might have on Mrs. Westington if it was done in front of her. The commotion would be too much, but I had to show her that I hadn't deserted her.

When we turned into the hospital parking lot, I looked about quickly for Skeeter and Rhona's van. I didn't see it and first wondered if they had already been here and gotten what they wanted out of Mrs. Westington. Perhaps we were too late. I found two empty parking places wide enough for the motor home. As soon as I pulled in, I hurried Echo along and we crossed the lot to the hospital entrance. Of course, I knew what I looked like to everyone, rushing about in a frenzy, my hair a mess, with Echo clinging to my hand, her own face still tear-streaked and her hair just as wild. I was sure we both made for quite a sight.

As soon as we stepped out of the elevator onto Mrs. Westington's floor, I thought finally, finally, luck had decided to smile upon us. There at the end of the hallway, in conference with a nurse, was Doctor Battie. He glanced in our direction, looked briefly at us, and then down at the chart before lifting his head again with surprise.

"I thought you had left the area," he said as we approached him.

"She lied to you. I have to speak with you," I said, eyeing the nurse, who looked at us with curiosity and interest. "Privately, please."

He nodded and led me and Echo down the hallway to an empty patient's room.

"How is Mrs. Westington?" I asked before saying anything else.

"I'm not seeing enough improvement yet to be comfortable with her having any other procedure. Something is really upsetting her," he added. "What's happening here?"

How do I begin? I wondered. Without speaking, I showed him my wrists.

"What's that from?" he asked.

And then I told him. He listened, his face changing from mere curiosity to concern and then anger. He signed with Echo and learned her story as well.

"You were right not going directly to Mrs. Westington with all this," he said. "Wait here."

He left us and when he returned, he had two hospital security guards with him.

"I've called the police," he said. "They're on their way. I just spoke with Mrs. Westington and without revealing anything, asked her when her daughter was coming to see her. She told me she was supposed to be here in about twenty minutes. She had phoned her from some attorney's office."

"What should we do?" I asked him.

"Just wait here. I'm having one of the nurses bring you something to drink and eat. I've asked her to attend to your wrists as well. Just sit in that chair and rest," he said, his face taut with anger.

"We would like to see Mrs. Westington."

"Soon," he said.

He pulled the security guards aside and spoke to them before leaving again. The nurse brought us some food and juice and we ate and waited. She put some antiseptic on my wrists where they were skinned and then bandaged them.

A policeman arrived with a detective shortly afterward. She introduced herself as Detective Temple. I told her what had been done to us. She was very interested in knowing more about this man Bill, who supposedly was keeping my car. I told her I didn't know anything else. She asked me a lot of questions about Skeeter. When I described his tattoos, she looked very happy.

She stopped talking when we heard Doctor Battie in the hallway. He was speaking to Rhona and Skeeter, who had just stepped out of the elevator.

"Your mother has been moved to another room," he said loudly enough for us to hear. "The first door on the left down the hall," he told them, which was where we were.

The hate, anger, and fury I had in me was soon to plant a smile of satisfaction on my face, a smile as full of delight and contentment as one on a well-fed cat. Rhona, her right hand grasping her portfolio of documents, entered first. Skeeter followed with his hands in his pockets, his eyes down, his lips in a grin. She stopped and gasped and he looked up, the shock reverberating through his lips and into his eyes.

"How the hell did you two—" he began.

"Shut up," Rhona said, looking at the policeman standing to their right and the detective on their left. The hospital security guards stepped up behind them.

"Sanford Bickers," Detective Temple said, "you're under arrest for parole violation, suspicion of drug trafficking, grand-theft auto, and illegal detention of a minor."

The policeman with her stepped up to Skeeter and put his hands in cuffs.

"Rhona Westington, you're under arrest for illegal detention of a minor and suspicion of accessory to drug trafficking and grand-theft auto."

She was placed in handcuffs as well.

"This is ridiculous," Rhona said. "That girl is making all this up. She's a lesbian, a stray my foolish and sick mother took in, and she was raping my daughter. We caught her in bed with her. Just ask my daughter. Go on. Ask her," she said.

Detective Temple ignored her and recited their Miranda rights. All the while Rhona glared at me and I stared back at her. I had Brenda's eyes now. They wouldn't waver.

"You won't get away with this!" she screamed at me. Skeeter kept his head down.

They were both led back to the elevator.

"I'll be up to the house in about two hours," Detective Temple told me. "I'll get a full, detailed statement from you and I'd like you to show me where you were kept and with what you were tied up as well."

All the while I hadn't looked at Echo, who had been sitting frozen in the chair to my right. No one had really looked at her. While Rhona and Skeeter were arrested and read their rights, she had been crying and she still was. I jumped up to comfort her. Doctor Battie came in and helped me calm her. He told her that her grandmother was asking for her and it was very, very important that she not look upset or it would agitate her grandmother. She sucked back her tears quickly. I took her into the bathroom and helped her wash her face and fix her hair.

"Don't tell her anything about what they did to us," I signed and spoke. "It could make her sicker." She understood and nodded.

Then we went to see Mrs. Westington. The moment she set eyes on us, her face lit up with such joy that it brought tears to mine. Aside from my own parents, I doubted anyone would be as happy to set eyes on the likes of me. Echo ran to her and hugged her.

"I knew that girl was lying to me about you. I pretended to believe her," she said. "There's more than one way to skin a cat and she's a cat that needs skinning. Now what's going on here? When am I going to hear the whole truth, every nitty-gritty detail?"

Doctor Battie, who was standing right behind me, cleared his throat. I looked up at him.

"You're not making things any better, Mr. Smarty Pants, by having my children keep things from me," Mrs. Westington told him. I didn't miss her referring to me as one of her children.

"You're not making things any better by insisting on getting right into the muck before I give you the go-ahead," he replied. "Now when you behave and let me get that blood pressure down so we can get that pacemaker started, we'll tell you all the miserable, dirty things you want."

Even she had to laugh. She turned to me. "At least tell me about Trevor," she said, eyeing the doctor. "Where is he? Why haven't I heard a peep out of him?"

I explained where he was and why.

"I guessed as much," she said. She turned to the doctor. "Well, how long are you going to keep me in here?"

"It's up to you," Doctor Battie told her.

She sighed. "All right, all right. I'll calm down," she promised.

She turned to Echo and began to sign. I watched her carefully and I watched Echo's responses as well. She kept to her promise and told her nothing terrible. A little over an hour later, we left, assuring her we'd return in the morning. She didn't wonder why we weren't coming back that evening. She could see the fatigue in my face and just nodded.

"Come closer," she said, and I leaned over. She reached up to hug me and bring her lips close to my ear. "I don't have to know what happened exactly," she said. "But I know I should thank you for my granddaughter."

I said nothing. My throat closed with my effort to keep myself from bursting into tears. I kissed her cheek and then took Echo's hand and walked out of the hospital room. Doctor Battie approached us before we got onto the elevator.

"You all right, April?"

"I think so. I'll just get some sleep, after we have a good, hot meal."

"Okay. You can call me if you need anything. I'm keeping my fingers crossed. The cardiologist and I would like to take care of her tomorrow or the day after the latest."

"Good," I said. "We need her home."

We got into the elevator and went down to the hospital entrance. I could tell from the way some of the staff was looking at us and some of the other security personnel that our story was spreading quickly. For a few moments after we entered the motor home, I just sat in the driver's seat staring out at the small patch of woods across the way. I was really very tired. I shouldn't have been so brave and independent. I should have had someone else drive us back, I thought.

"Do you always have to be such a wimp?" I heard.

I had thrown my voice again. It seemed appropriate to do it in the motor home, even without Destiny alongside us. It was still coming from her.

I laughed to myself, started the engine, and drove out of the parking lot. When I gazed in the rearview mirror, I saw Echo sprawled on the sofa, asleep. She looked younger, more like a six- or seven-year-old. What a difficult journey she had been on during her young life, I thought. The two of us were like the sisters of misery. We were in the same hard-luck family. Maybe now it was going to change. Maybe we had both rounded an important corner. Maybe we could dream again.

Despite what we had accomplished, Echo was still frightened when we arrived at the house. I could see it in the way she looked about and at the front door. I imagined she was wondering if her mother and Skeeter could somehow have managed to return here. I put my arm around her shoulders and smiled.

"We'll be all right now," I promised. "They're not coming back. Don't worry." The sign for *worry* required a bit of acting. The right fingertips were to be drummed against your forehead and you were supposed to frown and looked very concerned.

She laughed at my signing and we went into the house. I checked to see what we could have for our dinner. I thought we'd have an early one since we had really skipped lunch and breakfast. Shortly after, I heard the doorbell and went to greet Detective Temple. She was accompanied by another detective, a tall, lean, dark-haired man she introduced as Lieutenant Hampton.

"I hate to put you through it again," she told me. "But we need to have all the information, details, and evidence."

"It's okay," I said, and led them upstairs to the guest room and the closet where I had been imprisoned. The wires, the sock were all where we had left them. Detective Temple looked at me closely as I described the details and then she suddenly took my hand, nodded at Lieutenant Hampton, and pulled me aside.

"What else did he do to you?" she asked.

I started to cry.

"I know how hard it is for you. I've been involved with a number of rape victims. What I want to do is have him locked up and the key thrown into the Pacific."

I nodded and described what he had done and tried to do while I was bound up in the closet. I explained how Echo had interrupted it, but I didn't mention Destiny. I thought that would only confuse her. She took notes. Lieutenant Hampton took pictures of the room, the closet, and then they went into Rhona's room and searched their things. Apparently, they found drugs and information that made them happy.

"We'll have your car back here before morning," she promised. "We know where it is and with whom it is. We've been watching these people and the investigation is all coming together now."

"Is Rhona really part of all that?" I asked.

"She's associated with them and certainly involved to some extent. My guess is she'll get frightened enough to turn on them. It usually happens. Her mother is not going to be there for her this time, I'm sure."

"Nevertheless, I'm sure Mrs. Westington would have preferred to have been able to be there for her," I said.

"Yes, I suppose so. Any mother would rather that. Get some rest. We'll be talking to you again over the next few days."

She and Lieutenant Hampton left and I suddenly felt like I would keel over if I didn't get some rest. I told Echo, who was just as tired as I was. She was still frightened and insecure. I ended up sleeping in her room beside her on her bed with Mr. Panda between the both of us. Just for a few seconds, I hesitated, remembering Rhona's accusations, but I wouldn't let her twisted, dirty mind stop me from giving Echo comfort. The truth was I didn't mind her being beside me. We were comforting each other.

"Wait," she signed just as I started to close my eyes. I watched her get out of bed. She turned and smiled back at me at her closet door.

Of course, I thought.

She opened the door and I joined her quickly to bring Destiny out. Echo wanted her watching over us as much as I did. I set her in the chair to the right of us. Echo then crawled into bed.

"Thank you, Destiny," I said.

I didn't have to throw my voice through her. I heard her in my mind.

"You're welcome."

I got into the bed and then Echo said, "Wait," again.

What was it this time? She rose quickly and went out of the bedroom. When she returned, she had the dream catcher we had put in Rhona's room.

"Very good," I said, attaching it above us. If there was ever a night we needed it, it was this night, I thought.

Echo smiled again and finally closed her eyes. I brushed some hair back off her eyes just the way my mother would brush mine. And then I lay back on the pillow. I fell asleep so quickly, I don't think I turned over once afer I closed my eyes.

When I woke, it was dark outside and Echo was not beside me. For a few moments, I was terribly confused, but it all quickly came back and with it, a new panic. Where was she?

I sat up. It was so quiet in the house. Then I heard what I was positive was someone talking. I heard a laugh and my heart nearly bounced into my throat.

I slipped off the bed, put on my shoes, and scrubbed the fatigue out of my cheeks. Incredibly, I gazed at myself in the mirror and fidgeted with my hair. Female vanity, I thought. There was no way to get away from it.

I descended the stairway and walked to the living room. Sitting beside Echo was Tyler Monahan. He looked up quickly when I appeared in the doorway. To me he looked like a frightened puppy cowering with its tail between its legs.

"Hi, how are you?" he asked quickly.

"I'm all right," I said.

"Everyone is talking about what happened up here. People came into our store to tell us because they knew I had been tutoring Echo."

I nodded and folded my arms under my breasts. I saw he was uncomfortable, but I wasn't about to be so forgiving so quickly.

"You know why Rhona was able to threaten me and blackmail me, don't you?"

"I figured that out after my mother told me what she had told her. I'm sorry about . . . about what I did. I didn't know Rhona would use it against you like that. I let my mother know she had done a bad thing, too."

"Uh-huh."

"No, really, I did."

I stared at him. He looked at Echo, who was smiling with such admiration at him.

"You should have. I'm glad."

"I made a decision," he said. "I've decided I shouldn't waste my education and my skills."

"What does that mean?"

"I called the school that we want Echo to attend and as it turns out, they have an opening and a need for someone like me, so I'm taking a job there. I was just explaining it to her," he said.

"Really? That's wonderful, Tyler."

"I think so," he said. "I told my mother I would be showing her more respect by using the gifts she had given me. She understands now. At least, I think she does," he said.

"If she doesn't, she's a fool," I said. I wasn't in the mood to candy-coat anything. In many more ways than I thought, I had turned into my sister, my tough, competitive sister.

He nodded meekly. "How's Mrs. Westington taking all this?"

"She doesn't know any of the nitty-gritty details and we're not letting her know until the doctor gives the okay, but she's pretty smart and knows we went through something very unpleasant."

"Yeah," he said, looking down. "I'm sure you did. I'm sure it was horrible."

"We're okay," I said firmly. "Both of us are okay."

"That's good." He raised his eyes and then smiled at Echo and stood up. "Well, I just stopped by to see how you two were and to tell you my plans. Everything's still on go for her and the school, right?"

"I'm sure it is," I said.

"Something smells pretty good," he said, and I suddenly realized there was something cooking on the stove. I hadn't done it, of course.

I signed to Echo and she signed back that she had put up a casserole her grandmother had made and left in the freezer.

"I guess I slept through it all," I said. "I guess she's capable of a lot more than everyone thinks."

"She is and she'll grow even more so when she enters the school. By this time next year, you won't recognize her."

"I won't be here that long, Tyler."

"No. Of course not," he said.

"But I'll come visit."

"Sure," he said, smiling.

We stared at each other for a moment.

"I'm sorry," he said. "I really acted—"

"Let's stop apologizing, Tyler. I'm hungry," I said, and he laughed. "Echo," I said, turning to her and signing, "should we invite Ty to dinner?"

She nodded so quickly and emphatically, I thought her eyes would roll.

"Then let's set the table," I said.

We all went to work. It felt good to be happy, to joke and to enjoy ourselves. Moments after the table was set, the doorbell rang and we greeted two police officers. Looking past them, I saw my car. They asked me to sign that I had received it and then I thanked them and they left.

Just as we sat at the table to begin to eat, the phone rang. Tyler and I looked at each other, both holding our breath. I rose and answered it in the kitchen. He remained at the table with Echo.

"Hello," I said. Every time this phone rang, it made my heart pound.

"It's Doctor Battie. Just wanted to let you know that we will be doing the pacemaker tomorrow morning. She's not exactly where I'd like her to be, but we decided not to wait any longer on it."

"What time?"

"Early. It should all be over by eight o'clock," he said.

"We'll be there," I told him.

"Okay. And how are you two doing?"

"Much better," I said.

"Good. Don't worry," he said.

I thanked him and hung up.

Don't worry?

I gazed at my reflection in the kitchen window and then signed to myself: right fingers on my temple and that over-the-top grimace.

The strings that tied us all together were wobbling. I only could pray they wouldn't snap in the morning and put Echo into that limbo I had been fleeing ever since my parents died.

15

Encore

Tyler didn't want to go right home after I told him about Mrs. Westington's surgery in the morning. We of course agreed Echo should not yet be told. In the morning I would take her to the hospital pretending it was just another visit. We decided we'd amuse her until she was tired enough to fall asleep and that way keep her from thinking about the bad things that had happened and could happen. Actually, it did the same for me.

Tyler helped me bring all Uncle Palaver's magic tricks down and carried Destiny down as well so I could perform a magic show in the living room. I returned to the motor home and brought in more of the illusions that we used in the road shows. We had Echo sit on the sofa and Tyler stood to my right and signed and explained everything I said.

I began by pretending to hypnotize a handkerchief

so it would straighten up on its own in my hand. It was an easy illusion because a flattened straw was sewn in the hem of the handkerchief and I just pressed on it to make the handkerchief rise.

Using Destiny, I went through card tricks, disappearing ball tricks, and a variety of coin and mirror tricks. Tyler sat in a chair while I magically pulled a handkerchief through his head and then levitated him a few inches off his chair. Even he was amazed and impressed. I ended up with the answering pendulum trick, which was as close to real magic as anything I had seen. At the end of a string, Uncle Palaver had a small fishing weight. He then would have a member of the audience ask a question and the ball would either swing in a straight line for a yes response or swing in a circle for a no.

"How does it do that?" Tyler asked me after I had Echo ask a question. She asked if the casserole she had heated up for us was delicious. It went into a straight line. She clapped her hands and then asked if she would have any nightmares tonight and it went into a circle.

I shrugged. "Uncle Palaver couldn't explain it either. He said it was like an old-fashioned divining rod. Maybe it's our subconscious thoughts that influence it." I smiled. "And then again, maybe not."

Tyler nodded. He gazed at Destiny, who had her arms raised as she shook her head, and he laughed.

"I guess it wasn't all bad for you on the road with your uncle."

"No, but as Mrs. Westington says, you can't stay on the road forever and run from yourself, put your head in the sand."

We saw Echo yawn.

"Time to go to sleep," I told her. I nodded at Destiny, whose eyes closed.

Echo asked Tyler if he was returning in the morning and while he glanced at me, he told her he would see her at the hospital because he was going to visit her grandmother, too. That pleased her. She asked me if I was going to sleep now as well and I told her I would be coming up soon. I wanted to put away my magic show. She looked at Tyler and then at me and nodded. After she left, Tyler helped me take the tricks and illusions out to the motor home.

"Destiny stays in the house with us," I said.

We then went upstairs to check on Echo and found her asleep, embracing Mr. Panda.

"I see you have a dream catcher, too," he said. "Not taking any chances, huh?"

"Not anymore."

He smiled. All that had happened appeared to have freed him inside so that he wasn't as guarded about his feelings and as afraid of trusting them.

We went downstairs again. I saw how he was hesitating.

"You don't have to hang around any longer, Tyler. We'll be all right."

"If you don't mind, I'd like to," he replied. "It helps me to feel better."

"Okay," I said, surprised.

We sat on the sofa in the living room and talked about his new plans and mine. I tried to keep awake, but after a while, my eyelids just shut down and I felt myself leaning more and more against him. He rose and fixed a pillow under my head and then he sat across from me in Mrs. Westington's chair. When I opened my eyes with the morning light streaking through the window, he was still there, asleep himself.

I sat up and he opened his eyes.

"Hey," he said, looking about. "What time is it?" He checked his watch. "Wow. I guess I was more tired than I thought, too."

"I've got to get Echo going. I'll get her some breakfast and then we'll drive over to the hospital."

"Right. I'll meet you there," he said. He rose and stretched. Then he smiled. "Great show last night."

"Thanks."

"See you soon." He hurried out.

I wondered what he would be telling his mother when he got home or if that even mattered anymore.

Echo and I showered and dressed. I made some coffee. I was unable to eat very much. My stomach felt as if it were full of baby snakes. Echo had some juice and a little cereal. I thought she was suspicious about my moving her along quickly and getting us out so early, but she didn't ask anything about it. We got into my car and started away. I couldn't stop my nerves from twanging. Although getting a pacemaker was usually not a terribly dangerous procedure, it was for Mrs. Westington at her age and under her circumstances. As she would be the first to tell me, I knew enough to be dangerous. Mostly, I knew the doctors were afraid of her having a much more severe stroke.

Tyler was already in the parking lot waiting for us when I drove in. He got out of his car quickly to greet us. Echo was happy to see him, but very surprised as well. She kept looking at me for more of an explanation. I knew we could hold back the truth only a few more minutes because once we were inside and she saw we weren't going to her grandmother's room, she would know something more was happening. I was glad I had Tyler with me to help explain it all with his expert signing.

At the reception desk, we found out where to go to wait. When we reached the lounge, Tyler and I finally told Echo exactly what was going on. She sat there absorbing it all and looking very frightened and small. I held her hand and tried to reassure her. By doing that I was reassuring myself. A little after eight o'clock, Doctor Battie appeared. I held my breath until I saw him smile. As he spoke, Tyler signed to Echo.

"It went well," the doctor said. "That woman's got spunk. Give her a few hours and then we'll have you visit. I'll let her know you were here and were updated."

Joyous and feeling as if a ton of trouble had been lifted from our shoulders, I declared I was finally hungry. Tyler confessed to not having had much breakfast either so we headed down to the hospital cafeteria. Echo had a better appetite as well. The three of us sat at a table and watched hospital staff, other visitors, and doctors going in and out.

"I'd like to work in a hospital someday," Echo told us, "and help people."

"After you go to school, you can be anything you want," Tyler signed, and she smiled.

"What is it really like for the hearing impaired as far as careers go?" I asked him.

"Their opportunities have improved considerably. She's a ways off from making a career decision, but you'd be surprised at how much she can do. Maybe she will work in a medical lab someday or even become a doctor."

"A doctor?"

"Who knows? She's bright enough to do most anything."

Suddenly, Echo's eyes widened. I turned to look in the direction she was facing and saw Trevor coming toward us. He looked angry enough to tear the cafeteria into shreds. His eyes went to Tyler and then to me.

"She's all right. We're all right," I said quickly.

Trevor's shoulders relaxed. "Why didn't you have the police call me at my cousin's home?" he asked. "When I phoned the house and couldn't get anyone, I called a friend of mine in Healdsburg at the Mars Hotel. Seems the whole town's talking about what happened. When I heard the grisly details, I got an earlier flight out and just drove right to the hospital."

He sat. "They both in jail then?" he asked me.

"Yes, Trevor. Skeeter was wanted for a lot more and Rhona's in big trouble now."

"I'm not surprised and not disappointed either," he said.

"Can I get you a cup of coffee, Trevor?" Tyler asked.

Trevor glared at him a moment and then nodded. "Sure. Black, no sugar," he said, and Tyler leaped to his feet. "How's Mrs. Westington doing now then?"

"She had a pacemaker put in this morning and the doctor says she's doing well, Trevor."

"And the little one here?"

"She's all right now. She's going to be fine. We all are, Trevor."

"That's good. I'm sorry I wasn't here," he said, shaking his head. "I knew I shouldn't have left you with those two. You didn't tell me the whole truth about what was going on in that house, I bet. You didn't want me to stay and you knew I wouldn't leave if I knew everything."

"You were where you had to be."

"I'm not so sure. You can give me the details later," he said. He jerked his shoulder toward Tyler. "I thought he was gone from the scene."

"He's sorry he left us," I said. "He's taking a job at the school Echo will attend, too. It'll make it easier for her."

"That so? What's his mama got to say about that?"

"Not much it seems," I said, smiling.

"Looks like a lot more than I knew went on right before my eyes," he said, smiling.

"Mrs. Westington's going to be even happier when she sees you and knows you're back," I said to change the subject.

"Oh, she'll find something to blame me for. Don't you worry about that," he said, and I laughed.

Tyler brought him his coffee. "Sorry to hear about your mother, Trevor," he told him.

Trevor looked up at him. "Thank you. April here told me about your new career plans."

"Yes," he said.

"Sounds good," Trevor said.

Tyler nodded. "Maybe the jury's finally in on me," he told me, and we both laughed. Even Trevor thought that was funny and Echo laughed because she was wrapped in our good feelings.

When sufficient time had gone by, we went to see

Mrs. Westington. Normally, the ICU nurses wouldn't have let us all in at once, but I think they were just as afraid of hearing Mrs. Westington complain as they were of hearing their superiors complain. We gathered around her bed. She looked at our faces and nodded. Then she turned to Trevor.

"How did you get back here so fast?"

"Put my whole mind to it," he replied, and she smiled.

"Don't you all stand there looking down at me like I'm hovering above my grave."

"What are you telling us?" Trevor asked her. "That old man you saw through the window of your soul ain't looking in on you anymore?"

"He'll come around when I tell him he can and not a minute before," she replied.

"I bet he won't," Trevor said, laughing. "I just bet he won't."

The doctors wanted Mrs. Westington in the hospital one more day. Of course she complained, but she gave up when she realized she was actually going to walk out of there. She promised and swore that she would behave and not do too much too quickly, but we all knew those promises were as good as the air they were written on, as she would say about other people's promises. After she came home, I tried staying on her, taking things out of her hands, moving to do things before she could, and constantly pleading with her to sit and rest. She bawled me out for being a Nervous Nelly.

Trevor gave me as much help as he could with her, and so did Echo, who probably had the most influence. Tyler came over almost every night and we had some fine dinners and times together. The day after Mrs. Westington came home, Detective Temple came to see me again and to tell us that Rhona and Skeeter had been arraigned and a hearing before trial was being scheduled. Skeeter was also wanted in two other states and would be extradited to stand trial there as well.

Despite her anger and disappointment, Mrs. Westington suffered some quiet moments of regret and sorrow about Rhona. She talked about the mistakes she might have made bringing her up and declared that she bore some responsibility for her whether or not she liked to admit it. In the end she decided to pay for an attorney, not to get Rhona off scot-free as much as to provide for her having some hope somewhere down the line.

"It's throwing good money after bad," she told me, "but I can't help it. You'll discover that you do many things you don't want to do because of your parental obligations sometimes, April."

Who said I would ever be a parent? I thought. She saw the doubt in my face.

"Don't count yourself out of anything, girl. You're too young to come to any of those kinds of conclusions," she advised.

Maybe she was right, I decided.

When Mrs. Westington was strong enough, we all went to the school Echo would attend to meet with the headmaster and some of her prospective teachers. We were shown the dormitories as well. I watched Mrs. Westington's face the whole time. I could see the battle going on in her mind. She was impressed with the facilities, the achievements of the students and their interaction, but she also saw her grand-daughter drifting away from her. The ties that had bound them together were snapping loose. She was wise enough to recognize that some of those ties kept Echo far too constricted and trapped her in a little girl's world when she should be expanding, growing, maturing, and becoming independent.

"Funny," she said as Trevor drove us home that day, "but I think I'll have had more success bringing up a girl with a hearing disability than one who was healthy in every way."

"Not every way," Trevor said, scowling back at her. "She inherited some rot from some ancestor. Of course, not on your side of the family," he added, and she smacked him playfully on the shoulder. Echo and I watched it from the rear and both laughed.

"Stick to our grapes," she told him.

"Our grapes? Now they're our grapes?"

"They always were. I just humored you so you'd do a good job."

"Well, I'll be . . . you hear that, April? Is this woman the mother of all deception or what?"

"Oh, go eat your hat," she told him.

The following day we returned to the mall to buy Echo some more new clothes. It was Mrs. Westington's idea after she saw what the other teenagers at the school were wearing.

"I guess if they all want to go on looking foolish and clownish with those baggy pants and cut up blouses and pants, there's nothing I can do about it," she decided. "I just hope she doesn't go and get rings put through her nose."

The purchases delighted Echo. I couldn't remember seeing her happier and neither could Mrs. Westington. Echo and I carried everything up to her room and I helped her organize her things for her move to the school in what was now two more days. Her preparations reminded me of my own first days at school: the anticipation, the nervousness, and the hope.

Late that same afternoon, I received a phone call from the lawyer who had been taking care of Uncle Palaver's estate. He told me it was now possible to put the motor home up for sale and he had arranged for someone to come by in the morning and drive it over to the auctioneer. He wanted me to be sure I had taken everything out of it that I wanted.

I had known this news would be coming anytime, but actually hearing it put a chill in my heart. I told Mrs. Westington and she saw it all in my face.

"You've got to let go now, April," she said. "You've got to cut the past away. I know what I'm talking about. I've done it many times and I'm doing it now. Sometimes it's painful and sometimes it's not, but it has to be. We move on."

"I know," I said. "I guess I'd better go through the motor home and get what I don't want thrown out or taken by someone."

"You want me to help you?"

"Oh, no. I'll be just fine," I said. Of course, we both knew that was a boldface lie.

When I entered the motor home, I simply stood there looking at everything at first, not knowing where to start. I went through all of Uncle Palaver's drawers, putting things in small bags and cartons. I discovered old pictures of him and my mother, even pictures he had saved of Brenda and me when we were much younger. There was one picture of him and Daddy that brought tears to my eyes. They both looked so young back then, so young and full of hope and energy. If only there was a way to bring pictures back to life, to return to those happier times.

I found another cache of money hidden in a pair of Uncle Palaver's socks. And then, I found a shoe box with clippings and pictures of the real Destiny. There was a great deal of illusion in this motor home, I thought, after I had gathered all the tricks and paraphernalia that were part of Uncle Palaver's act, but there were many fine memories of real and happier times stored here as well. What I would do with all this, I did not know, but I spent hours going through everything, separating what was obviously no longer important from what was.

Trevor stopped in to help me carry it all out. He found a place for me to store it in his winery until I had decided what I would do with it all. Mrs. Westington told me to put the linens, towels, dishes, and silverware, as well as any insignificant household items in cartons that Trevor would bring to the Salvation Army. Echo decided to help me do all that. We worked until dinnertime and afterward, we loaded everything into Trevor's truck. He would take it away in the morning.

The auctioneer's man arrived just as we were getting ready to have breakfast the next day. I had spent a night tossing and turning over it all. Once the motor home was gone and Uncle Palaver's things given away or stored, that part of my past was over, I thought. I felt as if I was cutting some umbilical cord and leaving myself totally alone, floating in the space of indecision and uncertainty.

I had to sign some papers and then the man climbed into the motor home and started the engine. Echo came out to stand beside me and watch him drive it off. I didn't cry, but the ache in my heart was so painful, I had trouble breathing.

"It's the past," Mrs. Westington insisted. "Think only about the future."

I nodded, but I didn't say anything and I didn't eat much breakfast. Afterward, I helped clear the table, get the dishes and silverware washed and put away, and then went out by myself and walked down to the lake. Echo was up in her room looking over all her new things. She was as excited now as any young girl about to begin in a new school, whether it was a school for disabled children or not. I didn't need anyone to tell me that soon I would be less important to her. There was nothing wrong with that. She desperately needed to be with her peers, have friends who had things in common with her. Her life in so many ways was just beginning.

Maybe mine was, too, I thought. As if the future was full of bells that rang to signal a new turn and a new direction, I heard Mrs. Westington calling to me from the front porch. I hurried back to the house, worried something might be wrong with her.

"It's your sister," she said. "She's on the telephone."

"My sister?" I ran into the house and picked up the receiver. "Hello, Brenda?"

"Hi, April. I'm flying into San Francisco tomorrow. I'll be there by eleven. I have a three-hour layover and then I'm going on to Seattle." She gave me the name of the airline and flight number. "We can meet and have lunch and talk," she said. "If you still want to, that is."

"Yes, I would like that very much, Brenda. How have you been doing?"

"Our team lost only one game. I met a lot of interesting people," she added. The way she stressed *interesting* made my heart skip a beat. Did she mean someone in particular? "And how have you been?" she asked.

She had no idea why, but her question made me laugh.

"Why are you laughing?"

"I'll tell you when I see you," I said. "But I'm fine now, Brenda."

"Okay."

I told her about Uncle Palaver's things and what our attorney had told me about his estate.

"We have a little money, an inheritance."

"We do have what we need from what Mom and Dad left us, you know. You ran off before I could get into that."

"It wasn't important to me then."

"You have what you need for your college education," she said. "You do intend to go to college, don't you?"

"Yes," I said. "I do," I told her firmly.

"Good. See you tomorrow."

"Okay," I said. I let out a deep breath.

"Well?" Mrs. Westington asked as soon as I walked out of the kitchen and into the living room.

"I don't know yet, Mrs. Westington."

She nodded, thoughtfully. "You know you'll always have a home here," she said. "No matter what."

"Thank you."

I never imagined that I would be so nervous about meeting my sister. A part of me desperately wanted her love and a part of me still feared her. I was so afraid that when she heard what had happened to me since I left her, she would just shake her head and, as she had done so many times in the past, call me a hopeless case, a loser who would only be a weight around her ankles. Maybe we were just too unalike to ever get along. I knew I would have trouble sleeping, anticipating.

Mrs. Westington had insisted I take Rhona's room back. She had Lourdes clean it as if someone with a contagious flu had been sleeping in it. It was clean enough to be used as a surgical station in a hospital. I kept saying it was good enough and Mrs. Westington kept finding something else to wash or polish. Even Lourdes looked at me as if Mrs. Westington had gone mad. In the end I appreciated it, however.

I placed Destiny in a chair near the bed and slept comfortably up to the night before, when I had been troubled about selling off Uncle Palaver's motor home, and now I feared I'd be tossing and turning most of the night again.

"Stop all this worrying," my voice thrown through Destiny told me. "What will be will be."

I finally fell asleep. Echo was very curious about where I was going and why right after breakfast. When she learned I was meeting my sister, her face filled with concern. Even though she was going off to school, she had harbored the belief I was remaining behind to live with her grandmother. Neither Mrs. Westington nor I had spent any time telling her that. Most likely I would be leaving, too.

Later, Echo stepped out on the porch to watch me drive away. She looked so sad I was tempted not to go. I signed I would be back soon and she smiled and waved. I looked at her in my rearview mirror and saw she didn't go back inside until I was turning out of the driveway.

Our lives are filled with so many good-byes, I thought. There were good-byes to our parents and grandparents, of course, and good-byes to our other loved ones, but we also said good-bye to ourselves, to our youth especially. As I drove to the San Francisco airport to meet Brenda, I did feel older, almost battle weary, a scarred veteran of wars, toughened, perhaps more cynical, but certainly more self-confident. It was something Brenda saw immediately.

She came walking out of the gate to meet me and paused for a moment, her eyes blinking as though she had to be sure she was looking at me before continuing. She had her knapsack on her and carried a small athletic bag. She, too, looked different to me. She had her hair cut the same way and she looked to be the same weight, but she wasn't as tall and intimidating as I remembered. Perhaps, without my realizing it, I had grown a few inches.

I had my hair brushed back. It was longer than she would have remembered it.

"Hi," she said.

For a moment we were both unsure of what to do next. Should we hug each other? She moved first, putting the bag down, and we did. Then she stepped back.

"You look like you lost a few."

"A few," I said.

She stared at me. "I forgot how much you look like Daddy."

"I never thought so."

"Oh, yeah. You have his eyes and his nose. They say as you get older, you start to look like your parents more and more. Where can we get something to eat? I'm starving. I hated the plastic food on the plane."

"Down here is a sort of cafeteria-style place," I said, pointing to the right. She picked up her bag and we started toward the restaurant. "Was it a long flight?"

"Long enough. I've been on so many planes, I can't distinguish one from another anymore."

We entered the restaurant and I chose a salad and a bottle of water. She said nothing, but I caught her watching me choose food for myself just as she always did. She did fill her tray with hot food, some juice, bread, and a fruit dessert. We sat at a table in the far corner.

"Where should we begin?" she asked, buttering her bread. She looked up when I didn't respond.

"I don't know. Probably with my meeting up with Uncle Palaver."

She nodded. "Good. I don't want to talk about Celia."

"You haven't heard from her since—"

"No. That's over. Go on, tell me what it was like being on the road with him, doing those shows."

I described it as best I could. She ate and listened, but I felt she was looking past the stories and the descriptions. She was studying me so hard. When I described Uncle Palaver and his Destiny, she shook her head.

"I really did use to wonder about that. He never brought her around. There was always one excuse or another. How sad. Where's the doll?"

"I still have it. I won't let it go."

"I see. And after he died, this old lady just took you into her home to be with her deaf granddaughter?"

"Yes," I said. "Mrs. Westington."

"Well, what's that been like, living there?"

I talked so long and enthusiastically about Trevor, Echo, Tyler, and Mrs. Westington, Brenda's eyes just remained wide the whole time. She smiled and nodded and then, when I began to talk about Rhona and Skeeter, her face darkened. I told her what they had done to Echo and me, about their arrest and their upcoming trials.

"I'll have to be a witness, of course."

"All this just happened to you?"

"Yes, and to Echo."

"Did he actually rape you?"

"Almost," I said. "But there are enough charges beside that against him to put him away for a long time."

She looked away and then took a deep breath. I couldn't be sure, but it looked like she was pulling back tears.

"I felt terrible the day you ran off and not because of the reasons you think. I knew Mom would have wanted me to look after you and Daddy expected it. I left you out there all by yourself."

"No, you didn't, Brenda. Besides, I was with Uncle Palaver."

"He left you, too. You were with strangers."

"Not long. They've become my family."

She winced. "That's good," she said. She played with her remaining food for a few moments. I took advantage of the silence and ate some of my salad. She continued, her head down. "I made a terrible mistake with you, April. I should have been more truthful and forthcoming about my sexuality."

"No, you—"

"Yes, I should have. Even back when we were in the public school together. I should have taken you into my confidence. I know how confusing it must have been for you when you first realized and how that must have impacted on your own identity. It's very important to be comfortable with yourself, with your own sexuality, no matter what that might be."

"I think I am. Now," I said.

"Good, but I left you out there to wallow in all this . . . distortion. I'm sorry. I've been too involved with myself."

"I don't blame you for anything, Brenda."

"You should, but okay, I'm glad if you don't," she said. "Anyway, what do you want to do now? Will you come live with me in Seattle?"

"Will I be in the way?"

"Never. I'm not going to lie to you, however. I'm with someone again, someone not as absorbed with herself as Celia was. She's an assistant coach, and I know you'll like her. As a friend," she added quickly. "We've got this four-bedroom house with a real yard and an office you can use for your schoolwork. You still have to finish your senior year, right?"

"Yes. I thought I would just take an equivalency test, but I think I'd like to enroll and have at least part of a year's worth of real school."

"Good." She looked at her watch and then she dug into her athletic bag. "Here's all the information you need about contacting me. You'll drive up as soon as you can. I'll see about the school and get that started for you. Can you head up there right away?"

"Yes," I said.

"We don't have much, I guess, just each other now."

"We have a lot more than many people have. I've learned that," I said, and she smiled.

"You're very grown up, April. I can feel it. You've grown up quickly, mainly because you had to. I hope you haven't missed anything important on the way."

"We all do, Brenda, but I'll make up for it."

She pulled her head back. "Who's given you all this wisdom?"

"A little old lady who dips into her well of experience and gives me a cup of this and that."

She laughed. "Sounds like I should meet her."

"I hope you will someday."

She rose. "I got to make the plane."

"Right."

Off to my left, I caught a woman signing to a little girl. Brenda saw where I was looking.

"What is she telling her?"

"She's telling her not to be afraid. She's promising she'll always be right beside her. It's probably going to be her first plane trip."

"You understood all that?"

"Bits and pieces, enough to figure it out."

"Maybe you found yourself a career," Brenda said with a look of admiration.

I shrugged. "Maybe. What I did learn was people with good hearing don't always listen to each other as much as people without any hearing at all do."

She tilted her head. "Yeah," she said. "I want to meet this old lady."

"I'll arrange it," I called after her. "But you better not call her an old lady."

She turned and laughed and in that moment, I saw my father and my mother standing beside her, the same smile on their faces, and I remembered what Mrs. Westington first told me about how your loved ones who have gone could still be watching over you: "They do their best to watch over us and lead us to happiness."

Why can't it be true? I thought.

Epilogue

I had mixed feelings about still being there to accompany Echo to her school. I could feel the way she was torn, looking back at us and then looking at the school and all it promised to be for her. She hugged and held on to me as if she believed she would never see me again. I promised I would be back. I explained that for one thing, I had to be back for the upcoming trials.

Tyler came out of the building and escorted her in and helped her get settled. It obviously made a huge difference. After he got her settled in, he and I walked back to the parking lot while Mrs. Westington remained with Echo to help her unpack her things.

"She'll be fine here," he said.

"I know. It's just hard for Mrs. Westington. It's like bringing your child to her first day of school."

"Well, it is her first day, really. So, you're headed up to Seattle then?"

"Yes. My sister's getting me enrolled in the school there. Thanks for helping me with the equivalency preparation. I'm sure it will come in handy when I'm actually in classes."

"I expect it will. You'll be a good student," he said, slipping into his cool, evaluative manner. He realized it immediately and smiled. "Drop me a line when you can and let me know how you're doing."

"I will and you write back, too."

"Absolutely. I'll keep my eye on Mrs. Westington as well," he said when we reached the parking lot. Trevor was waiting in the car and Mrs. Westington hadn't come out yet.

"That'll be nice."

He thought a moment and then turned to me. "Look, April, I'm really sorry about—"

"Don't," I said. "Let's pretend none of it happened, okay? I'll be back and I'll be different and you'll be different and we'll see what that means for us then."

He smiled. "Right. Say good-bye to Destiny for me, will you?"

"You know I will," I said, and he laughed. He started to turn back to the building, stopped, and took my hand again to draw me closer and kiss me.

"Bye," he whispered, and walked back to the building. I watched until he went inside. Then I went to the car. Trevor had seen it all, but he said nothing. Moments later, Mrs. Westington appeared and he got out to open the door for her. She bawled him out for that.

"I don't need a chauffeur," she snapped. "You're not driving Miss Daisy."

He shook his head and got back behind the wheel. On the way home afterward, Mrs. Westington was terribly silent. Trevor and I talked continuously so there'd be no long moments of silence.

When we reached the house, she wobbled a bit more than usual when she stepped out of the car this time. "Starting to feel my age," she remarked. "Guess I'll have to ease up on that gas pedal."

"What did you tell me once? You think bad things and bad things will happen. Don't go giving advice you won't follow yourself," I lectured, and she laughed.

"Look what I turned loose on the world, Trevor," she said, looking back at him.

"Yes, Ma'am. You did good."

She nodded and then looked off in the direction of the school. "I hope she's not frightened tonight," she said.

"I gave her Mr. Panda. She'll have him beside her," I said.

She raised her eyebrows as if she was getting ready to make fun of the idea and then she just nodded. "Most likely that'll help," she agreed, and we went into the house.

I had to get my things together. Brenda had called to let me know everything was set up at the new house and to give me clear directions. I didn't have all that much. Trevor put some of the cartons with Uncle Palaver's things in them in the trunk and back-seat beside Destiny.

"You're going to get some looks driving around with that doll in your car," he said. "On the other hand, you've got to get real close to see it's just a doll."

"It's when you get real close that you realize it isn't just a doll," I told him, and he looked at me and smiled.

"I'm not going there," he said. "My great-grandma had a magic doll, something akin to voodoo. I never mention it to Mrs. Westington. She makes fun of my superstitions and such as it is. I'm putting a case of the wine in your car, too. Maybe your sister and her friends will like it."

"I bet they will. Thank you, Trevor."

I looked back at the house. Saying good-bye to Mrs. Westington was going to be difficult, even with the promise to return soon. She was keeping herself busy in the kitchen, pretending that nothing different had occurred or would.

"I made some sandwiches for you," she said when I appeared in the kitchen doorway. "No need to stop and eat that ratty road food they serve in some of those run-down places truckers go to."

"Thank you," I said, taking the bag.

"You sure you got everything?"

"Whatever I forgot, I'll get when I come back."

"Right," she said.

"You know I have to come back."

"Of course you do."

"You're not going to get sick on me while I'm away or anything, are you?"

"Now who you asking that?" she said indignantly. "I have plenty to keep me busy and healthy here. Who has time to get sick? I can't depend on that man or that maid to keep this place up to snuff."

"Good," I said. "I want to thank you—"

"Stop before you start," she said sharply. "Strangers go through all that thank you for this and thank you for that business. We're beyond it. Just go do what you have to do and make yourself successful. That's the way to thank me, girl."

"Okay. Can I kiss you good-bye?"

"No. Just kiss me and get yourself on the road and you drive extra carefully, too."

"Yes, ma'am," I said. I hugged her. She felt so fragile and small and yet, she felt like a world of love. I didn't want to let go of her anymore than Echo wanted to let go of me. But I did. And I smiled and didn't cry.

"That maid of mine is late again," she muttered, turning away quickly. "Don't know why I keep her."

"Yes," I said, as if I had heard it a million times and would hear it a million more.

I walked out slowly. I didn't expect her to follow and wave to me from the porch. Trevor was at my car, washing off the windows.

"All right then," he said. "You take care, hear?"

"I will. And I'll be back for your harvest to help."

"Long as you remember to handle those grapes like liquid gold."

"I will. I promise. Take care of her," I said. I hugged him and he held on to me, too.

"Take care of her?" he said after I got in. "Fat chance. She'll be taking care of me until one or the other goes trotting off into the shadows."

"You keep those shadows back," I said.

"Yes, Ma'am."

He stepped away. I started the engine, glanced

back at Destiny, who looked very thoughtful to me suddenly. And then I drove out, pausing at the end of the driveway to gaze back at the house.

She was in the front window, watching.

Despite herself.

She was there and always would be.

SIMON & SCHUSTER
PROUDLY PRESENTS

BROKEN FLOWER

VIRGINIA ANDREWS®

Coming soon from
Simon & Schuster

Turn the page for a preview of
Broken Flower . . .

My mother grasped my shoulders and even shook me as she spoke.

"Never, never let Grandmother Emma see you without any clothes on, Jordan," she warned in a loud whisper. "Don't tell Ian and don't even tell Daddy about this yet. He's liable to slip and say something. Your grandmother watches every little thing we do in this house as it is," my mother added and let me go.

Why would all this anger my grandmother Emma? I wondered. If she did find out, would she tell us to leave her house? Would Daddy be just as angry?

Mama read my fears in my eyes.

"I'm sorry, honey. I didn't meant to frighten you. It's not your fault. Everything that is happening to you is just happening to you too early," she said in a softer voice. "It's too much of a surprise. It's just better if no one else knows for now, okay?"

"Okay, Mama," I said. She looked relieved, but I was still trembling. She helped me into my pajamas and into bed.

Suddenly, something else occurred to her and she went to the dirty clothes hamper in my bathroom. I had no idea what she was doing, but she reached in and began pulling out my socks, panties, and shirts. She held up my panties and looked closely at them before tossing it all back into the hamper.

"What are you looking for, Mama?" I asked her.

She thought a moment and then she sat on my bed and took my hand into hers.

"You're way too young for this conversation, Jordan. I don't even know how to begin it with you."

"What conversation?"

"The conversation my mother had with me when my body started to change, but you're not even seven and I was nearly thirteen before she decided I had to have the most important mother-daughter talk with her. Something very dramatic happened to me first."

"What?" I asked, my eyes wide with expectation.

"I menstruated."

"What?" I scrunched my nose. It didn't sound very good or like any fun.

She was quiet. I saw her eyes glisten. She was holding back tears. Why?

"I'm not going to have this conversation with you," she suddenly decided firmly and stood up. "This is just not happening. We don't need to talk about this yet. Remember my warning, however," she added, nodding at me. "Don't let anyone else see you naked. Especially Grandmother Emma," she emphasized.

My mother hated the idea of our moving in to live with Grandmother Emma. I think the saddest day in her life was the day we walked out of our home and came here. In the beginning she would often forget, make wrong turns and head toward our old home, not remembering it was no longer her house until she nearly pulled into the driveway. On a few occasions, I was the one who reminded her. She'd stop and look and say, "Oh," as if she had just woken from a dream.

I had lived there five and a half of my six years and eleven months. Ian was just a little more than eight when my parents bought the house. Before that they had been living in one of my grandfather's apartment buildings. In those days there was supposedly a great deal of hope and promise. After all, how could my father not succeed? He was the son of Blake and Emma March, and my grandfather Blake March had been a vice president of Bethlehem Steel during its heyday, what Grandmother Emma called The Golden Age, a time when Bethlehem Steel supplied armies, built cities, and had a fleet of twenty-six ships. If she had told me about it once, she had told me a hundred different times.

"You have to understand how important it was," she always said as an introduction. "Bethlehem Steel was the Panama Canal's second-best customer. Lunch each day for the upper management of which your grandfather was an essential part was held at the headquarters building along Third Street and was equivalent to a four-star dining experience. Each department had its own dining room on the fifth floor and each executive enjoyed a five-course meal."

Once Grandmother Emma permitted me to look at her albums and I saw pictures of their lawn parties during the summer months. Other executives from Bethlehem Steel and their wives and children would be invited, as well as many of the area's leading businessmen, politicians, lawyers and judges. There was music and all sorts of wonderful things to eat. She told us that in those days the champagne flowed like water. She pointed out Daddy when he was Ian's age, dressed in his suit and tie and looking like a perfect little gentleman, the heir to a kingdom of fortune and power.

My mother always said my father grew up spoiled. Whenever she accused him of it, he didn't deny it. In fact, he seemed proud of it, as proud as a prince. For most of his young life, he was attended by a nanny who was afraid of not pleasing him and losing her job. When he was school age, he was enrolled in a private school and then a preparatory school before going to his first university. He flunked out of two colleges and never did get a degree. My grandfather eventually set him up in business by foreclosing on a supermarket which was renamed March's Mart in Bethlehem. It was expected that because the business now had the March name attached, it could be nothing but a success and the expectation was he would eventually create a supermarket chain.

However, Daddy's supermarket business was always hanging by a thread or as my grandmother Emma would often say, "Was always doing a tap dance on the edge of financial ruin." Our expenses grew and grew and our own home became too much to maintain. Since my seventy-two-year-old grandmother lived alone now in this grand house after my grandfather had died, she decided that it made no economic sense for us to live elsewhere. Economics reigned in our world the way religion might in other people's lives.

Mama always said, "For the Marches, the portfolio was the Bible with the First Commandment being *Thou shalt not waste a penny.*"

Even so, my father never had much interest in being a businessman. He hired a general manager to run the market and was so uninvolved in the day-to-day activities that it came as a surprise to him to learn it was on the verge of bankruptcy. My grandfather invested twice in it to keep it alive, and after my grandfather's death, my grandmother gave my father some money, too, but in exchange she forced us to sell our home and move in with her. Daddy was permitted to have assistant managers, but he had to become the general manager.

After that, Grandmother Emma took over our lives as if my parents were incapable of running their own personal financial affairs. "Practice efficiencies and tighten your belts" were the words we heard chanted around us those days. Once I heard Mama tell Daddy that Grandmother Emma had cash registers in every room in her house ringing up charges even for the air we breathed. I actually looked for them.

It didn't surprise me that my mother had complaints about Grandmother Emma. I don't think my mother and Grandmother Emma were ever fond of each other. According to what I overheard my mother say to my father, my grandmother actually tried to prevent their marriage. My mother came from what Grandmother Emma called "common people." My mother's father also had worked for Bethlehem Steel, but as a steel worker, a member of the union and not as an executive. Both her parents had died—her father from a heart attack and her mother from a massive stroke. Mama always said it was stress that killed them both, whatever that meant.

My mother had an older brother, Uncle Orman, who was a carpenter and lived way off in Oregon where, according to what I was told, he scratched out a meager living, working only when he absolutely had to work. He was married to my aunt Ada, a girl he knew from high school, and they had three boys they named after The Beatles: Paul, my age; Ringo, a year younger; and John, two years younger, all of whom we had seen only once. They were invited to visit us, but never came, which was something I think pleased Grandmother Emma.

"Your grandmother thinks your father went slumming when he dated me," Mama once told me. I didn't know what slumming meant exactly at the time, but have since understood it to mean she thought he should have married someone as rich or at least nearly as rich.

However, even though Grandmother Emma scrutinized us like an airport security officer when we entered a room, I didn't think it would be too difficult to keep my new secret from her. Since we had moved into her house, my grandmother had not once set foot in my room. She didn't even come over to our side of the house and said nothing about our living quarters except to warn my mother not to change a thing. She had set up imaginary boundaries so that Ian and I were discouraged from going into her side as well.

We were now living in what had once been the guest quarters in what everyone in our community called the March Mansion. It was a very large Queen Anne, an elaborate Victorian-style house Grandmother Emma described as romantic even though it was, as she said, a product of the most unromantic era, the Machine age. She often went into great detail about it and I was often called upon to parrot her descriptions for her friends.

The mansion had a free classic style with classical columns raised on stone piers, a Palladian window at the center of the second story and dentil moldings. The house had nineteen rooms and nine bedrooms. Although a great deal had been added on and redone, the house was built in the early 1890s and was considered a historic Pennsylvania property, which was something my grandmother never wanted us to forget. Her lectures about it made me feel like I was living in a museum and could be sat down to take a pop quiz any moment of any day, which is what would happen if she asked me to recite about it to her friends.

Ian wouldn't mind being tested on the house. He could not only get a hundred every time; he could give my grandmother the quiz, not only about the house, but all the history surrounding it, even the history of her precious Bethlehem Steel Company.

Daddy's old bedroom was on my grandmother's side of the house, but we knew the door was kept locked. It was opened with what Ian called an old-fashioned skeleton key. Only Nancy, the maid, entered it once a month to dust and do the windows. I was always curious about it and longed to go into it and look at what had once belonged to him as a little boy. As far as I knew, Daddy didn't even go in there to relive a memory or find something he might have left from his younger days.

Mama told me this house was full of secrets locked in closets and drawers. She said we were all better off keeping them that way. Opening them would be like opening Pandora's Box, only instead of disease and illness, scandals would flutter all around us. I didn't know what scandals were exactly, but it was enough to keep me from opening any drawer or any closet not my own.

Ian's bedroom was next to mine but closer to our parent's bedroom, which was across the hall and down toward the south end of the house and property. Although they were originally meant to be guest rooms, all of our bedrooms were bigger than the bedrooms we had in our own house. Even the hallways in the March Mansion were wider, with ceilings higher than in any hallways in any home I had ever entered.

Along the walls were paintings my grandparents had bought at auctions. There were pedestals with statuary they had acquired during their traveling and at estate sales. My grandmother was supposedly an expert when it came to spotting something of value that was underpriced. When she was asked about that once, she said, "If someone is stupid enough to sell it for that price, you should be wise enough to grab it up or else you would be just as stupid."

So many things in my grandmother's house once belonged to other wealthy people who had either bequeathed their valuables to younger people who didn't appreciate them or know their value, or things belonging to wealthy people who had simply gone bankrupt and needed money desperately.

"One man's misfortune is usually another's good luck," Grandmother Emma said. "Be alert. Opportunity is often like a camera's flash. Miss it and it's gone forever."

She tossed her statements at us as if we were chickens clucking at her heels and waiting to be fed her wisdom or facts about the house and its contents. The truth was there was so much about it that I, even so young, thought was breathtaking, and I couldn't help being proud when other people complimented me on where I lived. Even my teacher, Mrs. Montgomery, who had been at Grandmother Emma's house once, made flattering comments, comments that caused me to be more conscious of its richness.

Some of the grand chandeliers hanging over the stairway, hanging in the hallways below, and hanging in the dining room, came from Europe, and one was said to have once belonged to the King of Spain.

"The light that rains down on us now, once fell on royalty," Grandmother Emma was fond of saying.

Did that mean we were magically turned into royalty, too, when we stood within its glow? She certainly acted as if she thought so. She walked and talked and made decisions like someone who expected it all to be written down as history. After all, the mansion was historic, why wasn't she?

No two rooms had the same style furniture. Ian and I were often given sermons about it so that we would fully appreciate how lucky we were to be living in the shadows of such eloquence and culture. Everything, even the knobs on doors, had some significance and value. She made the house sound like a living thing.

"Each room in a house like this should be like a new novel," Grandmother Emma said. "Every piece should contribute to some sort of history and tell its own story, whether it be the saga of a grand family, or a grand time."

Some of the pieces of furniture in the same room could have different background and heritage, as well, whether it be a picture frame, a stool, or a bookcase.

The dining room had a table, chairs, and a buffet that was vintage nineteenth-century Italian and had once belonged to a bishop cardinal. The sitting room, which was different from the living room, had a Victorian parlor settee, a Victorian gossip bench, and a Victorian swan fainting couch I loved to lie on when my grandmother was out and about and wouldn't see. The wood was mahogany and the material was a golden wheat brocade with a detached roll pillow.

All of her furniture, despite its age, looked brand-new, and there was always this terrible fear that either Ian or I would tear something or spill something on a piece and bring down the family fortune. Our own grand heritage and glory would be lost, for we were never to forget that this family once paraded through the Bethlehem community with great pomp and circumstance, our family crest flapping in the breeze.

There were often overnight guests here and grand dinner parties during Grandmother Emma's Golden Age. She would describe them to us with a bitter underlying tone as if it were our fault she no longer had them. I knew she couldn't blame us for her not having guests anymore. There was still another guest bedroom downstairs and Daddy's old bedroom on her side, so there was plenty of room for someone to sleep here. She maintained a maid, Nancy, and a limousine driver named Felix, and a man named Macintire whom everyone called Mac, to oversee the grounds. He lived just down the street, so it wasn't a question of extra work for her either. Money was certainly no problem, although I often heard my father complain that his mother held such a tight grip on the money faucet, there was barely a drip, drip, drip.

I didn't doubt that. Grandmother Emma was always criticizing my mother for being extravagant. I thought that was at least part of the reason why she stopped going regularly to the beauty parlor and stopped buying herself new clothes. Like someone living on a fixed income, Grandmother Emma would complain about the electric and gas bills, too.

"If you would stay after your children and have them turn off lights when they are not necessary and close windows when we're heating the house, we wouldn't be throwing money out the window," she lectured. She threatened to fine us for every unnecessary expense.

"They're not wasteful," my mother said in our defense. "Especially not Ian."

Grandmother Emma would only grunt at that. She couldn't argue about Ian doing anything illogical or unnecessary. If anything, he was looking after wasteful practices on her side of the house. He would venture over at least as far as the switch on the wall and deliberately turn off a hall light. If she complained about having to navigate in the dark, he would say, "I didn't think it was necessary with so much natural light coming through the windows, Grandmother. Perhaps you should fine yourself."

My mother might smile at that behind the hand she held over her mouth. My grandmother would shoot a reprimanding look at Ian who would stare back at her without so much as a twitch in his lips. He had two licorice black eyes with tiny white specks and when he looked at someone so intensely, he didn't even blink. Mama was always telling him not to stare at people.

"It makes you look like an insect and not a little boy," she told him. Other boys his age might have been upset about that, but Ian looked pleased. I knew that sometimes he did deliberately imitate creatures so he could better understand them.

"What would it be like to only be able to crawl?" he asked me when I saw him doing it in his room. He'd walk about the house with his arms pressed against himself so he resembled a Praying Mantis. Or he would wonder what it would be like to be a Venus Fly Trap and have to wait patiently for your meal to succumb to deception. He would sit with his mouth open for as long as he could stand it. He was studying carnivorous plants as well as insects. He was truly interested in everything.

Grandmother Emma was often disturbed about something he would do, especially when he stood very still and jetted out his tongue like a snake.

After trying to reprimand him for staring at people, my mother would only shake her head and walk away.

Grandmother Emma would do the same. I envied the way Ian could make her shake her head and retreat.

When it came to Grandmother Emma's criticism of Daddy, however, she was relentless and unswerving. She never failed to tell him he was lazy and wasteful. She found ways to blame that on my mother, claiming she just didn't inspire him to be better or try harder.

"At times I think you are completely void of ambition and self-respect, Christopher."

She would say these horrible things to him right in front of Ian or me and even in front of my mother at times. Her sharp, surgical comments were never dressed in euphemisms or subtleties. She refused to rationalize or make excuses for Daddy and especially not for my mother and us. On occasion, my mother would try to stand up to her.

"Is it wise to be so critical of Christopher in front of his children?" she once asked her.

"The sooner they learn to base respect upon reality and not false promises, the better off they'll be. As ye sow so shall ye reap," she added.

"So do you blame yourself for Christopher's failings?" my mother dared to follow up.

Grandmother Emma faced her firmly and replied, "No, his father."

"That woman has an icicle for a spine," my mother muttered to me.

At the time I was young enough to believe that was literally true. I wondered how she kept it from melting.

There was so much tension and often so much static in our house, or I should say my grandmother's house, that sometimes I'd look down the hallway toward the circular stairs and think of the inside of the mansion as having its own weather. I'd imagine clouds or storms no matter what was happening outside. Shadows in the house could widen or stretch so that I would feel as if I was walking under a great overcast. Even in the summer months, it could be chilly and not because of too much air-conditioning either. Fair weather days were happening less and less, not that there were all that many after we were forced to move in with Grandmother Emma, anyway. It was no wonder then that my mother was adamant, even terrified, about Grandmother Emma finding out about me.

I suppose anyone would wonder how someone so small could command such obedience and fear. She was just five feet tall with small features, especially small hands, but I never thought of her as being tiny or diminutive. Even in front of Daddy, who was six feet one and nearly two hundred pounds, she looked powerful and full of authority. She had ruler perfect posture and a commanding tone in her voice. When she spoke to her servants, she whipped her words at them. She rarely raised her voice. She didn't have to shout or yell. Her words seemed loud anyway because after she said them in her manner of speaking, they boomed in your head. No one could ignore her, no one except Ian, but he could ignore a tornado if he was thinking or reading about something that interested him at the time.

My grandmother was always well put together, too. She never appeared out of her room without her bluish gray hair being brushed and pinned. She liked to keep it in a tight crown bun, but on rare occasion she would have it twisted and tied in something called a French knot. That was when she looked the prettiest and youngest, I thought, although she was very careful not to dress in anything she believed was inappropriate for a woman of her age. Everything she wore was always coordinated as well. She had shoes for every outfit and jewelry that seemed to have been purchased precisely for this dress or that sweater. There were butterfly pins full of emeralds and rubies, diamond brocades, earrings and bracelets that were heirlooms, handed down by her mother and her mother's mother, as well as my grandfather's mother.

I couldn't help but secretly admire her. In my mind she really was as important as a queen. When she criticized me for the way I stooped or ate with the wrong knife and fork, I didn't resent her as much as Ian did when she said similar things to him. I swallowed back my pride and tried to be more like her. I watched how she sat at the table, how she ate, how she walked and turned her head. I think she saw all this because once in a while, I caught her looking at me with the tiniest smile on her lips, and I wondered, could it be that she likes me after all?

I was afraid that if she did, Mama would hate me and might even think I had betrayed her somehow.

But I was also afraid that if she didn't like me, Daddy would be disappointed.

Did she or didn't she?

In my heart of hearts I knew that finding out would be something I would do on the journey toward discovering who I was.

And so with trembling feet, I stepped into my future.